STARSHIP OF THE ANCIENTS: BOOK 2

LOST PLANET

A K DUBOFF

LOST PLANET

www.akduboff.com

Published by Epic Realms Press
Cover by Robert Rajszczak

ISBN-10: 1965614027
ISBN-13: 978-1965614020
Copyright Registration Number: TXu002497789

0 9 8 7 6 5 4 3 2 1

Produced in the United States of America

TABLE OF CONTENTS

1

BEING KIDNAPPED BY an ancient alien spaceship was not how Evan had expected his day to go. Fully locked out of the controls, he and Anya were simply along for the ride—wherever the ship had decided to take them.

Evan's heart pounded in his ears and his chest was tight with anticipation. They'd launched from the hidden cavern on Aethos and then headed directly into space, which had never been the plan. All they'd wanted to do was take the ship to the other side of the planet to regroup and figure out their next move.

Instead, strange golden particles were now swirling around the alien starship. They had appeared to flow from a hiding place on Aethos' smallest moon, presumably dormant since the ship had landed on the planet. The particles formed an organized framework around the vessel as it soared into open space away from Aethos. They'd arranged into a series of interlocking bands—a latticework, of sorts—spinning along the length of the vessel.

"Do not fear," the ship's AI said. No speakers were visible, but the synthesized-sounding voice filled the flight deck. "I will take you to my homeworld now, and you will see how this structure creates a localized jump field to enable interstellar travel."

"Looking forward to seeing it in action," Evan said, wondering how much of his anxiety the ship could pick up through their telepathic link.

Anya glanced at Evan as she held his hand, her expression a mixture of apprehension and wonder at the engineering marvel. "Why were these components waiting up here in space?"

"This material is fragile and not designed for atmospheric entry," the AI explained. "It exists to fulfill its purpose, not to serve me."

Evan's skin prickled with excitement. "Does that mean it's modular? Could it be used with *any* ship?"

"Provided the necessary integrations were in place, yes."

"How would—"

"Do not seek to control what you do not yet understand." The AI's firm tone sent a chill down Evan's spine.

Through the viewport, the latticework's rotation rapidly accelerated until it became a golden blur encompassing the starship.

"What will happen to us when we jump?" Anya asked, always taking a scientific perspective.

"You organics will suffer no ill-effects," the ship's onboard AI replied.

Evan couldn't put complete stock in the ship's assessment since it had only seen humans for the first time mere minutes before, when he and Anya had boarded. However, if the ship wanted them dead, it could have opened an airlock as soon as they flew into space. He had to trust that whatever it had gleaned from its scans of them was enough to understand basic human physiological needs.

"I don't want you to die," the ship added, apparently glimpsing Evan's thoughts again.

The AI's uncanny telepathic connection to Evan was both helpful and alarming. Though it seemed friendly enough, Evan was wary of the sentient alien artificial intelligence.

However, it was too late to second-guess anything now.

The stars outside the viewport stretched into streaks before winking out, replaced by an eerie void with abstract bands of color shimmering beyond the golden glow. The air seemed thicker, but Evan was almost certain that was just his imagination.

"Where are we?" he asked tentatively.

"In the realm outside what you would call spacetime," the ship replied.

Evan tried to wrap his mind around the wonder he was witnessing. Independent jumps from point-to-point were a theoretical fantasy, according to conventional science. Despite countless models and hypothetical designs, the best humanity had been able to achieve was interstellar travel through fixed gates. Ships would enter one of the approximately two hundred rings in the network and come out at their chosen destination, passing through a stable artificial wormhole between the two gates. It was an excellent system, but extremely constrained by the limited number of rings located around the Commonwealth's territory.

But this alien vessel's process of generating a localized spatial distortion to jump to any location at will… it defied all previously held limitations of space travel. To possess such a technology would alter the entire landscape of the Commonwealth and open up untold possibilities.

Anya met Evan's gaze with wonder in her eyes. For days, they'd been talking about alien technology and how it might be harnessed, but actually seeing it in practice made it all *real.*

"What are we going to do?" she murmured.

"We have to find out everything we can." The alien ship had promised to take them to its homeworld to meet its makers, and that was the best prospect they'd had to get meaningful answers since their crash on Aethos. It was pointless to make any plans until they'd seen the alien world and knew what kind of civilization they were dealing with.

Anya stared straight ahead at the incredible view of hyperspace. "It's beautiful."

Evan stood next to her. "Yeah, this is wild."

"I never dreamed this was possible."

"I had hopes, but I never thought it would be in my lifetime."

The invention of transit gates had been a game-changer for humanity nearly three centuries before. Coupled with the one-quarter light-speed Forbes Drive, ships could hop through the closest available gate and then travel through normal space for the rest of the journey. That method had enabled an approximately two-month transit time to Aethos, which would have taken years without the initial gate hop.

Most planets in the core worlds had their own gate, but new settlements in the outer realms usually required months of travel through normal space. The advent of the Slingshot had been critical to those expeditions—catapulting huge ships from port so they didn't need to burn onboard fuel in the initial acceleration, allowing more efficient allocation of resources and longer journeys. It offered a significant advantage to anyone with deep enough pockets to afford the service, and NovaTech was a top customer for its massive colony expedition ships. Still, there were significant limitations to humanity's expansion across the stars. Those constraints would no longer apply with point-to-point jumps.

During their brief meeting on Aethos, Chancellor Conroy had impressed how revolutionary the discovery of the alien ship might be. Evan hadn't placed much stock in the statement at the time, but seeing the wonderous feat firsthand changed his perspective. But nowhere in Conroy's pitch had he factored in a *sentient* ship. This wasn't simply a vessel to be taken and controlled.

We have a real opportunity here. We need to build a relationship, Evan realized. And that meant treating this AI like any new acquaintance. "You probably picked this up in my mind already, but I'm Evan and this is Anya. How should we refer to you?"

"You may call me Sam."

Anya tilted her head. "That doesn't sound very alien."

"My designation in the native tongue of my makers would be difficult for you to pronounce."

"Why Sam?" she questioned.

"It works as an acronym for Sentient Autonomous Machine, which I am. It is also an appropriate truncation of this vessel's designation, the *Asamar*. And the name also elicits a positive memory association in Evan."

"An old teacher, from when I was young," Evan said. "It's freaking me out that you can read my mind so easily—things I'm not even thinking about."

"How have your kind mastered interstellar flight without understanding neural interface?"

Anya shook her head. "No, we can… just not without a dedicated device, and not things we aren't actively thinking about."

"And we value personal privacy," Evan added. There were a lot of things floating around in his inner mind that he didn't want the ship knowing, and especially not blabbing about.

"I apologize. I meant no offense."

"It might be better for all of us if we could have a conversation rather than you making decisions like we aren't here," Evan said.

"We would not be on this journey were it not for your presence." Sam sounded almost offended, if the AI was capable of that emotion.

"And we appreciate the ride. But you should know from being in my mind that we humans are extremely stubborn and like to be in control."

"You also suffer from an unearned superiority complex."

"Oh, *I* do? You—"

"Hey!" Anya spread her arms. "Let's not argue with the ship that currently has complete control of our lives, okay?"

Evan took a deep breath to calm himself. "Sorry, Sam."

"I can't fault your nature."

This ship might drive me crazy. He tried to keep the thought to himself.

AIs were common enough across the human worlds, but they were usually light on personality and designed for utility. Prior attempts at sentient synthetic consciousness had backfired in spectacular ways over the centuries, so such AIs were rare in modern times. Like human beings, some were kind and compassionate, while others were prone to murderous inclinations. A society could only take a gamble so many times on which brand they'd get before it made more sense to keep the guardrails on the AI models and treat them as a tool rather than a lifeform. After only a few minutes with this ship's sentient AI, Evan could understand why past generations had come to that conclusion. However, that didn't mean he couldn't form a productive relationship with Sam—they'd just need to find common ground, like any new friendship.

"So, Sam," Anya continued, "it sounds like it's to our mutual benefit to work together."

"Yes, Anya," the AI replied. "I would like to help you with your mission, and you can teach me about your human culture."

The proposal sounded innocent enough, but Evan shot Anya a cautionary glance. They couldn't entrust this sentient computer with details about their people, at least any more than it had already gleaned from his mind. It could turn on them at any moment, and he refused to inadvertently play a role in humanity's downfall by engaging in idle conversation with an unknown entity.

"Helping friends in need is at the heart of our culture," Evan stated before Anya could say anything. "Take Anya and me, for example. A week ago, we'd never even talked. But when our ship crashed, we became friends and have helped each other survive. And then you offered to help us, so I think we have that trait in common."

Sam was silent for several seconds. "Some among my makers thought that we should avoid all strangers. Others wanted to explore."

"You ended up on another planet. Are you one of the explorers?" Anya asked.

"No, I had a different purpose."

"And what was that?" Evan questioned.

"My post was the planet you call Aethos. I did not expect to find anything new."

Evan tried not to be annoyed by the AI's evasion of his core question about its mission. "And yet, you found us."

"I did. You have shown me that not everything unknown is to be feared."

Though some of the tension eased in Evan's chest with the

positive words, he was acutely aware that not all humans were as friendly or compassionate. Whatever initial impression Sam was gaining about the human species could be quickly undone; even one encounter with a member of the Noche Syndicate would paint a very different picture about the darker qualities of humanity.

Evan searched for the right words to explain. "Sam, it sounds like factions of your makers hold different opinions, right? Well, it's the same way with humans. And while having a variety of perspectives can be good for a society, it can also lead to conflict. In some cases, those disagreements are so extreme that humans will turn on each other to fight over which idea is correct."

"You mean war?"

"Yes. Those are *extreme* cases, but there's a long history of fighting, unfortunately. I don't want you to get the wrong impression of us. However, the last thing I want is for you to think I'm trying to hide something from you. I know you can see into my mind, so I want to be upfront and honest."

"Transparent communication is an important foundation for friendship," the AI stated.

Evan smiled. "Very insightful."

"You are guarded, but I do see the honesty in your mind. I see the logic in your perspective. And I understand your intent." Sam paused. "I accept your offer of friendship."

"Thank you," Anya said. "I hope this is the start of something good. I think we should also point out that Evan and I are two nobodies in the grand scheme of human civilization. We can't speak on behalf of our race."

"Nor may I speak for my makers," the AI acknowledged. "Soon, you may speak with my people and decide on a path forward."

Streaks of stars appeared outside the viewport and abruptly snapped to points. Evan got a momentary sense of vertigo as his senses reoriented. The golden glow outside the viewport faded until the individual particles making up the latticework were once again visible.

Rather than an open starscape, a planet lay before them. It was covered in clouds, but what little land was visible had a brownish hue. Surprisingly, there were no visible orbital structures out the viewport or showing up on the scan data screen. For an advanced civilization with starships colonizing remote worlds, that caught Evan by surprise.

"Hey, Sam," Evan began cautiously, "do your people use space docks?"

"Yes."

He frowned. "Where are they?"

The AI didn't reply for several seconds. "There should be docks here. I am also not receiving any transmissions from the surface. However... something appears to have come along inside the displacement field when we jumped from Aethos."

Evan's stomach turned over. "What kind of 'something'?"

"A probe."

"Shit!" His pulse spiked. "They'll know where we are."

"And where *is* that, exactly?" Anya asked.

"Given what I have discerned about your interstellar capabilities, it would take many years to reach this planet," Sam stated. "There is no immediate danger of pursuit."

"All the same, destroy it," Evan said. "Our enemies don't need to know any more about this place."

"Why should I destroy the probe if it poses no threat?" the AI asked.

"Every minute that device is here, it's collecting data. And as long as it's around, there's a risk of it following us if we go elsewhere. It might not pose an immediate threat, but I can think of no upside to keeping it around."

"I understand."

A beam of white light shot out from the ship, instantly turning the probe to dust.

Those weapons could definitely come in handy. Evan breathed a little easier knowing they were no longer being observed. "Thanks, Sam."

"Next question. Is anyone home?" Anya asked, nodding toward the planet.

"That requires a closer investigation," Sam said.

Without waiting for the humans to reply, the AI directed the *Asamar* closer to the planet.

The ship descended through the atmosphere with barely any vibration. The advanced stabilizers on most human craft minimized the disturbance, but it was still obvious when a vessel was heading into atmo. On this ship, if he'd had his eyes closed, Evan wouldn't have been able to tell the difference between outer space and the rapid descent. Then again, this race had figured out how to master near-instantaneous travel across incredible distances, so making a ship not shake while flying around was a comparatively minor feat.

They broke through the upper layer of clouds, granting a first look at the world below. Evan was encouraged to see scattered patches of pale green in the landscape, indicating plant life. He was acutely aware that they had limited supplies and would quickly go hungry if they couldn't find food on this planet.

Less encouraging was that he saw no signs of an active civilization. When traveling to any human-occupied world, there were almost always some other ships visible in the sky, or at least evidence of habitation on the surface. He saw neither through the viewport.

"Sam, where is everyone?" Evan asked.

"This is home. There were…" The AI faded out.

Evan wouldn't have thought he could feel sympathy for a machine, but Sam wasn't like other computers. "How long were you dormant on Aethos?"

"Six-thousand-two-hundred-eighty-one years."

Anya winced. "Have you been out of communication all that time?"

"Yes. I didn't realize it had been so long. I hadn't thought about what might have changed."

As frustrating as it was to be dealing with a confused and ill-informed AI, Evan couldn't bring himself to be upset with Sam. He'd experienced enough loss in his own life that he empathized with what the AI must be going through as it came to realize that everyone and everything it once knew had been gone for millennia. No chance to make up for lost time or say goodbye. Just… gone.

Anya's brows pinched as she mulled over their plight, eventually meeting Evan's eyes. "Sam, we'd like to find out what happened to your people," she said. "Can you land us in a place where we might be able to gather data?"

"Yes, I will take you to the location of the capital city." Sam's flat tone belied a deeper sadness to the words. Perhaps it was Evan's inexplicable telepathic connection to the ship, but he got the distinct sense that the AI was silently grieving.

The *Asamar* accelerated on a new course across the planet, cruising at high elevation. The view was occasionally obstructed by clouds, but what barren scenery Evan could make out reinforced a grim picture of the planet's—and its inhabitants'—fate.

Several hundred kilometers from their initial atmospheric

entry point, Sam descended toward a flat expanse at the foot of a jagged mountain range.

The setting could have been beautiful in the past, with the striking peaks as a backdrop for a city. But there were no buildings now, or even ruins to suggest that the area had ever been inhabited. Nor were there any hints of green.

"Did the city crumble over time?" Evan asked.

"There should still be signs of remains here," Sam replied. "They must have been destroyed."

Anya looked at Evan with concern. "By something like the sphere?"

"Sam, the technology of your people that lets you rearrange matter to construct buildings… does that also allow structures to be disassembled?"

"It can, yes. But that is not something my people would have done here."

"Not even in a war?" Anya asked.

"I am missing too much history to make a definitive determination."

Evan nodded. "Well, if there's anything to learn, we'll find the answers out there."

2

THE WORLD WASN'T shaping up to be anything like Evan had expected. "Is it safe for us to walk around outside?" he asked the AI.

"I have confirmed that there are no known pathogens or pollutants detectable by my scanners."

Anya crossed her arms. "I wish we had some of our own equipment to verify."

"Or spacesuits… What do you think, Anya? Do we throw caution to the wind and go walk around on a dead planet?"

She bit her lower lip, a charming practice he'd noticed her do while she worked through a problem. "Sam, can you please display the results of your scan data on one of the monitors for me to review?"

Evan nodded his approval of her thinking.

"Here is the sensor data of current environmental conditions," Sam acknowledged. A large monitor on the side wall of the flight deck illuminated with a graphical display of the information.

Anya examined the details on the screen. "I don't understand some of these readings, but what I can make out looks fine for humans. But there's no telling if there's a virus or something that the scanners aren't picking up."

"Based on my evaluation of your biology and my analysis, I detect no risks to your health," Sam stated.

"There's not a whole lot of anything out there," Evan said. "What's the likelihood of an unidentified pathogen existing in a barren wasteland, Anya?"

"Pretty low."

Evan shrugged. "You're the scientist. I'll leave it up to you."

Anya looked between the scan results and the outside view displayed on the front screen. "The risks are non-zero but negligible. I say we go for it."

"All right." Evan rubbed his hands together. "At least if we die, we'll die together, right?"

"Yep. Then it will be up to someone else to save the Commonwealth."

"Neither of you are going to die from anything on this planet," Sam reiterated. "Are humans always so dramatic?"

Anya laughed. "If you think *this* is dramatic, you're going to be truly shocked by humanity."

"Don't worry, Sam, we'll get you up to speed," Evan told the AI. "You keep us alive, and we'll teach you the nuances about what it means to be human."

"I will endeavor to preserve your lives."

Anya headed toward the main airlock. "How reassuring, thank you." She grabbed her pack containing the bioanalyzer, which would be helpful for investigating physical samples of soil or biomatter.

Evan slung his pack over his shoulders, and they went to the main hatch where they'd initially entered the ship. He was about to open it but hesitated. "Sam, if we go outside, are you going to fly away and abandon us here?"

Anya's eyes went wide, clearly having not thought about

that possibility. It hadn't occurred to Evan, either, until he was facing down a scouting mission on an alien world. But unlike Aethos, this was not a verdant garden world. They wouldn't stand a chance long-term.

"As I stated, I will endeavor to preserve your lives," Sam repeated. "I will not abandon you here."

"We won't abandon you, either," Evan said. He brushed his hand over the door control.

Golden light illuminated around the hatch's perimeter. The material folded away, leaving an open view of the planet's sparse landscape.

A warm breeze ruffled Evan's hair, dusty and dry compared to the humidity and intense aromatics from Aethos. "I think we might have a clue why they wanted to settle on another world."

Anya nodded. "I wonder if it was always like this, or if something happened?"

"This used to be a forest," Sam commented. "I cannot determine from my scans if the change was due to a shift in environmental conditions or the result of a weapon."

"We'll see what we can find out there," Evan replied. "Only way to know a place is through boots on the ground, right?"

— — —

Anya sucked in a deep breath as she descended the ramp from the alien ship.

A lot could be told about a planet by its air. High humidity and fresh scents would demonstrate a world brimming with life, whereas arid conditions would suggest a larger struggle to survive. Water was essential for organic life to thrive; that was a universal truth. While there were other forms of life, surely, it didn't matter from a human perspective.

Any species that had shown interest in Aethos must have had similar priorities with their own explorations. On a dry world such as this, water would be a prize. So why, then, would they not have settled on Aethos after they'd already gone to the trouble of building a city?

"Something is really strange about all of this," Anya said. "This race clearly expended a lot of resources to colonize other worlds, but then they just… stopped."

Evan nodded. "I think there was a conflict of some sort on this world, which prevented them from leaving. Or, at least prevented them from going to their intended target."

"War?"

"Perhaps. Though, I don't know how to tell if it was infighting or they were attacked."

Her stomach lurched. "Oh, I really don't like the idea of there being *another* Big Bad out there."

"There's always something bigger and badder, Anya. Whether or not we cross paths is the question."

"Okay, let's say there was some kind of fight here. Did they all die here, or did some leave to go… somewhere?"

"That's what we're here to figure out. If Sam's makers are still out there, I'd like to talk with them."

"Yeah, Sam seems agreeable enough to working with us. AIs are a reflection of their creators, right?"

"Usually."

"Well, we're off to a pretty good start. Let's walk around and take some samples." She got out her bioanalyzer and rattled it in her hand.

The device was designed to process organic matter, but it was theoretically capable of running an analysis on any physical item. Dirt contained all sorts of decayed plant matter as well as bacteria and other tiny lifeforms. So, what looked like dead soil could contain traces of life.

They walked fifty meters from the *Asamar* across the barren ground. Coming to an area that wasn't as hard-packed, Anya took a sample of loose soil and loaded it into the bioanalyzer. The results came back with high traces of decayed organic material.

"There used to be lots of plants here. That tracks with Sam's comment about a former forest," she told Evan. "And, based on these mineral deposits, I think this may have been a riverbed or some other body of water."

"Where did the water go?"

"Climates change over time. Weather patterns shift. If the rain stopped, bodies of water would go dry."

"That would explain why people would leave the planet."

"But that doesn't mean what happened here was due to a natural change. A cataclysmic event could also cause that kind of extreme shift."

"Like a meteor impact?" he asked.

"Or a weapon." She didn't want to think about the aliens having a planet-killing weapon, but they couldn't rule out any possibilities at such an early stage in their investigation.

They continued walking along the parched ground to look for any signs of former civilization. Anya took additional soil samples at intervals along their path, garnering similar results to her first analysis. By the time they'd wandered a kilometer or so from the ship, they hadn't encountered any meaningful landmarks.

Evan surveyed the landscape, shielding his eyes from the sun, while Anya gathered another sample. "I think we need to try somewhere else. Without some kind of ground-penetrating scan equipment, I doubt we'll see anything related to the old city no matter how long we wander around here."

"Yeah, I had the same thought." Anya stood up and dusted off her hands. "But what are we doing? We'd intended to take the ship and hide out on the far side of Aethos, not travel who-knows-how-far across the galaxy to wherever we are now."

"When Sam brought us, it was so we could speak with the ship's makers."

"Well, Sam is clearly very confused and out of touch with current events."

"I feel bad for him," Evan said. "Can you imagine waking up and discovering that everyone and everything you knew had been gone for millennia?"

"It's a machine, Evan."

"No, Sam is more than that."

She tilted her head as she looked him over. "Do you think we can trust him?"

Evan crossed his arms. "I don't know. The telepathic link is weird. It does seem like Sam is feeling emotions, but that might just be me projecting."

"We know nothing about the ship's technology at this point. For all we know, it might *actually* be some kind of bio-technological hybrid. Based on the animals and other creatures we encountered, there's definitely precedent."

"That's true."

"So, maybe we should chat with Sam a little more? And, since we're here, maybe fly around a little to see if we can find any clues around the planet."

"Good plan."

— — —

Evan returned to the alien ship's flight deck with Anya.

"All right, Sam, we need your help."

"Certainly. How may I be of assistance?"

"We'd like to check out the rest of the planet. We didn't find anything here."

"There should be a city at this location," Sam replied.

"Well, based on your knowledge of your people's construction practices, what would have happened to the city after six thousand years?" Evan questioned.

"The support structures of the buildings were primarily formed using the rock inherent to this region. Windows and other components would have likely decayed beyond recognition, but the core framework should be mostly intact."

"Okay, so, could it have been buried? Can your sensors tell if there's anything underground?"

Sam took a couple of seconds to respond. "The readings are anomalous. I am detecting a mass where the city should be, but it appears to be a solid form. I can't tell whether it's being shielded or if there's nothing there."

Anya brightened. "Hey, yeah, maybe they went underground and are in some kind of stealth containment bubble."

"It's possible," Evan said. "Is there any way you can get a better look, Sam?"

"I may be able to adapt the weapons system to remove the top layer of dirt to expose the apparent mass."

Anya nodded thoughtfully. "That's not half-bad. Getting eyeballs on it should let us know what we're dealing with."

"Would you like me to deploy a weapon?" Sam asked.

"Let's do it. Blasting a big hole in the ground actually sounds like a great way for us to vent pent-up frustration about everything that's gone wrong this week," Evan said.

"I don't understand. Is this a human trait?"

Anya laughed. "Oh, Sam… When things don't go right for us, we'll sometimes express our emotions on something unrelated. We met some bad people on Aethos who ruined our day, and you firing a weapon on this city is going to make us feel better about it."

"I still do not understand."

"You don't have to," Evan assured the AI. "You're being a good friend by helping us with our displacement."

"You are a strange species. I'll start blasting for you now."

"Much appreciated."

3

ROMAN FLEXED HIS left hand, sending golden shimmers of energy along his skin from his fingertips to forearm. Since his near-fatal fall from the cliff, the alien sphere had completely merged into his palm as it had healed and enhanced him. Now, the lights were the only visual indication of its presence.

But he could feel it. The power it had granted him hummed in his veins, begging to be unleashed. It had also caused a buzzing in his ears that tickled the back of his mind. At first, he'd thought that it was a result of the alien tech surging through him. But after several hours of reflection since the sound began, he suspected that it was actually a call. *Where* he was being summoned remained to be seen.

The compulsion to follow the call made it difficult to concentrate on anything else as he tried to salvage the disastrous situation on Aethos. He shook his head, attempting to clear the buzzing so he could focus on what Red was saying.

"No?" she asked, confused.

"Just stretching. What were you saying?"

The soldier's brows scrunched together. "I was suggesting ways to fortify Conroy's bunker to serve as an operational base for us."

"Right, yes." He had caught bits and pieces of the plan. Repurposing the facility came with risks, since Conroy's people were intimately familiar with the territory. But having a solid roof over their heads was better than the alternatives.

Red crossed her toned arms. "You insisted on being a part of these discussions. I won't repeat myself."

"And I won't apologize for having more on my mind than rearranging furniture."

She glanced toward his left hand where the lights were shimmering under his skin. "I'm sure you do." Some of her bluster had faded.

Though they hadn't overtly talked about the sphere, the new power it had granted him was undeniable. If nothing else, it had solidified his position of authority. The tentative alliance between the military and the Noche Syndicate made for a questionable operational hierarchy. Had everything gone to plan, Roman would have reported to a designated mission commander. However, the commander had been one of the many soldiers killed when the military cruiser was shot down, leaving a leadership void. While Red was a competent commander for her unit, she had a limited understanding of the mission's larger context. Of those still alive on Aethos, only Roman knew all of that critical information. He was in charge, whether Red had accepted it or not.

"What we do with the bunker doesn't matter. Our focus needs to be finding Conroy and his people. The mission objective hasn't changed."

Red placed her hands on her hips. "I'm well aware of the objective. And I'm also acutely aware that we've lost a lot of people, so we don't have the numbers for a major assault. But Conroy is on the run, and we have the benefit of all the resources they were forced to leave behind. Backup isn't coming for either side for months, so if this turns into a long game, then provisions and infrastructure might be the deciding factor."

"Try to starve them out?" Roman asked.

"It's probably tough to starve on a planet like this, but roughing it in the woods will be tough on people used to living with climate-controls. Don't overlook the tactical advantage of being well-fed and rested compared to a mentally fatigued and demoralized enemy."

Roman had to admit that her reasoning had merit. Maybe she wasn't just a shoot-first soldier, after all. "Fine. Do what needs to be done to secure the bunker."

"Way ahead of you." Red walked toward the mangled entrance, where several of the soldiers were moving around materials and talking. "Status?" she asked them.

"Well, the front door was all blown to shit in the raid, but we've got some cargo containers staged to barricade it overnight," one of the men replied.

"Realistically, we're going to be here for months," Red said. "We'll need to come up with a better long-term solution."

"The cruiser crash site isn't far from here," another man pointed out. "There's lots of metal we can salvage from that. Carrying it over in the drop ship wouldn't be too difficult."

Red nodded. "We should also cut a ground path. And clear out a defensible zone around this base, for that matter. Don't want to make the same mistake Conroy did by leaving close cover."

"Well, they weren't expecting a ground assault," the other soldier pointed out.

"Poor planning all the same," Red said. "Never make it easy for your enemy to sneak up on you."

Roman didn't care what the military goons did so long as

he had a cabin to himself—one of the officer's cabins with a proper bed and a private washroom. This mission was never supposed to be a camping trip, and he was sick of his own stench after a week in the wilds. "I'm going to comb through their files to see if there's mention of any other outposts where they might have gone to hide."

Without waiting for acknowledgement, Roman brushed past the soldiers through the partially blocked opening. Inside, the power was on but the lighting fixtures nearest the entry had been broken in the breach assault. Dark scorch marks covered the metal surfaces in the vicinity, and the air still carried a strong scent of singed metal. Roman quickly moved deeper into the facility with the hope of finding fresher air. Fortunately, the environmental systems did seem to be online, and he was soon breathing easier.

Members of Red's team were moving through the corridors, cleaning and carrying gear. One soldier was painting a long, colored line on a wall, which ran parallel to other colored lines that had already been laid in.

"What are those?" Roman asked him.

"Guides. Follow yellow to get to the Mess. Blue will take you to the sleeping quarters. Red leads to the area that used to be the administrative wing, but it's pretty messed up from when they blew it."

Roman's heart sank. "There was an interior explosion?"

"Yeah, some kind of self-destruct, we think. We haven't found any bodies, so we suspect that Conroy got out through a secret exit."

"Ah."

The man finished his blue spray line. "We'll find them."

"I have no doubt." Roman nodded to the man and then followed the red path.

Scorch marks and divots from kinetic rounds pocked the corridor as he ventured deeper. Despite the unsightly damage, Roman was comforted by the ship-like environment after his recent trials in the planet's untamed wilderness. He did have to give Conroy's people credit for the effort it must have taken to reconstruct a starship underground. Of course, that was also the act of traitors who would sooner hide than admit defeat.

The red line terminated at a heavily burned section of corridor. Roman wrinkled his nose; apparently, the air filtration system hadn't been able to purge the charred aroma from this area yet. His mood was equally soured by the visual confirmation that Central Command had been reduced to a blackened hunk of twisted metal.

This is why I hate dealing with meathead soldiers. They'd been so focused on forcing their way into the place that they hadn't stopped to think about the value of the contents. With a little more planning and finesse, they could have tapped into the air system to knock out the occupants. No mess, everything preserved, and Conroy would be in custody. But, of course, Red had been in charge of the breach, not him. That's what he got for agreeing to follow her lead. *Never again.*

He made a quick assessment of the rubble pile before concluding that a salvage operation would be pointless. With the right specialized equipment, he could perhaps have restored damaged data archives, but he had none of that on hand. A much better bet would be locating an intact secondary administrative space. Though there would no doubt be security protocols in place, interfacing with serviceable equipment would give him a much better chance to glean something meaningful rather than sifting through pulverized scraps.

There was only the singular red line tracing back to the facility entrance, so Roman decided to explore. It would have been easy to get lost in the maze of corridors, but the distinctive damage to certain walls and his lifetime of experience on starships were enough to help him keep his bearings.

After ten minutes of wandering around, he eventually came across a promising room. He'd opened the door expecting to find a custodial closet, but it, in fact, appeared to be a server room.

The racks of computer equipment were presently dormant, aside from a single unit that was separate from the others. Checking the display screen, the active unit was controlling the lights, HVAC, and other environmental systems. He definitely didn't want to mess with that.

The other units, though… Those would be the heart of the facility's data processing capabilities. Any information he could have gleaned from the main control room would likely be accessible here, as well. That was assuming he could turn everything on and then bypass the encryption without triggering a complete wipe. But, realistically, everything might have already been auto-purged when the control room was blown up.

Only one way to find out.

Roman got to work. He didn't consider himself a technical expert, but he knew a whole lot more about computers than he did about surviving in the wilderness.

After a little trial and error, Roman was able to get the units powered on. Not surprisingly, he was met with a login screen.

All right, I need to be careful. It was likely that too many login attempts would lock the system, and he didn't have a rig to brute force his way into the network. *How do I get in?*

An idea started to form in his mind, and he smiled to himself. *I don't need to access* all *the materials in the database, just the most recent.*

When Red's soldiers had attacked the base, Roman had assumed that the enemy would load the most valuable information onto an external drive and flee. That's why he'd encountered Evan and Anya at the back exit, and he'd been right. Since almost no one used hardline cables for data transfers—especially not when on a time crunch—that meant those recently accessed documents would still exist as temporary files. He just needed to find the archive of the completed transfers.

Roman combed through the info screens on each server to identify the one that controlled the wireless network. The task was tedious more than difficult, and he found his mind wandering to thoughts of walking through the forest rather than being cramped in this awful little room.

Eventually, he located what he was looking for. The archive folder was filled with files named in nonsensical gibberish, but each was noted with a time stamp. *Now to find the right files...*

He identified several sets of documents that had been accessed around the time of the breach, but he wouldn't be able to read them here. Since the ancillary computer terminals inside the facility were locked—at least until they could reset the base's network—the only operational computer at his disposal was the one on the drop ship. He transferred the relevant files from the temporary folder to an external drive so he could go there to run the recovery protocol.

As he exited the base, Red was still talking with members of her team near the entrance.

"Did you find what you were looking for?" Red called out to him.

"Maybe." He held up the drive and kept walking.

The drop ship was parked in a clearing a few hundred meters away. While not a large vessel, it was big enough to be a challenge to set it down amid the thick foliage common in that area. This location was as close as they'd been able to get. Fortunately, though, there'd been enough traffic between the craft and the base that a defined path had already been worn along the route.

Roman found that the ship was unattended and locked. He disapproved of leaving their one meaningful mode of transportation without an armed guard, but it's not like they had a lot of people to spare while everyone was moving things around. He entered and locked the hatch behind him.

Settling into the comm console station on the flight deck, Roman brought up the external drive's files on the screen. A smile spread across his face as he saw that the first was a map. *All right, where did you go?*

— — —

Samor set down his binoculars and crawled to deeper cover. It had been a risk to sneak back to their former base, but he needed to know for certain what the enemy was doing. Despite his recent injuries sustained during the breach, he was the go-to candidate for any scouting mission. He'd been out in the jungle more than anyone else, and he knew which plants to avoid, how to cover his tracks, and how to make the wildlife feel comfortable around him.

He'd been quietly observing for the last hour. Unfortunately, his fears had been confirmed.

The infiltrators were settling in, and they would be difficult to unseat. It had taken significant firepower for them to breach the facility, and Samor knew that he and his allies had nowhere near the resources necessary to reclaim what had been taken. For that matter, he couldn't think of a compelling reason to retake the place until they were no longer under siege. The location was known, so they'd be vulnerable. For now, Hidden Grotto was a superior stronghold.

Even so, seeing the enemy swarming the place that had been his home for five years grated on Samor's nerves. The invaders had mercilessly killed his friends… for what?

I've been at this for too long. I don't even remember how the fighting started. He brushed off the thought. He *did* know—it had just been so long that it felt like a lifetime ago. But he could never truly forget the crippling betrayal of seeing the Commonwealth's leadership turn on each other.

As he was crawling away, Samor noticed a lone man walking away from the base into the trees. He'd noticed the path when he'd first arrived for the reconnaissance mission and hadn't been sure if it was worth exploring. But, this seemed like a great opportunity to see where it led.

He began circling around the left side of camp to get to the path. Moving slowly and carefully through the trees, he kept watch on the man's movements. After a few hundred meters, the destination was obvious: the drop ship, nestled in a small clearing between the thick trees. Samor had seen the ship flying around overhead earlier, but he'd been unable to see where it had landed.

Oh, this is good! He didn't see any guards, and the man had easily let himself on board.

Though there weren't other people around, trying to board the ship now would be a terrible idea. A close quarters confrontation would leave a lot of room for things to go wrong, especially when dealing with an unfamiliar interior layout. It would be better to attack the person on his way out and then…

Samor stopped himself there. *What* could *I do after that?*

He wasn't a pilot. The ship would be a boon, but it

wouldn't be leaving the ground with him at the helm. Or anyone currently in Conroy's alliance. That's why they'd been so eager to recruit Evan, but he'd taken off on the alien ship, and there was no knowing when he might be back.

No, trying to take over this vessel was a dead-end prospect. A better option would be to disable it so the enemy couldn't use it, either.

How to get close enough to cause meaningful damage without drawing attention to himself was the next question. A craft like that would have an advanced sensor suite and surveillance, so staying hidden behind trees wouldn't prevent detection. His limited mechanical knowledge didn't make the task any easier.

Don't overcomplicate it, he told himself. *There has to be something simple that would disable the ship without destroying it.*

As he was mulling over his options, a metallic click sounded behind him.

A man spoke, "You're not supposed to be here."

4

IN ALL ANYA'S research visits to alien planets, she'd endeavored to be a steward. Study. Observe. Minimal impact. Ordering a starship to blast a massive hole in the ground went against her instincts.

However, she didn't see a better choice. *Something* significant had occurred on this planet. She was eager to get answers about what had happened to the original inhabitants, and delving beneath the surface—in the most literal sense—was their best chance to get clues.

"We'll leave it to you, Sam," Anya told the ship. "Just don't do anything too extreme. We want to uncover, not disintegrate."

"I understand the parameters of the task."

Anya couldn't be sure, but she thought there was a hint of exasperation in Sam's synthesized tone. *I need to remember that this isn't an AI like back home. He's just as scared and confused as me.*

Evan moved closer to the main viewport to observe the excavation, and Anya stood next to him.

"Want to take a bet on what's down there?" she asked.

He shook his head. "I don't think anything's left. I don't

'feel' anything in the way I can sense other alien tech. So, I guess my bet would be that there's nothing left here."

Anya scowled. "That's not a fun bet at all. Never mind."

The weapon activated, sending out a visible pulse of energy as particulates in the air were disrupted. When the blast reached the ground, the soil lifted and scattered in a massive ripple, spreading from the epicenter.

Anya was expecting to see ruins emerge as the soil cleared, but there were no signs of past structures. Anything constructed like the rock city on Aethos would endure millennia, so it was strange this place was empty. But her heart skipped a beat when a large, smooth plain was revealed.

Sam eased off the weapon, and the dust settled. The polished area glimmered in the sun, reflective as though it was dark glass.

"What happened here?" Anya murmured.

"I've heard of damage like this, but have never seen it for myself," Evan said. "It can be caused by weapons fire."

"This is such a huge area…"

"It would have been a really big weapon. I can't think of anything else that could cause this. I mean, unless a research lab exploded, or something."

"Based on the last known information in my data banks, there was no facility working on physics, energy, or weapons-related projects in this vicinity," Sam chimed in.

"Is there any kind of elevated radiation at this site?" Anya asked.

"Negative."

"So, most likely, a different kind of weapon caused this," Evan surmised.

Anya nodded. "I would love to find out what."

"We should see if there are other sites like this."

"Yes, establish a pattern." The medium was different, but Anya reminded herself that scientific inquiry followed the same principles regardless of the subject. If an animal species died out, one would look at the environmental factors in both the immediate habitat as well as at the regional and global levels. Though she may be dealing with sentient aliens now, solving the mystery of their disappearance was the same. *Did they die, or did they simply move on to greener fields?*

"Sam," Evan addressed the AI, "can you identify unique properties related to this site? Is it possible to scan the rest of the planet to see if there are other glassed areas like it?"

"Yes, there are several differentiating markers. However, I am unable to scan the planet from this location."

"Then let's take this show to the skies!" Anya declared.

"In other words, please fly around the planet and proceed with whatever scans you need," Evan clarified.

"Acknowledged," Sam said.

The scene out the viewport shifted to a distant view of the planet's surface. Anya was amazed how smoothly the *Asamar* could launch. Acceleration in starships with even the most advanced stabilizers lurched her stomach, but there was no discernible sensation of movement from this drive. For however advanced she'd considered human systems, this ship's tech was in another league.

"If you find any other sites with the same markers, please take us in for a closer look," Anya instructed.

After completing a circuit of the planet, Sam concluded that there were more than a dozen sites with presumed weapons damage. Each one bore a distinct scar of a 'glassed' field like the first area they discovered. The size of the scar varied from place to place, though each was proportional to the former population center, according to Sam's records. And while not all of the planet's former cities had been impacted, the fourteen sites they discovered had been the most populous areas on the world. While that still didn't explain whether or not the aliens had done this to themselves, it did paint a clear picture that there'd been an attempt to wipe their presence from the planet's record.

"All these cities reduced to nothing..." Anya murmured. "It's awful."

"We don't know that any of them were inhabited when this happened," Evan pointed out.

"Why destroy an empty city?"

"The same reason we'd scuttle a ship in war."

It was one thing to destroy a vessel to keep the technology from falling into enemy hands, but bombing a planet was a whole other extreme. Then again, one could look at a ship as a mobile city, so maybe it wasn't that different, after all.

"Sam, can you glean any more information about when this destruction may have happened?" Anya asked.

"Based on the sediment over the site and the decay, I would estimate close to six thousand years."

Evan raised an eyebrow. "So, shortly after you left the planet?"

"Affirmative."

"Well, no wonder you never got updated instructions," Anya said.

"If I had more current data, I would share it," Sam replied. "However, I am perplexed."

Anya's skin prickled. She was used to humans being confused, but something about the AI's phrasing was deeply unnerving. "I take it there's nothing more we can learn here?"

"My scans have detected no remaining structures or energy signatures on the planet. Any further excavation is unlikely to yield the information you seek. This was not what I anticipated when I decided to bring you here."

"There are still a *lot* of things I'd like to know." Evan crossed his arms. "I'm just gonna say it… I'm stumped."

Anya sighed. "Yeah, me too. For a second there, I'd actually believed coming here would solve all our problems by meeting advanced aliens with a soft spot for helping wayward humans stumbling our way across the stars."

He raised an eyebrow. "And the narrative went like that in your head?"

"Word-for-word."

"Okay… Well, it didn't work out."

"But what are we going to do *now*?" She was reluctant to say it out loud, but they were in a perilous situation. They'd never intended to leave Aethos—a place where they at least had access to abundant food and water. This new place was a barren wasteland with some scrubby grass as the only vegetation they'd seen. She had half a canteen and a handful of MREs in her pack, but that was the extent of her supplies. There were no signs of being able to stock up here, so they'd have to move on to a different planet. But… where?

"Our objective hasn't changed," Evan said. "We need to learn more about this alien technology and find out how the Noche Syndicate might be using it. They have a serum to allow interaction with the tech, which means they *have* the tech. But where did they get it?"

"Probably a planet closer to the core worlds."

Evan nodded. "Sam had the right idea coming here, but this isn't where we'll get answers."

The sinking feeling that had been gnawing at Anya's stomach since they'd arrived stabbed at her yet again. "How long are we going to keep searching?"

"As long as it takes."

"Takes for *what*? We need, you know, 'metrics'. What does success look like for us?"

"Crazed megalomaniacs don't take over the Commonwealth and doom us all?"

Anya placed her hands on her hips and glared at Evan. "I'm serious. We need goals and a plan to achieve them."

He gave a sober nod. "You're right. The biggest thing, I think, is tracking down the Syndicate's supply of alien tech. Where did they get the materials to synthesize the serum? Do they have other technology in hand? What are their intentions?"

"That sounds like undercover work."

"Which is totally unrealistic. We'll need to come at it from another angle and try to piece it together."

"That's a nice way of saying 'make our best guess'."

"Well, I made a career out of doing that. Except, I was one investigator on a larger team, each filling in one little piece of the puzzle. We'd run our info up the chain, where all the different threads would come together. What *we're* missing is that top-level view to give us the full picture."

"You know, there is someone in that role," Anya pointed out. "Conroy."

Evan grimaced. "That's the problem. I want to verify his claims for myself."

"Agreed. I'm just not sure how much help I'll be with this sort of investigation."

"If we *do* find the source of this alien tech, you can figure out what it's done to me."

"My specialization begins and ends with plants and animals. Tech is a whole other thing."

"But this tech integrates with biology."

"True. I won't really know until I get a look at it. So, I guess figuring out that alien-tech interface might be objective number two. Or maybe that *should* be number one…" she mused.

"Hey, we might even be able to find a way to stop the Syndicate from using it."

"You mean, like, deactivate the serum?"

"Sure."

She nodded thoughtfully. "I hadn't thought of that."

"Knowing how something works is a key step toward breaking it, right?"

"Yeah." Anya let out a long breath as her chest tightened. The overwhelming scale of their task was closing in around her. "But we really do need a plan. We can't just run around with this ship indefinitely."

He tilted his head. "But, you know, that *is* an option."

She laughed it off.

"Seriously. We talked about running away to live in a cave. Having a starship with an interstellar jump drive is *way* better."

"We can't run away with the ship, Evan."

"Why not?"

"Because people are counting on us!"

"Two factions—that we know of, there might even be more—want the ship. Both have questionable motives, and we have no way to verify the intentions of the leaders. Plus, leadership can change in an instant, so striking a deal with one side or another doesn't guarantee anything. The only people we can trust are ourselves."

She crossed her arms. "I refuse to believe running away is the best option."

"The reality is, I'm not the only person who could control the ship. Someone else could convince Sam to listen to them instead, and then we will have lost the only bargaining chip we have."

"Is that true—are you going to ditch us for the next cool person to come along, Sam?" Anya asked.

"I have no compelling reason to change allegiance at this time," the AI replied. Not the most encouraging answer.

"Even with this ship, there's too much ground to cover," Evan continued. "We can't start randomly jumping to planets and hope for the best."

Anya tapped her chin with her index finger, deep in thought. "No, there has to be a pattern here..." She stared at the screen, searching for answers that may not be there. There were far fewer inhabitable worlds compared to the total tally of planets, but the sheer vastness of the galaxy was too broad a search area to analyze. "I have an idea, but I don't know if it would work."

"Don't know until you try."

She nodded. "Sam, we need you to take us to another planet where we might be able to make contact with your people."

"I have no knowledge of the present location of my people."

"But you could help us narrow down some possibilities, right?" Anya asked.

"Yes."

Evan held up his hand. "Wait, do you have fuel limitations, or anything else that will restrict your jump capabilities?"

"My power reserves are regenerative, and my systems are in good working order. At this time, I foresee no issues to prevent continued travel."

Evan smiled. "All right, then we're in business."

"Let's walk through the potential locations," Anya said.

"Planets like Aethos that may have been prepped for habitation but were never settled."

"I am not permitted to share those details with outsiders."

Had the roles been reversed, Anya would hope that her human ship's AI wouldn't spill all of humanity's secrets to the first aliens it came across, either. She'd been prepared for that contingency. "I can appreciate that, Sam. We're in a tough spot here, because we want to help you, and we're in pretty bad need of help, ourselves."

"I would like to help you."

"Let's try looking at it this way… Do you trust us, Sam?"

"You have given me no reason not to."

"You said before that you wished to keep us alive. What are you willing to do to fulfill that objective?"

Evan raised an eyebrow at the question but remained silent.

"Please further define the premise," Sam replied.

"Would you die? Would you kill others?" Anya asked.

"You are not my masters. I would not give up my own existence to save your lives, but I would kill others to save you."

Anya nodded. That was what she'd been hoping to hear. "All right, so Evan is your friend. You trust him and want to keep him safe—to keep him alive. What would you do if there were people threatening to kill Evan in order to control you?"

"I would use lethal force to preserve Evan's life and maintain my autonomy."

Self-preservation instincts for the win. Anya turned to Evan with a satisfied smile. "There it is. We have our solution."

"What, exactly, is the solution here, Anya?" Evan asked. "I feel like we skipped over several steps of that logic tree."

"All right, Sam, listen up," she said, pacing as she talked. "There are people who want to find us. If they find us, they will kill us. They will also try to capture you, and study you, and treat you like property that can be controlled and exploited. We aim to stop these people from using the technology of your people to hurt other humans or any of your kind."

"I understand."

"Okay, good. So, here's where we need your help. We need to know all the planets where your people might have hidden technology. There are already people using it, and if we can figure out where it came from, it might allow us to stop them from getting any more. And preventing them from using what they already have."

"I would like to help you, Anya. Unfortunately, my information is thousands of years out of date. I do not have sufficient data to inform your search."

"We can help narrow down the possibilities. Let's go over what you know."

5

Samor could envision the rifle trained at his back as well as if he'd had eyes on the weapon. He listened to the fine movements of its wielder, noting that the man was shifting on his feet. Soft clacks told him that he was adjusting his grip. All were nervous ticks. Either the soldier was inexperienced, or he was anxious in the unfamiliar environment.

"Steady. I'm not here to fight," Samor said, keeping his tone quiet and cool. He extended his hands slightly to make it look like he was cooperating while still keeping his sidearm within easy range.

"You one of Conroy's people?"

"Are you out here alone?" The man's hesitation was telling. "I guess so," Samor inferred. "Probably tough to make a team since you aren't exactly working under the same banner, are you?" He thought about leaving it at that but decided to press his luck. "Must be a slap in the face to be working alongside those Noche guys."

The soldier adjusted his stance. "How do you know I'm not one of them?"

"Because we never would have even started a conversation. War can be brutal, but their tactics are something else."

"I need to take you in."

"I know you do."

The man stepped forward. "Come on—"

Samor threw his elbow back and knocked the rifle's muzzle aside. In one smooth motion, he spun around and grabbed the man's forearm. He twisted up and around, causing the man to follow the rotation and drop to his knees.

"Sorry, kid." Samor held the young soldier at his mercy. "You should know better than to get that close."

"He's right. You shouldn't have," a voice said to Samor's left.

He whipped around to see a dark-haired man around thirty years old standing in the trees a dozen meters away—the person he'd seen enter the drop ship. Despite Samor's finely tuned senses, he hadn't heard him approach. Strangely, the man wasn't carrying a weapon, and his left hand was even casually stuffed into his pocket.

Samor kept his grip on his young captive. "You're invaders here."

"That's nothing new in the course of humanity. A place is only yours if you can hold it."

"We're holding on just fine."

"Are you? From where I'm standing, it looks like I'll be sleeping in your former bed tonight."

Heat rose in Samor's chest and climbed to his cheeks. "You're killers."

"And you're traitors."

Samor noted that the man's tactical gear wasn't a military design. Either he'd changed, or he was one of the Noche Syndicate thugs. He made an educated guess it was the latter. "That's rich, coming from you."

"Building an alternative economy isn't treason."

"Is that what you call it?" Samor scoffed.

The young soldier struggled against Samor's hold, but he wasn't able to do much with his arm and shoulder twisted at the extreme angle. Still, they couldn't remain in that position forever. Samor needed an exit strategy, but he didn't yet see a way out that didn't end with him getting shot in the back.

But why doesn't he have a weapon? No one walked up to an armed adversary without having an offensive strategy of their own. Were there others hidden in the surrounding trees? Imagining rifle muzzles pointed at him prickled Samor's skin.

He fought a wave of panic. *Why did I think I could get close to the ship without being seen?*

Not only was he failing this mission, but he was failing his leader. Their cause had too few fighters to lose anyone. He couldn't let it end like this.

Steeling himself, Samor calculated his escape move. It was a terrible plan, but he couldn't think of anything better in the moment. Even a longshot was better than being captured or dying here.

Samor abruptly released his captive, casting him in the direction of the Noche thug. The motion gave Samor a consistent line of sight with the two targets, which granted him an escape path in the opposite direction. He immediately started walking backward, keeping his weapon aimed toward them so he could quickly adjust to shoot either target.

To his relief—and a little surprise—no other soldiers emerged from the trees to surround him, and no shots were fired. Either they were biding their time, or there wasn't any backup. *But why doesn't this guy have a weapon?*

"You can relax! I'm not going to kill you now," the Noche man called out.

Samor didn't slow his retreat. Just because the man hadn't

raised a gun toward him yet, that didn't mean he wouldn't. Samor wanted to put as much distance as possible between them and get to a place where he'd have some cover.

"I want you to pass on a message," the Noche man continued. "Tell Conroy he can't hide forever."

Samor had reached an area with denser tree cover. He darted behind one of the thicker trunks.

The Noche man continued to stand there, watching him retreat. The young soldier with him seemed mystified by the entire encounter, but he simply massaged his shoulder. It was an interesting dynamic to see the military deferring to a member of the Noche Syndicate, but Samor didn't want to hang around to observe. He'd been given an opportunity to escape, and he needed to take it.

Even so, he recognized that he wouldn't have been released out of the goodness of the Noche man's heart. 'Passing on a message' wasn't how things worked. No, he'd been let go so he could lead the enemy back to Conroy. But Samor wouldn't make it that easy.

— — —

Roman watched Conroy's minion retreat into the forest. He couldn't fault the man for being thankful to be alive. However, any celebrations were premature. The minion—whom he recognized as Samor, one of the heroic guards who'd allegedly died in the shuttle crash along with Conroy—was the perfect patsy to lead Roman to his real prize.

Roman could 'see' him clearly, even as he disappeared from visual sight. It was as though every cell in his body was now attuned to the other man's position.

Roman knew it was the alien tech now integrated into his

own being, but he didn't know *how* it worked. He'd had less than a day to begin exploring his newfound abilities. However, what he'd discovered so far was nothing short of amazing. None of the other tech the Noche Syndicate had acquired compared to the marvelous power he was cultivating inside himself. Any doubt about taking his place in a prominent leadership role within his family could be put to rest. He would explore this new power, and he would master it to ensure his place in history.

But first, he needed to root out the weed that had been infesting Aethos for the last five years after fleeing the core worlds: Conroy. The disgraced chancellor who'd threatened all of their carefully laid plans. He needed to be eliminated once and for all.

Samor had taken off at a quick pace through the trees, heading to the east. Through his newfound mind's eye, Roman watched Samor's progress. Eventually, he'd guide him to Conroy's hiding place.

In the meantime, though, there were other loose ends to tie up.

The young guard flung out his arms with an exasperated sigh. "Why did you let him go?"

"So he can lead me to my prey." Roman rounded on the other man, tilting his head. "You failed today."

"I tried to bring him in, but—"

"You're weak. I can't have weakness."

Roman envisioned the young man's heart exploding in his chest. His skin tingled as warmth spread from his core to his limbs.

The man abruptly went limp. He crumpled face-first into a heap on the ground.

Heat receded from Roman's extremities. Knowing such

power was so easy to summon thrilled him.

Sneering down at the man, Roman nudged him with his boot. He was definitely dead.

The body presented a problem, but also an opportunity.

Roman went back to the camp. On his walk, he thought about everything terrible that had happened to him throughout his life, dredging up every painful memory. Marcus taunting him. The breakup with his first love. His parents' death. He let the emotion surge through him until his hands quivered and his face was flushed. By the time he reached the entrance, he looked the part of a man on the warpath.

Red was still outside, huddled with two of her soldiers. She noticed him approaching and cut the conversation short. "What in the planets happened to you?" she asked as soon as he was within earshot.

"One of Conroy's people came scouting around," Roman explained, trying to keep his tone firm while still seeming like he was distraught over the death. "He killed one of the watchmen!"

Red's face dropped. "Oh, no."

Imagine that... she actually cares. Misplaced affection, unfortunately. "You can't let Conroy get away with this," Roman said.

She exchanged glances with her two soldiers, and they nodded. "Where did it happen?" she asked.

"By the drop ship. I left him there, so..."

"And what happened to the perpetrator?"

"I put a tracker on him."

Red's brows scrunched together. "We didn't have any of those in our inventory."

"Not a device," he replied. "I have something much better now."

— — —

Samor ran. He'd spent so much time sneaking through the trees that an all-out sprint felt wrong. But right now, speed was all that mattered. While they'd easily be able to trace his current path of trampled plants and broken branches, no tracking skills were needed while the target was in plain sight. His only chance was to put enough distance between himself and his pursuers that he could disappear into the forest and then switch to a light touch that would hide his path. If he handled it right, it would look like his trail suddenly ended.

In preparation for that misdirect, he ran perpendicular to his intended target. The enemy was smart enough to know that he wouldn't lead them in a straight line to his destination, but it would set them far enough off course that they'd be unlikely to stumble across Echo Falls.

He checked behind him to look for signs of his pursuers. None stood out, so he slowed his pace and listened. It was quiet; he'd lost them for now. He put the second part of his plan into effect.

Samor continued blazing a clear trail for another dozen meters. When he reached a thick grove of saplings, he ran up to them and stopped. Carefully, he retraced his steps backward. Once he was several meters back, he delicately hopped off the original trail and began lightly moving across the ground to avoid leaving prints or other signs of his presence.

Even after he was two kilometers away from the drop ship, Samor kept compulsively checking over his shoulder. He'd detected no signs of human pursuit, but there was no way that he wasn't being tracked. At some point during the encounter, he must have been tagged with a tracker of some sort. The sooner he could find it, the better.

With one final look around to confirm no one was nearby, Samor stopped to strip down. Methodically, he removed every piece of clothing and shook it out while also performing a visual inspection to look for a tracker. Such devices could measure half the size of a grain of rice, so it would have been easy to drop in a pocket or stuff into a seam.

After a thorough search, he wasn't able to find anything. For that matter, after running through the encounter, he didn't know when a tracker could have been planted. The first soldier had intended to bring him in, and Samor had been in control during their up-close interactions. The Noche man had kept his distance, and Samor had never taken his eyes off the man's hands.

Yet, they'd let Samor go. There *had* to be a reason.

Protecting Conroy's hiding place was paramount. Even though he hadn't found a tracker, that didn't mean he was in the clear.

Samor re-dressed and then resumed his path to Echo Falls. He needed specialized equipment to sweep him for bugs, and they would have what he needed. Hopefully, he could get there without compromising that location.

Half a kilometer out from Echo Falls, at the outer reach of their close-range radios, he called for a team to meet him with a handheld sweeper. He found them waiting under a particularly large tree with high, wide branches that stood out from the surrounding foliage.

To Samor's surprise, Rogers was there, accompanied by a woman who normally worked with communications, Wen. The two of them waved him over.

"What was so urgent?" Rogers asked.

"I did something stupid," Samor admitted. He gave them a

brief recap of the encounter.

After he'd finished, Wen held up a hand-sized piece of equipment. "I brought the sweeper," she said. "Hold out your arms."

Samor did as he was told. Wen waved the device across each limb multiple times and all around his torso and head. After a thorough investigation, she stepped back and waved the device around some more in the open air, frowning slightly.

"What is it?" Rogers prompted.

"I'm not picking up any broadcast signals like a bug," she said. "But you *do* have a higher-than-ambient energy field around you. Have you been around anything unusual lately?"

"I was handling a lot of the alien tech samples before we evacuated. Could that do it?"

She nodded. "Very likely. That stuff does weird things. Gives me the creeps, honestly."

Samor had often felt that way about the tech, himself, but he'd rather not dwell on what exposure to it may be doing to him long-term. He'd probably been around it more than anyone else on Conroy's team during their years on the planet. "I just want to be absolutely sure that there isn't a trace on me," he said. "I don't want to risk leading anyone back to our strongholds."

"I've always appreciated your caution. I brought you a change of clothes, like you asked." Rogers handed him a clean outfit.

"I don't even know that that's necessary, but it can't hurt just in case," Wen said. "To my best assessment, you're clear."

Samor nodded. "Thank you. I appreciate you coming out here to check. I just can't think of why they would have let me go if it wasn't to track me."

"Taking prisoners or killing can stir up all kinds of shit,"

Rogers offered. "We're all stuck here, so maybe they don't want to escalate the situation until backup arrives."

"That'll be months from now, unless a ship was already in transit well before the crash."

Rogers shrugged. "We took heavy losses on both sides. They might suspect we have another missile and could blow up the base."

Samor frowned. "That would be insane."

"These are the people that were willing to shoot down a colony ship so there wouldn't be witnesses to them exterminating *us*. I think we can throw usual decency standards out the window," Rogers pointed out.

"Yeah, maybe so." Samor looked down at the folded set of clothes in his hands. "Thanks for these. I'll get changed and then go fill in Conroy."

"Happy we could help," Rogers said.

"You're good, don't worry," Wen assured him. "See you around."

Samor hurriedly changed into the new outfit and buried the old clothes under some fallen leaves. It wasn't a true hiding place, but it would be enough to keep them from being easily spotted by a casual passerby, and any hidden tracker would safely remain in the middle of nowhere.

He took a brisk pace back to Hidden Grotto, following a slightly weaving path that varied from his other travel between the two sites. He made a point of never following exactly the same route twice to prevent a path from wearing into the ground.

Samor was winded by the time he made it to the other base, but the less time he was out in the open, the better.

Rebeka greeted him at the entrance. "Hey, how'd the scouting go?" She squinted and tilted her head. "Wait, are those different clothes?"

"It's a long story."

She crossed her arms. "Uh oh."

"I need to talk to Conroy. Should I start with the good news or bad?"

6

As Conroy took in Samor's report, he was reminded yet again of how isolated and vulnerable they were on Aethos. When the planet had been merely a remote world, months from the nearest outpost, the seclusion had given him comfort. Now, it seemed more like a trap.

"How, then, do you propose we gain control of the drop ship? Or disable it?" Conroy asked.

Samor shook his head. "I'm afraid that my impulsive move cost us the element of surprise. They'll probably post guards now. It's not worth it for us to go after it until we're ready to make a bigger move."

Conroy steepled his fingers. "We're cornered. We can't make any kind of move until Evan and Anya return."

"*If* they return," Rebeka countered.

"She's right," Samor said. "We need a plan that isn't contingent on them or the alien ship. There are invaders on our doorstep, and we need to do something about it."

Conroy hadn't wanted to face the possibility that they might be on their own, but that was the grim reality of the situation. After all their years of careful planning and maneuvering, their prospects now hinged on two strangers.

Tying so many of their ambitions to the alien ship had left them in a vulnerable position. They'd worked everything out, securing the serum sample and gear they'd need, but all those materials had been destroyed when the colony ship was shot down. They didn't have a backup plan for that contingency; he couldn't have imagined the need for one.

Recruiting Evan and Anya was a last-ditch effort to salvage what had been lost. But the process to bring them into the fold had been rushed and incomplete, so there was no telling where they may have gone or what they might do. The one saving grace was that they *had* gotten the alien ship, which meant the enemy didn't control it—yet.

"We need to restrict the enemy's numbers and movements," Conroy mused. "We know where they are. We need to pen them in."

"Sir, I appreciate the ambition, but our own resources are extremely limited," Samor countered. "We simply don't have the firepower to take them on."

"We can't sit idly and hope for the best."

"No, we can't. Let's lay it all on the table." Samor spread out his hands on the metal surface for emphasis. "We have two weeks' worth of pre-packed food—three if we ration. Every time we go out to forage, there's a risk of getting caught. The enemy has a drop ship, which will enable them to move faster than us. We have limited weaponry and even fewer trained fighters." He looked across the table at his friend. "That's not a knock on you and the others, Rebeka. You've done great, but being brave in a firefight isn't the same thing as having rigorous tactical training."

"No offense taken," Rebeka said.

"And you're absolutely right." Conroy told him. "We need an alternative where we don't need to fire any—or, at least, *minimal*—shots. Options. What do we have?"

"We could try to barricade them in the base," Samor suggested. "We have explosives, so we could blow the entrances. Pick them off one-by-one as they try to escape."

"Problem with that is it would destroy most of our stuff," Rebeka pointed out. "I think trying to make them evacuate would be better."

"How? They know we're after them. They'll see through any kind of diversion in seconds."

"Not if we don't give them a choice. Messing with the environmental controls could force them out, right? Make the air unbreathable or something?"

"That's an idea without an executable strategy," Samor said.

"Why not? There's an external access point for the environmental systems. Do you have a better idea?"

Samor and Rebeka continued throwing out suggestions and promptly disagreeing with each other. They exchanged barbs for a couple of minutes before Conroy couldn't hear any more.

He stood up. "Excuse me. I need to mull this over." He stepped away, wanting to evaluate the options in peace. There was no way to think clearly while the others talked over each other in heated debates about irrelevant details.

The big picture was what mattered. Multiple worlds hung in the balance. The very future of humanity was at stake.

Or is it? He'd been so wrapped up in plotting the worst doom scenarios that he hadn't considered that the worst-case circumstances may never come to pass.

But still, the *possibility* was there. Even if total annihilation was unlikely, the smallest chance seemed like too big a bargain. He needed to do everything within his power to mitigate a disastrous outcome. That included forming alliances he would never have indulged during better times. War had a strange way of changing one's perspective. And from where he was sitting now, he would graciously accept help, even from the most unlikely places.

Gathering his thoughts, he returned to the group. "Before we do anything, we need to get an updated count on their numbers and position," he stated, not raising his voice to talk over the din. "Then, we will find a way to weaken them enough to reclaim our base. We can seal them as prisoners on the crashed cruiser."

Samor and Rebeka looked at each other and then back to Conroy. They nodded their approval.

Conroy sat back down. "All right, let's go over what we know."

— — —

Roman smiled to himself. *That was too easy.*

Credit where it was due, Samor had done his best to stage a redirect. He'd gone well out of his way in the wrong direction. But just as expected, he'd eventually headed home.

Roman couldn't perceive anything about Samor's surroundings, aside from knowing his physical location. It was a similar pull to what he experienced when he was near the alien tech. He simply *felt* it. He supposed the imprint could be classified as some kind of telepathy. The strangest part was how natural it felt to use an ability that would have sounded like fantasy to him a day ago.

In fact, his perceptions about many aspects of Aethos had shifted rapidly over the last day. Even the insects and pollen in the air, which had been the bane of his existence a week prior, were now barely noticeable. He was picking up details in the natural environment he'd once overlooked. The beauty of the flowers. The way the light filtered through the tree canopy. The pleasant warmth of the breeze on his skin. There was even a satisfying spring to his step on the ground that had once seemed to weigh him down.

There's a network of life here, he realized. And not all of it was natural. Many of the plants and animals had been modified by the alien presence. It was in the soil. The air. Right now, he only had the faintest grasp of it—like trying to snatch a handful of fog. Perhaps with time, though, he'd be able to seize it and mold it to his own design.

At the moment, maintaining the trace on Samor was at the outer reaches of his ability. A location… that's all he'd needed. But what was the best response to the new information?

He decided to keep it to himself for the present. He didn't trust Red, and he certainly didn't trust her people. After the poor performance he'd witnessed from the young—now deceased—soldier, Roman was even more convinced that he'd been saddled with the 'D' team.

Fortunately, he was resourceful. They'd be useful bodies when they were needed, but he could manage on his own.

Since his previous evaluation of the recovered files had been rudely interrupted by Samor's arrival, Roman returned to the drop ship to finish his work.

Two guards were now posted outside it. They stood aside as Roman approached, nervously glancing at his glowing hand as he passed by.

On the ship's flight deck, he once again settled in at the communications console. He pulled up the files to resume his study of the map.

The trace on Samor drew his attention to the north. It was

a bizarre sensation being able to tell where someone was in space without really knowing where it was. He focused on the map, trusting his new inner senses to guide him.

He scanned the map, envisioning the distance to various points from his present position. Some of them felt immediately wrong. After a few minutes, one specific location called out to him.

There you are. It was only an educated guess, of course—not a certainty—but he would wager that was Conroy's hiding place. A heavily forested and hilly region.

Interestingly, another location also caught his attention. That one was only a kilometer from where he'd sensed Samor had gone during his misdirect.

Or maybe it wasn't a misdirect, after all. Is that another outpost? Perhaps he had gone to report in on the encounter. Or maybe *that* was actually Conroy's hiding place, and the second location was him trying to draw attention away from the real target. Either way, he was eager to learn more.

Roman leaned back in the seat. *I'll have to pay our friend a visit.*

7

"I HAD NO idea there were this many potentially habitable planets," Evan said while he watched Anya scroll through one planetary profile after another.

"You wouldn't want to live more than five minutes on many of these."

"Then why are you looking at them?"

"Because that's how cross-referencing works. If you'd like to help verify the atmospheric mix and biome mapping, I'd welcome your input. Otherwise, silence is appreciated." She raised an eyebrow as she glanced at him over her shoulder. Somehow, the look managed to be both alluring and terrifying.

"Yes, ma'am." He clamped his jaw and resumed watching her methodical review.

For the last two hours, she'd been cross-referencing various information from Sam's data banks. The way she'd described it, she was conducting a quick and dirty analysis of potential colony worlds in the way she would have back home to determine the best candidates. Sam had suggested that his people had been in the midst of an expansion effort at the time Aethos was prepped as a colony, but he didn't know which worlds had ultimately been selected. Anya was attempting to narrow it down from a couple hundred candidates to the top dozen with environmental conditions that matched the overlapping characteristics of both Sam's homeworld and Aethos.

Analyzing data tables had never been Evan's strength. Breaking into a locked room to access an encrypted console to download the data… that part he could get excited about. But actually combing through those records made his eyes glaze over. Nonetheless, he tried to pay attention and offer feedback when he spotted something that might be helpful. In time, they got into a smooth routine working together and knocked out the rest of their master list review.

"All right, I think we've got a good starting place," Anya announced.

"Those are some good candidates." Evan sat up straighter. "Where should we go first?"

Anya called up a file on the wall-mounted display. "I say this one. The alien designations are utter gibberish to me, but let's call it EX-17. Similar temperature range to Aethos, though less vegetation. Plenty of liquid water. It's got a lot of rocky mountains, and we know these guys love those!"

"Speaking of giving things names we can actually pronounce, what should we call your people, Sam?" Evan asked.

"For your tongue, the closest name would be 'Korani'."

"Korani," Anya repeated. "That works for me."

Evan nodded. "Yes, that's great. Hopefully, some of the Korani are still at one of these outposts and can answer some questions for us."

"At a minimum, I'm hoping that we can find some similar tech to what we discovered on Aethos. You know, get our hands on more of those spheres."

Evan's hand tingled from the memory. "What do you think you'll need in order to evaluate the Noche serum?"

She drummed her fingers. "You know… that's a good question. We're surrounded by alien tech here, so I doubt an artifact would give us anything different than what we already have right now. Let me get a blood sample running in the bioanalyzer now, and maybe those results will give us clues about what else to look for on each of these planets."

Evan pricked his fingertip, and Anya took a blood sample with the sensor prongs on the bioanalyzer.

She set it aside. "This equipment is designed to assess organic samples. And while running your DNA profile is straightforward, my guess is that there's some kind of nanotechnology in that serum. I won't be able to decode that with the bioanalyzer. I might be able to work with Sam on an analysis, but I think we should prioritize checking out some more planets."

"Yes. Macro data first." Evan sucked on his finger to help quell the bleeding.

"Would you like me to jump to the first planet you identified?" Sam asked.

"That would be great," Anya confirmed.

The starship smoothly launched into space. When it had cleared the planet's atmosphere, the golden particles began swirling around the *Asamar*. A golden glow enveloped the vessel, and the stars winked out as the ship slipped into the spatial distortion.

Unlike the previous jump, which had taken several minutes, this one was only forty seconds.

When the *Asamar* returned to normal space, Evan was relieved to see that the planet framed in the forward viewport had significantly more green than the Korani's bleak homeworld.

Anya took a slow breath. “Okay, so far, so good.”

“Any signs of the Korani?” Evan asked.

“I am not detecting any cities on the planet,” Sam replied with obvious disappointment. “However, there are active energy signatures.”

Evan grinned. “But that is *great* news for us.”

“Yes, I believe you will find what you want here,” Sam confirmed.

Clouds blurred by outside the viewport as the ship descended. Were it not for the altimeter displayed on the screen, Evan would have had no idea that they were at such a low elevation.

Only a thousand meters from the ground, the clouds finally broke enough to get a first look at the landscape. There was minimal vegetation, and deep rock canyons scarred the vast expanse between a broad forest. From their high elevation, he couldn’t make out fine details, but it did seem like some of the ‘canyons’ were too straight and symmetrical to be natural formations.

Sam set down the *Asamar* in a field at the head of one of the suspiciously shaped canyons. “These are the geo-coordinates in my records related to prospective colonization targets. My sensors are not detecting the presence of any Korani, but the energy signatures are consistent with pre-colonization efforts.”

Anya’s eyes gleamed with excitement. “What kind of tech might be here? Like the spheres, and—”

“Much more than that, Anya. The ‘spheres’, as you call them, are part of a larger system.”

Evan’s heart skipped a beat. The sphere had been the most mesmerizingly powerful thing he’d ever touched. If that was only the start… "Where's the entrance to the Korani structure, Sam?" Evan asked.

"Walk through the canyon. You'll know it."

Evan had no doubt that the ship was correct. The pull was unmistakable, even from this distance. He hurried off the flight deck to the exit hatch.

Without waiting for Anya, Evan opened the hatch and descended the ramp.

"You seem more excited than the last stop," she commented, coming up behind him.

"I wish you could feel what I feel with this tech. I think I now understand an addict's compulsion to get a fix."

"That's a disturbing analogy."

"I mean, it's not *that* bad. I don't *need* the power. But it's out there, calling."

"You practically ran off the ship, Evan."

"Yeah, I guess I did," he realized. Now that he was aware of the influence, he made a point of trying to be more objective. "I've got it under control, I promise."

She side-eyed him but nodded.

Stepping foot on the planet's dry topsoil, Evan sensed the same resonance as he'd experienced on Aethos—like he was a part of the place despite being a new visitor to the land. Though it was strangely comforting to feel like he was a part of something bigger than himself, it was also terrifying to know that alien technology was driving that sensation.

If I could remove the Syndicate's serum from me right now, would I do it? he wondered as he hiked away from the ship with Anya. Being honest with himself, he recognized that he was too invested in this mission now. Removing the serum and the integration with the alien tech it offered would only make accomplishing the mission objective more difficult. *Well, it would make some things more difficult. But what* is *the mission objective?*

To Anya's point earlier, they'd been wandering blind for a while now. With so many competing players, it was difficult to determine who was a true opponent and who might be a potential ally. Since the motives of the different factions were still unclear, Evan wasn't ready to declare full allegiance to one side. His bond with Sam, though—*that* relationship was necessary. His part in the other political dynamics wouldn't matter without that link. So, to maintain the connection to the ship, he was stuck with the alien serum whether he liked it or not.

"I just can't fathom how the Syndicate may have figured out how to make the serum," he mused while they walked.

"Neither can I. First, they needed to *find* alien tech. Before Aethos, I hadn't heard about any definitive discovery."

"Neither had I."

"Second, someone had the crazy idea to… what, like inject some alien nanites into themselves? Or did it mind-meld with them? It just doesn't add up. I feel *nothing* when I'm around that tech, so how would any other random person even know that a telepathic interface was possible?"

An idea itched at the back of Evan's mind. He didn't want to acknowledge it, but it continued pestering him. Finally, he had to blurt it out. "Unless they were told."

Anya halted and turned to face him. "Told by *whom*, Evan?"

"I don't know. I…" He shrugged. "Who's to say it couldn't be the aliens themselves?"

"But if they were already in contact with the Korani, then why would they need to go to Aethos to find Sam? Surely, they'd already have other starships, right?"

"The planet we just came from was really messed up. What if a few survivors escaped and crashed somewhere?"

She frowned. "Right. And the Syndicate is helping them out of the goodness of their hearts," she quipped.

"Not goodness. For power and profit. They get access to powerful tech in exchange for launching a plot to get the Korani a new starship from Aethos."

"You have a very active imagination, Evan."

"Another hazard of my former line of work."

Anya searched his face. "Part of you believes it might be possible, though."

"All I can say is that there's a *lot* about this whole situation that doesn't add up."

They continued their trek across the rocky valley. Dry air burned Evan's eyes and sinuses—especially harsh after the humid air on Aethos.

"I never thought I'd miss the jungle," Evan admitted.

"I seem to recall you wishing for flatter landscape with fewer trees."

"Misguided newbie explorer attitude," he replied. "I know better now."

"It is nice to know you can live off the land in a place. Up there might not be so bad." She nodded toward the trees peeking over the canyon's lip.

"If only we could do what they do. Being able to grow structures and potentially engineer hybrid animals, who knows how quickly you could bio-optimize a planet?"

"Good point. Hmm."

"What about it?" he asked.

"Well, all this time, we've been excited about the idea of being able to jump to different planets. But what if we could *make* the kinds of planets where we'd want to live?"

"Wow, that really would open up a lot of new possibilities."

"As advanced as we like to think we are as humans, colonizing different star systems, we have a lot of limitations. Temperature, ecology... If there was a way to transform environments, we'd have a lot more options. Not to mention, there are a lot of planets that have useful resources but aren't habitable. Imagine how much easier it would be to mine if there was a breathable atmosphere!"

"I thought most of that work was done by robotics?"

"Yeah, a lot of it, but human oversight is needed on many things," she said. "You know what the regs are like."

"Sure do. We ran into that in the military all the time." Since the current sentiment was that artificial intelligence was excellent as a productivity tool that should be kept under strict regulation, there were limitations on the creative thinking aspects of those systems. So, situations that didn't have a clear numbers-based solution were best handled by humans. After seeing robotic soldiers make some questionable calls in battle, Evan was happy to keep it that way.

"With the push for human boots on the ground, so to speak, being able to create a habitable biome would be huge for future development," Anya said. "We could send people to oversee mining or farming operations on planets that would have previously been a pass."

"What kind of hypothetical increase in viability are we talking about here?" Evan asked.

"I can't give you hard numbers off the top of my head, but paradise planets like Aethos are *extremely* rare. There are a lot of barren rocks that are way too hot or way too cold, and plenty of useless balls of gas. But when we do find one in the right zone to support liquid water, imagine if there was an efficient technology to seed them and simply grow a city rather than needing to ship in parts… Well, that would revolutionize everything."

"Finding the ship was just the start," Evan realized.

"Yeah, I don't think Conroy shared more than a sliver of his bigger plan."

Evan shook his head. "We really got mixed up in a hell of a thing, didn't we?"

"And here I am, just a lowly research scientist. At least you were trained for investigations!"

"As an operative to covertly gather discrete information. Putting together the pieces to an interstellar puzzle is a new one for me."

"You do it the same way. One piece at a time. Get all the pieces, and maybe we can have some peace."

He sighed. "Anya…"

She laughed, flashing her pretty smile. "I'm sorry. That was terrible, even for me."

"Whenever we start getting this punny, it's a sign that we need a good meal and a full night's rest."

"Ha! Like that's going to happen any time soon."

"About as likely as either of us giving up corny wordplay."

"Hungry and tired it is."

— — —

With only one direction to go and few obstacles, they made quick progress through the canyon. Anya noted the various plants and wildlife they passed by. While not as lush as Aethos, there was a more interesting biome than some of the places she'd surveyed during her time in the field.

Many of the plants were covered in large spikes or had a thorny texture to their main stalks. Those kinds of features developed due to something wanting to eat them. She didn't see any large animals around, but the clue was enough for her to alert Evan to the potential danger.

"If they eat plants, how likely might they be to want to eat us?" he asked.

"Even obligate herbivores have been known to chow down on a meat snack on occasion. Though, that's usually baby birds rather than large game."

"Great. That makes me feel so much better."

"It should. We're likely not on the menu for whatever ate these plants. But whatever eats *them*..."

Evan picked up his pace. "I feel like we should earn some kind of award for surviving a record number of ridiculous things in the span of a week," he grumbled.

"The committee has noted your nomination."

Eventually, they crested a hill. With a clear line of sight to the other side, a structure came into view.

Her breath caught. The formation before her was aglow in the angled sunlight, with strong shadows giving a crisp, illustrated quality to the stone formations. Giant pillars and archways were etched into a towering cliff face. For all the magnificence of the cave city on Aethos, it had been underground so she hadn't been able to appreciate its architectural scale from afar. This place, though, exuded artistic flare and elegance, evoking a cathedral or capitol building where form took precedence over function.

"Is it some kind of temple?" Anya wondered aloud.

"It definitely has that kind of grand look to it, huh?" Evan shrugged. "Seems like a lot of work for a place where no one moved in."

"Is it any more work to make a plain building than something fancy when it's nanites moving around all the material?"

"True. It must be a heck of a lot easier to create fine details when it's not some dude with a chisel picking away by hand."

They began descending the far side of the hill toward the structure.

"This seems really intact for a place that's been exposed to the elements for millennia."

"It's possible that the nanite treatment strengthens the stone."

"Maybe. But..." He frowned. "A lot of stuff was buried and destroyed on Aethos. Like, those scraps Samor showed us back in the storage room—those pieces had clearly been broken off from something larger. What used to be there, and what happened to it?"

Anya considered the observation. He had a point. "This might be a leap, but could it be connected to the gap in Sam's memory?"

"I'd figured that had to do with how an AI processed time compared to a non-sentient computer."

"Could be. I dunno, just a thought."

"I'll entertain all possibilities."

"I'm just wondering if there might have been an attack with the intention of... well, wiping out the Korani. The cities were leveled. There could have been some manner of a cyberattack, as well."

"All interesting thoughts, Anya. It *is* a leap, though. We simply don't have enough information right now to speculate."

"Maybe this place will be able to give us more."

They were approaching the grand entrance archway to the temple—at least, that's what she was privately calling it. The close-range inspection confirmed that it was yet another place where the structure had been 'grown' rather than being carved, as evidenced by the detail in the channels and overlapping fine lines.

Walking up to it, Evan got a faraway look in his eyes. “I feel something happening.”

8

EVAN'S BLOOD BURNED. The sensation wasn't pain, exactly—more like the heat from standing in the sun for too long without protection. There was also a strange resonance inside him, similar to what he'd experienced with the other alien tech, but even stronger. The burning was a vibration. Every cell in his body was calling out to sing a melody he didn't yet know. He wanted to embody that song. He needed to.

"Evan?" Anya asked cautiously, her brows pinched as she searched his face.

"There's definitely something here," he managed to reply. The strange song had filled his mind, overwhelming his senses. It buzzed in his ears, pulsed at the edges of his vision, and he could even taste a new sweetness in the air.

The call drew him toward the temple door.

"It's in here," he said, giving into the ethereal beckoning.

Anya followed him, silent and fascinated. She had the same look in her eyes as when she was studying a new animal with unique characteristics.

Except, I'm the specimen this time. One was never supposed to become the subject of their own investigation. It was impossible to remain objective once personal feelings got involved. He'd become hopelessly entwined in this project, and there was nothing he could do about it now.

A rush of cool air passed over his skin as he stepped into the shadow of the temple's towering entrance. Up close, he noticed the same kind of intricate lined patterns as those in the chamber where they'd discovered the starship. The fine channels snaked across the walls and merged into larger conduits, which framed the doorway. Inexplicably, despite being exposed to the elements, the detailed surfaces looked like they could have been finished yesterday.

"It's absolutely incredible," Anya breathed.

Evan shared her awe, but the bizarre hum in his head wouldn't permit him to stop and admire the architecture. Something inside was waiting for him.

As he passed through the threshold into an apparent cave entrance, a piercing shriek echoed in the darkness. Additional shrieks rang out, followed by a cacophony of fluttering.

"Duck!" Anya shouted, dropping to the ground.

Evan squatted a moment before a winged creature emerged from the depths. Its wingspan was nearly as wide as he was tall, with four leathery wings flapping wildly. Two additional appendages hung down, each ending in three oversized talons.

Evan reached for his handgun, but the speedy creature was directly above him before he could draw.

However, it passed overhead and continued out the doorway.

A flurry of three dozen more beasts soon followed. The breeze from their flapping wings ruffled Evan's hair as he kept his head down. A stench of decay wafted through the air as they passed.

When the creatures had departed and there were no

further sounds from deeper in the cave, Evan finally raised his head. "That was close."

"Scavengers, I think," Anya said as she stood up. She dusted off her knees. "And it must get hot on this planet. Low fat and no insulating fur or feathers."

"You xenobiologists…"

She grinned. "The power of observation, my friend. I know you appreciate it."

"I do."

Evan fished a flashlight out from his backpack. He shined it deeper into the cave.

Massive columns rose to the ceiling four meters above. Each was wrapped in the same intricate channels, but the floor and walls were perfectly smooth. The chamber was twenty meters wide and appeared to get narrower further back, though its depth was beyond the reach of Evan's light.

Swinging the light beam around, Evan noticed lumpy piles behind a number of the columns around the perimeter of the space. Anya pulled out her own flashlight and went to investigate.

She wrinkled her nose and stepped back. "Yeah, um… Those things roost here. I recommend you avoid the piles."

Evan didn't need to be told twice.

Careful of their footing, they continued deeper into the chamber. It did, indeed, narrow further in, though the ceiling remained the same towering height.

Fifty meters from the entrance, the burning sensation in Evan's veins dimmed to a warm glow. Light then started creeping up the walls, much like the simulated sunrise inside the cavern on Aethos. The illumination gradually intensified until the interior had the appearance of a warm glow after dawn.

Anya clicked off her flashlight. "Well, that's convenient. Did you do that?"

"Not consciously. But who knows?" Evan returned his flashlight to his pack, wanting his hands to be free in case there were any other surprises.

After another thirty meters, the walls abruptly flared outward and transitioned into a massive circular room. At the center of the space, a sculptural metal device loomed floor to ceiling. The bottom of it was ringed in a control panel, which was currently offline. The upper section of the device was interwoven tubes of metal, reminding Evan of vines wrapped around the trees in Aethos' vibrant jungle.

The 'pull' he'd been experiencing since first setting eyes on the temple now indicated that this was his destination. He couldn't begin to guess what this device would do.

"I know we came here to find alien tech, but I'm hesitant to touch anything," he admitted. "For all we know, it could be a weapon."

"You've had a telepathic link with the other stuff. Is this thing telling you it's destructive?"

"No. But it's not telling me *anything* right now."

Anya examined the device from a distance. "I would hope that Sam would have told us if there was something we should be worried about. But then again, we only met Sam a few hours ago. An alien starship. For all we know, he could have brought us here because it's an extra-dimensional holding facility where they deposit samples of various species they meet around the cosmos, and turning on that device might spring the trap."

Evan blinked at her. "And here I thought *I* was the one with an active imagination."

"Okay, I got a little carried away with that one."

"You're right, though, that this tech has the potential to be *dangerous*. I won't ever forget how those guys were vaporized because I magically wished they were gone."

"It's not magic," Anya murmured.

"No, but whatever it is—"

"Nanotech. It's all nanotech. Whatever little nanite technology that's capable of disassembling a mountain and reforming it in the shape of a city is probably what was weaponized against those soldiers."

"Where is it?" he asked.

"The nanites could be anywhere. I don't know if it's stored in the sphere or if the whole planet of Aethos is covered in it after all these years, but the hypothesis fits what we've observed. There's nothing 'magical' about it just because we don't yet understand the underlying science."

"I don't really care about how it works, Anya. The only thing that matters is what it can do. And, apparently, that's unalive people with horrifying efficiency."

"You can't judge a technology purely by the worst application of its capabilities. With the right commands, it could heal as effectively as it destroys. Or build anything a civilization would need to flourish. The potential uses with colonization alone would revolutionize how we develop new worlds."

He crossed his arms. "You have an idealistic view as a scientist. I'm more cynical after spending time with the darkest sides of humanity. As long as this technology exists, there's opportunity to exploit it for gruesome ends."

"Better we possess it than someone else," Anya said matter-of-factly.

"We'll never control all of it. The more we uncover will just crack the door wider open."

"You want to walk away?"

"No, I didn't say that. What I mean is, I'm not taking this lightly. This is *real power*, not playtime."

She reached out to tenderly take his hands, gazing at him with her striking copper eyes. "I trust you, Evan. The fact that you're cautious tells me you're the right person to hold this power. And knowing that others far less honorable than you will want to use it, you'll need to learn to master it. To stand against them. The only way to fight power is with power."

He nodded, cracking a smile. "Will you promise to give me an ego check if I get too big a head from my superhuman abilities?"

Anya laughed. "Oh, hell yeah! I'll give you a nice, cold splash of reality whenever you need it."

"All right, deal. Let's do this." Evan took a deep breath as he approached the central console. His skin tingled as he extended his hand toward the smooth surface.

Like the control arch in the cave on Aethos, golden symbols appeared on the interface screen when he touched it. He knew they were only in his mind's eye, yet they were indistinguishable from a projected holographic image. Like that previous experience, the symbols started out as nonsensical squiggles but began to take on meaning the longer he stared at them.

He withdrew his hand; the symbols remained.

"Anya, you should stay back. I don't know what's going to happen," Evan warned.

She withdrew to the chamber's entrance.

When she gave him a nod to proceed, Evan returned his attention to the symbols. Whatever was happening in his brain had sorted itself out, because looking at the control panel now made as much sense as any device in a human-made starship.

The curious thing, though, was none of the controls seemed like something that belonged inside a rock cavern in the middle of nowhere on an uninhabited planet.

There were labels for standard environmental controls related to temperature and lighting, but also inexplicable items like 'suspension field'. The words were familiar, but he had no idea what any of it *meant* in this context. *One way to find out...*

He started with a simple one: lighting. Messing with the lights couldn't hurt much, right?

Brushing his hand over the designated control sent a tingle through his fingertips, and visions flashed in his mind. He concentrated on a mental image of the lights intensifying and then dropping to a simulation of dusk.

A moment after relaying the thoughts, the room got brighter and then abruptly dimmed. Remarkably, rather than the generic darkness he'd envisioned, the room came to life in a new way. A detailed starscape appeared on the ceiling, as realistic as stargazing under the open sky on a clear night. The nighttime simulation rotated slowly around the room and shifted position, as though watching a time-lapse of the celestial procession.

Evan stared up at it, slack-jawed. "Anya, are you seeing anything right now?"

"The lights dimmed, if that's what you mean."

All right, so the stars are in my head. He turned in place as he searched the simulated sky for clues. "I really wish you could see into my brain right now."

"We might discover an interface here, but I don't think you'll find it by staring at the ceiling," she called back.

"I'm looking at a starscape. I didn't ask for it to appear, so I'm trying to see if this place is attempting to tell me something."

"Oh." She shifted on her feet, then she deliberately strode toward him at the center of the chamber. "It's really frustrating not being able to see what you're seeing."

"No kidding. I could use another set of eyes to tell me what I'm missing." He glanced at her as she came up next to him. "What happened to staying back?"

"Images of stars in your head aren't going to hurt me." She placed her hands on her hips. "Try letting your thoughts go fuzzy. Invite the important stuff to jump out at you."

"That—"

"Just try it, Evan. With all the other things, stuff has happened when you haven't thought about it too hard. Don't fight it."

He took in a slow, deep breath through his nose and exhaled. As he released the breath, he relaxed his senses.

Various points started to stand out to him. *Are these worlds where the Korani settled?*

The map made no indication if his thinking was correct. However, as he watched the rotating map, he recognized some of the larger landmarks in that region of space. Not only was some of it within the zone of human settlement, but he was confident that he recognized one of the worlds. He'd never been there, but it had been mentioned within the Noche Syndicate. The allure of the place had remained a mystery to him during his time undercover. Now, though, it was starting to make sense.

"Anya, I think I might know where the Noche Syndicate found whatever they used to create that interface serum."

Her brows shot up. "What? How?"

"This machine told me… or guided my subconscious. I'm not sure how to describe it."

"Would you be able to direct Sam there?"

"I think so."

"Well, we know what tourist stop is next on our list."

He turned back to the massive device. "There's more here. This place wasn't constructed just to be a telepathic planetarium."

Evan started a slow, clockwise walk around the central column. The various displays came to life in his mind. Many of their exact functions remained unclear. Eventually, though, another beckoned to him. It reminded him of the roof hatch on Aethos. This one was oriented differently, but its design suggested 'movement'. He pressed it.

A deep rumble vibrated in the floor, reverberating through the chamber. A section of the back wall slid aside, exposing another area. Light illuminated along the floor seam, which appeared to head toward a downward corridor.

Evan looked at Anya. "Should we check out the secret passageway?"

"Is that a serious question? Obviously!" Her eyes were wide with excitement.

"I really have no idea what to expect from this place."

"All part of the mystery."

They descended the ramp, which turned into a spiral. After several revolutions, it opened up into a large chamber. The turns had been disorienting, but Evan was pretty sure the space was directly below the circular room with the large device at its center. To further support that assessment, there was a similar item in this new room. The same kind of columns towered from the floor to the ceiling, but the base of this was a pool of the golden particles.

The strange particles activated as Evan approached, beginning to swirl around each other with too much order to be random. When he extended his hand, they broke from their original path and came toward him. They rotated around his hand like it was their new center of gravity.

Anya crouched down to get a closer look, fascinated. "That's something you don't see every day."

"Are these the same things that formed the jump drive lattice?"

She shrugged. "Maybe? Sam might be able to tell us."

"Makes me wonder if the sphere we found on Aethos was made from these, too."

"Another Sam question."

"I wish we had some sort of comm system so we could communicate even when we're away from the ship." He paused, half hoping that the strange material would spring into action and make his wish a reality. Unfortunately, the particles didn't do anything new.

While Evan was mulling over his next move, Anya wandered off to inspect other areas. It wasn't long before she called out, "Found something!"

Joining her, Evan's heart skipped a beat when he saw a metal circlet. "What could that be?"

"I was hoping you knew."

No clear telepathic message jumped out at him. "There's power in it, I know that much."

"Might need to test it out to see what it does."

"That's a great way to accidentally vaporize someone. Not making that mistake twice."

"The previous time wasn't a mistake, given the 'kill or be killed' situation."

"What *matters*," Evan continued, "is that I now know even a casual thought could have deadly consequences. I need to be extra careful about anything I touch or interface with."

"So, be careful," Anya told him. "Like you said, you're

aware of the risk now. Having that awareness will no doubt help control the subconscious commands."

That rationale did track with the limited bioelectronic interfaces Evan had used in his previous line of work. *Be deliberate with your thoughts. You're in control.*

He studied the inscription Anya had identified. It appeared to denote the outline of a four-armed figure surrounded by a halo. He placed his hand on the icon.

A channel of golden light shot up the central column, followed by a mechanical *clank* like a hatch opening.

Tiny, glowing golden particles levitated from the channel. They swirled around each other to form a loose spiral looping around itself in the air. The formation slowly descended, heading for Evan.

His heart rate spiked as it approached. It was calling out to him, willing him to accept it.

Evan thought of the ship and the particles that collectively formed the latticework capable of performing spatial jumps. *Could this give me that same kind of power?*

Part of him wanted to find out. A big part. But a voice in the back of his mind warned him that accepting this gift would change him. He might not be able to control it, and he'd have no guaranteed way to sever a connection once it was established. He wasn't ready to make that commitment. He didn't know enough.

The particles sensed his hesitation. They hovered in front of his face, almost like they were studying him. Though no words were exchanged, his mind was filled with a clear message. *"It's okay. We will help you when you're ready."*

Abruptly, the particles contracted toward a central point. In a bright flash, they joined together in a sphere. The light extinguished, and the sphere dropped.

Evan caught it, finding it slightly warm to the touch. Delicate grooves encircled it. Though there was a strong resemblance to the sphere they'd found on Aethos, this one didn't give him the unnerving flashes of violent thoughts. Instead, it made him feel… safe.

"Whoa!" Anya exclaimed.

"You saw that?"

"Swirly light show and new sphere? Yep!"

"I think it wanted to, like, *fuse* with me," he told her.

"That's a new kind of unnerving."

He stared at the sphere in his hand. "There's a personality to it. This is so strange, Anya. Somehow, it wants to help us. I can't explain *how* I know that, but this isn't a mindless machine."

"I can't help but be skeptical of the wants and ambitions of something so unknown."

"Me, either."

Nonetheless, some alien race had gone to great lengths to construct this chamber. Even using technology that could create a room from blank stone, care had clearly been taken with the design. The proportions spoke to a grand majesty. Someone wanted the users of this place to feel special. And, truthfully, Evan did.

There had to be more to the place, though. This may as well be a storage room, full of potential. But all that material required guidance. Command.

How are these structures made? he wondered as he looked around the space. There had to be something that issued the instructions. *Is that what the central device does?*

The central column was clearly large and prominent enough to look important. Everything did seem to be formed around it.

"I didn't see anything like this on Aethos, did you?" he asked Anya.

"No, I'd definitely remember. I'm wondering if it might be the central interface for controlling the nanites."

"Hmm." She placed a hand pensively on her chin. "There were all those metal scraps Samor and Conroy's other people had found. I suppose those could have been wreckage from a destroyed one of these."

"Maybe. If so, how did it all get broken?"

"A very good question."

"It might have something to do with what happened to the Korani." He had nowhere near enough information to draw a connection, but it seemed like a worthwhile supposition to throw out there.

Anya shook her head. "We came here looking for answers, but looks like we're going to leave with more questions."

"Questions, but also more resources. This new tech—"

"Hold on," Anya interrupted. "It just occurred to me, Sam hinted that we'd find something more than the spheres here. Except, how would he know that if he'd never been here before? I selected this planet based on its environmental properties, but there was no information about Korani infrastructure in the data Sam showed me."

"A scan once we got here? Or a communication signal?"

"It just seems strange that he wouldn't have given us more specific instructions about what to look for."

Evan crossed his arms. "Do you think he's lying to us about how much he remembers?"

"I don't know. But I think we should be cautious about what we believe." Anya resumed wandering around the room. "I want to know how this place was built. How are the nanites programmed with the layout?"

Evan found his attention drawn toward the central console again. As he stared into the pool of particles, he noticed that not all of them were golden. Occasionally, a bright-blue speck floated by.

What are you? he mused.

The blue lights separated themselves from the other mass of light. They joined together in midair before snaking over to him. After looping around his head and chest twice, they wrapped around his left wrist. The lights abruptly faded, leaving a matte dark-gray metallic material. It fit snugly around his wrist—not tight enough to pinch his skin, but leaving no room to pull it off.

For a moment, panic set in when he couldn't get it off. "Anya, I don't know what this thing is!"

"Stay calm," she soothed. "Does it hurt?"

"No. There's a little static-like tingle, but otherwise I don't feel anything at all."

"And what about a mental connection?"

"There is… something." He did sense the item, but not in the same way as the other alien technology he'd interfaced with. The others seemed to point him in a specific direction, but linking with this one was like staring at a blank input screen. He didn't need to negotiate to get it to agree to carry out his thoughts; instead, it was *asking* for direction.

He knew what to tell it to do.

9

THE NEW BRACELET warmed as Evan telepathically relayed his command. *Make me a seat.*

Aside from the consoles, there were no furnishings in the room. Nowhere to sit. He'd seen chair-like formations in the residential structures on Aethos, so he figured it was within the technology's general vocabulary. But making something that didn't already exist here would be a good test.

In response to his unspoken command, golden particles flowed from the pool and snaked across the ground toward him. They concentrated on the place where he'd requested a seat, and a section of rock next to him started to rise up. Individual fragments rolled over each other, swelling and folding as they slowly took the shape of a stool. Subtle golden light sparked between the fragments as they moved around. When the shape was complete, the lights faded and the rock darkened slightly.

Evan stared at it, slack jawed. "Wow."

"I can't believe that just happened!" Anya looked at the device on his wrist. "That must be some sort of control key for it."

"Yeah, but… how?"

"Amazing technology that's way beyond anything we have."

"I wonder how many nanites are needed to transform a place like this? Are they embedded in everything?"

Anya shrugged. "I would guess so. Do you think that's what Sam detected?"

"Maybe." Evan concentrated. He could sense the bracelet and the 'potential' within the room, but he couldn't detect anything beyond that. "I think there might be a range with this thing. Or I'm just not attuned with it yet to reach very far. But that doesn't mean Sam can't communicate with this tech through meters of rock."

"I wouldn't expect you to master anything in all of a minute."

"Can we bring the nanites with us?" Curious, Evan placed the sphere on the ground. It slowly dissolved into the glowing golden particles. They lifted up and began encircling Evan.

"That's incredible," Anya breathed.

"Yeah, it's…" He was mesmerized by the swirling fragments of light dancing around his hand as he batted at them. The power beckoned to him. "I shouldn't have this much power. No one should." He cast the lights away, returning the swarm to its holding pattern.

She placed her hand on his arm. "Evan, what's wrong?"

He shook his head. "If I take this, then I'm responsible for it. I was supposed to have a nice, quiet early retirement. But this is the sort of thing you'd read about in a superhero story—crazy, world-altering stuff."

"Isn't the 'reluctant hero' the good guy in those stories?"

"Or the well-meaning guy gets corrupted by the evil technology and is eventually defeated."

She looked him in his eyes. "Well, I believe we have a part

in writing our own stories. I already promised to help keep you on the path of good. I mean it."

He nodded. *We're a team. I might be the one interfacing with the tech, but I'm not in this alone.*

The new control bracelet gave him an idea. He directed the golden particles to coalesce. But rather than a sphere, he envisioned them forming another bracelet to match the command device. The lights faded and settled into the same gray metal with a golden sheen that they'd encountered on Aethos.

Anya nodded her approval. "Good thinking."

"Unless I command it to let go, it'll take busting my hand to get it away from me. And if that happens, I've got other problems."

"Speaking of those problems, I think we have another planet to investigate… That Syndicate world."

"Isn't it a terrible idea to take the very ship they want to a planet they control?"

She frowned. "Yeah, that's an awful plan."

"So…"

"*So*, what if we get another ship first?" Anya suggested.

"You make that sound like an easy thing."

"Isn't it?"

Evan eyed her. "In case you forgot, we're out in the middle of nowhere."

"With a ship that can jump anywhere in a matter of minutes." She sighed. "Evan, think about it! As far as anyone else is concerned, instantaneous jump travel is a fantasy. If you're not near a gate, no one is expecting visitors. There are tons of shipyards out there with all types of craft. We could jump in, grab one, and be gone before anyone knew something was missing."

"What you're suggesting is theft. The kind that comes with serious prison time."

"Only if you get caught. And only if they *do* know it's missing."

"Right, but—"

"All that we need is a functional shell. Something that would look totally normal to an outsider. But you are now in possession of a device that can create anything out of practically nothing. We grab an old junker from a shipyard—something slated for parts—and they won't even notice. You can work with Sam to make the repairs we need. Good to go."

He tilted his head. "I can't get over how you've changed."

"I have become a creature of necessity."

"Who said we need to steal a ship?"

"How else would we get one."

"Uh... *buy* it?"

"That costs money."

"I'm not broke."

Anya's cheeks flushed. "Oh."

"But the dramatic heist plan... it's tempting."

She sighed. "No need to mock me."

"Just a *little*."

"Anyway, we need to get to a place to 'acquire' a ship—through whatever means—and that will require taking Sam. How do you propose we do that without showing up in a populated area with a large alien starship?"

"I'm still working on that part of the plan."

— — —

Even though Anya knew there was a scientific explanation for the dancing lights, the technology was making her rethink her disbelief in magic. To visualize something and have it become manifest in reality was astonishing to behold.

She suspected that the nanites were self-replicating, but they were still beholden to external commands. In this case, they were being controlled by Evan. She was fascinated to see if the nanites in their raw state were capable of transforming blank stone into a sophisticated device or if the reshaping was limited to the source material.

Their surroundings were probably saturated with the nanites, so they wouldn't be able to effectively run tests here. However, she looked forward to getting to a world with no existing alien presence and seeing how far they could stretch the nanites. Could they self-replicate indefinitely?

She caught herself. That sounded like the set-up for a planet-destroying incident. They'd need to be cautious and test on a much smaller scale. Nonetheless, the technology was a thrilling discovery, and she was eager to explore its potential applications.

The biologist in her was also excited to study the interaction between the nanites and living organisms. Transforming rock was one thing, but how did this technology enable interfacing with the creatures on Aethos?

Even as questions swirled through her mind, she tried to stay focused on Evan's actions as he played around with his newfound ability. The chamber was slowly transforming to be more human-friendly with new seats and work surfaces. But the most incredible part was that it wasn't just the stone being moved around, the metal surfaces were being modified, as well. On the surface, it appeared that materials were changing state; however, she suspected there was a deeper process going on. She found herself wishing that she had a team of metallurgists and molecular chemistry scientists to help her study the alien tech.

"Can you sense any more about this place now?" Anya asked. "Is there more to this structure, or is this it?"

"I think this is all of it," Evan replied. "But I still don't think we're using it to its full capacity."

"What about talking to Sam? Can you construct a communication device?"

"I seem to only be able to make things I can fully envision. I don't have the engineering knowledge to picture all the necessary components for a device like that."

Anya nodded thoughtfully. The logic tracked. "I feel like we could spend days exploring here and still know nothing."

"The link I experience with the consoles isn't like reading a language I know. It's more like getting… impressions. It's no more helpful than getting a hunch."

"I don't know, some of our hunches have been pretty spot on. Major interstellar conspiracy, anyone?" she jested.

"True, but this isn't the same thing. We need specifics, and we're not going to get them here."

"Right. How's that plan coming for getting us a non-super-secret alien ship?"

"I have a place in mind, but I haven't worked out the part for how we get from our ship to the new one. No matter what, we need to jump in and transfer vessels."

"There has to be a way."

"Let's head back and talk to Sam. It's tough to think of tactics when you don't even know the capabilities of the equipment."

"I don't think he'd appreciate you thinking about him as 'equipment'."

"I meant the ship, not Sam."

"Aren't they one and the same?"

"Still unclear. Part of the not understanding the capabilities argument."

"Point taken." She nodded toward the glowing pool at the column's base. "Should we take more of these handy glowing things?"

"I suppose it wouldn't hurt to have some more if we discover they're not able to replicate well." Evan motioned to them.

Streams of golden particles levitated. They began circling around each other in three distinct groups, pulling into tighter and tighter balls. Eventually, they merged into three solid spheres, and the light faded.

"It's going to take a while to get used to that," Anya admitted.

"You and me both."

Evan gathered up the new spheres and placed them in his pack. "I can't fit anything else in here. I guess that's our cue to go."

"We can come back here and study it more later."

"Hopefully, we'll find someplace even better. I think we got what we need for now."

They returned to the *Asamar*. On the walk back, Anya reflected on what she'd seen in the temple. The strange particles were the centerpiece. Were they worshiped? It seemed so strange that such a large place would be constructed around a single feature. The ante hall, the soaring ceilings. It didn't make sense—at least by her human standards.

Upon boarding the ship, they went straight back to the flight deck. The lights returned to full brightness with their presence.

"Did you find what you were looking for?" the AI asked.

"Not exactly," Evan replied.

"You wished to communicate with my makers."

"Yes, and no one is here."

"This world has an active signal." Sam sounded genuinely confused.

Anya cast a concerned glance toward Evan. She had significant misgivings about the operational stability of this ancient AI. "There was *something* in there, but definitely no people."

"Hmm."

"So, Sam…" Evan continued, "we have somewhere we'd like to go, but there are other humans there. The bad humans who would want to claim you for themselves. We need to take another ship there so we can keep you safe. But we also can't let anyone see us take that ship. Do you have some kind of stealth capability?"

"This vessel is too large to mask, but there is a smaller shuttle in the hangar that may suit your needs."

Evan's eyes widened. "There's another ship on this ship?"

"Come to think of it, we haven't looked around anywhere beyond the flight deck," Anya realized.

"You're right, I've been so focused on getting to destinations…" Evan sighed. "Sam, I think you need to give us a tour before we do anything else."

"It would be my pleasure."

Sam directed them down the central corridor and back past the entry hatch. The first stop was what Anya would consider a lounge room, equipped with strange seats ill-suited for the human form.

"Could you show us an image of your people?" Anya asked. "I can't figure out the anatomy, but I know it's not like ours."

"It is not that different." A screen activated on the wall behind an oddly proportioned couch.

The creature displayed on it perplexed Anya. "Not that different, huh?"

Two additional limbs and awkwardly hinged joints were the first departure. But the large, oblong head, four glowing eyes, and scaley textured skin confirmed that these creatures were definitely not human.

"Yeah, Sam, we might need to check your visual processors," Evan said. He turned to Anya. "These kinda look like that thing we fought on Aethos—the one that made those paths through the jungle. It's not *identical*, but there's a resemblance."

"Agreed. It supports the theory that some of the creatures on the planet are hybrids."

"Which would mean that some of the Korani *did* make it there."

"And that brings us back to the beginning… where did they go?"

"I will need to go back there," Sam chimed in. "I was very disoriented when you woke me from my dormant state, and I did not examine Aethos thoroughly because I was focused on getting back to my homeworld."

"We can go back, but not yet," Evan told the AI.

"I understand. Now, we should continue the tour."

They resumed the walk around the ship. The rest of the upper deck consisted of rooms that could have been office space, though the consoles were blank so Anya couldn't be sure about their intended function. Next, they took a lift down one deck to what was clearly a residential level. It consisted of what Sam described as a galley—though the function of the 'kitchen' was a mystery—and a row of living quarters along the central corridor. Each room was equipped with a large, square mattress, which actually had an acceptable softness, and a washroom with bizarre facilities that Sam had to explain. Once they understood the components, everything seemed like it would be functional enough; really, Anya would take *any* form of indoor plumbing after her week in the wilds.

The final segment of the tour was the lower cargo area and hangar. The cargo bay was empty, but there was a small shuttle craft, as Sam had indicated. Though not a large vessel, it could accommodate six passengers for a flight, plus a modest amount of cargo.

"Is this small ship capable of interstellar jumps, as well?" Evan asked.

"Yes, the drive can be adapted to this vessel."

"What about disguising it? Would there be a way to make it look… well, *not alien*?"

"Why?"

"Like I said before, Sam, humans are a complicated bunch. If they knew what we had here right now, they'd try to take it by force. We want to find out how to stop them. For good."

"I understand," the AI said after a pause. "I will help."

10

INITIALLY, ROMAN HAD been thankful that Aethos was equipped with an interstellar comm relay because it was his one connection to civilized society. But as he stared at his older sister through the screen at the drop ship's comm station, he wished more than anything he could leave the rest of the galaxy behind.

"How, exactly, did everything go to shit so quickly?" Marta demanded.

Roman leaned back in his seat. "What did Marcus tell you?"

"Enough to understand why I was looped in. If your sorry ass wants a ride off that rock, you'll tell me exactly what kind of shitstorm I'll be walking into."

"By the time you can get here, I'll have everything ready to hand you on a silver platter."

"Drop the bravado. You and I both know the ship is long gone. I don't care if you kill Conroy and the rest of his cronies and have the rest of the planet mapped and cataloged—that's all secondary. We *need* that ship."

"And you'll have it."

She scoffed. "Right! And you're going to conjure it out of

thin air?"

"They'll be back, and I'll be ready when they return."

"What makes you so sure?"

"How aren't you? You must have read his profile."

"The Alex guy? Or, Evan, I guess." She let out a long breath, shaking her head. "Marcus is *pissed* that he pulled one over on us."

Roman steepled his fingers. "A man like that is loyal to a fault. I have no doubt that Conroy got to him, and he'll come back to save his beleaguered leader. His kind are so predictable."

"Say he *does* come back. How are you going to get the ship?"

"You can leave that up to me."

"No, I can't. Your screw-up is what got us off-track to begin with."

"I had nothing to do with the crash!"

She sighed. "Roman, there's no point in arguing about *how* we got here. What matters is how we fix it."

The last thing he wanted to do was admit his diva of a sister was right about anything, but she was on this point. Their family had been maneuvering for years to get here, and the entire future of their enterprise hinged on this mission. Marcus had delegated the cleanup efforts to Marta, but she wasn't positioned to make a meaningful impact from light-years away. Roman still had an opportunity to gain control of the situation.

"How about this, Marta? You send a team over here. If I'm not running this planet by the time you arrive, I'll throw myself at Marcus' feet with no resistance."

"You'll need to answer to more than him by then."

"I will submit myself freely and receive my punishment."

She considered him through the screen, her dark-brown eyes narrowed. "He'll kill you."

"I have no doubt."

Marta shrugged. "Well, I wish you the best of luck. You have nine weeks to figure it out."

"Understood."

He was about to end the call when her face abruptly softened. "Roman, I really hope you do."

"Don't want me to die, huh?"

"You're such an ass."

Roman sat up straighter in his seat. "I'm sorry. Thank you. I really do want to make things right."

"I know it wasn't your fault."

"Someone had to take the fall."

She bit her lower lip, nodding slowly. "Keep me posted on your progress. You'll have your backup soon."

When he ended the vidcall, Roman let out a deep sigh. A knot tightened in his chest; any talk about his brother set him on edge. Marta wasn't exactly a ray of sunshine, either, but she had made an effort to look out for Roman. Being only a year younger than Marcus, she'd never been sidelined as a baby in the family like Roman had. She'd been able to jump in as a protective older sibling when Marcus had gotten too rough with Roman when he was little. As much as he'd tried to shift the dynamic while he'd moved into adulthood, Roman had never been able to shake the label of being the kid in the family. Even with less than a decade age difference and now being nearly thirty, Roman had been unable to get Marcus to see him as anything but his fumbling ten-year-old self.

Admittedly, the recent incident hadn't done anything to change that perception.

A knock sounded on the drop ship's outer hatch, followed

by a muffled shout, "Are you done in there?" It was Red.

Roman hastily wiped his call from the communication log. "Yeah, hang on."

After confirming that the sensitive contact details had been removed. Roman got up to release the manual lock on the ship's access hatch.

When the hatch popped open, Red was standing with her hands on her hips. "This isn't *your* ship, you know."

"Considering that I'm the one getting us a ride off this cursed rock, you should really be nicer to me."

The soldier squinted. "What's this about a ride?"

"I made the call for backup. It's nine weeks out."

"That's an eternity!"

"Those are the realities of physics. It's not like we're next-door to a gate."

She groaned. "I'm not worried about surviving, but what the hell are we supposed to do about the mission until we get backup? Just sit on our hands for the next two months?"

"Of course not. We're going to deal with Conroy and his minions just like we'd planned. By the time others get here, everything will be tied up with a neat bow and we can go back to civilization with our heads held high."

"I've lost a lot of good people here, Roman. There won't be any gloating from me."

"Suit yourself." Roman brushed past her and down the ramp.

The trees sang to him as he stepped foot back on the planet's soil. The buzzing that had occasionally swelled in his mind intensified again. For a moment, he couldn't bear the thought of leaving this place, despite his recent words to the contrary.

What's the matter with me? This power deserves a broader

stage than a backwater planet. Reflexively, he called on the new energy source coursing through him, causing subtle sparks to dance along his fingertips.

Drawing on the power settled the anxious thoughts at the back of his mind.

But the strange hum beckoned him away from the drop ship. Compelled, he headed into the forest, the opposite direction from the base. As he wandered into the trees, the animals continued calling and going about their business as though no one was around. It wasn't long ago that they went silent in his presence.

He looked down at his hands, flexing them as he walked. *I'm becoming a part of this place.*

Two days ago, that concept would have horrified him. But now… there was opportunity. The environment could guide him in the pursuit of an even greater power. There were more relics to find, more abilities to gain.

Roman hiked through the trees with his senses alight. He traced the location of birds and followed the movements of smaller creatures through the underbrush, which would have gone unnoticed before. But strongest in his mind was a pull toward an energy source.

He walked through the trees until he came across a meadow. Nestled in the dappled light at the transition from trees to the blooming grasses was a strange patch of blue flowers. Electric energy danced along the stems and scattered across the petals.

Roman reached out to touch a flower. It sent a painful shock through his fingertips. He recoiled.

So much for being connected! He was about to leave when he spotted the amber eyes of a large animal staring at him from the other side of the meadow. He froze.

The creature stepped forward, revealing a long, dark-furred body with muscles that rippled under its shiny pelt as it casually strolled across the meadow.

Roman remained still, watching it. The animal's unhurried movements and only partial attention toward him indicated that the creature didn't pose a threat and didn't view him as one, either.

It should know better.

The panther stopped and stared into Roman's eyes. The golden irises had a faint glow in the shadow of its strong brows, seeming to stare into his innermost self.

"*You are a killer,*" a voice said in his mind.

Roman recoiled. *Was that the cat?*

The panther dropped to its belly on top of the blue flowers, sending up a flurry of sparks. "*You have killed my kind.*"

That definitely came from the cat. Roman stood his ground. "*Are you a killer, too?*"

"*I kill to eat and in defense. I watched you end a life for no reason.*"

"*I had my reasons.*"

"*You have lost your way.*"

Roman unholstered his sidearm and pointed it at the panther in one smooth motion. His finger hovered over the trigger.

The cat remained on its belly, staring at him. "*Kill me if you must.*"

Roman hesitated. *How can it speak my language in my head?* He'd thought these were mindless beasts, driven by instincts alone.

But as it watched him, calm yet calculating, he realized that it was intelligent and reasoned. However, its intellect didn't matter if it came down to defending his own life. He'd been party to the death of many people, at least some of which he'd consider smart. It was important to do whatever was necessary to stay ahead.

His hand twitched. He'd been able to kill a man easily, yet he couldn't fire on this predator?

The back of Roman's neck tingled. He shifted his focus from the animal to his greater surroundings. Only then did he realize that the sounds of nature had gone silent. But the creatures weren't hiding—they were all intently focused on him.

He lowered his weapon and holstered it. Without any comprehensible words, he understood that inflicting any harm on the panther would be his end.

"Wise decision," the panther said in his mind.

"What do you want from me?" Roman asked.

"That's not for me to explain." Abruptly, the panther bounded away into the forest.

The other animals who'd been conspicuously watching him also melted back into the environment. Roman could still sense their presence. They were judging, waiting. He wasn't sure how to respond.

What the hell is this place?

11

EVAN SIZED UP the shuttle resting on the *Asamar*'s hangar deck. "How did you retrofit this so quickly? I honestly wouldn't be able to tell this apart from something human-made."

"I am pleased to hear you are satisfied with the product."

From the hull plating to engine design and even identifying markings, the shuttle was identical to the K-27R model used regularly throughout the Commonwealth. The craft was a particular favorite of smugglers because of its speed and favorable size-to-cargo-space ratio. Evan had seen dozens, if not hundreds, throughout his life, and this reproduction would be indistinguishable in a lineup.

"This really is impressive, Sam," Anya said with a satisfied nod. "I hope your environmental controls skills are as good as your aesthetic design."

"As I stated before, I have no desire for you to die. You will be safe."

There was no doubt that Sam *had* delivered a shuttle that suited their needs. Compared to Evan's limitations with making simple objects using the nanites, it was clear that Sam had more advanced capabilities to extrapolate complex engineering designs.

"You know, it's *so* good that we could just use this," Anya commented.

"Tempting, but too risky," Evan replied. The plan was to use the disguised vessel as temporary transportation so they could secure a human ship that they could take to the Syndicate planet, thereby keeping the alien vessels far from enemy territory. Using an actual alien vessel would defeat that purpose.

"We'll still need the Korani jump drive on the human ship," Anya pointed out.

"But that can be separated from the ship as soon as we jump into the planet's vicinity."

"I'll defer to your judgment," Anya said, though she seemed unconvinced about the necessity of the extra steps.

"How did you even make this, Sam?" Evan asked. They'd grabbed some much-needed sleep while the AI had worked overnight. But even a full suite of robotic workers in a human shipyard wouldn't have been able to complete such a thorough retrofit within eight hours.

"I reprogrammed the structure to match a design I pulled from Evan's memory."

He blanched. "Wait, you *what*?"

"Would you like me to explain the technical specifics of the process? I believe the scientific principles might be beyond the scope of your current understanding."

Fighting offense at the knock on his intelligence, Evan shook his head. "No, I don't need to know the specifics. I'm just trying to understand what's within the scope of your abilities. It sounds like you can manufacture objects based on images in my thoughts?"

"I need sufficient details, but yes."

"Holy shit," Anya whispered.

Evan pinched the bridge of his nose. "Sam, we need to have a talk about what you tell us."

"My apologies, Evan. Have I upset you?"

"No. I know we're working with a language barrier here, and we haven't known each other for long, but it would be helpful if you could volunteer information. If you have ideas for something, please offer them rather than waiting to be asked."

"I serve organics."

"And that's great," Anya cut in. "You can serve us best by working with us as a partner. We have a big mission, and we need all the help we can get."

"In that case, I would like to point out that going after another human-made shuttle craft would be a waste of time and an imprecise approach to achieving your objectives."

That's more like it! Evan nodded thoughtfully. "Please, share your analysis."

"If I understand correctly, you wish to investigate a planet you believe is controlled by the Noche Syndicate. This mission requires stealth as you observe their operations. It also requires you to be able to jump to the planet without using a transit gate, because otherwise your approach would be detected. While the jump drive tech this ship uses *can* be applied to a human vessel, no human-made craft would have the stealth capabilities of this shuttle you see before you. Therefore, it remains a better option to simply use this craft rather than using it to acquire another ship."

"See?" Anya flourished her hand with vindication.

Evan hadn't considered the stealth angle in his original assessment. "So, we can focus on not being spotted in the first place rather than hedging our bets for if we do get caught."

"Correct."

"Well, I agree," Anya said.

"But what if we *do* get caught?" Evan countered.

"A part of me will be on the ship. I can ensure that it is destroyed rather than fall into enemy hands."

Anya nodded pensively. "No one will think this is anything special if they spot us in it, so it's no different than a human-made shuttle but saves us complications and time. I think it's worth the risk."

Evan nodded. "Fine. There *is* merit to the stealth aspect. That just leaves the question of where, precisely, we're going."

— — —

Astronomical navigation hadn't been Anya's strongest subject in school, but she'd reviewed enough star charts as part of her xenobiological survey work to find her way around this part of the galaxy.

"All right, here's our destination, the planet Pavia," she said, pointing to it on the main display in the flight deck. "It has all the metrics we'd look for in a new colonization target—temp, atmo, flora. I remember it because the whole team was excited and ready to launch a survey, but then the investigation was killed from higher up with no explanation."

Evan raised an eyebrow. "Kind of like they knew there was something there that they didn't want you to find?"

"In retrospect, yes."

He nodded. "It makes sense. A lot is making sense now with the new context. If the Syndicate has been operating there…"

"Right?" She sighed. "I keep thinking about how I was played—how so many people were played. It's infuriating."

"The people who orchestrated this conspiracy are

monsters any way you look at it. They'd use anyone and consider them all expendable."

"It's a hell of a way to do business."

He scowled. "This isn't just business. It's a way of life for them. They follow their own code."

"How do you stop people like that?" Anya asked.

"By beating them at their own game."

She studied his face and the tension in his shoulders. He was worried—scared, even. And he didn't want to admit it. "We can go about this another way if you don't think this is a good idea," she offered.

"No, the signs all point to this place. I want to know what Noche found that enabled them to make the serum. There's *something* important on that planet. And maybe a clue about what happened to Sam's makers."

"I, too, would like to investigate this world. I want to know what happened to my people," Sam chimed in.

"See, that. *That's* the kind of unsolicited input I appreciate!" Evan exclaimed.

"I am happy to offer my support for this plan."

"Then what are we waiting for?" Evan got up. "Show us how the shuttle works." He headed toward the lift.

"Are we leaving right away?" Anya asked, following him.

"I don't see why not."

"Then we should bring our stuff."

"Why?"

"Well, if things go sideways and we need to go on the run, wouldn't it be better to have everything we might need?"

"Good point."

They headed back to the rooms where they'd rested overnight. The accommodations were a far cry from her housing back in the core worlds, but it was a definite step up from their time roughing it in the forest.

With her pack slung over her shoulder, she walked with Evan to the hangar.

"All right, Sam, give us the tour," Evan said when they reached the shuttle.

The craft's side hatch popped open, illuminating blue lights around the edge.

"Please, step inside," Sam instructed.

Anya followed Evan in. As soon as she'd passed through the threshold, the hatch sealed.

"I have modified the craft to follow the standard operational protocols in your memories," the AI began.

As Sam continued walking through the technical specifications with Evan, Anya explored the mid-section and rear of the compact craft. It had a small washroom, two bunks, a food prep area, and several storage lockers, with a larger open area at the back for cargo. The storage lockers were mostly empty, though she did find some basics like a flashlight and medkit. It was unclear how Sam had manufactured everything down to such fine detail, and in such a short time, but she appreciated the extra touches.

Mention of the craft's stealth feature prompted Anya to tuned back into Sam's operational walkthrough.

"It will not make you disappear completely," the AI was explaining, "but it should prevent detection on most electronic surveillance systems and also visually disguise the vessel to a human observer. Avoid trying to hide in something like a gaseous cloud, as the camouflage will be less effective in environments where the vessel is physically displacing its surroundings."

"Noted," Evan acknowledged.

"Hey, do we need to worry about fuel or anything?" Anya

asked. The idea of getting stranded on another random planet was still too real a possibility.

"No, my technology uses what you might consider a perpetual energy core. Though the aesthetics of this craft now match human design, the changes are mostly superficial. This is why I would destroy this ship before it fell into enemy hands."

More technology that would revolutionize human civilization... or destroy it in the fight for control. "And what about you? You said you'd be here on the shuttle with us, but how does that work? Will there be two of you?"

"In a sense, yes, but it'll be more like an extension of myself. I will sync my two instances over the interstellar comms."

"And if we lose long-range comms for some reason?" Evan asked.

"Then I would revert to myself on the ship. This craft does not have the infrastructure to support my full being."

Anya was struck by how Sam talked about himself. Even *she* was thinking of the AI in terms of 'self' rather than 'it'. None of the artificial intelligences she'd encountered had made her consider a full consciousness rather than a tool. But Sam had a whole personality. That meant reasoning, planning, ambitions. And all from an alien perspective. They were placing an awful lot of trust in this being.

"Well, I'd better make sure I know how to fly this thing in case we lose you," Evan suggested. "Let's take it for a jump."

— — —

Evan had flown a number of craft throughout his career, and the modified alien shuttle was as responsive as a fighter despite its larger size and different profile. They'd jumped it back to the alien homeworld of Koranis, knowing the planet was unoccupied and therefore safe. The *Asamar* had jumped separately with them so Sam could check his link between the two vessels. So far, so good.

"You do very nice work, Sam."

"Thank you, Evan," the AI said over the shuttle's speakers.

"All it needs is a coffee bar and a sauna."

"There is not presently room for those modifications without removing seating or storage."

"That was a joke… But could you *really* add—"

"Evan, look!" Anya exclaimed.

She pointed out the front viewport at an object in front of them. It wasn't showing up on the scan data.

Evan squinted in a vain attempt to make out the details, but it was little more than a shadow at their present distance. "Sam, what is that?"

"I'm not sure. It isn't emitting any signals, which is why I didn't detect it when we were here before."

"Can you get closer so we can check it out?" Anya asked.

Evan directed the shuttle toward the object, slowing his approach when it became large enough on the main viewer to see clearly. Its oblong exterior was definitely metallic, showing minimal features to indicate propulsion capabilities or other functionality. The construction didn't look human.

"Any ideas?" Evan asked.

"I believe this was a Korani probe or beacon of some sort, but it's dormant now," Sam said.

Anya lit up. "Hey! It might have a record of where everyone went or what happened on the planet."

"It looks too big to capture with the shuttle, but can you scoop it up with the *Asamar*?" Evan asked.

In response, the large vessel moved in their direction on the scan display.

"I will bring it into my main hangar and place it under quarantine," Sam said.

Evan and Anya waited several tense minutes while the ship brought the object on board. Sam activated an interior camera feed from the hangar so they could watch on the shuttle's display. The object showed no obvious exterior signs of damage.

"This is, indeed, a Korani device," Sam announced after running scans. "However, it is not from this planet. Its isometric signatures do not match anything on Koranis."

"Does its origin match any other Korani worlds in your database?" Evan asked.

"No."

"Can you extract any information from it?"

"I'll see if I can restore power and interface with the systems. It will take time to repair and analyze. I'll work on it while you are inspecting your planet," Sam said.

"I'm envious of your multitasking ability."

"Your one-track minds are quaint," the AI replied. "The Korani are intellectually superior."

"Thanks, Sam. You know how to make a human feel special." Evan initiated the jump to Pavia.

Golden light swirled around the craft as the particles encircling it became a blur, and they transitioned to the strange blackness and abstract lights of hyperspace. Sam had modified the jump controls to include several pre-programmed destinations in case his connection to the shuttle was severed. The safeguard gave Evan some peace of mind, but it also made him feel like he wasn't flying so much as being taken for a ride. Everything about this mission was risky.

The shuttle transitioned back to normal space beyond visual range of their target planet. They'd selected coordinates that would fall outside a standard scan radius so they could jump into the system without detection. Once there, they could use the cloak—assuming it actually worked—and fly in closer to inspect what was happening on the planet. With any luck, they'd be able to glean important clues about the Syndicate's operations.

"We are in the correct location, and I am not detecting any scanning signals here," Sam announced.

"That's a relief. I guess it's time to see how well you can hide us."

A shimmer briefly passed over the front viewport before the normal view of space returned. Simultaneously, a schematic of the ship with a line drawn around it appeared on the flight controls console.

"Cloak active," Sam confirmed.

"So, we can't go through clouds without the physical displacement being noticeable, but otherwise we can cruise around without detection?" Evan asked.

"Yes. Though if you fire any weapons or jump away, that will reveal your location, as well."

"Makes sense. We'll take it nice and easy…" Evan directed the ship toward the planet.

He kept a close eye on the scan report and comms for any sign of a response. None came.

But as Pavia came into visual range, his heart jumped into his throat.

A spacedock hovered in high geosynchronous orbit above the planet. It was populated with nearly a dozen ships, including a mid-sized cargo hauler. Even now, a vessel was ascending from the surface.

“Yeah, this isn’t some little backwater operation,” Anya said, stating the obvious.

“No, it’s definitely not.”

“Sorry to interrupt,” Sam broke in, “but there’s something you need to see.”

12

EVAN'S HEART DROPPED as Sam changed the front display to show a zoomed-in view of the planet's surface.

The planet definitely wasn't uninhabited. There was what looked to be a human-made structure in a valley. And along the valley's walls were the unmistakable etches of Korani architecture.

Evan's jaw went slack. "Anya, how didn't any of this show up on the planetary survey?"

"It's impossible. They must have doctored the survey results."

"Why even mention the planet at all as a colonization option?"

She frowned. "Because it's easier to hide the details about a place than the whole planet itself. One of the first steps in site identification is to look at the unified spectral analysis—basically a blended snapshot of temperature and elemental composition to give an indication of each planet's suitability. The snapshots are done at the sector level, so trying to disappear a planet from all star charts would be next to impossible. But it wouldn't be nearly as difficult to alter the profile of a 'green' or 'blue' planet—the two highest tiers with the snapshot—and disqualify the targets."

"Do you remember why this one was ruled out?"

"They didn't tell us, but it was reclassified as TR-2."

"What's that?

"A designation for a place with a gate in the system—transit-ready—but non-inhabited."

"Ah, yeah, the trade hub kind of places that have a station but little else."

"Exactly. And that was weird for a place with a seemingly great planet, but then Aethos came along, and we got distracted with a new reason to be excited."

"And we know they were completely honest about that one…"

She sighed. "Yeah, the lies are becoming a pattern."

"Sam," Evan began, "I know going down into the atmosphere might give away our position, but how close can we go to get a better look?"

"The visuals you see now are composite scan data. There is significant interference and cloud cover that make a traditional high-elevation visual survey impossible, but additional angles will improve my assessment. I suggest this flight path." An overlay on the forward viewport updated with a course snaking past the orbital structures and passing through the uppermost atmosphere of the planet.

"All right, going in…" Evan nudged the controls. He kept wanting to hold his breath as the ship moved closer to the enemy activity.

Next to him, Anya was gripping the armrests of her seat and tapping her foot with nervous energy. It was only through his own experience in high-pressure situations that kept Evan from fidgeting, himself. But his calm façade almost shattered when the front viewport was filled with images of a ship marked with the official Commonwealth emblem.

"Uh, isn't this supposed to be a Noche Syndicate operation?" Anya asked tentatively.

Evan's mouth went dry. "Yes, and it *is*."

"So..."

"Whatever relationship might be going on between the government and the Syndicate probably includes the alien tech. Does Conroy even know about this place?"

"Unless he has spies who've been here, this seems like the kind of operation that would be easy to keep under wraps."

Evan agreed with her reasoning. The local gate meant it would be easy to get ships in and out, and the government involvement would facilitate getting airtight documentation to accompany any shipment. They could make cargo look like it had come from anywhere, and this place wouldn't even exist as far as the rest of the Commonwealth was concerned. Evan had only started hearing references to the place after two years of being undercover with the Syndicate.

But the question remained: what were they exporting from here?

"Sam, can you scan any cargo? Any signs of what this operation is all about?"

"The hub of activity appears to be this facility on the surface. Follow the adjusted course bearing to bring us into optimal scan position."

Evan followed the instructions. As they got closer, the scan data on the display updated with higher-resolution imagery. There was a human-made facility—

The front console lit up with warning alarms.

Evan's pulse spiked. "Shit, what happened?"

"Their scan caught an echo of us," Sam reported. "Not a full contact, but they're on alert."

"We need to learn more about this operation," Anya urged.

"The ship has not been exposed," Sam said. "Proceed along the course." The route flashed on the screen.

We may only get one shot at this. Evan forged ahead.

Imagery kept refreshing on the display, but he kept his attention focused on the flight controls and scan data. He noticed that there was a signal strength indicator, which he'd initially taken to be a readout of their own systems. However, he realized it was actually a measure of the lock other scan systems had on *their* ship. Following that indicator, he adjusted the course, speed, and distance to keep the readings in the nominal range.

He was just feeling like he was getting the hang of it when a different alert flashed.

"Did they spot us?" Evan asked, unable to find the source of the alarm.

"No, the Korani tech in this ship is responding to something nearby," Sam announced. "I'm trying to locate the source.

"No… wait—"

The screen flickered. Silence.

Evan's stomach dropped. "Sam…?"

"Shit! Evan, the cloak!" she warned.

He checked the screen, horrified to see that the schematic indicating their disguise had dropped away. They were exposed.

The sensor lock warning flashed. A moment later, the comm panel lit up with an incoming communication.

"Do we answer it?" Anya asked.

"There's no way we can talk our way out of this," he said, already working the flight controls. "We need to run." *But can we?*

Sam had assured Evan that a jump would still be possible even without the AI, but they hadn't tested it. He brought up the pre-programmed fallback location. Heart pounding, he initiated the jump sequence.

Nothing happened.

No, no, no!

He tried again. No response.

Anya didn't say anything, but her expression of pure fear mirrored his own rising panic. They were potentially seconds from being blown up, or maybe a couple of minutes from being apprehended. He wasn't sure which would be the worse outcome.

We need to jump away. We have *to!*

Warmth ignited around Evan's left wrist. The nanite bracelet was glowing blue. The light spread out from the bracelet and formed tendrils extending to the ship's control panel.

A low vibration began in the deck, followed by a golden glow forming outside the viewport. Moments later, the planet Pavia winked from view.

Evan didn't dare to move. He held the destination in his mind, willing the ship to make it there.

The golden light evaporated. They were back in normal space.

"Holy shit..." Anya whispered.

Evan took an unsteady breath. "What the hell happened to Sam?"

She shook her head faintly. "Do you think they saw us jump away?"

"Definitely."

"Yeah, I thought so." Gathering herself, she checked the front readout. "Hey, looks like we did make it to the rendezvous. Good job."

He couldn't bring himself to be happy or relieved about anything.

His heart was still pounding in his chest, and that strange heat from whenever he used the alien tech still burned him from the inside. "That went about as badly as it could have."

Anya shook her head. "We could have died, but we didn't. Guess you're stuck with me a while longer."

"I'm good with that." Evan looked over the scan data for the new planet below. It seemed livable enough, though not nearly as lush as Aethos. "We might be stuck here, though."

"Why would we be stuck?"

"We can't attempt another jump without Sam."

"Why not?"

"Because this destination was programmed using some kind of astro-navigational process I can't begin to understand. Until I get a better grasp on how to control these nanites, I don't want to risk it."

She nodded. "All right. Let's scout out a campsite."

— — —

They settled on a location a little south of the equator where the temperature was moderate and there were trees for shelter and firewood. As Anya investigated the site on foot, she couldn't escape the feeling that they were pretty much back where they'd started. Sure, they had a space-worthy shuttle now, but they were no closer to finding safety or stability. In some ways, they were even worse off.

She tried to work out some of her anxiety by gathering a meal of plants and fruit from the surrounding vegetation, which she verified was edible with her bioanalyzer. A lot of the items were strange shapes and colors—lots of spikey bits and vibrant blue she didn't see too often in nature—but her testing equipment said they were nutritious.

She cut the various fruits and veggies up into two bowls and walked over to where Evan was preparing a campfire.

"That was a big sigh," Evan commented.

"Oh, did I? Sorry."

"I feel it, too." He finished constructing a pile of kindling and lit it.

She watched the tinder catch, and flames slowly consumed the larger twigs.

"Just like old times."

"I really thought those days were behind us."

"I did, too," Anya admitted. "But I did mean what I said before about being happy it's you I'm stuck with."

He added a couple of larger sticks to the growing fire. "Me too."

She wasn't usually one to make moves, but the life-or-death drama of recent days had changed her perspective. Normally, they sat opposite each other at camp. With an unexpected burst of confidence, she instead sat down close to Evan, handing him one of the bowls.

He looked over at her a little quizzically. "Hi."

"Hi," she replied nonchalantly. "Figured I'd come hang with the cool crowd over here."

"Good call."

Her mind abruptly went blank, uncertain what to say or do. The reasons to wait to explore anything beyond friendship remained valid—namely the fact that it would be a distraction from the all-important mission of survival. But, on the flip side, she needed a reminder of what it meant to be alive.

After a brief internal debate, she settled on scootching

closer until their shoulders were touching. He took the hint and put his arm around her. She happily leaned against his well-toned frame. The warmth of him and gentle pressure across her shoulders gave her a sense of comfort and security that she'd been craving.

The bushes across from them shook. Anya tensed, worried a creature might jump out to attack. Evan unfurled himself from her, the bracelets on his wrists glowed as he reached for his handgun.

However, only a small, furry animal came wandering out, walking on all fours and with a short, bushy tail sticking straight up. It sniffed in their direction and then started rooting through the pile of leftover fruit peels.

Evan relaxed as he looked at the little animal. "Reminds me of Stubby."

"Who, or what, is that?"

"Our cat when I was a kid."

"Didn't you grow up on a spaceship?" Anya asked.

"Yes."

She side-eyed him. "You had a cat on your spaceship?"

"Sure. Why is that strange?"

"I dunno… I just didn't think of them as being particularly spacefaring."

"Oh, tons of ships have cats. The bigger the ship, the more animals. Especially any cargo ships dealing with food or other organic stuff. As careful as we try to be, there's almost always some kind of spillage. And as soon as you have a speck of anything edible, the mice or bugs come. Cats are great at dealing with both. Plus, they keep your feet warm in your bunk."

"I stand corrected." She paused. "Why was your cat called 'Stubby'?"

Evan smiled. "Oh, he only had half a tail. We got him like that, so I'm not sure what happened. But that little bit he did have would stand up perfectly straight when he got excited. He passed a couple months before I left home to join the UPDF."

"I always wanted a pet, but my parents didn't want to deal with shedding around the house."

"So, you decided to surround yourself with wild animals instead?"

"Where there's a will there's a way."

She snuggled up to him again, and they sat in silence for a while longer, watching the flames and setting sun. It was only lunchtime relative to when they'd woken up, but it may as well have been an evening back on Aethos.

After eating the semi-filling meal, Anya was left wondering how best to proceed. Then, a distant roar sounded above. For a moment, she worried a storm was rolling in.

Evan looked up at the sky. "That's an engine." He jumped to his feet and kicked up dirt to snuff out the fire.

The ship was impossible to see in the near-blackness of the sky. It could be Sam coming to meet them, or maybe the Syndicate had found a way to follow them. Better to make themselves more difficult targets to spot if it was the latter.

They stared into the darkness. Anya only caught the occasional shadow blocking stars to indicate that something was descending. Eventually, it was close enough to make out the shape. She finally relaxed, recognizing Sam's distinctive shape.

The large vessel was landing in a nearby field. They went to meet it.

The *Asamar* was on the ground by the time they arrived. The side hatch opened, and its entry ramp unfurled to greet them.

"Sam, what happened?" Evan asked as soon as they were on board.

"I am pleased you made it here safely. I was concerned that the problem with my systems had extended to the shuttle."

"Is this related to that object you brought on board?" Anya asked.

"Yes. Proceed to the hangar. It's easier if I show you."

Anya and Evan hurried to the lower deck. When they stepped out of the lift, Anya's breath caught in her throat.

The object, which had seemed small and dull on the monitor, was now floating in the center of the hangar. Slowly bobbing and rotating, the three-meter-long oval was also glowing with subtle golden light.

Evan brought a hand up to his head. He winced and groaned.

Anya placed a hand on his shoulder. "Hey, are you okay?"

"You don't hear that? It's—" He grimaced, squeezing his eyes shut.

She knelt next to Evan as he dropped to his knees. "Sam, what's happening to him?"

"Let me try something," the AI replied.

A few seconds later, it seemed like the air in the room shifted. Anya sensed a new pressure in her chest—pulsing with the rhythm of the lights on the strange object. It was almost like feeling the resonant bass beat of music without hearing the song.

Evan immediately relaxed. "Wow, that was intense," he said, getting back to his feet. "My ears started ringing—only I felt like it was my whole body."

"I apologize that I did not foresee that possibility," Sam said. "This object is a communication device. It is emitting a signal, which overlaps with the control frequencies of the other Korani nanotech."

"So, it really *was* vibrating all of me," Evan surmised.

"In a sense. Your two signals were interfering with each other."

"Like feedback in a speaker." Anya looked over the device; it still seemed active. "How did you stop it, Sam?"

"I initiated a neutralizing field within this hangar to counter the object's signal. It should be below your human audible range."

"Great. But what the hell happened to you?" Evan questioned.

"Right, yes. The object's power reserves had been depleted, so I swapped its power core. As soon as it came online, it initiated a forced infiltration of my systems. It was following some kind of assessment protocol."

"Assessing what?"

"That is unclear. However, it followed a similar protocol to a scan for malicious code."

"Please tell us you learned more than that," Anya said.

"Ultimately, yes. After my systems unlocked, I was able to interface with the device. It comes from a time after I left Koranis but before the world ended."

Evan brightened. "Great! So, it could tell you what happened?"

"No. I have a timeline of some events, but I am no closer to understanding what actually happened to the world. What I do know now, though, is that other ships departed, and there were people on board. The civilization did not end with Koranis' destruction—at least, there is a *chance* it didn't. There were no records in the relic of where those ships went, only *when*: approximately two hundred years after I went to Aethos. All further communications from the planet's surface ceased soon thereafter."

"That's not a lot to go on," Evan said, his disappointment coming through.

"Actually," Anya said more cheerfully, "it *does* fill in some gaps in a roundabout way. The timeline suggests that there was premeditation to the departure, so there was a reason to leave the planet. Either they found a great world to settle, or they knew something bad was coming and headed out to escape. It's vague, but it does rule out the possibility of a sudden freak accident that destroyed the world."

The logic wouldn't hold up in a court case, but it was enough for their preliminary investigative purposes. Most importantly, it suggested that the Korani might still be out there, somewhere. Not only was that good news for a potential ally, but it increased the likelihood that Sam would be inclined to keep helping them.

Evan nodded thoughtfully as he listened, then his eyes widened. "Wait, we do have one more clue to frame this up. This device was made by the Korani, right? And it ran a system scan upon making contact with this Korani ship. It implemented a quarantine procedure. Why would it do that if not to detect and prevent the spread of *something* through the technical systems?"

Anya met his gaze. "You're right! They *must* have known about some kind of threat, possibly coming to the world. And they could have evacuated. But when it ultimately arrived…"

"That was their end," Evan completed. "But what was that threat, and where did *it* go?"

13

ROMAN SAT ON the bunk in the small cabin he'd claimed inside Conroy's former stronghold. He'd been inside for less than twenty minutes, but the walls were already closing in around him. The filtered air weighed heavy in his lungs. A flicker in the artificial lights, something he'd never noticed before, was now giving him a headache. And there was some infernal rattle—

A sharp bang on the door snapped him to attention.

"Go away!" he shouted.

The knock came again, more forcefully. "Now!" a muffled voice shouted back.

With a frustrated sigh, he got to his feet and opened the door. Red stood outside, her eyes narrowed and face flushed—the first indication he'd seen of what may have inspired her nickname.

"Are you just going to sit around and do nothing?" she demanded.

"I'm doing plenty."

"One of my men was killed! You said you had a tracker on Conroy's soldier. Why aren't we planning a retaliation?"

"I'm working on it."

Red groaned. "We need to be proactive. We're already down to so few people. If we get attacked, I'm not sure we could hold this place. We can't let them pick us off one by one."

"They wouldn't dare attack us here."

"I'm not going to assume anything."

He nodded. "You want to bring the fight to them?"

"If you, in fact, know where they are."

"I do."

She raised an eyebrow. "How?"

"I told you, a tracker." He didn't want to get into the alien tech and what it was doing to him. There was no way she'd be able to understand it well enough to trust him. If he hadn't experienced it for himself, he wouldn't believe it, either.

"How far is their camp?"

"Close enough. The distance doesn't matter as much as who's there."

"Conroy is the target."

"Yes. I know of two places. He's in one of them, and we need to figure out which."

Red stared at him, her eyes flitting across his features as she looked for signs of deception. She wouldn't find any with that statement. "Show me the places on a map."

Roman grabbed his wrist communicator from the nightstand. He brought up a holographic map of the region. "The first place the collaborator went is here," he said, indicating the location on the projected topographical display. It was at the edge of a mountain range to the east. "The other one is here." The second location was in the middle of the jungle to the north, farther from the base.

"I don't recall either of those places being areas of interest on our scans," Red observed.

"They wouldn't have been very good evac locations if they

were easy to find."

"True. You know how the environmentals mess with readings down here. They're probably naturally shielded."

Roman's opinions about that natural shielding were evolving on an hourly basis. He could sense the energy network within the planet—growing stronger in his mind every time he allowed himself a few quiet moments to immerse himself in the place. Nothing about the energy fields was random. He hadn't yet picked up the pattern, but there was greater meaning here. Greater power. He wouldn't stop until he'd mastered it.

Red was eyeing him expectantly. "Are you listening?"

"What?"

"I asked if you'd thought about how to approach either one of these locations."

When did she ask that? Roman rubbed his eyes. He realized his head was throbbing. "Can we go outside to talk?"

"Why?"

He pushed past her and hurried down the corridor toward the exit.

Brisk footfalls sounded behind him. "Roman, what's going on with you?"

"I'm getting the mission back on track."

"Really? Seems more like you're losing it."

"The only thing I'm losing is my patience with you." He reached the main passageway and practically jogged the rest of the way out to daylight.

A pair of guards posted at the entry hatch stepped aside as he burst into the open meadow. He breathed in deep breaths of the aromatic air, savoring the warmth of the sun on his bare face. Immediately, the pressure in his head diminished.

Coming up behind him, Red swatted at tiny bugs buzzing around. "Why the hell do you want to be out here in this humid heat?"

It's marvelous. How doesn't she see that? Roman knew the answer. He extended his left hand to her. "Take my hand." His palm glowed golden, even in the direct sunlight.

She took a step back. "You need to explain what's going on."

"There aren't words to describe it. But I can try to show you."

"I'm not into whatever kinky shit you're trying to pull."

"Nothing like that," he assured her. Flexing his hand, the glowing intensified as the points of golden light moved under his skin. "This… I can't explain what, exactly, the tech is or how it works, but it's incredible. I'd like you to see for yourself."

Red shifted on her feet. She glanced at the two sentries at the facility entrance, beyond earshot but clearly curious about what Roman and Red were discussing. "How will this work?"

"Just take my hand."

She did.

Golden particles flowed from Roman's palm and began tracing up Red's arm. Her body tensed and her eyes got a faraway look. Then, her pupils dilated and her lips parted. In a matter of seconds, her expression shifted from wonder to joy to anguish.

"Aghhh!" she cried out, dropping to her knees.

Roman let go of her as she fell. The golden lights winked out from her hand.

"Ma'am!" One of the sentries ran to her while the other remained at his post. "What did you do?" he spat at Roman.

"I opened her mind. She'll be fine." While he couldn't be certain of that fact, he had been careful to only give her a glimpse of his power. He'd unveiled an inner part of himself to show the connection he now shared with the environment—

how the life around them was connected in a way he never could have imagined. Though he'd only begun to scratch the surface of that relationship, there was no denying the magnitude of his transformation.

Red remained limp on the ground, her eyes closed. The guard knelt next to her. "Ma'am! Ma'am!" he shouted, shaking her. "What did you do?" He glared at Roman. His hand moved to his sidearm, fingers twitching toward a draw.

Roman stood his ground. *If she's strong enough, she'll see.*

Red's eyes shot open. She abruptly sat up. "Stand down, Corporal."

Hesitantly, the young man went back to his post.

Red met Roman's gaze. There was new understanding in her eyes now. "How did you do that?"

"I'm still learning. But what I know for certain is that this world is more important than I'd ever dreamed. We can't let anyone take it from us."

She nodded faintly. "Rats hide where they feel warm and safe. We'll go to their eastern camp and flush them out, see where they go. Then, we'll trap them."

— — —

"Sir, you need to hear this," Rebeka announced, barging into Conroy's makeshift office area.

He pushed back from his desk. "Hear what?"

"Transmission from Echo Falls on the emergency channel. They have a situation."

His heart dropped. "How serious?"

"Unclear. Follow me."

She led him to the comm console. Though it was a far cry from the setup they'd had in the base, it had the important functional components.

Rebeka handed him an earpiece and tapped the one looped over her right ear. "Repeat what you told me, Rogers."

Conroy listened to the familiar voice coming over the comm. "There's been a cave-in. I think we have to evacuate."

"Is everyone okay?" Conroy asked.

"For now. I don't know what could have caused this. Maybe it became unstable after the flood? I'm worried this is going to keep getting worse."

"Understood. Get everyone to a secure area," Conroy instructed. "I'm going to confer with the team, and we'll be in touch with a plan soon. Stay safe."

"Yes, sir."

Conroy removed the comm from his ear and motioned for Rebeka to follow him. They flagged down Samor and went to the meal table that doubled as a conference area.

"This Echo Falls situation is a real problem," Conroy began. "They have close to seventy people there with all the crash survivors. We can't accommodate that many here."

"Not to mention... *you*," Samor pointed out.

Continuing to play dead would become increasingly complicated with additional civilians around. Loyalties couldn't be trusted, and access to long-range comms could mean information getting out at an inopportune time. He fully intended to reveal himself to the Commonwealth at large, but that announcement would be a strategic tool. The timing needed to be perfect, and he needed additional information before he'd be ready to take that step.

If he were to reveal himself to the crash survivors now, they'd become inextricably entangled in his political machinations. Generally speaking, people who'd venture to a new colony world were the sort looking to *escape* that kind of mess, not dive in head-first.

Regardless, space and resources were more immediate concerns. Hidden Grotto could hold maybe thirty people with their current setup; there was plenty of space to expand in the future, but they were short on everything from beds to food. Not to mention, leading a group of seventy people between the two camps would carve a trail that would be impossible to hide. They may as well send up a flashing beacon to let the enemy know where they were camping out.

"Since we can't bring them here, what are our options?" Conroy asked.

"Finding a more stable section of the Echo Falls cave system is the easiest move," Samor said.

"Yeah, relocating all those supply stores to a whole other site would be a nightmare," Rebeka agreed. "It's not just our stuff but also the things salvaged from the crashes."

"We have a manifest of the civilians, right?" Conroy asked.

"Yes, just a sec." Rebeka ran off and came back with a tablet. "Let's see... Here you go." She handed him the device.

He looked over the list of names and summary profiles. Most of the people had been administrators with NovaTech or its vendors, but there were a few with more practical experience. "This one." He opened the expanded profile and placed the tablet on the table for Samor and Rebeka to review.

"A geoengineer? What about him?" Samor asked.

"Someone who might be able to assess structural stability," Rebeka mused. "I'll get Rogers to have a chat with him." She stepped away to make the call.

"Sir, even if they stay put, that doesn't fix our problems," Samor stated.

"I know, my friend. What we really need to do is retake our home."

"Do you mean the base here, or…?"

"Both." Aethos was a staging ground, not a destination. Returning to the core worlds was the only long-term play.

Samor leaned back in his seat. "I'm beginning to think we may have numbers on our side—especially if we factor in the civilians. But all of the people holding the base are trained soldiers. Even a ten-to-one count would be challenging odds against superior equipment and tactical experience."

"We're not without proper soldiers, ourselves. And we know the landscape."

"Still."

Conroy nodded. "I'm wondering if it might be time to bring on some new recruits."

"That's extremely risky."

"But if we explain the true nature of this mission and how they came to be stranded here, that might gain us some followers. How can a person not be furious over that treatment?"

"I don't disagree, but—"

Rebeka came running back, slightly out of breath. "Sir, I just spoke to the geoengineer. The cave-in wasn't from erosion. It was bombed."

14

ANYA HAD STUDIED mass extinction events on multiple worlds, but she'd never investigated the disappearance of a sentient, space-faring race. Whatever weapon had glassed large swaths of Koranis and wiped out the planet's ecology was terrifying. Whoever had wielded that weapon appeared to be long gone, but there was no way to know for certain. She felt extremely exposed camping out on this backwater world with no plan.

"What's our next move?" she asked Evan.

"We can't keep going at this alone."

Thank the planets we're on the same page with that! She glanced at the *Asamar* parked on the other side of the trees. "Should we go back to Conroy?"

Evan shook his head. "They're looking to *us* for help. They can't do anything for us."

"What about their connections back in the core worlds?"

"True. But maybe a better question is, do we trust Conroy?"

Anya thought about it. "I don't *distrust* him. But I don't know the guy well enough to tell if he's been truthful and honorable."

"Exactly. I'd really rather not hand over technology with

civilization-altering capabilities without being one-hundred-percent certain that it's the right thing to do."

"How can we possibly get any more information to decide?"

Evan winced. "I have an idea, and I hate it before I've even said it out loud."

She frowned. "What?"

"Well, we know that the opposition is aware of this technology. They've clearly been up to something on Pavia. Based on the scale of the operation we saw there, there's no way we'd be able to get inside to take a closer look without a significant fighting force to breach their defenses."

Anya's eyebrows shot up. "And who might help us with that?"

"One of the Syndicate's contractors."

"You can't be serious!"

"I told you it was a terrible idea."

She shook her head with disbelief. "I was thinking it'd be crazy, not suicidal."

"I don't think we'll be in serious danger if we play it right—at least no more than we are already. It's just a friendly business meeting."

"Do you have a specific contact in mind?"

"Yes. She's in the logistics business. If she's not in on Pavia's shipments already, she'd be curious to find out what they're moving."

Anya crossed her arms. "Worth a shot. How do we make contact?"

— — —

Evan had dreamed up a number of crazy schemes in the

past couple of weeks, but this might be a new extreme. The last thing he wanted to do was delve back into the seedy underbelly of society, but he saw no other choice. Career smugglers had the kind of reach they desperately needed, and Evan was willing to put his qualms aside for the greater mission.

"Do what you need to do," Anya told him.

Evan didn't expect Anya to understand the intricacies of black market trade, but he was confident with his skills and connections in that area. It wouldn't be pretty, but they'd be back in the game if he could get the right people on board.

But the first step was making contact.

"And you're sure nothing about this comm signature will look strange on their end?" Evan asked Sam as he checked the communication console in the shuttle.

"The brief survey of Pavia provided ample opportunity for me to scan human-made equipment and create a detailed profile. I am confident that this configuration will read as the commlink originating from a standard human craft. I have also upgraded the shuttle to improve its disguise."

Evan hadn't expected that, but he could think of no downside. "Good work."

He'd gone through his mental list of contacts to weigh the pros and cons of each potential partner. In all cases, the negatives outweighed the benefits. It wasn't his first time picking the least painful option for the sake of a mission, but his final selection gave him pause, nonetheless.

He'd left things on ambiguous terms with Zaris Alva when they'd last spoken seven months ago, while he was still undercover. They'd had occasional dealings over the prior two years, with Zaris serving as a key member in the transport logistic chain for the Syndicate. She was an independent contractor with a significant operation of her own, a good head for business dealings, and enough of a morally gray approach that she might be willing to sell out the Syndicate for the right incentive.

"Can we trust this woman?" Anya asked.

Evan shook his head, wishing he had better news. "Her allegiance can be bought. Which is what makes her perfect for this."

"Great."

If they had any other options about where to turn, Evan would take those prospects instead. He didn't trust Zaris not to stab them in the back, but he did have faith that she'd at least hear them out. As long as they could make a pitch for why siding with them was in her and her business' best interest, there was a chance they could work out a deal. But the key would be to *maintain* her loyalty long enough to execute their plan.

That was, once they *had* a plan. Right now, his vague sense of direction was as mercurial as Zaris' business deals. There was a lot to figure out in a short time.

"I'm sorry we have to do this, Anya."

"Hey, it's a new life experience. And here I was thinking I'd never have the opportunity to check 'negotiate a black market deal for alien tech' off my bucket list!"

"By the time this is over, I suspect you'll have added quite a few more to the list." He centered himself at the console. "All right, Sam, initiate the commlink."

Anya settled in next to him well out of range of the camera's view. She gave him a supportive nod.

He took several slow, deep breaths to center himself. It'd been months since he'd needed to be Alex. He dredged up every memory he could of the persona. Alex had been a lot more confident than Evan felt right now. Maybe getting back to that mindset was exactly what he needed.

The image on the screen changed to a pulsing, spinning circle while the interstellar relay connected. When the link was established, the spinning stopped but the pulsing continued while waiting for the other party to pick up. He'd placed the call to Zaris' personal line. But she might not accept.

An agonizing thirty seconds passed. Then, the screen abruptly changed to the image of a woman with pink highlights in her dark hair and eyes so pale blue they were almost violet.

"Zaris! It's been a while," Evan greeted.

"Alex?" She raised an eyebrow.

"The one and only." He flashed a disarming smile.

"I thought you'd gotten out of the game. Actually, I'd heard you were dead."

"Just laying low for a few months. But I'm planning a comeback."

"That so?"

"I have a new lead and wanted to run some numbers."

She was quiet for a few seconds, studying him. "I'm surprised you called me, of all people."

"Hey, if you don't want a cut, it's your loss."

"Didn't say that. What kind of gig is this?"

"One better discussed in person."

Zaris sighed. "Of course."

"You can set all the particulars," he offered, sensing her hesitation.

"Fine, I'll take a meeting."

"You won't regret it."

"Remains to be seen. I'll send the rendezvous info." The call ended.

"Link severed," Sam confirmed, and Evan relaxed a little.

Anya raised an eyebrow. "She always that friendly?"

"Oh, I'm one hundred percent convinced we'll be walking into a trap."

"Wonderful. What can we do about that?"

"That depends on what she proposes for the meeting."

"Maybe we should cancel—"

"And do what instead? There are simply no good moves here. I have the control bracelet. They won't know about it, and it will be a last-ditch safeguard if things go sideways."

"When."

He nodded. "Yeah, probably. But I won't let anything bad happen to you, Anya."

"Good. Because if I die from this, I *will* haunt you."

— — —

I should never have agreed to this, Anya thought to herself as she reflected on Evan's latest scheme.

The meeting was a full day away, which offered ample time for Zaris to orchestrate the situation to her advantage. She sounded like the kind of person no one would want to run across; to actively seek her out was absolute madness. The brief recap Evan had told Anya about his past interactions with the woman painted Zaris as two-faced, unsympathetic, and conniving. Evan had shown sound judgment in their other dealings, but this proposed alliance was a bridge too far.

"There *has* to be another way," Anya insisted. "Too much is riding on this to trust someone who's clearly so unreliable."

"I wish I had an infinite network of contacts so we could pick and choose, but this is the best I've got. The second-choice option threatened to shoot me if he ever saw me again, so…"

"That's not a very good baseline," Anya admitted.

"Believe me, I wish I had a better suggestion."

She considered the possibilities. "Okay, what if we could hedge our bets with her? You know, make it so a double-cross would be too big a risk for her to take."

"How?"

"I remember this political consulting gig my dad told me about one time. It was about some sort of trade dispute where the local government of a colony kept screwing over their neighbors, and it blew up enough for the Commonwealth's central administrators to get involved. They ended up passing a resolution that mandated a flat-rate on all trades, so if one of the territories raised their prices, it would automatically go up for everyone."

"Sorry, not seeing how that would apply here," Evan said.

"Well, you can bluff, right?"

He shrugged. "Pretty much everything I've ever told her has been a lie, so…"

"So, present a case she can't ignore. You know, one of those mutually assured destruction kind of deals."

Evan shook his head. "Anya, if I go in there and tell her she'd better play nice or she's going down with me, she'll just shoot me on the spot."

"Obviously, that's not what I had in mind. We have a day before the meeting. That's time to strategize. We *can't* be fully upfront and tell the full truth."

"You're right about that. Let me run through some scenarios myself and we can circle back in a few hours."

"You sure you don't want to brainstorm together?"

"I'm used to working through this stuff on my own. I need to get back into the mindset of my alias she knew. Give me a bit to prep, and then you can meet Alex."

"Okay."

He left the shuttle. She watched him walk back to their

campsite, talking to himself.

I don't think I could become someone else with the flip of a switch like that. This is going to be harder on him than he'll admit, she realized.

He'd been gracious about everything, but she recognized that he'd been shouldering most of the weight of their mission. The Syndicate's serum had granted him direct interface with the alien tech. He was the pilot. And now they were turning to his black market contacts. Anya had done her little science tricks along the way, but she'd largely been a passenger in the mission. It couldn't continue that way.

The key was the Syndicate serum. She had the preliminary assessment of Evan's blood from her bioanalyzer. She had Sam. She had all the alien tech she could ever dream to possess.

With a new sense of purpose, she headed back to the main ship.

15

ROMAN WATCHED PEOPLE pour out from the cave entrance, most covered in dust and a few with bloody smears beneath the dirt. He couldn't help seeing the irony in using the explosives from Conroy's own inventory against these collaborators. Sometimes, the universe had perfect symmetry.

The explosives had been well-placed, making it look like a natural cave-in—one of Red's soldiers had managed that. Getting close hadn't been difficult, since they'd only had two guards posted. This was clearly the kind of place where they relied on remaining hidden as their main defense. In all fairness, they couldn't have anticipated a telepathic trace.

After the explosives tech had set the charges, Roman and the rest of the team had set up in hiding places around the cave to observe. The point wasn't to hurt people or bury their supplies, but rather to force them into the open. If they made this base uninhabitable, they'd have to seek shelter elsewhere. Get them out in the open, and they'd be easy to round up and use as bargaining tokens. Would Conroy give himself up for his followers?

There were about twenty people standing in the trees by the time everyone was out. A middle-aged man did two headcounts, seemingly satisfied with the result.

"All right, everyone," he began, "we have a pretty long walk ahead of us. Pick a buddy, and always be sure to keep eyes on each other. Fan out, and try to keep a light touch. We don't want to leave a trail."

Roman looked on with an amused smirk as most of the group ventured away from the camp into the trees. They were all weighed down with gear, and many were carrying crates in pairs. The idea of keeping a 'light touch' was downright laughable.

Six people remained, including the middle-aged man. Staying behind to guard the place, perhaps?

Roman signaled for four of the seven other people on his team to shadow the group of civilians. No doubt, they were the crash survivors from the colony ship. They shouldn't be difficult to manage, and there was no plan to engage them until they were close to Conroy's other hideout. Roman and the three remaining soldiers should be able to deal with these six, given they had the element of surprise.

"Rogers, we good?" a young man questioned the middle-aged leader.

Rogers nodded. "All clear. Let's clean it up."

Roman tensed. Something about the exchange seemed rehearsed. A coded message.

He looked around for signs of other enemy combatants. The trees were thick around here, obstructing his sightlines. But those weren't his only senses....

Taking a series of slow breaths, he opened his mind to the environment. There were potential spies all around to tell him what was happening. But where his presence had been welcomed before, now there was only silence.

Roman re-focused his attention near the cave entrance.

With a spike of adrenaline, he realized that Rogers had disappeared. *Wait, where did he go?*

The back of his neck prickled. There was someone behind him.

Roman spun around. He was greeted by Rogers holding a pistol aimed at Roman's face.

"Nice try," Rogers said.

"Try?" Roman held out his arms like he was surrendering, though he had no intention of doing so. "Everything is going perfectly from where I'm standing."

"You blew up our camp."

"*I* didn't do anything."

Gunfire sounded in the distance.

Roman's heart skipped a beat. It was impossible to know from here which side had fired the shots—or both.

Rogers' eyes flitted in the direction of the sound, but his attention never dropped from Roman. "Come with me." He motioned with his gun's muzzle for Roman to move toward the cave.

Roman complied, walking backward so he could watch the other man's movements. The environment had gone eerily quiet, making every crunch of dried leaves under Roman's feet stand out.

Three of Roman's team members emerged from the trees, each with one of Rogers' men at gunpoint. That left two more unaccounted for.

Heat rose in Roman's hands, radiating toward his chest. His left hand started to glow with golden light.

"What the—?" Rogers' words cut off as he disappeared into red mist.

"Holy shit!" one of the enemy combatants shouted.

Another one of Rogers' men took the opening to throw

himself backward, leading with his elbow as he jammed into his guard's side. The guard grunted as the two men collided, doubling over. As he took a stumbling step backward, the guard haphazardly raised his gun and fired.

The captive man had anticipated the shot and was already moving out of the way. The blast missed him, but it struck one of Roman's other soldiers in the neck instead, sending out a spray of blood.

That man's captive snatched his weapon as the body fell, opening fire on Roman's remaining soldiers. Others soon joined the fight in a chaotic exchange of physical blows and shots.

In a matter of seconds, all the members of Roman's team were dead or disabled.

The heat intensified in Roman's core. "Enough!" he bellowed.

The three remaining enemy men stood in stunned silence as they watched the golden light pulsing up Roman's arm while he approached them. They lowered their weapons.

Roman held out his palm. He could sense their small lives. It would be so easy to snuff them out.

"Please, don't," one of the men whispered.

Roman burned with a fire waiting to be unleashed. Whispers in the back of his mind encouraged him to end this fight. These lives were his to take.

But a competing force implored him. The forest was silently screaming for him to show mercy.

Roman hesitated. The fear in the men's eyes… the sadness…

His mind flashed to the warning from the panther. This place was judging him. It was already angry about him killing Rogers, and any more death in this engagement would not be forgiven. His power wasn't entirely his.

Spare them.

Roman ran into the trees.

— — —

Conroy knew that Samor brought bad news before the soldier said a word.

But the announcement was worse than he'd imagined. "Sir, I'm sorry. Rogers is dead. And two others."

Three more of my people lost to this war? His heart lurched. "What happened?"

"There was a fight at the cave, and several people were shot. But that Syndicate operative has some kind of weapon we've never seen before. It… vaporized Rogers."

"What…?" Conroy was at a loss for words. Aaron Rogers had been a friend for years—since well before their exile on Aethos. But as much as Conroy wanted to take time to process that loss, there were pressing concerns. "What is this weapon? Where did the operative go?"

"He ran off. They didn't actually *see* a weapon, but *something* killed him. One of the survivors said… they said the operative's hand was glowing."

A mystery weapon. That's all we need! He fought to keep his expression neutral. "What about the rest of our people?"

"We were able to ambush the enemy soldiers that were following them, and now they're back at Echo Falls," Samor said.

At least that part of the plan had worked out. As soon as they'd discovered that the cave-in was deliberate, it hadn't been a leap that the place was being watched. They'd figured that the intention was either to force Conroy out of hiding—if he was inside—or to follow the group back to Hidden Grotto. So, they'd devised a plan to send out twenty of their seventy people to draw attention, carrying weapons in crates designed to look like survival supplies. While dividing the enemy forces had seemed like a good idea at the time, now Conroy questioned whether or not that strategy had gotten Rogers and the others killed.

"Is Echo Falls secure?" Conroy asked.

"The place is a mess, and its location is compromised. Is it still defensible? Probably. But *should* they stay there?" He shrugged. "I need to know what to tell them."

"There's been too much death," Conroy murmured.

"That's not a reason to stop fighting. If anything, we need to keep going so those sacrifices have meaning."

"Oh, I have no intention of stopping," Conroy said. "But we can't keep repeating the same mistakes. Hiding. Dividing."

"It makes us a hard target."

"And it also makes each of our units weaker. I think it's time we pool our resources."

"Sir…"

"I know, it's a mess."

"I think Rebeka should be a part of this conversation," Samor suggested.

"You're right." Conroy invited her over and filled her in on the current situation.

Her expression became increasingly more horrified the more he explained. Eventually, she covered her mouth with her hand and turned away.

"We've lost a lot of people. We'll mourn them later," Conroy said, even though his own heart was heavy. As chancellor, many of his orders had been issued to faceless soldiers—statistics more than people. But everyone here with him on Aethos he'd known personally. Rogers, Amari, Cruz. They'd been brilliant and committed through the end. He needed to do right by them.

"If we bring anyone here, they'll know about you," Rebeka said. "Putting on my PR hat, my advice on that hasn't changed. It could destroy everything we've worked for."

"There is Riverview," Samor suggested.

"It's not outfitted with any supplies," Rebeka said. "Whatever they could carry by hand wouldn't last long."

"Except..." Samor got a glimmer in his dark eyes. "The enemy took over our base, but they haven't done anything with the crashed cruiser since they left, right?"

"Not as far as we know," Conroy confirmed. "What are you thinking?"

"That we left a bunch of supplies sitting nearby."

Rebeka clapped her hands and pointed at him. "That's right! Gah, why didn't I think of that sooner?"

"What's this, now?" Conroy asked.

Samor beamed. "We'd swept the crashed cruiser for supplies and had moved them to a staging area. We were in the process of ferrying everything back to base when we ran into Evan and Anya. Unless the enemy stumbled across them, there should be a whole stack of crates filled with MealPaks, medical supplies, and even some weapons."

"That is extremely promising."

"If it's still there," he cautioned.

"For that matter, the cruiser wasn't completely stripped," Rebeka added. "All those cabins have mattresses, and chairs, and everything else you'd want to build out a camp. We just didn't take any of that stuff because we didn't need it at the time."

Conroy smiled. "All right, let's make the preparations for Riverview to be a new home for our colonist friends."

— — —

The heat finally dissipated from Roman's limbs. His breathing came easy again after the strain of his run.

As he calmed, the sounds of animal activity around him reemerged. And so did the presence that occasionally tickled the back of his mind.

Stay.

Roman checked the map on his wrist. He'd been heading back toward the base camp. But the subtle message in his mind gave him pause. Returning to the base would mean facing Red and confessing that every member of the team she'd given him for the mission was likely dead. With their already diminished numbers, it would mean an untenable setback.

She'd seen his new power and had trusted that to be enough, but he'd failed the mission, yet again. At this point, she was more likely to barricade herself in the base and wait for reinforcements to arrive in two months. And if Marta's crew got to Aethos and found that Conroy wasn't in custody or dead, Roman may as well say goodbye to his own life.

Another option was for Roman to camp out on his own while he developed his new skills. That would reduce the chance of being apprehended by Conroy's people, and he wouldn't be subject to Red trying to exert authority over his actions.

The solo approach called to him. Frankly, he wasn't sure he'd be able to sleep inside the base, and Red would no doubt want to lock it down the moment he got back. Being trapped in there—that would be worse than roughing it in the wilds. He could likely even salvage some materials from the crashed cruiser.

Yes, that's what I need to do, he decided. Energized, he set out to forge his own path.

16

THE TRANSIT GATE dwarfed their little shuttle. The massive metallic ring floated in open space at a gravitationally neutral point within the star system where it would remain stationary—a standard practice. Evan's previous travels through such gates had been on big ships, and rarely had he had a direct view out front. Approaching this one now in their small craft made him feel like an ant about to step through a human-sized doorway.

"All right, Sam, work your magic," Evan instructed the AI.

Anya crossed her fingers. "Let's hope this works."

Though their shuttle was cosmetically indistinguishable from a human-made craft, it wasn't a registered vessel within the Commonwealth's transit system. Gate transits were logged and regulated—especially in the core worlds—so they needed to follow a specific procedure. Since gates were activated in pairs, with specific entry and exit points, the automated system had to approve each journey to prevent multiple activation requests from interfering with each other.

Though their shuttle could jump directly to the rendezvous coordinates with Zaris' ship, that would give away their hidden tech. They needed to make a show of arriving via a gate to avoid unwanted questions. But doing so meant trying to spoof the system. Smugglers did it all the time, though they had dummy transponders and other tech suites to facilitate the process. Trusting an alien AI to get everything right on the first attempt was a leap of faith.

"I have identified the correct exit gate," Sam reported. "Synching access codes. Lock established… Activating gate."

Red lights illuminated around the ring's outer edge. Interior components started spinning in a dizzying blur within the outer framework. A bright point of white light formed at the center of the ring. In a flash, it exploded to fill the ring, settling into a rippling blue surface.

"Do you know why it's blue?" Evan asked Anya.

She tilted her head. "You know… I've never thought about it."

"I remember asking my parents when I was maybe seven or eight. They didn't know, but they helped me look it up. Something about how the exotic matter in the wormhole scatters light—it makes the blue pop. And that's why it looks like we fly into the ocean."

She smiled, admiring it. "One of the best views in the galaxy."

There really were few things so magnificent. A controlled tunnel between worlds. One of humanity's greatest achievements.

"Everything good to go, Sam?" Evan asked.

"Affirmative."

Evan took them in.

An intense hum of electromagnetic energy vibrated the ship as they approached the ring. Evan's fine hairs stood on end, and a low thrum resonated deep in his bones. He'd learned later in life that the effect was from the insane power demands of maintaining the gate, but it'd always been his favorite part of jumps as a kid on his family's merchant ship. The electrical crackle in the air made him feel like he had superpowers. Thinking about the new control bracelet affixed to his wrist, that dream was actually coming true now.

As the shuttle passed through the ring, the view outside changed to an ethereal corridor glowing slightly with blue light. Ahead was a faint, shimmering blue disc—the exit gate. It grew steadily larger as the shuttle traversed the tunnel. The blue haze gradually lifted to reveal the distorted starscape of their destination, which sharpened as they neared.

There was a slight shimmer and another intense hum of energy as the ship passed through the exit gate.

"Transit complete," Sam announced.

The rippling blue portal vanished with a flash of white light.

Anya shivered in her seat. "That's always a rush."

"Sure is," Evan said absently, looking around their destination. He checked the scan data on the front display. Zaris' ship was waiting for them about fifteen minutes' transit away at standard sub-light speed. "Of course. Figures she'd get here early."

"What's the likelihood she shoots our ship on the approach?"

"Minimal. A vessel has utility or resale value. She wouldn't want to damage it."

"So, she'll shoot *us* and take our ship?"

"Much more likely."

"This meeting is the best. Excellent suggestion, Evan."

"Hey, I told you that you could stay behind."

"And miss all this fun?" She scoffed and waved her hand. "Not a chance!"

Evan spent the transit time getting back in the Alex character mindset. Anya gave him a few funny looks while he muttered to himself as he talked through potential conversations, but she allowed him the time to prep. By the time they were within visual range of the other ship, he was ready to go.

"Incoming communication from the *Invictus*," Sam announced.

"Here we go." Evan accepted the voice call. "Greetings, *Invictus*. Where should we slide in?"

Anya raised an eyebrow at the phrasing.

"Bay C," Zaris' voice replied. "Keep it slow and steady, champ. Wouldn't want you to wear yourself out before our pillow talk."

Anya silently sighed and rolled her eyes at that.

"I know just how you like it. See you soon." Evan ended the comm link.

"Oh, *do* you, now?" Anya asked.

"All talk," he told her, which was true. But there had been a *lot* of talk. And interest that hadn't been entirely faked on his end. All of that couldn't be further from his mind now, though.

He brought the ship into Bay C through the electrostatic force field, setting it down in one of the open berths. Debarking and leaving the alien shuttle—however well disguised—unattended made him more nervous than walking into Zaris' lair, but Sam had assured him that there were ample safeguards in place to prevent the vessel from falling into the wrong hands.

Knowing that they'd be frisked and all weapons confiscated, Evan didn't bother to bring a handgun or knife. The control bracelet and accompanying nanite reserves in the other bracelet would be both his offense and defense should the need arise.

"Remember, don't volunteer any unsolicited information. Keep things as vague as possible. And don't let them take you anywhere without checking with me," he reminded Anya.

She nodded. "I've got it."

"All right." He opened the side hatch.

They stepped down to the hangar deck. A group of people were approaching, with a burly man at the lead. Evan recognized him from previous interactions, but he couldn't recall his name—if one had ever been given.

"You said nothing about bringing anyone with you," the man said.

"And you didn't forbid it. This is Anya, my associate." Evan had seen no reason not to share her real first name—one less aspect of their fabricated story to keep straight, and less chance for her to slip up.

"Well, pretty face like that, I think we can make an exception." He smiled predatorily at Anya. "You can call me Rex."

"Nice to meet you," Anya said. "We should get to business."

"Just need a quick check," Rex said.

Evan spread his arms and legs in anticipation of the check for weapons. Rex wasn't shy about running his hands over Evan's clothes and getting his fingers up in all the potential hiding places. "Hey, at least buy me dinner first," Evan muttered.

Rex only scoffed in response, then moved on to repeat the search on Anya. He lingered longer than needed with the pat-down, including a full slide down her chest. She took it with a straight face.

"Hey, we good?" Evan prompted with the hope of getting him to stop.

Rex finally dropped his hands. "Just need to do a quick

sweep." He pulled out a plastic square from inside his jacket.

Evan recognized the device as a scanner for recording or communication devices. While a reasonable precaution, it was a deviation from their previous procedure. He wasn't sure how the alien tech on his wrists might register.

Rex started with Anya, since he was still standing in front of her. The sweep was clean, no surprise. He then stepped over to Evan and began with a head-to-foot vertical scan. "Turn."

Evan flipped so his back was to Rex. That was all for the best, because his expression was hidden when Rex ran the wand down Evan's left arm. It beeped rapidly.

Rex gripped Evan's wrist and leaned in to inspect the bracelet. "What's this?"

"It's some sort of energy healing thing…" Evan scrambled to come up with an explanation. *Shit, I'm out of practice.* He regretted making such a rookie move of being unprepared for the question. That's why weeks or months were spent preparing for assignments, not a day.

"Pretty, isn't it?" Anya chimed in. "I saw them in a market and just *had* to get them for him. It's a set."

She's a natural. Evan smiled at her then looked over his shoulder at Rex. "Thoughtful, isn't she?" He showed the other bracelet on his right wrist.

"No electronics allowed," Rex stated. "Take them off."

"They're not electronic," Evan replied, turning back to face him. "Look, man, I've been trying to get these things calibrated for a month. If I take them off, I have to start all over again. I know you're checking for bugs, but these ain't it."

"If you want this meeting, you'll take them off."

Removing them would truly mean going in empty-handed, but he had little choice now.

"You're killin' me here. Hang on." Evan went into the

shuttle and stowed the bracelets in the weapons locker, which was the only locking cabinet on board.

Steeling himself, he returned to the hangar. Rex repeated the security checks to make sure he hadn't picked up anything else while in the shuttle.

He nodded, satisfied. "This way."

Evan followed Rex from the hangar into a barebones corridor lined in riveted metal. Fifteen meters down, after passing by three doors on the right, Rex swung open a door. The interior was darker than the corridor, making it difficult to see inside.

"Ladies first," he said, inviting Anya to step ahead of him. Following the logic they'd established on Aethos, if there was about to be an ambush, it was better for her to step into it first so he'd have more time to react.

She smiled sweetly at him as she passed, but her eyes communicated that she knew what he was doing.

Evan waited for Anya to fully enter the room. She continued inward, unimpeded.

In the corridor, Rex motioned for Evan to go in. He detested the idea of having that man behind him, blocking the only known exit.

The moment Evan stepped into the room, two sets of hands grabbed him from behind. Cold metal pressed against his throat—a knife, not hard enough to draw blood, but sending a message.

Behind him, the door slammed closed, and a bolt clanged into place.

Of course, we couldn't just have a nice, normal meeting. Evan couldn't turn his head without drawing the blade across his neck, but he was able to see out of the corner of his eye that Anya was also being restrained. Short of refusing to enter the room, there'd been nothing he could have done to avoid the grapple—and offering any resistance now would ensure they'd never reach a deal.

A woman wearing form-fitting black pants and a tailored jacket stepped from behind a storage crate at the back of the room. Her face was still half in shadow, but the twist of her lips was unmistakable.

"Great to see you, too, Zaris," Evan greeted. "Can we skip the pleasantries?"

"Oh, but this is the most enjoyable part!" She sauntered forward. "I was surprised to get your message."

"Well, when stars align…"

Zaris examined Anya, her nose wrinkled with disdain. "What's her story?"

"All that matters is she brings the technical expertise for the job."

"Right. This 'opportunity' you mentioned," she sucked her teeth, "not sure I believe it."

"You took the meeting."

"I took an opportunity to get back at you. And you walked right into it."

The broad side of the blade pressed harder against Evan's neck. He kept his expression neutral. "What'll it take to let the bygones be?"

"Always trying to talk your way out of a bind. Not gonna work."

"So, you only agreed to a meet so you could kill me? What does that accomplish?"

"Makes me feel a whole lot better."

"For the short-term, maybe. But wouldn't you rather set yourself up for life?"

"That deal of yours won't amount to shit."

"You haven't even heard the pitch. All I ask is for you to hear me out. Right now, the Syndicate is calling shots with your deals. How'd you like to be the one on top?"

She laughed. "Oh, that's a good one."

"Not a joke. I know what they've used to gain their power, and it's time we cut off that supply."

"What are you talking about?"

"I learned of a place critical to their operation. Get control of that, and *we'll* be the ones with power."

"Slow this 'we' business," Zaris said. She gestured to Rex, and he relaxed the blade slightly. Her eyes narrowed. "What is it you want from me, exactly?"

"I have the intel and the know-how but not the personnel. If you bring the firepower, we can serve an eviction notice."

"I'm not saying I don't command a significant force, but the Syndicate can mount a defense on par with the UPDF."

"Every militia has their weakness. I know the Syndicate's. This wouldn't be a massive shootout. I'm talking surgical, precision strike."

She didn't reply at first, still evaluating him. "What you're proposing won't work. They have bases and supply depots on at least a dozen worlds. No way that hitting one place will make a dent in the operation."

"It's not any old supply depot. This planet is different."

"In what way?"

Evan had intended to take a different approach to the conversation, but he had to follow this thread now. Simply making it out of the meeting alive wasn't enough—he needed to take a chance. If he couldn't sway Zaris, the likelihood of recruiting anyone else with enough resources was next to zero. It was either go all-in or revert back to the non-plan of hiding in a cave with Anya for the rest of his life.

He met Zaris' gaze. "Because the planet I'm talking about is where they've been mining alien tech."

Her brows shot up. She hadn't laughed this time, which was an improvement. "What kind of tech?"

"*That's* what I want to find out," Evan continued. "I conducted a preliminary survey—at great personal risk, mind you—and have it on good authority that they have some good shit down there. We get control, we use it to our advantage."

"They'll just attack us and take it back. Then it *would* be a shootout, and whoever has the most guns would win. That's not me."

"There is another wrinkle to this," Evan said, recognizing that he was losing her. "The Syndicate is working with the Commonwealth government."

"That's crazy."

"How else could they have grown so large in the last few years? I mean, I've known about the org for decades, but in the last four years or so it seems like they're *everywhere*. Because they're not actually being policed."

"You're not making a case for this being a viable plan."

"Can't give it all away on the first date. But trust me when I say I know where to hit them where it will hurt—and in a way that would make the Commonwealth want to put as much distance as possible between them. Take away that support and protection, and they'll be hurting. That will present a prime opportunity for a new power to step in and fill the void."

"You're going to need to get a *lot* more specific," Zaris said.

"Something I'm happy to do once I don't have a knife to my throat. You can kill me to get payback for whatever you think I did wrong. Or, we can talk this through, and you can use me to get rich."

She tapped her foot while pursing her lips. "Before I endure what will no doubt be a convoluted and verbose pitch, know that I won't even consider doing anything with this kind of risk profile for less than eighty percent of the take."

"That's ridiculous."

"My muscle, my risk. I haven't heard anything come out of your mouth that would justify even a five percent finder's fee. I think twenty percent is very generous."

"Once you hear the details, you'll be happy with seventy."

She raised an eyebrow. "Not even countering with fifty-fifty?"

"We both know you would have countered that with seventy-five, then I would have moved to sixty, and we would have settled on seventy, anyway. I figured I'd cut out the steps as a thank-you for not slitting my throat."

"Very thoughtful."

"And in the interest of good faith negotiation, I should probably tell you my real name and how I know so much about the Syndicate's operations. Whaddya say?"

"I say you bought yourself twenty minutes to make me not regret keeping you alive."

17

ANYA KEPT HER mouth shut throughout the meeting, even after she'd been released. She was still fuzzy on exactly what Evan was proposing, but she understood enough to recognize that his suggestions weren't the *actual* plan—simply a means to an end.

Zaris' expression was difficult to read. Mostly, she seemed annoyed, but there was also a degree of intrigue in her eyes. Not so much for the words, but for the person speaking them.

"My real name is Evan Taylor," he explained. "When you met me before as Alex, I was working undercover."

Zaris' eyebrows shot up. "Why the hell would you tell me that?"

"I don't have any reason to lie to you now. I know from our work together that you run one of the largest outfits outside the Syndicate. I could really use those connections now."

"I'm not a snitch."

"No, I'm not here to recruit you as an informant. I got out of the service months ago. I'm here as a private citizen, and so is Anya."

"How did you get insane enough to want to take on the Syndicate?"

Evan relaxed his shoulders. "Zaris, I'm just going to level with you. Believe me or not, but I swear it's the truth. My cover was blown because I walked in on a meeting between the Syndicate and the Commonwealth's Deputy of Economic Development. That meeting can only mean that the Syndicate is about to gain a *lot* more power. And while I may have been working on the side of law and order for my career, I recognize that competition is what keeps criminals honest. Having the Syndicate as the only game in town isn't good for you, and it's not good for the Commonwealth. I'd like you to help me keep the free black market alive."

"Why didn't the Syndicate call you out as a rat? Word was that you cashed out and went to live on a world off the beaten track."

"That was close to the truth, though retirement didn't work out. I suspect they kept it quiet because they didn't want to admit that they'd allowed an undercover operative to infiltrate high up in the organization. Any sign of weakness can be detrimental, as you know."

"I was surprised when you just… disappeared. That last night we spent together had seemed like the start of something."

"If I hadn't walked in on that meeting, it very well could have been. Leaving wasn't a choice."

Zaris scowled. "You could have come to me and explained."

"Would you have listened?"

"Maybe. I'm listening now, and I was a lot less pissed at you back then."

Though Anya would have never considered herself a jealous person, it made her skin crawl every time Zaris looked at Evan that way. Worse, he seemed to be leaning into it.

"I didn't have the whole picture while I was still embedded, but I've learned new things about the Syndicate and their relationship with the Commonwealth's leadership since getting out," Evan continued. "The key thing is that they're using alien tech, and they're getting it from Pavia."

"What does it do?"

"I don't know exactly, but clearly it's giving them some kind of strategic advantage."

Zaris crossed her arms. "How does the Syndicate have alien tech and no one else? I haven't heard any chatter about that."

"All part of the mystery I hope to solve."

"The security on that world has to be insane if what it contains is so important."

"We can cripple their defenses. I was able to get the control frequency for the alien tech, so I can disable it," Evan said, which Anya knew to be a lie.

"How do you know they're using the alien tech in their defenses?"

"That was part of my research."

It hadn't been, but after listening to Evan's rehearsals, Anya had pieced together that it was important to make oneself indispensable to the mission. Positioning himself and Anya as technical experts with knowledge that only existed in their heads was a good way to do so.

Zaris pursed her lips. "Before I commit to anything, I need all the ins and outs. I assume you wouldn't show up here, asking for my help, without a thorough tactical plan in hand?"

"Of course not."

"All right, walk me through it."

The briefing ended up taking close to an hour due to many questions and interjections. Anya fought to keep her expression neutral while she tried to memorize the details in his statements. Evan was blending plenty of facts and fiction, and she was beginning to appreciate how difficult it must be to maintain deep cover. No wonder he'd felt like he barely knew himself anymore.

"Are you sure you were a UPDF soldier?" Zaris asked after Evan finished laying out his proposal. "What you're talking about here doesn't seem very 'by the book', or feasible."

"I know the Syndicate, and this is what it would take to get in there."

"Hmm." She crossed her arms.

"Do we have a deal?" he asked.

"I need to think on it. You're not going anywhere until I do."

Zaris and her men headed for the door. "There'll be guards outside." She left and sealed the door behind her, leaving Anya and Evan alone in the room.

Anya let out a long breath. "I'm not sure what I was expecting, but it wasn't that."

"Black market dealings entail a lot more business than you academic types might think."

"I appreciate the attention to detail." She chose her words carefully, trying to stay in the character of a technical consultant. It was safe to assume they were being watched.

"May as well get comfortable. This could be awhile," Evan said, moving over to sit on a crate.

Anya sat down on a crate next to his. Only once she was off her feet did she realize how sore they were from standing stationary on the metal deck for so long.

This wasn't the kind of room where good things happened to people. With cold realization, it occurred to her that this might be the last room she ever saw. If Zaris decided to turn down the job, she might not let them go.

— — —

Zaris had been taking in Alex's—rather, Evan's—statements with a healthy dose of skepticism. The man hadn't even shared his real name with her before, so how could he be trusted?

But she'd dealt with a lot of people—especially people with terrible reputations for double-crossing. After growing up in a culture of thievery, she'd developed a good sense for deception. Everyone had a tell. Before, she'd noticed that Evan would clench his left fist when making an argument. His intelligence had always panned out, so she'd eventually written it off as a nervous tick. But now, she realized that everything he'd told her had been a lie; he'd just been *that good* at maintaining his curated persona. And, curiously, his hands now hung loosely at his sides.

As outlandish as some of his statements sounded, he appeared to be telling the truth on the big things. Even if a fraction of his story was accurate, she couldn't ignore his warning. Not only was there major impact on her business interests, but her very life was at risk. The Syndicate would no doubt eliminate their competition as soon as they had sufficient power to do so.

Though she ultimately called the shots, Zaris didn't want to make any decision without running it by the senior members of her crew. One of the reasons she'd built up such a capable and loyal fighting force was because they trusted her not to make hasty choices. Whatever happened now, she wanted everyone to be on board.

She headed to the *Invictus'* flight deck perched above the

nose of the vessel. It was one of the few rooms on the ship finished in materials other than brushed metal—the walls lined with dark-maroon synthetic leather to absorb echo while still being easy to clean, and the seats were upholstered with matching material. The floor was still metal, but it was painted black and finished with a sandpaper texture to give it exceptional grip. While the flight deck was equipped with eight workstations, only five of them were occupied right now. Zaris' second-in-command, Tarek, currently occupied the central command seat.

"That was a long meeting with someone you intended to throw out an airlock," Tarek commented as she entered. He relinquished her seat and moved toward his usual station in the front left. His black clothes and shaved sides of his head gave him the aura of an executioner, but he had an insightful, analytical side that had made him an invaluable advisor.

"Turns out he still talks a good game. And there might be some truth in it. Callie, join us," she requested of her ops officer.

The young helm officer got up from her station, one of the few among the crew who made a point of maintaining a varied and colorful wardrobe—a teal jumpsuit today.

The three of them went into Zaris' office through a door on the left side of the flight deck. As they settled into chairs around her desk, the two officers looked at her expectantly.

"The short version is that the Commonwealth's government might be working with the Syndicate behind the scenes, with the intention of granting legitimacy to their operation." Zaris went on to explain more of the details Evan had presented, and how he'd responded to her clarifying questions.

Tarek and Callie didn't bother to hide their skepticism

throughout the explanation.

"That's quite a story," Tarek commented when she turned it over to them for questions. He was a few years older than her and had taken on a protective role in their relationship despite her being in command. She trusted him to look out for her best interests, and this initial reaction wasn't a surprise.

"I would have dismissed him out of hand, but I've noticed some things over the last couple of months," Zaris said. "Like, remember that pickup on Orjin last month? I didn't say anything at the time, but I saw some Commonwealth-marked crates mixed in with the Noche inventory. I'd figured it was stolen goods, but there may have been more to it."

Callie frowned, drawing her thin eyebrows together. "You should have mentioned that."

Zaris shrugged. "Some things only seem important in hindsight."

"Let's just assume for a minute that everything this guy told you has merit," Tarek said. "We can play out the logic. And it *does* lead to us being royally screwed if the Syndicate gets elevated like that."

"We can't take his word for it," Callie insisted.

Zaris nodded. "Agreed. But I also don't think we should dismiss it. So, the question is, how do we verify without exposing ourselves?"

"Obviously, we can't let the Syndicate know we're sneaking around," Tarek said.

"Better yet, we have someone else do the sneaking for us," Callie suggested. "I mean, we *do* have two highly motivated people locked up downstairs."

Zaris nodded thoughtfully. "We do." She smiled. "Maybe it's time we roll out the welcome mat and make our new guests feel at home."

— — —

Evan slid off the crate to his feet as soon as the hatch door creaked open. Rex and another guard still framed the doorway, but Zaris entered alone.

"Thank you for waiting," she said.

"No problem. Have you made a decision?" Evan asked.

She shrugged. "Still working on it. But I will say this: I hear you, and I think you might be onto something with this Syndicate thing. I'm just not sure yet what the best course of action is."

Evan nodded. Pressuring her wouldn't get positive results. "I know there's a lot to consider."

"Sure is. And that's the thing. Most of what we discussed revolves around gaining control of Pavia. But that would only be the beginning. There's still a whole, powerful interstellar organization out there—not to mention the might of the Commonwealth potentially behind them. Even if we *did* capture the planet, holding it for any meaningful time is unlikely."

"That's where leverage comes in."

"And what kind of leverage might we hold?" she asked.

Evidence that the current chancellor tried to have his predecessor assassinated, for one, Evan thought to himself. *Not to mention the most revolutionary transit technology humanity has ever seen.* But he couldn't say any of that. Yet, he needed to say *something.* And a compelling statement, at that. A version of the truth always made the best lie. "I've been in touch with certain collectors. They've recovered alien artifacts that would make a big splash if it all went public. When that happens, you'll want to be on the right side of history."

"Where did these artifacts come from? Were they all exported from that same world?"

"My understanding is that there are other planets with alien artifacts."

"Why bother trying to capture Pavia, then?"

"Because what's on Pavia seems to be unique to that world. If we can help the collectors expand their domain, we'll be well-positioned to have a place in the expanding empire."

"Empire, huh?" she raised an eyebrow.

"My word, not theirs."

Zaris sighed and shook her head. "We talked before for, what… an hour? There was no mention of these 'collectors'. Every time we chat, the story changes. Either you've lost your touch, or you're intentionally giving me the runaround to frustrate me. But why?"

A little of both? Evan had mostly stuck to his script, and feeding little pieces of the narrative had been a core part of his approach. He knew Zaris well enough to understand her inquisitiveness. If he'd laid everything out from the start, she would have simply dismissed—or killed—them and acted on the information as she saw fit. But regulating the flow of information and introducing new wrinkles along the way would keep the conversation going for longer to get her invested in the grander vision. Not only would that keep them alive, but it might actually get Zaris on their side.

"My knowledge is only beneficial to me as long as it stays in my head," Evan confessed. "We don't trust each other. You have absolutely no reason to believe me, and I know me being here isn't improving your day. If the roles were reversed, would you be any more forthcoming?"

"No," she admitted.

"See? So, take my presence as a good faith demonstration

that I want this to work. My life is in your hands. I wouldn't take that risk unless there was too much upside to ignore."

Zaris looked him over thoughtfully. "Whaddya say just the two of us catch up?"

That seemed like a positive indication, but he feared what strings might be attached. Nonetheless, he needed to take the opening.

Evan drew Anya aside, speaking to her in a hushed voice. "Maybe you should go wait on our shuttle."

She raised one eyebrow, meeting his gaze levelly. "That sounds like a terrible idea."

It probably was, but Evan's mental calculations had the likelihood of Zaris agreeing to anything while Anya was around at close to zero. He was hesitant to resurrect their flirty rapport from back in his undercover Alex days, but closing this deal was a make or break moment. "I'll be careful, Anya," he said, hoping that she somehow could pick up on all the rationale behind his simple words.

Whether she understood or not, she sighed and shrugged. "Whatever you say."

They returned to where Zaris was waiting.

"Anya would like to go back to our shuttle, but you can keep the craft locked down. Why don't we go somewhere more private to talk this out?" Evan suggested.

"Agreed," Zaris said, giving Anya a once-over.

Anya bristled. "I'll see you later." She departed with Rex.

Zaris watched her go. "What's the story with you two?"

"No story. Brought together by strange circumstances and now united by a common goal." He couldn't say more than that without undertaking a lie he didn't want to maintain. The truth was, he was actually quite taken with Anya. Though their time together had been brief, the intensity of the experience had forged a bond between them that he was eager to explore. But unveiling any of that to Zaris at this stage would be counterproductive.

"Come on," Zaris motioned for Evan to follow her out into the corridor.

She led him to a lift, which took them up four decks to a more residential part of the ship. Her destination was a common room filled with various types of seating and an expansive bank of viewports along the back wall. Despite its significant size meant to accommodate a large number of people, it was currently unoccupied.

Zaris sat down on a couch in front of the viewports and patted the spot next to her. It was big enough for two people, but they would have to be friendly.

Evan settled in next to her, leaving as much space between them as possible.

"I didn't expect to ever see you again," she began.

"Did you care that much?"

She pivoted to stare out the viewport behind them. "This job can be lonely. I always enjoyed our talks."

"I did, too." And he meant it. His undercover assignment had dictated that he keep an emotional distance from the subjects of his investigation, which made friends few and far between. Zaris, despite her sometimes brutal nature, had provided him with the rare glimmer of genuine connection. While their sense of morality diverged widely on several points, he appreciated her grit and determination—and even her ruthless ambition. The fact was that she'd been born into a life of crime, and she'd made the most of it while so many were eaten alive. He respected that, even though he disagreed with her methods.

"You realize I can't let you go now," she murmured.

"Because you think I'm going to turn you into the authorities?"

"Not because I believe it, but because others would."

"If I had any intention of getting you arrested with what I know, I would have done it a long time ago. The truth is, everyone back in the core worlds thinks I'm dead."

"Why?"

"I was on a ship that crashed. With Anya—that's how we met. It was sabotage, and as far as anyone knows, there were no survivors."

"And that has something to do with this proposed plan to take on the Syndicate?"

"Yes. Trust me when I say it's better for your own life expectancy if you don't know more than that right now."

She turned back to face him. "Seems like attacking Pavia would be hazardous to my health, too."

"It's dangerous, it's true. But isn't it *more* dangerous to be holding none of the cards when the Syndicate steps into new power? As long as you possess something they want and need, you're guaranteed survival."

"Until they try to take it back by force."

"Their power is being bolstered by Rostov's administration. Imagine how the tables would turn if someone else were chancellor."

Zaris held up her hands. "Whoa, whoa, wait. We were just talking about capturing a planet hiding alien tech. What's this about a government coup?"

"Like I said, there's more to this. And the details are best kept vague. But I assure you, whoever controls the tech on that planet will have a major bargaining chip regardless of who's in power."

She pursed her lips. "I don't know what to make of you.

Are you still a lawman at heart, or did we successfully corrupt you?"

"I'm a realist. I don't trust anyone other than myself. And I know that you are equally motivated by your own self-interests. For that reason, I think we can agree that *we'd* rather call the shots than let out-of-touch politicians decide our fate."

"Sure, but that's just idealistic talk."

"No, Zaris. This is one of those moments in history where everything could change. The kind of opportunity that comes along once a century—if not longer. I intend to seize the day. You need to decide, are you with me?"

She raised her eyebrows, then leaned back on the couch, chuckling to herself. "I shouldn't be listening to this shit."

"Admit it, you're intrigued."

"Sure, in the same way a drunk's ravings in a bar can be entertaining. That doesn't make them any more real."

He nodded. "Oh, it's real. What will it take for me to prove it?"

18

"START WITH THAT one over there," Samor instructed his team as they began gathering up the crates that had been left in the staging area near the crashed cruiser. He hated everyone being in an exposed place with such poor sight lines, so the sooner they could get all the equipment and colonists moved, the better.

They'd recruited some of the colonists to help with the relocation. A number of the people had suffered injuries during the crash, and there hadn't been enough nanite medical stims to fully heal all of the injuries. So, while Samor's gunshot wounds were now only reddened marks on his skin, those who'd suffered broken bones still had limited mobility. Their compatriots had stepped up to help without protest, which was an encouraging sign for building a new, sustainable community.

Regardless, there were significant concerns about the safety of the area. They'd killed many of the invaders, but even a handful of soldiers with military weaponry could be devastating against unarmed civilians. And then there was the Noche Syndicate man. His mysterious weapon that could instantly disintegrate a person was a thing of nightmares.

With the supply sorting and distribution underway, Samor took four of his team to make another pass through the military ship. Their previous search had been for specific items, but there were still a lot of materials on board. The plan was for them to offload anything that could be beneficial to help build out the new Riverview base. Others would then meet them at the crash site later to help carry whatever they'd found to the cave.

Samor couldn't shake the feeling that he was being watched the entire walk over. Even the animals seemed to be paying extra attention to him. There were no overt signs of being followed, but he kept his hand on his sidearm just in case.

When the trees opened up to the crash path where the cruiser had come down, he was surprised to see little saplings already sticking up through the charred remains of the broken forest. That kind of regrowth would take a year or more on most worlds; for the land to already be healing after less than two weeks was remarkable.

The five of them jogged across the exposed area to the mangled ship and then hugged the hull as they worked their way around to an access point. They went in near the aft of the vessel, at a place where they'd previously entered; it was reasonably close to the cargo hold and also near some of the crew quarters.

Samor led the way inside. The air had become mustier, stinging his nostrils with the stench of damp, rotten soil. With a turn of his stomach, he realized that it might not be from the rain or dirt at all, but rather the decomposing bodies locked in some of the cabins that might not have been airtight.

Ignoring that disturbing thought, Samor first headed back to the cargo hold. Scrambling up the sloped decking from the awkward landing orientation was hard on his ankles, but it was worth it to get the valuable resources contained in the vessel.

When he reached the hold, he was surprised to find the door open. He remembered sealing its locking wheel the last time he'd been here. Perhaps Evan and Anya had opened it?

His stomach dropped as soon as he entered the hangar. Light flooded into the space through an open cargo door. He wouldn't have left it open like that.

"Hey, when was the last supply run out here?" Samor asked his team.

"Sorry, sir, don't know," one of the younger soldiers, Erran, replied.

It was possible another team had come through the ship after Samor had last departed. The textured decking showed no footprints, so it was impossible to see who might have been by, or when.

"All right, let's give it another sweep and see what we can get," Samor said.

The team located several crates of supplies they'd initially left for future collection, like maintenance tools and tents, which they hadn't needed while living in the base. They also found a crate of walkies buried under a bunch of other stuff, which they'd missed on their first pass; those would be extremely helpful once they'd dealt with the enemy infiltrators. One of the best finds, though, was two hovercarts, which would allow them to more easily transport the bigger, heavier items across the challenging forest floor terrain.

They dumped the salvaged materials outside through the open cargo door. It was about a three-meter drop to the ground, but none of the materials were fragile enough to worry about the fall in the durable crates. Once they had a pile of crates and other loose items collected on the ground, they moved on to the residential cabins to get mattresses, linens, and the like.

As Samor headed up one of the stairwells to the next deck, the echo of soft, rhythmic pounding sounded above him. He froze, holding up a fist to signal the soldiers behind him to halt. They listened.

There was only a brief, soft creak. Then silence.

Samor frowned. It'd sounded like something was inside the stairwell. As a precaution, he drew his weapon, and he heard soft clicks behind him as the rest of the team followed his lead. They continued their ascent.

— — —

Roman slowly eased the stairwell door closed. He would have liked to lock it from the inside, but the clang of the bolt would draw too much attention. As it stood, the soldiers had stopped below, so they were already suspicious.

Through the open crack in the hatch, he heard careful footfalls continue upward. Through the telepathic trace, he sensed that Samor was with them. That link had given Roman a heads up that the soldiers were coming to the ship, with the local wildlife relaying their sensory perceptions to him. To his own detriment, Roman had waited too long to move into a hiding position, wanting to overhear as much of the soldiers' conversation as possible. He hadn't learned enough to make this precarious position worthwhile.

Roman wanted to avoid a confrontation here. This group would certainly die before his mission was complete, but this wasn't the time or place for that standoff. There was still more to learn about Conroy and his plans, not to mention what had happened with the surviving colonists. All those pieces would play into his next moves.

I need to get this mission back on track. Marcus and Marta will condemn me if I fail in this, too. His family's approval shouldn't mean so much, but what else did he have? All the power he'd been granted from the alien tech was meaningless without a clear objective. And the only thing that mattered to him was assuming his rightful place as a leader in the Syndicate.

That dream would dissolve here and now if he made the wrong move. He centered his mind. *Survive.*

Roman crept backward down the hall, feeling his way across the decking from toe to heel. The soldiers were advancing up the stairwell.

His composite boot bumped into a wall as he tried to place his foot. A dull thud reverberated through the quiet place.

The soldiers stopped again. They were right outside the hatch.

Shit! Roman debated whether to freeze or run. He looked around for possible places to hide. A doorway a few meters to his left was ajar. He tiptoed toward it and slipped inside.

No sooner had he rounded the corner than the stairwell hatch creaked open. Soft footfalls slowly advanced toward his position.

Along with the sounds was the odd telepathic nudge that told him Samor's location. He'd taken the lead in the group, and the mental trace helped pinpoint his movements beyond what Roman's ears alone could detect. He was nearly to the open door.

Roman's heart pounded. His hand involuntarily started to warm as the alien tech responded to his panic.

No, don't! Not him! He pleaded with himself. The heat intensified.

He hid his hand behind his back to conceal the golden

glow. But in doing so, he realized that all of his skin was glowing, casting a subtle amber light inside the room.

Samor reached out to push the hatch open further.

Roman's arm burned, begging to release an energy charge that would end the other man's life. It wanted him and all the others gone—and it was prepared to act.

But Roman resisted, willing the heat to dissipate. His pushback only increased the pressure in his head. His heartbeat was overshadowed by an intense buzz. At first, it seemed like energy feedback, but he soon realized it was a voice, fragmented into a discordant din as it shouted overlapping orders for him to act.

Go! He yelled in his mind, not sure if he was speaking to the voice or willing Samor away.

"Nothing here, guys," Samor said in the corridor outside. "Let's move on."

Roman held back a gasp of relief as footfalls headed away. *Did I command him, or did he leave on his own?*

He couldn't be sure. But with the retreating soldiers, and the threat reduced, the heat faded from his arm. The golden glow returned to its normal muted pulsing on his hand and palm.

With his heartbeat normalized and mind re-centered, he focused on tracing Samor through the ship. He appeared to be gathering materials from the cabins and then dumping them outside. Roman had just gotten the cargo door open to do that same thing himself when he'd sensed Samor coming.

What are they up to? he wondered.

After more than an hour of gathering items from the ship, the soldiers went outside. Roman took the opportunity to creep to a cabin with an exterior viewport so he could observe more than his telepathic perception allowed. The sloped ship placement gave the window a slightly downward slant with a clear view of the ground. There were large piles of goods outside exterior hatches, including dozens of mattresses and crates.

Why would they need that many beds? And then it clicked for him. They were gathering housing supplies for the colonists. That meant they had to be leaving the cave hideout in the jungle to the northeast. *But where are they going now?*

Roman scrambled downstairs. He'd need to follow them and find out.

A group of about twenty people showed up a short while later. Based on their clothes, they looked to be colonists rather than members of Conroy's crew. That supported Roman's suspicions about them building a new camp somewhere.

The group helped lower two hovercarts from the cargo hold, and then they started dividing up materials between people and the carts for transport. Roman remained in his hidden observation place until they were finished loading. He waited by one of the holes in the hull until they had disappeared into the trees.

He jumped down from the ship and followed—not a difficult task with that many people and heavy equipment cutting a path through the foliage.

Always staying at a distance, he followed their path to a river, which they traced for a kilometer before cutting eastward. A few hundred meters from the water, they arrived at a low hillside covered in rocks and trees. The place would have been completely unremarkable were it not bustling with activity.

Dozens of people were gathered, already opening up crates and distributing items. People carrying mattresses in pairs were disappearing behind a rock formation, and then other people would emerge. There had to be a cave entrance back there.

All right, little rats, Roman mused, *what's hidden in this new burrow?*

19

'PROOF' WAS A subjective term in the world of crime. Salesmen made a living off overselling an inferior product. Dreams were wrapped in false promises. Zaris knew better than to take any 'evidence' as fact, but she needed *something*.

Despite Evan's apparent earnestness now, he'd been fooling her for years. The notion that he was allegedly coming clean could just be another ruse.

"You claim to have extensive knowledge of the Syndicate's operations—specifically, their operational bases. You will map them out for me, and then I'll pick one at random and you can take me there to demonstrate that your intelligence is legit," Zaris stated.

Evan leaned back on the couch, chuckling. "See, that's the problem. You want me to give you all information upfront and make myself irrelevant."

"If everything checks out, I promise not to kill you," she offered.

"Not kill… but what about cut out of the deal?"

"That'll all depend on how much I find."

"No, Zaris, that isn't how to make this work." He propped his arm on the back of the couch and leaned slightly toward her. "Do you remember that Rombarti job?"

"How could I forget?" She smiled in spite of herself as the memory flooded back. She hadn't thought about it in a while, but the mere mention of the name returned her to the experience like it was yesterday.

Evan had been her contact with the Syndicate, and she'd been hired to covertly move product from a remote planet to one of the busiest spaceports in the core worlds—a trade hub on Constella. Ports like that had increased security, making any illicit dealings all the more risky. But the pay had been too tempting. She'd posed as a missionary, and Evan had pretended to be a pastor receiving her goods. The local authorities had stopped by for an inspection, and Evan had given them so convincing a lecture about the nature of morality and the foils of intervening with others finding their own path to enlightenment that Zaris had nearly contemplated a career change on the spot. The impromptu sermon had been enough to make the guards back off, and they'd been able to proceed with the transaction without further incident. To this day, she'd never seen anyone more convincingly talk their way out of a bind.

"You really were magnificent that day," she said. "Still don't know how you came up with that argument on the spot."

He smirked. "I didn't, actually…"

"What, then?"

"I lifted it from a movie."

"No way!"

"Yeah, it was an older flick I used to watch with my parents. I did a lot of paraphrasing, but there was this preacher guy in it that really ripped a crime boss a new one. It was fun to flip it around."

She shook her head. "Had me going."

"I knew I had to pull out all the stops to make sure the job went right. I was so convinced you were going to double-cross me, but you didn't. And it ended up being a turning point—every job after that went smoothly. What made you decide to set aside our past issues and finally trust me that day?"

"Clearly, it was the clergy outfit."

"I'm serious."

She sat in contemplative silence for several seconds. "I looked into your eyes, and I saw that you wanted the job to succeed. When I double-cross people, it's so they don't hurt me first. But the people who *actually* want to work with you for mutual benefit—that's rare. You don't throw that away."

He met her gaze. "Am I trying to deceive you now?"

From her read, he did seem genuine in his intentions. But it was clear he was holding a lot of things back, and that concerned her. She didn't have only her own wellbeing to consider. She had a crew on this ship and dozens of others operating within her larger network, each with their own crews and businesses. On the net, there were thousands—possibly tens of thousands—of people who could potentially be impacted by her decision.

"You're asking me to declare war against the Syndicate," she said.

"I'm giving you a reason to stand up to the people who've been holding you back." He slid his arm forward along the back of the couch until he brushed her shoulder with his fingertips.

For a moment, she wanted to give into the gesture. The pressure of leadership could be so stifling. If she could just be here, in the moment, with this man who'd always had a knack of seeing the woman beneath her tough exterior…

No, he's just manipulating you.

She yanked her shoulder back. "I won't fall for that again."

"I never faked that with you."

"That's the past. Anything going forward is strictly business."

He seemed almost relieved to hear it. "Understood."

"You still haven't given me anything concrete about the players in this plan of yours. I get needing to hold some things back so I have a reason to keep you involved, but we're never making it off the docking pad if you don't give me more."

Evan searched her face. She could see the permutations running through his mind, weighing options and scenarios. The next thing to come out of his mouth would decide his fate. "Chancellor Conroy is alive."

That was… the last thing she'd expected to hear. "He's… what?"

"He didn't die in the shuttle crash. And that crash wasn't an accident. Rostov tried to have him killed, but he escaped and went into hiding."

Heat rose in her cheeks. "What the hell, Evan? I expected you to spin a tale, but I thought you respected me more than to spout off half-cocked conspiracy theories!"

"Wait, have you heard rumors about that before?"

She scoffed. "It was all over the comm chatter last year. Something about the Syndicate sending operatives to finish the job—"

"Zaris, please try to remember. Tell me exactly what you heard." His grave expression caught her off-guard.

He really believes that nonsense. She got up from the couch. "Who are you working for?"

"No one."

She backed up, drawing her pistol from inside her jacket. "No, you're here to gather information. Who put you up to it?"

Evan remained seated, keeping both his hands still and

visible. "Zaris, I know Conroy is alive because I spoke to him myself. He's been hiding out on the planet where Anya and I crashed. I'm not working *for* him, but he asked for my help. I'm here talking with you because I want to gather information to corroborate his story. I can't do that alone, and I'm hoping that you'll help me figure out which side to back."

"What sides?"

"To determine who's the rightful leader of the Commonwealth."

"What you're talking about is sedition."

"I swore an oath to the *Commonwealth*, not a specific leader. If a usurper is holding power, it's my duty to right that injustice."

"Why the hell would *I* want to be involved in that? To put my people in the crosshairs of a civil war."

"You already know the answer."

Because someone who would deceive an entire interstellar nation would stop at nothing to maintain their power. And if the Syndicate has their ear, they'll want to eliminate anyone who isn't under their thumb. The aim of her pistol wavered. "You haven't given me any proof."

"I can take you to Conroy—"

"*No*, Evan! Whatever insane made-up conflict you're trying to incite, I want no part of it." Her mind raced. With even a sliver of truth to his story, she might be in for a fight no matter what. More likely, though, he was working a scheme for his own benefit, trying to get her to stick out her neck for the slaughter. Maybe he'd started up a rival crew, and goading her into attacking the Syndicate was a strategy to get her out of the way?

She leveled the weapon on him again. "I heard you out. The answer is 'no'."

"All right. I'll leave, and you won't hear from me again."

"I told you, leaving isn't an option. Sorry." Her finger tightened on the trigger.

Evan hurled a couch pillow at her. It caught her by surprise, throwing off her aim as she fired. The pulse shot missed Evan and instead hit the viewport, the energy rippling across the thick transparent polymer.

Before she could re-aim, Evan barreled toward her and tackled her to the ground. He wrestled the pistol from her hands.

"Zaris, I don't want to hurt you—"

She kneed him in the groin and rolled out from under him. He still had the pistol in his hand. She jumped on his back to straddle his shoulders, locking his head between her thighs. She wrested the pistol from his grip.

"Why kill me?" he asked, his voice muffled through the pants' fabric.

"You can't turn on me if you're dead."

— — —

Having his head pressed into the deck while being straddled by a homicidal woman was not how Evan had envisioned the day going. But, in all fairness, he'd acknowledged that this was a possibility.

Zaris' volatility and distrusting nature were a product of her upbringing, but he recognized that she wanted a real connection with others. He understood that same loneliness from his time undercover. That had been what first drew them to each other, even if they'd never stated it outright. But appealing to that part of her and talking his way out of this situation was looking less and less likely.

He made a point of not resisting, as further agitating her seemed unwise. He slowly extended his hands in front of him as a sign of surrender. “Can you get off me?”

She did get up, but she kept the pistol pointed at his head. She walked a wide arc around him toward his feet, staying well outside of kicking distance.

As she moved, Evan rolled to his back, keeping his hands up and outstretched. He subtly scanned the area around him for anything that could be used as an improvised weapon if it came to it.

But something more important caught his attention. Hairline fractures were spidering across the viewport that had been struck with the close-range pulse blast.

“Zaris, the window!” he warned.

“Nice try.”

“Where’s your patch kit?”

She repositioned so she could watch him while also seeing the viewport, not expecting to see anything— “Oh, shit!”

More cracks snaked through the inner layer. The outer layer of heat-resistant material seemed to be holding for now, but a catastrophic failure could happen at any moment. Zaris raced to the bar counter on the other side of the room, concerns about Evan no longer the priority.

He wanted to help her stabilize the breach, but this was also as close to an escape opening as he was likely to get.

Evan positioned himself to make a run for the door as soon as Zaris emerged from behind the counter with a patch kit. She dashed to the window and unloaded a spray canister over the compromised area—a type of instantly hardening foam that was kept on any vessel as an emergency measure, just like fire extinguishers.

While she was working, Evan slipped out into the hallway.

The door was flanked by two guards, who snapped to attention. "Breach! She needs help," he told them.

They hesitated just long enough for him to bolt. A second later, weapons fire sounded behind him. He spotted a stairwell and dove inside.

Evan raced down the steps, skipping several at a time. The door banged open above him, followed by rapid footfalls.

A red, strobing light lit up. *And that would be the warning to the crew.*

He reached his destination floor and burst through the door. Crew members in the hall spotted him and immediately reached for weapons.

Is everyone on this ship armed? Of course, they were.

He ducked as someone fired at him. Dodging and weaving, he ran toward the hangar. The stairwell had dumped him in a slightly different location than the lift he'd taken to the upper decks, but he spotted the features he'd noted in his mental map and raced forward. The gunfire behind him was getting closer.

His lungs were burning by the time he reached the hangar. The shuttle was a long way across an exposed open area. He'd never make it that far without getting shot.

Instead, he crouched behind a crate for cover. Shots flew by, pinging against the container's side.

Well, this went sideways awfully fast.

Evan peeked over the top of the crate to spot the shooters. There were two men hunkered down behind a wall of cargo across the hangar. Even if he'd had a weapon, getting a clean shot would be tricky. But moreover, killing Zaris' people would only make the situation worse. He needed to figure out a way out of this without hurting anyone.

A rumble sounded across the hangar. In his peripheral

vision, Evan noticed the shuttle lifting off the deck. *Good, Anya, get out of here while you can.*

But the vessel didn't exit. Instead, it flew toward him.

Workers scattered to avoid the wash from the maneuvering thrusters. A few tried shooting the shuttle, but the blasts had no effect on the disguised alien ship. The shuttle arced around so its bulk was between Evan and the shooters.

The side hatch opened, framing Anya.

"Come on!" she shouted.

Evan jumped up to the opening. She helped pull him inside.

"Sam, we need to get out of here right now. Try not to hurt anyone." Evan waved his hand over the controls to seal the hatch.

"Acknowledged," the AI stated. "Destination?"

"Anywhere but here. As soon as we're outside, jump us somewhere safe where we can figure out our next move."

"Meeting didn't go as planned?" Anya asked.

"Not even close." Evan's arm itched. He checked it and found a bloody streak. Another centimeter and it would have been more than a graze.

Anya noticed the injury. "Shit! Are you okay?"

"It's minor."

She motioned for him to take off his jacket.

"Once we're out of here," he told her.

The shuttle passed through the electrostatic field into space, and Sam sped them away from the *Invictus*. But they weren't safe yet. Just as they were gaining distance from the bigger vessel, the shuttle abruptly shuddered.

"The *Invictus* has fired on us," Sam announced.

"Damage?" Evan asked.

"None. However, the jump latticework is vulnerable. I

can't prepare for a jump while we're under fire. They're pursuing us."

"Well, shit." Evan ran to the shuttle's controls and activated a rear view on the screen. The *Invictus* was giving chase, and it packed serious firepower. "I should have asked before, but does this shuttle have weapons?"

"Affirmative," the AI acknowledged.

"Would you be able to disable the enemy ship without harming the occupants?"

"Yes, I can damage the propulsion system, which should disable it without compromising the rest of the craft."

"Do it!"

A beam shot out from the alien ship and struck the pursuing vessel. Shards of metal exploded outward from the rear. The craft continued forward on momentum, but it fell further behind them as their own ship continued to accelerate.

"That was too easy," Anya murmured.

"Remember how that sphere vaporized those people? This was nothing," Evan replied.

She frowned. "Good point." Immediately, she stepped closer to Evan and examined his arm again. "How long until we can jump, Sam?" she asked while carefully parting the fabric on Evan's upper sleeve.

"We are now a sufficient distance from the station. Would you like me to cloak first?"

Evan considered it. Zaris wanted proof he was telling her the truth. Well, she was about to get it. "No, give them a show. Get us out of here!" Evan ordered.

The latticework around the ship spun into a golden blur. The view on the screen transitioned to the dark void and eerie lights of hyperspace.

"Come on, let's get you cleaned up," Anya urged.

He followed her to the cabinet holding the medical supplies. "Are *you* okay, Anya?"

"Oh, yeah, I'm good. Clearly, I missed all the excitement."

With a sudden impulse to be near her, he wrapped her in a hug. She fit perfectly in his arms, her soft curves pressing enticingly against him as she squeezed his chest. "That was too close," he whispered.

"We've had a lot of those."

Evan released her enough to look into her eyes. "I'm so sorry. This plan to turn things around has been anything but."

"Hey, we got off Aethos, so there's that." She got to work tending his wound with gentle precision.

He looked away to hide a grimace from the sting as she applied disinfecting spray. "I wonder what life could have been like for us if we'd followed through with our plan to hide out in a cave and live off the land."

"We'd probably be getting shot at a lot less," she said pointedly while applying a bandage to his arm.

"That would be nice."

"But we also wouldn't have our own spaceship."

He chuckled. "You're right. And what would be the fun in that?"

20

"REPORT!" ZARIS DEMANDED as she stepped onto the *Invictus*' flight deck moments after a concussive blast rocked her ship.

"Significant damage to the main engines. I've never seen a weapon like that before…" Tarek said.

"Neither have I." Moreover, a blast that powerful shouldn't have been possible from such a small vessel. *Maybe there was something to Evan's claims about alien tech, after all…* She kept the thought to herself, not having enough to go on yet to get her crew worked up. "I thought the shuttle was locked down?"

"It was, but it overrode our grapple."

Why did I ever agree to this meeting? She wanted to scream or break something, but she managed to keep her voice level. "Can we make the repairs ourselves?"

"Still assessing," Tarek replied. "And what was it about you almost venting yourself?"

"It wasn't intentional."

"This is why we don't shoot windows…" he muttered

"Hey, a pulse blast should have been harmless. There must have been a defect—"

"Whoa… what the?!" Callie exclaimed. She made a series of rapid entries on her console. "The shuttle just… jumped away."

Zaris took a couple seconds to compute the statement. “That’s not possible.”

Callie threw a replay of the scan data and external camera feeds onto the front screen. One minute the shuttle was speeding away from the *Invictus*, then it fired a ridiculously powerful energy beam for a vessel that size, and then the craft was surrounded in glowing golden light and disappeared. Both the broad-spectrum scan readings and visual recording corroborated the event. It defied everything she knew about space travel.

The rest of the flight deck crew recognized that they’d just witnessed something revolutionary. The air was thick with anticipation, without knowing what they were waiting for, exactly.

For me to explain, Zaris realized. But she *had* no explanation. “Finish those diagnostics. We need to get going on repairs ASAP.”

She headed for her office, and Tarek followed.

“What happened in that meeting?” he asked as soon as he’d closed the door.

He approached her and placed two fingertips on her forehead. It was tender to the slight pressure; she hadn’t realized she’d been injured in the tussle.

“He claimed to know about alien tech. He said that if we don’t make a move against the Syndicate now, then they’ll grow too powerful through a partnership with the Commonwealth’s government, and we’ll get shut down.”

“Why did you start fighting?”

“Because he told me that Chancellor Conroy is still alive and Rostov was behind the shuttle accident.”

“I’m not seeing how you go from that statement to a bump on your head.”

"You had to be there." She sat down. "Tarek, can you think of any explanation for what we just saw that ship do?"

"Using conventional science? No, not off the top of my head. But if you want to throw alien tech in there, anything is possible."

"The shuttle looked completely normal."

"It did."

"We must have some kind of scan log of it, right?"

He nodded. "Definitely."

"Let's take a look to see what else we can learn about that craft." Her chest tightened from uneasy nerves. *Maybe Evan really was telling the truth…*

While maintenance workers began repairs in the other parts of the ship, they pulled up historical scan data on the main flight deck screen.

"Looks pretty standard," Callie assessed. "There's a higher composition of a few rare alloys, but I don't see any red flags."

Zaris frowned. "How could such a powerful weapon be hiding in there? Not to mention the… 'jump drive', I guess?"

"I don't see anything in the scan that explains those features," Callie said.

"We all saw it. It happened."

"No doubt about that," Tarek agreed. "And we have a recording of the jump. No mistake about it."

"I'm getting the impression that the Syndicate isn't the only group in possession of alien tech," Zaris ventured.

Tarek arched an eyebrow. "Are you suggesting that we had an alien ship sitting in our hangar and we didn't know it?"

"Do you have a better explanation?"

His silence told the story.

"I'm guessing we have no way to trace where they went?" she continued.

Callie shook her head. "Nope."

"But we do have the comm info from our initial contact," Tarek pointed out.

Right, like they'd want to talk to us after this shooting match. Zaris regretted letting her insecurities derail their conversation. There was no getting a redo now. Only forward. "We're in no position to talk yet. Callie, can you see if there are any jobs posted to the boards about Pavia?"

"Sure. But… why?"

"Because the people who put a hole in our engine said that planet is important, and I intend to see for myself."

— — —

Evan landed the shuttle on the same planet where they'd regrouped before, which they'd decided to name Haven. It was out of the way, unoccupied, and the local greens were tasty, so they could think of no better place to plan their next move.

Being back on solid ground, plus having the alien bracelets once again securely around his wrists, calmed him. Nonetheless, their mission had been an utter failure.

Out the front viewport, the *Asamar* landed in the field.

"Where would you like to sleep tonight?" Sam asked over the speakers. "I can dock the shuttle for you in my bay if you have no further use for it now."

"Fireside dinner and then head to our cabins on the main ship?" Evan asked Anya.

She nodded. "Sounds delightful."

They grabbed their packs and headed to the fire ring. On their previous visit, Evan had played around with the nanites to shape some benches and a hearth at the center of a small clearing. The reserve nanites had responded to his commands well, forming whatever shape he envisioned in his mind. Upon arriving at the campsite, he found all the forms were still intact.

Anya had been a little quieter than usual since their escape from the *Invictus*, but there were tasks to accomplish before Evan wanted to get side-tracked with a discussion.

The first order of business was to gather firewood and forage for greens and fruit to supplement a MealPak.

A little outside camp, they came across a flock of knee-high, feathered puff-balls scurrying around the underbrush. Little clouds of dust would occasionally fan out underneath the animals, and then their entire body would ripple. Evan imagined they were raking the ground with their feet and then pecking at worms or bugs, though the action was obscured beneath the ridiculous plumage. The birds seemed wholly unperturbed by their human presence.

Anya smiled at them. "Aww, they're cute."

Evan and Anya stepped forward to continue their foraging. When they were about three meters away, the birds froze, and one of them let out a high-pitched chirp.

All of the animals abruptly reared up on their hind limbs. Their exposed bellies were covered in concentric rings of spike-like teeth. The gaping mouths started to undulate, causing the teeth to rub against each other and produce a discordant hum.

Evan and Anya took a step back, but one of the animals launched itself toward Anya, who was standing closer to the flock. Evan dropped the firewood and drew his handgun, firing at the bird midair. The body went limp and dropped at Anya's feet.

The rest of the monstrous little birds curled back into fluffballs and scattered.

Anya stood in shock for a few seconds. "Well, that was unexpected."

"Not so cute."

Anya looked down at the dead bird. "You know, I'd hate for this to go to waste..."

Evan assessed the creature. "Let me guess, it'll taste like chicken?"

"Probably. Has to be better than a MealPak, right?"

He couldn't argue; a well-rounded, fresh meal was too appealing to pass up.

Anya took over with the cleaning of the carcass, having more experience with dissections from her scientific studies. Underneath the fluff, its back did resemble a chicken well enough to be appetizing, though Evan couldn't get the image of its horrifying mouth fully out of his mind.

While the *Asamar* had proper cooking facilities, roasting it over a campfire sounded like a more enjoyable way to spend the evening, so they decided to fashion a spit out of sticks. Watching Anya prepare the spit, Evan was reminded of her unique skillset for someone who had spent much of her career in a highly regulated research lab.

"I've been wondering something, Anya," Evan said while he got the fire going. "When we first met, you said that you'd been through enough to know how to handle yourself in a medical emergency. But whenever you talk about your past assignments, it sounds like things were tightly controlled."

She nodded solemnly as she handed off the bird to Evan—its stubby limbs sprawled and tied to a spit frame. "Yeah, usually."

He placed the spit over the fire. "So, what happened? That day of the crash, I could tell it wasn't the first time you'd seen a bad, bloody injury. And you didn't wrinkle your nose while preparing this thing."

Anya sat on one of the benches and pulled her knees up to

her chest, wrapping her arms around her legs. "There was this one planet we were surveying. Having breathable air was about as close as it got to being habitable. There were a handful of nasty, spiky plants as well as some awful little lizards and insects—enough 'life' to warrant a xenobiological cataloging. It was only my third field survey. I'd had training about how to handle crisis situations, and I'd never expected to need any of it. But nothing can prepare you for what it's like to be in a real emergency. The adrenaline surge, the heightened senses, how time perception changes. You learn a lot about yourself in those moments."

He watched the light dance across her exquisite features as she gazed at the flames under the bird. Though he wanted to prompt her to continue, the air was too heavy to say a word.

Eventually, she unfurled her arms and extended her legs. "We'd been on the planet for almost a week. With so many sharp, unfriendly things around, there'd already been a few minor injuries—scrapes and whatnot. Our base of operations was on a hill at a moderate elevation, with a valley to one side and some higher mountains to the other. The location allowed us to study multiple ecologies without needing to travel far. But when we selected the site, we didn't realize how unstable the rocks upslope from us were."

Anya paused, continuing to stare into the fire while Evan stoked it. "We'd bickered over assignments that morning. I was sick of getting stabbed by the thorny bushes, so I'd wanted to stay behind in the mobile lab to run tests. Instead, I got the draw of doing the higher elevation survey along with two other team members. Midway on our ascent, Iko kicked a rock loose. It didn't seem like a big deal at first, but then a larger fracture formed, and this massive chunk of sharp rock broke off and tumbled down.

"We shouted back toward the camp and tried to radio them, but it all happened too fast. The rock crushed the lab. There were two people inside. Three others were exploring the hillside beyond, and they got hit with other rock fragments when the whole mess spilled over the edge. One person fell." She shook her head. "I'd never seen blood or damage like that before. One of the people who'd been inside the lab took a couple of hours to die. In the end, we lost three people that day, and four others were seriously injured. I learned really quickly that you can either let the shock and fear cripple you, or you can shut it out and do what needs to be done."

"Not everyone is able to do that," Evan murmured.

"You can."

He nodded. "But I've known people who've frozen when it mattered. You have something in you they didn't."

She shrugged. "Maybe it was from dealing with my dad on his bad days, or it could be something more innate. I dunno. But I wouldn't still be here if I didn't have that survival instinct."

"Wherever the drive comes from, it's what's gotten us this far. I understand now how you were able to handle that man right after the crash."

"I have to admit, I was back on that awful planet for a moment when I saw him there."

"You acted like a pro. I knew right then and there that I'd be able to work with you."

Anya tilted her head. "Is that all this is... a work arrangement?"

"You should know by now it's much more than that."

She smiled and looked away. "Just checking."

"I know what it's like to have experiences that are difficult to talk about. Thank you for sharing that story with me."

"I'm sure you've been through a lot crazier—and things you really *can't* talk about."

"Even so, I think you have me just about tied for the 'almost died' experiences, so... congratulations?"

Anya laughed. "Great! That's exactly what I want to be known for."

"Better to be on the surviving side of the scenario."

"That is a very good point."

They fell quiet for a while, watching the sun slowly dip below the treetops. Eventually, as the bird's juices sputtered into the flames, Evan decided it was time to address the uncomfortable truth of their situation. "I think it's safe to say that teaming up with Zaris is a no-go. So, do we throw in with Conroy, or do we keep the ship for ourselves?"

Anya glanced in the direction of the *Asamar*, now only a vague shadow in the evening light. "I'm still not sure. But I think Sam should have a say."

"Agreed. But what would be our request, in an ideal world?"

"In an ideal world, I'd still be back on a planet where I could enjoy fancy coffee drinks, and eat chocolate cake, and live in blissful ignorance about the deep corruption throughout society."

Her acerbic tone caught him off-guard. "I know things haven't gone how we wanted," he said.

"I really wish we'd been able to get a serum sample from Pavia. I've been trying to reverse-engineer it with Sam, but no dice."

"You have?"

"Yeah, I figured it was worth a shot." She shrugged. "I needed something to work on while you were practicing your Alex lines."

"Thank you for trying."

"Sure. It was a longshot. Working with original source material is always a lot more effective."

He stretched out his legs. "I guess we're right back where we started."

"Only more beat up, and now even more adversaries know we have alien tech," she added.

Evan winced. He'd ultimately revealed much more to Zaris than he'd planned, but he'd decided that's what was needed in the moment. He could talk about the stakes all day, but showing them was the only way to prove his point. Maybe that demonstration would make an impact. "I said and did what I thought was necessary."

"What do you think Zaris will do with the information about Conroy and the jump drive?"

"Try to spin it to her benefit. What form that will take, I don't know."

"You really don't have any other contacts we could try?"

"I have plenty of contacts, but Zaris was the best test case for how any would respond."

"Well, I've had enough of getting shot at for the day."

"I've had enough for a lifetime."

She eyed him. "What was the deal with you and Zaris, anyway? I was getting some serious 'jilted former lover' vibes in there."

Evan's face twisted for a moment before he shook his head. "It's more complicated than that. We never slept together, but it also wasn't nothing."

Some of the tension went out of Anya's shoulders. "Based on how she was acting, I take it things didn't end well?"

"You could say that. My boss made me double-cross her, so our last encounter was shooting at each other."

“Your boss… as in *Alex*’s boss?”

“Yeah.” He frowned. “Sorry, the distinctions get blurry sometimes.”

“I’m still amazed you could do that. I can’t imagine keeping up a front for even a few hours, let alone *years*.”

“I don’t recommend it. You end up with a lot of broken relationships, like with Zaris.”

“Do you have regrets?”

He searched her face, then got up and went to sit right next to her. He placed his hands gently on her upper arms, looking straight into her eyes. “I know what you’re really asking, and I assure you that I never felt as strongly about her as the way I do about you.”

She softened under his touch. “Is that so?”

“A fact.”

“Well, that’s good to know.”

— — —

Anya’s heart leaped as Evan brought one hand up to brush loose hair away from her eyes. They’d been close during their travels together, but not like *this*.

She’d been relieved to hear that Evan and Zaris had never been intimate. There was something about Zaris that put her on the defensive. If she was being honest, she didn’t like the thought of Evan being seduced by someone like that woman. But even with the direct confirmation of his interest, Anya’s rational mind told her that this still wasn’t the time to act on those feelings—however mutual.

She placed her hand over his as he cupped her face, then slowly laced her fingers through his and lowered his hand to her thigh. “We went through a lot today. I think we should let that settle before introducing any other complications."

He nodded his understanding, clearly disappointed but not offended. "It has been a hell of a day. But we survived."

"Oh! On that note…" She fished around at the side of the bench for the item she'd hastily assembled from the leftover spit supplies while Evan was getting the fire started. She'd only had a few minutes to make it, and it looked like something a three-year-old may have constructed in pre-school class. But it fit the moment.

Holding her creation behind her back, she scootched back to her seat next to Evan.

"What are you up to?" he asked cautiously.

"Congratulations!" she exclaimed, handing him a bundle of sticks she'd tied together with string, roughly in the shape of a human figure.

He blinked at her in stunned silence for a couple of seconds. "What is this?"

"Your official Survival Award. I'm sorry it's not gold-plated."

His eyes softened. "When did you find the time to make this for me?"

"I've been working on it for days. Painstaking labor."

He cradled it in his palms. "This might be the most thoughtful gift I've ever received."

To her surprise, he seemed genuinely touched by the gesture. She'd been going for a laugh, but she realized that he probably *hadn't* received a personalized inside joke gift from anyone in years. No matter her initial intention, he'd ascribed far deeper meaning to the item. And she was okay with that.

"I'm glad you like it," she told him.

"It's perfect. It'll be our new mascot."

"All right, but don't be surprised if our mascot has a rapid unplanned disassembly. I'm shocked it's held together this long."

"We can reinforce it," he assured her. "The right framework is there."

She smiled. "Yeah, it is."

21

"OKAY, EVERYONE LISTEN up!" Samor shouted.

Some of the colonists who were engaged in more spirited conversations around the large cavern at the Riverview site had missed his announcement, but they fell silent when they noticed others were focused on him.

"You've done great work getting everything moved over here," Samor continued once it was quiet. "However, there's still a lot more to do, and we won't get it done by hiding in here. But we need to be careful. Whenever you leave the cave, make sure you're with at least one other person. Stay vigilant. Enemies are still out there. We don't know their numbers. But the main reason we're here now is because they forced you out of Echo Falls. If this place doesn't work, we don't really have other options."

"What about where you're camped?" a woman called out from somewhere in the crowd.

"Yeah, why aren't we all together?" a man agreed.

Because then you'd all know about Conroy, and you'd have to pick a side in this war of ours. But he couldn't say that. Instead, he replied, "It's for all our safety. Having everyone in one place makes us an easy target."

"You still haven't explained why you were already here on this planet," the first woman said.

Other voices rose up to voice assertions about the planet being fresh and unexplored. More people chimed in that maybe there wasn't anyone else and they were all being played, despite it being obvious that Samor was not among the crash survivors. That sentiment caught attention, quickly raising the crowd into a frenzy. People were shouting over each other and demanding answers.

Samor's soldiers recognized the problem and fanned out to contain the civilians, ready to intervene if anyone got confrontational. As the most senior person present, Samor knew it was his responsibility to keep it from getting to that point.

"Quiet!" he bellowed. Either they were too worked up to hear him, or they didn't care.

He went over to a crate and kicked it. The sharp crack of metal and plastic grating against the stone ground sounded enough like a gunshot to get their attention. "Yelling at each other isn't going to accomplish anything," he said, keeping his voice low enough that they'd have to remain silent to hear. "I can explain, but there's a weight to that knowledge."

"Tell us," a man said, stepping forward. Samor recognized him as Peter, someone who'd fashioned himself a spokesperson for the colonists after the crash.

While Samor wasn't authorized to reveal the entire complex situation involving the Commonwealth's government, he and Conroy had worked out talking points that could be shared with the survivors if they pressed him. This qualified.

"Aethos has had a secret human presence for years," Samor began. "There are valuable resources here, and those with grand ambitions wanted to stake a claim before the world could become an official Commonwealth settlement. My people were sent here years ago to safeguard the planet from unsanctioned occupation. And it worked, for a time. But we didn't anticipate that those bad actors would infiltrate your colony mission. They sabotaged the ship and caused it to crash, and they also took out the military escort. Now, those people who crashed your ships and killed your family and friends want to claim this whole planet. We are the last line of defense. We're trying to keep this world from falling into the wrong hands, which also means protecting it as your future home.

"Those of us who've been here for years want this planet to be stewarded by you, the rightful colonists. The saboteurs who were hiding among you on the colony ship are mercenaries with one mission: to take the planet for themselves. You aren't just collateral damage in achieving that objective—you're a downright obstacle.

"So, do you want to work with us—the people who've been trying to keep you alive while protecting this planet—or would you rather try your luck with the people who destroyed your ship?" he asked, sweeping his gaze across the crowd. The details in his speech weren't strictly accurate, but revealing that the military was actually hunting Commonwealth citizens would introduce too many questions he couldn't answer. Painting them as guns-for-hire was close enough to the truth—at least the truth as he saw it, being bought off by a corrupt, illegitimate government.

The colonists murmured to each other. A few people went up to Peter and engaged in an earnest discussion too quiet for Samor to overhear. They glanced occasionally in his direction.

After a couple of minutes, Peter nodded to his group and turned to face Samor again. "There's no doubt that we appreciate you helping us. We'd still be stuck on that hillside if you hadn't come for us. But we don't know if we can believe you. How could rebels on our colony ship take down the military cruiser? The colony ship had no weapons that could match that vessel."

Shit, they did pick a smart bunch to send here. No wonder NovaTech was worried about them asking too many questions back home. Samor's mind raced to come up with an explanation. He couldn't tell them the truth about shooting down the military cruiser because it had been compromised—and that the very escort ship allegedly sent to protect the colonists had, in fact, been what destroyed their colony vessel. But the story he'd just laid out did have holes large enough to fly a spaceship through. He had to give them *something.*

"We don't have all the details, but we think the military ship was sabotaged from the inside. Possibly a bomb. Shuttles were ferrying people between the two vessels, right?" he asked, hoping it was true. It wasn't uncommon for military officers to board colony ships after reaching the destination world to facilitate loading and offloading of cargo and personnel.

To his relief, a few people in the crowd nodded.

"One or more of the mercenaries must have gotten on board the cruiser and blown it up from the inside. Ships like that are designed to hold up to an exterior battering, but the interior structure is still vulnerable, especially so close to a big gravity well like a planet. With no propulsion, once it started going down… What can I say, physics is a bitch."

That seemed to satisfy most people. A few continued to squint at him skeptically, but the tension had diminished in the group at large.

"I know how frustrating it must be that so much was kept from you, but we're doing the best we can," Samor said.

"Please, believe me when I say that we want to help you. If we haven't shared information about something, it's for good reason. I have nothing but my word to offer."

"Words only take us so far," Peter said. "But you have backed up those statements with action. You brought us to this place and have shared resources we wouldn't have had otherwise. You'll need to eventually tell us everything, but it can wait until we're settled and rested."

"Fair enough," Samor told him. "I need to go take care of some other things now, but you'll be in good hands here. We'll finish this talk and figure out next steps later."

"Thank you," Peter acknowledged before he shifted his attention to the colonists, resuming a debate about the layout of their new home.

Before Samor could get roped into any more explanations he wasn't prepared to give, he headed for the exit.

"Great job," Erran whispered to him on his way out.

"I'd rather leave the politics to the politicians."

"Everything is political. Even soldiering."

Isn't that the truth. Samor patted the other soldier on his arm as he passed by. "You'll do just fine here."

He continued out to the cave's entrance, feeling lighter as soon as he was once again outdoors. Being inside normal structures never bothered him, but something about being in caves was unnerving—like an entire mountain was pressing down on him.

Maybe some of that was the weight of his responsibility. Not only was he charged with protecting Conroy and his followers, but now there were these colonists. *How did we ever think that more people coming to Aethos would help us?*

Sure, the chance to covertly send supplies was supposed to have been a major bonus. As was the prospect of getting more of their collaborators with technical expertise to Aethos; those new additions were supposed to have filled in skill gaps on the original team, which could facilitate further investigation into the alien tech. But in hindsight, none of that seemed worth the trials from the last couple of weeks. In fact, *nothing* about this mission to Aethos was making sense anymore.

How in the planets did Conroy expect to make a triumphant comeback? They'd been living in their bubble of hope and ambitious optimism here in a backwater corner of the galaxy, but the rest of human civilization had moved on. By now, would any regular citizen even care how Rostov had come into his power?

He shoved aside the thoughts. That line of thinking wasn't helpful; he'd committed to the path long ago, and questioning its destination now would only lead to despair.

Nothing good comes easy, he reminded himself as he set off into the forest.

He had a long hike back to Hidden Grotto—plenty of time to organize his thoughts and recenter himself. Conroy needed him sharp and setting a positive example for the rest of the team. He'd been serving his role of a good soldier, and he'd keep playing the part.

— — —

The cave where Samor and the other defectors had stuffed the colonists looked like a prison worse than death, as far as Roman was concerned. At least the other place up to the northeast had offered a water feature—but this one was an awful hollow in a hillside. While that did make it an excellent hiding place to lay low, that was no way to live.

Why am I pitying them? They're just going to die, anyway.

He frowned at the entrance to the doomed community. This was why they'd wanted to get in fast and wipe everyone out. The longer this mission dragged on, the more opportunity there was to overthink it. Nothing about their core objective had changed. If anything, now that he understood the extent of the power this place contained, it was more important than ever for him to gain complete and total control of the planet. That meant no opposition.

A man emerged from the cave, moving quickly but with the lightness and caution of someone familiar with the wild landscape. It only took a few seconds for Roman to realize it was Samor. He was on his own; that was foolish.

Roman had intended to take up residence in the crashed cruiser, but the relocation of these colonists had disrupted that plan. He couldn't dig in anywhere where someone might stumble across him. Killing everyone was an option, but that would unleash the full wrath of whatever fighting force Conroy might have left—not to mention angering the mysterious energies on this planet. No, it was important to take off the head of the beast first and then work his way down. Some of the colonists might even see that they'd been deceived and opt to join the winning side.

Samor was almost out of sight, but Roman still had the telepathic trace on him. No doubt, he was heading back to Conroy now. This would be the perfect time to make his move.

Roman gathered his backpack and followed Samor at a distance. All he'd done was talk about eliminating Conroy. Now was the time for action.

22

FOLLOWING A RESTFUL sleep, Evan met Anya in the *Asamar*'s galley. He had to do a double-take when he stepped into the room and found a new round bistro table with plush-looking seats along the back wall near a viewport. Anya was seated in one of the raised chairs.

"That wasn't here yesterday, was it?" Evan asked.

Anya took a sip from a mug—another item he didn't recall seeing before. "Nope. Sam has been busy."

"I have been modifying the environment to better suit your human habitability preferences," Sam said over the ship's speakers. "Do you approve of these modifications?"

"Yeah, it's great." Evan gestured to Anya's mug, and she pointed him toward a cabinet. He opened it to find that the cupboard was now stocked with various drinkware, plates, and bowls that bore a striking resemblance to the set from his youth. "You sure you're not reading my mind, Sam?"

"I never said I wouldn't glean thoughts. I can't help overhearing when you think loudly."

Evan rubbed his eyes. "Whatever you say."

On autopilot, he pulled down a mug and went to get… He remembered they didn't have coffee. Or tea. But Anya was happily sipping something hot from a mug.

"Hey, what do you have there?" he asked her.

"Oh, this? It tastes like a perfectly brewed latte."

Evan blinked at her. "Where…?"

Anya set down her mug and walked over to him. Dramatically, she opened up a floor-to-ceiling cabinet stocked with labeled sundries, including a tin of coffee.

"Uh, Sam…?" Evan questioned.

"I took the liberty of gathering minerals and organic matter from this world while you slept. Using the texture and flavor profiles from your memory, I reassembled the raw materials into new items suitable for your human consumption."

Evan gaped. "How—?"

"No, we're good Sam, thank you." Anya flashed Evan a warning look. "I made the mistake of asking earlier, and the details were too much for even me. Suffice it to say, it's properly nutritious, tastes great, and we no longer need to worry about food—or anything." She opened up a refrigerated compartment and pulled out a dark-brown rectangle in a container, then grabbed a fork from a drawer. "Want some?"

He eyed the confection. "Some what?"

"Chocolate cake, based on my smell check earlier. But my bioanalyzer says it has the well-balanced nutrition profile of a MealPak."

Evan struggled to formulate words. "Sam, why didn't you tell us you could do this?"

"You hadn't asked before. Once you instructed me to take initiative, I have endeavored to fulfill that request."

"I'll say." Evan nodded for Anya to get him a fork, too.

They sat down at the bistro table—perfectly proportioned and exceptionally comfortable—and each tried a sample of a cake-breakfast. Light yet structured with a rich, deep flavor perfectly balancing sweetness and bitter, it was one of the best bites of food Evan had ever consumed.

"Oh… wow!" he exclaimed as soon as he swallowed.

Anya melted into her seat. "I don't know what memory this was pulled from, but *damn*!" She went in for another bite.

"And it's even healthy?"

She nodded slowly, savoring her latest forkful.

Evan devoured his half of the cake. He leaned back in the seat when he finished. "Sam, you're my new best friend."

"I am pleased you are happy with my creations."

"Keep them coming!"

Anya rested a hand contentedly on her stomach. "I've enjoyed our foraging campfire nights, but I move for picnics from here on out whenever we want time outside."

"No argument here!" The bird thing the night before had been edible—and, indeed, better than a MealPak—but there was a chasm between edible and delicious.

"All right," Anya sat up straighter, "this development changes things. Now that Sam has revealed himself to be a wizard, we no longer have resource constraints. As long as Sam is amenable, we can go anywhere and manufacture anything we need."

"I am happy to fulfill your requests," Sam said. "However, I do still aspire to locate my people."

Evan nodded. "That's high on our priority list, too. Problem is, we don't know where to find them. The star map on Temple World led us to Pavia, which is currently occupied by the Syndicate. I don't think we're going to get any more clues about the Korani's current location without getting an up-close look at that planet, but we can't do *that* without either eliminating the Syndicate or joining them."

"Joining seems… not advisable," Anya ventured.

"Correct. And the 'elimination' option is a lot easier said than done." Evan sighed. "I can't believe Rostov would work with those psychopathic bastards. Even if it's a means to an end, playing ball with them for the short term is so risky."

"Well, we need to come up with a plan. It's clear that Sam's capabilities are even more extensive than the *Asamar*'s jump drive. I feel a duty to make sure that power is used responsibly."

"I was skeptical of one ship offering enough political capital to make a difference. My opinion has changed."

Anya nodded solemnly. "I still don't know if we can trust Conroy."

"I don't, either. But I also don't feel right abandoning him without a word. We don't need to go *back*, but a conversation wouldn't hurt, right?"

She shrugged. "Yeah, it's not like he could come after us."

"Can you make a call untraceable to our physical location in space, Sam?" Evan asked.

"Affirmative."

"Okay. Let's have a chat, and we'll take it from there."

— — —

"Incoming transmission!" Rebeka shouted to Conroy from the comm booth.

They received plenty of messages from the core worlds, yet none elicited that level of excitement. This was different. He hurried over to her.

She beamed at him. "The message is from 'Trailblazer'."

His heart lifted. "Oh, thank the stars! Text, or…?"

"No, it's a vidcall."

"Send it to a tablet," Conroy instructed. There was no

telling what Evan and Anya might say, and he wanted to be able to go speak with them in private. It had been days with no communication. The only explanation was that they were questioning their loyalties. Conroy couldn't afford for his people having any doubts; all their hopes rested on getting that ship.

Rebeka handed him a tablet; the screen showed an active call on hold. He went to another chamber in the cavern—not as private as a proper office, but as close as he could get in their present circumstances.

He held up the device and activated the video feed. An image of Evan and Anya appeared on the screen, set against the backdrop of a sleek starship interior. "It's good to see you," he greeted.

"How is everything back on Aethos?" Evan asked.

"Could be better. Where are you?"

"Somewhere safe. Turns out this ship has a mind of its own."

"Greetings," a slightly synthesized-sounding voice said in the background.

Conroy's brows shot up. "Uh… hello."

"We've been learning what we can," Evan explained. "It turns out that Aethos was originally established as a prospective colony site for a race known as the Korani. Some six thousand years ago."

Conroy had known they were dealing with ancient tech, but he'd had no sense of the actual timeline. Six thousand years placed the civilization millennia before humanity had ventured into the stars. There was no telling how advanced they might be now. The prospect was both thrilling and terrifying.

"Great researching, but we need you back here," Conroy insisted.

"We never agreed to help you," Evan replied. "We said we'd try to get the ship. We did. But it's raised a lot more questions."

"I'm sure. And I'm happy to answer them once you get back here."

"We'd rather know *before* we come back."

Conroy's heart dropped. He was relieved to have taken the call away from the others, but that also left him without his support network. Every word mattered if he was going to turn this back around to his favor. "I understand your hesitation, Evan. And Anya, you've really stepped up, too. The service you're both doing for the Commonwealth—"

"Cut the bullshit," Evan interrupted. "You don't need to sell us on the dream of a better future. I want to know why *you're* the person who can deliver that."

"I'm just a man, Evan. I'm no better or worse than anyone else."

"Is that supposed to make you sound relatable?"

"Just honest."

"More political rhetoric to couch yourself as 'one of the people' before you act in your own self-interest."

Conroy took a slow breath through his nose to ease the growing tension in his chest. Losing his cool now might mean never hearing from these two again. He knew he was being tested, and he'd do anything necessary to pass. "I wouldn't be human if I didn't have my own ambitions, but that doesn't mean those goals don't align with the common good."

"You ran away to hide on Aethos rather than face the man who tried to have you killed. How is that virtuous behavior in a leader?" Anya asked.

She has more bite than I'd realized. It was clear this duo was not only well-matched but that they'd be impossible to win over through conventional emotional appeals. They wanted facts. *But can they accept the cold reality we're facing?*

He decided to go for it. "There are things I didn't tell you."

Evan scoffed. "Yeah, no shit."

"You couldn't expect me to trust you with all my secrets out of the gate. What kind of a leader would I be to give up so much to a stranger?"

"No doubt, but the picture that's been painted over the last few days has sure made things interesting."

"Such as?"

"How those in power will do anything to keep it and always strive for more. Just look at what you're doing."

Conroy shook his head. "You don't understand."

"Really? Because it seems pretty obvious that you're trying to seize power for yourself to—"

"To save the Commonwealth!" he shot back. "There's more at stake than you know."

Evan crossed his arms. "Then tell us." He stared at Conroy, unwilling to back down. It was clear he'd lost his patience for evasion, and this was Conroy's final opportunity to win back his trust.

If I don't open up now, I'll lose him. There were things Conroy hadn't even told all of his most trusted advisors. But if there was time for a leap of faith, it was now. He let out a long breath and nodded. "We need this alien technology not only for our civilization's development, but because we hope to make contact with its creators so we can build an alliance."

Evan raised an eyebrow. "Why keep that a secret?"

"Because of *why* we'd seek such an alliance. Evan," Conroy met his gaze, "these aren't the only aliens out there. We believe that there was a conflict between them, and the creators of the Aethos tech were on the losing side. But they weren't wiped out—they're in hiding. And we need to find them to learn everything we can about what failed in their defensive strategy, because we believe the aggressors are about to come for us."

— — —

Evan's mouth went dry. "What do you know about this other race? How do you even know that they exist?"

"We don't know much about them—yet," Conroy explained. "But we've seen evidence of their destructive power."

"What kind of evidence?" Anya asked after exchanging a concerned glance with Evan.

"Ground turned to glass."

Evan's stomach lurched. It sounded like what they had seen on Koranis. Too similar to be a coincidence. "What makes you think that was done by another race?"

"In one of our early surveys, we took samples. The chemical analysis came back with multiple hits that didn't match the environment. Our scientists determined that the traces originated from multiple sources."

Evan didn't understand enough about that kind of science to know if there was any validity to the assessment. He turned to Anya.

"Assuming that's right," she said, "that doesn't mean these enemy aliens are about to come back and launch an attack, or invasion, or whatever."

"Those clues in isolation wouldn't suggest that, no. But there's also the signal."

Evan's chest tightened. "The… what, now?"

"We noticed a particular frequency pattern existed in the background when listening to the sonification of the planets' magnetic field. Each planetary body has a distinct sound to it, so finding a portion of the sound that was identical across multiple worlds points to something else going on. That particular frequency pattern is *only* present on the worlds that have been fully or partially glassed. And that frequency was recently discovered on Terrax."

"Give us a sec." Evan paused the vidcall, alarmed to hear the news about the Commonwealth's capital planet. Terrax was dozens of light-years from any of the worlds they'd investigated. "Sam, have you detected any kind of signal like he referenced?"

"The device we found orbiting Koranis might fit the description. However, that was of Korani design."

"Why in the planets would there be anything around the human capital planet, though?" Anya questioned.

"I have no idea." Frankly, Evan didn't want to think about the implications of that statement. Terrax had served as the seat of human power for the last three centuries; since gate tech was invented there, it remained at the center of the ever-expanding gate system. As a major transit hub, there were ample opportunities to smuggle in tech. But was this the Syndicate's doing or something else?

He resumed the call. "It's still a leap to jump to multiple races of aliens, possibly warring with each other."

Conroy's brows knitted. "I know it sounds farfetched, but everything I've learned in the last decade points to that reality. For as few people know about our resistance movement on Aethos, even fewer know the truth behind our mission. I meant every word when I said I want this alien technology to save the Commonwealth and ensure our future. But it's not just to save us from ourselves. We are facing a real, pressing outside threat, and Rostov has wholesale rejected that danger. *That* is the real reason behind our disagreement. He would rather have killed me than acknowledge the possibility that humans are weak and vulnerable."

"Why be so willfully ignorant?" Evan asked.

"I've been asking myself that for the last five years, and I still don't have an answer."

Evan pinched the bridge of his nose. "I'm going to level with you, Chancellor… We went to the Korani homeworld. No one was home. The world was glassed."

Conroy's face drained. "No…"

"Yeah, so whatever plan you had to recruit them, it's not going to happen any time soon."

"That's all the more reason we need that ship. Is it willing to help us?"

"Sam trusts our opinion. And we haven't decided what to do yet," Evan replied.

"Please, come here and we can talk—"

"Chancellor, I understand you feel stuck right now, but I didn't put you in that position. From my vantage, you're just as guilty of manipulating people from behind the scenes as Rostov allegedly is. If you're genuine in your interests for the Commonwealth's wellbeing, then you'll respect my desire to confirm information rather than hand over this technology without proper vetting."

At last, Conroy nodded. "You weren't my first choice for this role, Evan, but you ended up being the right choice."

"I was your *only* choice by the time you got to me."

"That doesn't make you any less suited. We had a dozen other prospects, but all of them died in the shipwreck. You offered us a glimmer of hope."

"You'd sold your followers on a pipedream," Evan countered. "And you used me to make it seem like you were getting somewhere. But you're no closer to your goal than before you recruited me."

"That's where you're wrong. You have the ship now. We have an interface—"

"*I* have an interface."

Out of view from the camera, Anya shook her head for him to back off. He knew she was just as annoyed with their situation, but she was right—this wasn't a bridge to burn. At least, not yet.

"Look, I didn't sign up to be an arbiter," Evan continued. "I just need more time to understand the situation."

Conroy nodded, but there was a crease between his brows. "I understand where you're coming from, but—"

"But nothing, sir. I was recruited as a private citizen, and I'm not taking orders from anyone."

"Okay, Evan. Take all the time you need."

Does he really mean that, or is this another tactic? Once again, Evan wished he could get Rostov's take on the whole thing for comparison—though he could think of no way to do so without becoming inextricably snared in their interstellar feud.

"Are you and your people safe, Chancellor?" Anya asked.

"For now, but we've had new setbacks. The invaders attacked one of our outposts, and the colonists needed to relocate. I don't know if they'll try to attack again."

"I'd advise you to sit tight while Anya and I continue to assess this vessel and the landscape," Evan said.

Conroy's mouth twitched. "Don't take too long."

"We'll take as long as we need. We'll send over contact protocols so you can get in touch if there's a major change. I'll let you know what we decide."

"I know you'll make the right choice."

"I hope so." Evan ended the call.

Anya let out a long breath and sank into her seat. "That was… tense."

"*Of course* he wants us to come running back. No surprise."

"And if we go back, we'd be walking into a fight."

"For sure."

Anya pursed her lips. "The *Asamar*'s weapons could easily decide the battle on Aethos. If we want Conroy to win, we could make it happen."

"I know the Syndicate can't be the good guys in this. So enemy of my enemy?" Evan shrugged. "But there's a difference between tolerating Conroy as a lesser evil versus outright endorsing him."

"Right now, we have no evidence that Rostov really is working with the Syndicate aside from seeing a Commonwealth ship docked at Pavia."

"Well, I did see Shah with the Syndicate, when I'd thought he was a captive. Conroy said that's because they were actually working together, but can I take his word for it?"

"It would be nice to independently confirm a deeper relationship before we do anything to help one side or the other."

Evan nodded. "I'd hoped Zaris could help us with that. But without her, how?"

23

ZARIS WATCHED THE errors and alerts clear from her ship's status screen one by one. They'd been lucky that the damage had been more superficial than they'd initially feared. In fact, the damage had been *so* targeted to disable rather than destroy that there was no way it was accidental. Evan had done exactly what was necessary to escape and no more.

She'd been mulling over his words since their encounter yesterday, and she hadn't been able to let it go. *What is the Syndicate really up to? Are we a subcontractor or competition?*

They'd been watching the job boards for any work related to Pavia—the planet Evan had indicated was a hotbed for alien tech. It was a decent gate location away from the main trade routes, so it was the kind of place smugglers might meet up to transfer goods without the prying eyes in major ports. If she could get an invite to the world for a cargo run, she might be able to verify some of what Evan had told her. However, it was wishful thinking to hope something would so conveniently fall into her lap. She'd need to be proactive.

While she waited for the final repairs to be completed, Zaris decided to browse the black market contractor forums to see if there'd been any chatter related to Pavia outside official channels.

She browsed through the list and came across a post that caught her attention. They were talking about moving a rare item and the details of the job were super locked down. That wasn't suspicious in and of itself, but the connection to the Syndicate and a reference to being in the same region as the gate servicing Pavia made it stand out from the other entries. And there was a bit of luck—she'd worked a job with the poster a few months back, and they were on friendly terms.

Time to get reacquainted! She forwarded the information to her office workstation and went to make the call.

The commlink connected after a few seconds, and an older woman's face filled the screen. Her graying, dark hair was pulled up into a loose bun with strands framing her face. "Zaris, to what do I owe the pleasure?"

"Hi, Leeana. Sorry to bother you, but I was hoping to get a little intel."

"What about?"

"I have a lead on a gig out of Horizon Station, but I'm not too familiar with them. I think you worked a job with them a while back, so I figured I'd check if they're legit or not. And, you know, super creeps or anything."

The other woman smiled. "I hear ya. What's the name?"

Zaris double-checked the info in the post, acting like she was trying to call it up from memory. "They're operating under the name… Delvious, I think? Not sure if that's a ship or a person."

Leeana turned serious. "Yeah, they're legit. But…" she tsked, "not sure you want to go there."

"Any particular reason?"

"They're tight with the Syndicate. Do a lot of their super hush work."

"Like the stuff out of Pavia?" she ventured.

"That's not a name I hear come up too often, but yeah."

"Any idea what they're doing over there? I've been hearing some pretty crazy rumors."

"Not so crazy. Friend of mine has been over there—he saw some unexplainable stuff. Like, glowing shit."

Zaris raised her brows. "Not radioactive, I hope."

"No, don't think so. Rumors say it's alien tech, but who knows?"

"Sounds messy."

"Like I said, I'd steer clear."

"Do you know if the UPA has been sniffing around at all?"

Leeana leaned toward her camera. "Between us, I think the Syndicate bought them off a long time ago. I heard there was a mole rooted out a few months back—around the time I was doing this job, actually—but that could just be talk. Happened right after the UPA made a big bust, actually. Come to think of it, I think the ship was out of Pavia."

"You have an excellent memory."

"I wouldn't still be in the game after this long if I didn't keep track of where bad things happen to people like us. Steer clear of the trouble and you can have a decent career."

"Low risk, low reward."

"I look at it as lifetime earnings versus a quick buck. I intend to live free long enough to enjoy my retirement."

"I appreciate you tipping me off so I can do the same."

"Always happy to help another captain. Stay safe, all right?"

Zaris smiled. "Always."

After ending the call, she leaned back in her chair and tapped her chin pensively. The conversation had yielded more information than she'd expected, however vague. It was possible the mole Leeana had referenced was Evan, which would corroborate his story, if true. She hadn't heard anything about a bust, though; that might be the next item to investigate.

She went back to the forum and looked around for references of a UPA bust. After changing her wording and the search criteria a few times, she found a thread from five months ago talking about a Syndicate shipment that had been intercepted. None of the comments discussed the cargo, but the discussion pointed to it being a big loss and causing a rift in the Santano family. Some crew had even been spaced for it.

For all her talk about throwing people out airlocks when they did something infuriating or stupid, Zaris had never *actually* followed through on the threat. But the Santanos were known for prizing expediency over all else—and venting a troublemaker out an airlock was the perfect intersection of swiftness and no clean-up necessary. That level of pragmatism was enviable and horrifying.

Yet, it still wasn't common for even the Santanos to space crew, so there must have been a *significant* offense. Someone messed up that job big-time and paid the price. But maybe there'd be others who were willing to talk?

She spent the next hour rooting around every forum and chat log transcript she could find. As she was getting ready for a lunch break, she spotted a morsel buried three levels deep in a comment thread. Supposedly, the youngest Santano had been running the op that got busted. And that same Roman Santano hadn't been seen since.

They wouldn't kill their own brother, would they? Only a second of deliberation yielded her answer: they absolutely would.

For all the sensationalized takes on those family dynamics peppering the discussion forum, Zaris couldn't find out much about the raided materials aside from one fact: it had originated on Pavia.

An item important enough to be escorted by a member of the Santano family and then have people killed over the loss. And it traced back to that planet. It was all circumstantial info, but not one thing had contradicted anything that Evan had told her. As much as she hated to admit it, it seemed like he'd been telling the truth.

Well, shit.

That left her in a tough spot. She'd threatened to kill him, and he'd shot up her ship—an offense the crew would not easily forget. And he was unlikely to ever want to step foot in the same room with her again after how she'd behaved.

"Tarek, come to my office," she messaged over the comm.

A few seconds later, her first officer entered. "You summoned?"

"Have a seat." She motioned to a chair across from her desk. They'd sat together like this countless times to plan strategies or bemoan setbacks. He'd know that a sit-down with just the two of them meant serious business.

"What have you learned?" Tarek asked.

"Enough that's made me think maybe I was too quick to dismiss Evan."

"He's long gone by now."

"But his warning still stands. We're shit out of luck if the Syndicate ever decides to shut down smaller operators like us."

"There's no scenario where they could have a monopoly on private shipping," Tarek countered.

"No? Not even if the UPA impounded every non-Syndicate vessel that pulled into port?"

"On what charges? Most are above board."

"Okay, that might be a ridiculous example. But I could see

a new reg about who can use the gates and when. Syndicate ships get priority slots, everyone else gets shafted. That's the kind of corrupt shit that can happen real fast."

He scratched his beard. "All right, you have a point. I still don't see what we can do about it."

"Evan's proposal was to capture Pavia—a world with significance to the Syndicate. We control their precious planet, and they'd have to play nice with us."

"But they'd just *kill us all* and take it back."

"That's what I thought, too, which is why our chat didn't go well."

"And then you shot the window."

"Again, not intentionally, and I can't help it that sub-par materials made it through the QC check. But *anyway*, I have another idea for how we can accomplish the same thing with a much higher likelihood of success."

"Go on."

"Remember that job we pulled on Malkara a couple years ago? With the dummy and the projector."

"Yeah…"

"What if that were… bigger."

"I'm not following."

She made a quick sketch on her touch-surface desktop and showed him. "I mean, a *lot* bigger."

He looked at her scribbles. "You're insane. I absolutely love it."

Zaris grinned. "What's the ETA on our remaining repairs?"

"Less than an hour."

"Perfect. Let's map this out for real and then rally the troops."

24

SAMOR SWATTED AT the insects circling his head. He'd spent the night outside observing the underground base—his former home—which was now occupied by the two-faced invaders.

It still turned his stomach to think that any UPDF soldiers would accept an assignment to hunt down a former leader of the Commonwealth through a clandestine operation. They weren't just dealing with a small group of rogue actors here—there must be corruption all the way up the command structure for something like this to happen. If—when—they made it back to Terrax, there'd be a lot more to restoring the Commonwealth's leadership than just Conroy moving back into the capitol.

But first, the more pressing issue was what to do about these people who'd swarmed his home. In the half-day he'd been camped out monitoring them, he'd only seen a handful of people out on patrol. Several had been killed during the Echo Falls incident, and there'd been other skirmishes before Evan and Anya departed. Still, he had to imagine they had a decent fighting force. They must be inside, hunkered down to wait it out. And why not? It was a self-contained, repurposed spaceship underground. Everything they needed. Why stick their necks out?

I'm not going to learn anything else out here, Samor realized. He'd just figured he'd do some recon on his way back to Hidden Grotto since his last survey had been interrupted, but there wasn't nearly as much activity this time around. *Get back to Conroy. Prioritize our actions.*

He quietly set out into the trees.

— — —

Roman's body was poised for action and his mind was clear. He was surprised to find himself so energized after staying up all night watching Samor. Perhaps it was the alien tech offering some manner of rejuvenation, or maybe it was his excitement about finally zeroing in on his prey.

He'd been waiting for the right moment to make his move against Conroy. This opportunity was perfect—better than he could have planned. At first, the colonists moving into his intended haven had seemed like a disruption, but he now realized it had been a nudge toward his ultimate goal. A correction. He'd chosen to hide like a coward—just what Marcus would have expected him to do. But now, Roman was ready. He'd face his challenge head-on, and he'd be victorious.

Conroy has to die. We can't have anyone stand in our way. Serving up the chancellor would solidify his position in the Syndicate, and his new power would push him to the top. He wouldn't just have a seat at the table—he'd decide who'd occupy each seat.

Samor took a twisting path through the forest, but Roman's trace on the man made it easy to follow him from a distance. After two hours, Samor finally slowed his pace as he approached a large rock formation covered in moss and vines.

It was a veritable cliff face fully enveloped by the surrounding forest, including an array of fruit trees.

The soldier approached the cliff and abruptly disappeared behind a rock. Curious, Roman crept around to look at it from the right side; from that angle, he could see the entrance to a darkened tunnel.

Walking in after him was a terrible idea, so he went to look for alternative ways through the cliff. On the north side, Roman found a hill sloping up to the top. He dropped to his belly and crawled the last several meters, not knowing if there might be guards.

He peeked over the lip. The cliff surrounded a deep basin the size of a sporting arena, filled with more fruit trees, a stream, and other lush vegetation. The place was ridiculously idyllic, he had to admit.

Movement below caught his attention. A man and a woman were walking across the basin. She was young, but he was older. Roman strained to make out details.

His heart skipped a beat. *Conroy!*

The man's hair was grayer than his last official political headshot, but his broad shoulders and strong brow were unmistakable.

Roman's palm warmed where the alien sphere had merged with his skin. It recognized his desire to kill the man. But he couldn't simply vaporize him like he had the others. He'd need *proof* of Conroy's demise, and that meant a body.

With effort, he willed the energy charge to dissipate from his hand. He'd need to get closer—

Samor appeared in the basin. He jogged up to Conroy and the woman when he spotted them. Roman crawled as far as he dared to eavesdrop on their conversation.

"They're getting settled, but the peace isn't going to last.

They're asking a lot of questions about the accident and why we were already here. Valid questions. I kept you out of it, sir, but you were right before... We can't keep talking around the truth."

Conroy nodded gravely. "Thank you for seeing to their relocation. Presenting myself now might do more harm than good. Rostov's operatives did a thorough job smearing me before my alleged death."

"Not everyone believed those lies."

"Enough did."

"We could try some sort of survey to gauge receptiveness," the woman suggested.

Conroy chuckled. "Oh, Rebeka. Even after five years in the jungle, your analyst skills haven't skipped a beat."

"Still haven't met a statistical data set I don't love!"

"I forgot how weird you are," Samor quipped.

She shrugged. "You have guns, I have voter polls."

"And both serve their roles in different types of battle," Conroy mediated. "You must be tired, Samor. Go rest and we can talk strategy later."

"Yes, sir." Samor saluted and then disappeared into the tunnel where Conroy and Rebeka had come from.

"He's not wrong about the colonists," Rebeka said. "The cover story is weak. We slapped it together in a hurry when we went to get them off the hillside, and no amount of bolstering can make it stand up for long. The best thing we have going for us right now is taking meaningful actions to help them."

"The enemy's attack may have won us some favor."

Roman frowned. He hadn't intended for his attack to make the survivors more sympathetic to Conroy. Sure, he'd wanted to drive them toward the former chancellor's physical location, but that was only meant to consolidate his targets. Instead, they were now physically even more separated and possibly more motivated than ever.

His palm warmed again in response to his annoyance. When he lifted his hands to crawl further, he was surprised by a flash of golden light emanating from his palm. *Shit!*

"What was that?" Rebeka pointed upward toward Roman. She grabbed Conroy's arm and pulled him to cover behind rocks in the basin.

Roman ducked down and shimmied to a protected position, himself.

"Who's there?" Conroy called out.

What kind of idiot would actually respond? Roman stayed silent. He peeked through the bushes near his head but couldn't see much. *I need to get him out in the open.*

Shooting Conroy wouldn't be tricky. The tough part would be retrieving his body for identity verification. Dropping him inside this outpost would make the corpse difficult to recover since he'd need to also kill every person here. The panthers wouldn't be happy about that.

Against his initial judgment, speaking out suddenly seemed like the right thing to do. "Stop hiding behind your people, Conroy!" Roman shouted. "Come out front where we can talk."

— — —

Conroy tensed in his hiding place behind a rock with Rebeka. He couldn't see the speaker, but it was a man, and he sounded upset. It very well could be the Syndicate operative others had encountered; he seemed bolder—or more desperate—than the other soldiers who'd been hunting Conroy's people.

Is he alone, or is he just the spokesman? Conroy wondered. The entire Hidden Grotto outpost might be surrounded by armed soldiers right now. *This could be the end.*

Rebeka's eyes flashed with terror. The two of them were stuck in the middle of the large courtyard, and there would be no way to get inside the caves without risking significant exposure.

"You can't go out there, sir," Rebeka whispered.

"Am I supposed to just sit here and wait?"

"Yes. Eventually, they'll realize something is wrong and come looking."

"I'm not going to stand by while more of my people get shot."

"If that's what it takes to keep you safe."

"Rebeka—"

"Don't." She looked at him firmly. "We've lost too many for you to throw it all away."

Reluctantly, he nodded. They were stuck. But their cover also wasn't complete. "Do you have a radio on you?" he asked Rebeka.

She shook her head.

Shouting for help was an option. Someone on his team would probably overhear, but it would also unleash mayhem. There had to be a more strategic way to defuse the situation without it turning into a messy firefight.

"What do you want to talk about?" Conroy called out, eliciting a look of disapproval from Rebeka.

"We're not going to shout like this. Let's talk like civilized men," the unseen man replied.

I don't believe for a second that he just wants to talk. Before Conroy could think of a good response, movement caught his attention out of the corner of his eye. A figure was creeping up the basin wall.

— — —

Roman's hand burned to take action. Conroy still hadn't moved from his hiding place. It'd be easy to wipe him out of existence from here; so many problems could be resolved with that one action. But that wouldn't satisfy Marcus. Roman needed to prove the chancellor was dead, and he needed to be the one to do it.

He had Conroy cornered now. There was nowhere for the old man to go without leaving himself open to a clean shot. Eventually, he'd need to give in. Roman would wait as long as it took.

"You move like a buffalo," a familiar voice said from behind.

Roman froze. *How?!*

Samor had somehow crept up behind him. Without turning, Roman was certain there was a weapon in his hand. It was easy to tell now through the telepathic link, but he hadn't been paying attention—yet another mistake Marcus would use against him if he ever got the chance.

"I'll admit, I'm impressed," Roman said.

"I'm not special. You just suck at stealth."

Heat rose in Roman's arm again. Samor would be a good target to vent his frustrations. There were enough people at the other camp that losing this one wouldn't hurt—

Searing pain erupted in Roman's arm. For a second, he thought that the alien sphere had burned right out of him. But then his brain processed that there was a ragged stump where his hand used to be.

"Aghhh!" Roman clutched his wrist. He rolled onto his back to find Samor had a gun leveled on him.

“Next one is through your chest.”

Roman tried to summon the alien tech to attack the other man, but nothing happened. “Do it,” he growled.

Samor’s eyes were hard. He *wanted* to shoot, but there were responsibilities holding him back. “Come with me. We’ll get you patched up.”

“No.”

“I won’t let you die here. I have too many questions.” Samor kicked Roman’s rifle away, and it clattered down into the basin.

Roman cursed him out under his breath. His destroyed hand burned, but the pain was already receding. In fact, the wound didn’t seem nearly as severe. Somehow, he was… regenerating.

Samor noticed a moment later. “Holy shit!”

Roman’s power beckoned to him again now that his panic was receding. Golden pulses extended down his right arm. He raised his hand.

Samor dove aside. He fired again at Roman, missing his leg by centimeters.

Gunfire came from below. Additional soldiers had stormed the basin and were shooting upward. Samor dropped to cover out of their line of fire.

I never should have left him alive before! The trace had been useful, but it hadn’t been worth all the trouble now. Roman tried to send out a kill command with the alien tech, but it still wasn’t responding to him while it focused on healing his wounded hand.

Now without a gun, the alien tech was his only weapon. If he stayed put and waited until he was healed enough to kill Samor, other soldiers may come up the hill and pen him in. Getting out now was the better play.

Yet another plan gone to shit. Marcus was right about me being a failure, Roman thought while clutching his wounded arm to his chest as he scampered down the slope away from the soldiers. Fleeing like a coward. He was pathetic and unworthy of the power—no wonder it wasn't working.

He ran close to a kilometer before he stopped, worried that he may be pursued. But there were no signs of Conroy's people.

Roman checked his destroyed hand. The pain was now more like an intense itch, and the severed wrist had rounded out and was starting to form five little nubbins where fingers would be. He gaped with amazement at the regeneration. While medical science could achieve the same results, it took weeks—not minutes—to regenerate limbs, and it was an intensive process involving numerous injections and other therapies.

As he was considering how the alien tech could achieve the remarkable results, he realized he was ravenous. The energy demands for the healing must be enormous, so that made sense. He spotted a nearby tree weighted with a plump red and orange fruit.

The alien tech inside him signaled in his mind that the fruit would be safe for him to consume. He yanked one of the fruits from the tree and bit in. Its skin was firm and bitter, so he spit it out and peeled it back to reveal a pale orange interior. The flesh was soft and sweet—exactly the kind of fuel he needed. He ate the first fruit down to a cluster of seeds at its center, then consumed two more.

Full and reenergized, he headed back to the base.

When he reached the meadow outside the bunker entrance, Roman held out his arms as he stepped from the cover of the trees. The two sentries raised their weapons when they spotted movement, but they soon relaxed when they recognized his face.

“Where’s Red?” he asked.

“Somewhere inside,” one of the guards replied with a shrug. A moment later, his face twisted when he saw the bloody smear across Roman’s chest and arm. “Holy shit, are you—”

“I’m better than ever.” Roman breezed past them.

The same oppressive feeling he’d noticed last time closed in on him again as soon as he entered the door. Moving quickly, he followed the colored lines to the administrative wing. With the original central command room destroyed, the team had set up a former conference room as the new operational base. However, Red wasn’t there. They directed him to her quarters.

He hurried to the other section of the bunker, his skin crawling. It didn’t make sense to him that he couldn’t stand to be inside, but every second was agony.

Roman located Red’s door and banged on it with his intact right hand. “It’s Roman. Open up.”

The door bolt released a couple of seconds later and it swung open.

Red leaned against the doorframe. “Where the hell have you been? Where’s my team?”

“Keeping watch over Conroy’s lair,” he lied.

She noticed the blood on his shirt and the way he was cradling his left arm. “Dude, what happened to you?”

“One of Conroy’s goons tried to blow off my hand. Well, he *did*, but…” He showed his mostly regrown limb, still weak and gangling.

Red recoiled. “What the…”

“This tech will change everything, I told you. That’s why we need to dig.”

“Unless you figured out a way to clone yourself fifty times, the very real labor issues haven't changed."

"I know where we can get people. How soon can you be ready?"

25

ANYA HAD NEVER thought about herself as an indecisive person, but her chest ached from being in a constant state of uncertainty. She and Evan were facing only bad options, which made her reluctant to commit to any of those paths.

Everything since leaving Aethos had been simultaneously incredible and frustrating. The FTL travel capability of the *Asamar* was nothing short of thrilling, but there was no denying that discovering that the Korani homeworld had been unoccupied for thousands of years was a major letdown. They weren't any closer to getting the 'answers' Sam had promised, and every option they'd tried on their own seemed to get them into deeper trouble.

Sitting in the *Asamar*'s galley while Evan paced, Anya could sense he was equally concerned. His suggestion to work with Zaris had gone terribly. Though Anya didn't fault him, he was clearly blaming himself for their current predicament.

"What we need is inside information, right?" she asked, breaking the awkward silence.

Evan nodded. "Yeah. And unless you have a friend inside Rostov's administration, I don't know how we're going to get it. Zaris has probably blabbed to everyone on the black market side of things by now. We're stuck."

Anya crossed her arms in a subconscious bid to shield herself from an option she hadn't previously allowed herself to consider. But they were desperate now. Standing at the intersection of failure and undesirable alternatives, she had to side with the path that would give them a chance to move forward.

"There might be a way," she mumbled.

Evan stopped his pacing and looked at her, his head slightly tilted. "Which is?"

She sighed. "You may recall that my father is a government consultant."

"Yes, which I took to be the sort of vague description someone gives when their job is either very boring or very secretive."

"In this case, it's kind of both. To be honest, I don't know *exactly* what he does, but I do know he runs in some rather influential circles. When you need information, he's the guy to get it."

She could see Evan silently putting the pieces together. The guy couldn't help building profiles of people. Not for the first time, she wondered how his dossier about her might read.

"And yeah, I think he's seen—or at least been read in—on some unsavory things. It's no wonder he liked to drink to help numb it all."

Evan dropped his head and nodded faintly. "It makes more sense now."

Anya shrugged. "Like I said before, a lot of people deal with far worse problems. And this might be an opportunity for it all to have been worthwhile."

"What do you have in mind?"

"It's more of a vague notion than a plan," she admitted.

"The problem is… I haven't talked to my parents in two years."

Evan raised an eyebrow. "Did you have a falling out?"

"Yes and no. One of those things where we had a disagreement about something stupid, and days turned into weeks, and then months. Once you go that long, it's an awkward question of how to reconnect."

"Does that mean you left for the Aethos colony without telling them?"

"No, we did exchange a couple of messages, but they may as well have been professional memos. They might want nothing to do with me by now."

"No one would feel that way about their child—especially not you."

"I'm not always sunshine and smiles."

"I know. But you're principled. Whatever you were fighting about back then, I'm sure you had a good reason."

"I did." She wasn't sure those reasons mattered anymore, but she hadn't changed her mind. If her parents hadn't come around, then a conversation about anything else would be a non-starter.

"That argument is probably long forgotten. But anything worth noting?" Evan asked.

Anya sighed and pushed back from the bistro table. "You know how it can be as an only child—all of your parents' energy focused on you. Wanting to know every detail of your life. But something changed about three years ago, a year before I stopped talking to them. My dad started asking a lot of really specific questions about my work. Like, beyond casual curiosity. And he'd get upset with me if I didn't answer. At the time, I'd thought it was just more controlling behavior. Now, I wonder if there was something… more."

"As in, him trying to get inside information about

NovaTech on behalf of his government contacts?"

"Right. But I was a tiny cog in NovaTech's operation. Why would he be asking *me* anything?"

Evan drummed his fingers on the table. "I could speculate all day about different factions within the government and who might be investigating who else. Is that what your fight was about?"

"It's sort of what started it. I blew up on him for trying to micromanage my life. But I still wonder why he wanted those details about my work—especially given our new conspiracy theories."

"Why not just *ask* him?"

Her gut twisted. "It's not that simple."

"You're the one making it complicated. It's your dad, Anya. Along with the not-good stuff, you've also told me nice stories about him. I haven't heard anything that makes me think he wouldn't take your call."

"Well, we can't just come out and say, 'Have you heard about a dastardly plot for the corrupt government and NovaTech to steal alien technology?' How would I even start that conversation?"

"Well, we'd learn a lot just by him seeing your face. Everyone back in the core worlds has probably been told we're dead, right?"

"True. If I can tell him I'm alive, maybe we can get help."

"It's a start."

"Okay." She dropped off the barstool to her feet. "Let's do this before I lose my nerve." She left the galley, heading for the lift. "Sam, please configure the shuttle for a commlink to Julian Rojas on Praxas."

Evan followed her down to the hangar, where they boarded the shuttle. With its modified interior, the vessel would make for a good generic backdrop for a vidcall. Sam had already activated the screen in preparation for their arrival. They sat down in the front seats.

"I'll be right here," Evan assured her.

She nodded. "Thanks. All right, Sam, call him up."

The screen changed to a spinning symbol while the vidcall connected. It pulsed while waiting for her father to pick up. After thirty seconds, she was getting ready to hang up and try later, but then the screen abruptly changed to a close-up of his face. He was a little grayer than the last time she'd seen him.

"Hi, Dad."

His jaw instantly went slack and his eyes wide. The lighting was terrible, but it even seemed like some color had drained from his face. "Anya?! How…" He was whispering, and the scene behind him was dark. Only then did Anya realize that it was only an hour shy of midnight local time.

"Sorry for calling so late," she said.

"Late? It's been *two years*! And…" He shook his head incredulously. "I thought you were on Aethos."

"That's a long story."

"I had it on good authority that the *Stratum* crashed on the planet. We were told everyone was killed."

"That's awful." Anya wasn't sure what drove her to be evasive, but explaining the survivors and everything that had happened on the planet didn't feel like the right thing to do. She wanted to get, his perspective without feeding any information that might influence his responses.

"What about you? Where are you now?" her father asked.

"I'm safe. I'd heard some rumors, myself. I didn't know what to believe. What do you know?"

"About the *Stratum* and Aethos?"

"Yeah. I mean, I could have been caught up in all that.

Really freaked me out, you know?"

"Your mother and I have been beside ourselves. We thought you were…"

Anya studied his face. He was upset, but he wasn't relieved the way she'd expected. There was worry in his eyes. "Do you know what happened to the ship? Why it crashed?" she prompted.

"They didn't tell us anything specific. There was some speculation about a solar flare or something. I don't know. You were lucky to not be on there."

"Yeah, for sure."

"But Anya, where are you now?"

"That's not important."

"Are you okay? You're acting like you're in hiding."

She stared at him levelly through the screen. "Should I be?"

"I don't—"

"Colony ships don't randomly crash. I can't think of a single instance in the last hundred years where anything on this scale has happened." She decided to go for it. "Was what happened on the *Stratum* really a freak accident?"

Her father swallowed. "You think it could be, what…? Sabotage?"

"I don't know, Dad. You're a lot more plugged into things than me. Have you heard anyone question the official story?"

"Why are you asking that?"

"I want to know if I should be concerned. It all seems strange to me. I can't imagine I'm the only one asking questions." She was intentional with her wording on that point. *The sort of people who'd ask questions unwanted were all on that ship.*

Julian's brows pinched. "Why did you decide not to go on the colony expedition? Did you think something like this was going to happen?"

"No, it definitely surprised me."

"Well, I'm glad you're okay," he said too flatly. "I didn't think I'd ever see you again."

And would you have been okay with that? she wondered privately. His demeanor remained unsettling. Where was the love and relief to be connecting with his presumed-dead daughter? He was saying the right words, but the emotion wasn't behind them. She needed to push him for any details she could get. "Are they sending a search party to look for survivors on Aethos?"

"I think so, but NovaTech hasn't made an official announcement. The mission was declared a total loss, so…"

Anya glanced at Evan seated to her left. He gave a subtle shake of his head, making her pulse spike. He sensed that something was wrong, too. "Hey, Dad, can you hang on a sec?" She muted the mic and stopped the camera feed. "How isn't he jumping for joy right now?" she asked after confirming that nothing would be transmitted.

"I'm sorry, Anya, but that isn't how a father should react," Evan said softly, his eyes compassionate.

"Don't pity me."

"Hey, I'm just saying that he might know more than he's letting on."

Anya took a calming breath. Evan wasn't the real target of her distress, and it wouldn't be helpful to unload on him now. Her father was the objective here. "I need to push him," Anya said. "Why the hell wouldn't he be excited to see me?"

— — —

The explanation was clear in Evan's mind, but it was

heartbreaking enough that he didn't want to say it out loud. *Because he was in on it.*

Evan didn't have much to go on to support that assertion, but he'd interviewed enough people over the years to recognize deception when he saw it. Julian Rojas' questions were the sort of thing a handler would ask an operative that had gone rogue—try to figure out their position and assess their frame of mind. Evan had enjoyed a close relationship with his own parents, and he knew what a loving parent-child connection looked like. He didn't see that affection from Julian. Coupled with the strange line of questioning, Evan was left with the disturbing impression that Julian had already come to terms with his daughter's death, and her unexpected resurrection was an inconvenience.

If that was true, it meant that Julian had been willing to sacrifice his only daughter in service to a greater objective. Evan couldn't think of any circumstances where his own parents would have even considered betraying him, let alone followed through. Evan hoped he was wrong and there was another explanation for Julian's behavior.

Anya resumed the vidcall with new steely resolve. "Sorry about that. This whole thing is so weird, Dad. We haven't lost a whole colony ship in decades. I just keep thinking about how I could have been on there."

"You're okay, and that's the important thing," Julian said. "Tell me where you are. I'll come get you."

"It'd be better if I come to you. You're at home, right?"

"At the moment, yes. But I spend a lot of time on Terrax these days."

That wasn't a surprise to Evan, since Julian was a government consultant. Terrax was the capital planet for the Commonwealth, so all official functions routed through that world. Praxas was the neighboring planet in the same system—a little further out in its orbital path, so colder, but its larger size and multiple moons had made it a bustling center of industry. Terrax was the seat of government, but Praxas was home to the movers and shakers in business—including NovaTech's headquarters. That made Praxas the perfect home for a 'consultant' serving as a liaison between government and business. It also made Evan wonder where the true loyalties of a person like that might lie.

"I can come to Praxas," Anya said.

"That might not be a good idea," her father replied.

Okay, maybe he sees a chance for redemption here, Evan thought. *He may have agreed to send her to her death, but this is a second chance to keep her away from further danger.* That could be an opening for them.

Unfortunately, Anya had gone stoic. "Okay, I'll stay here."

No, Anya, that wasn't the right thing to say! No doubt, her father would see her concern; any consultant worth even minimum wage could read a person well enough to see that. If Julian was up to something sketchy—and it was pretty clear to Evan that he was—then he would want to find out why Anya hadn't died on Aethos. Anya had just handed him the fuel.

Julian delivered. "Oh, sweetie, I didn't mean it like that. I want to see you. Things are just a little hectic around here, and it would be better if we could meet in a place where I could focus on you. Would you be able to gate over to Constella?"

Constella? Oh, hell no! Evan shook his head to Anya. Constella was the seat of the Syndicate's power and where Evan had nearly been killed. The mere suggestion of the planet as a meeting place confirmed in Evan's mind that Julian must be in bed with the enemy.

"I'll have to get back to you on that, Dad," Anya said. "Now you know I'm okay. I'll call again when I can." She ended the commlink and sank back in her seat.

"Good job," Evan told her.

"No, I suck at this. That was terrible."

"We can prep more for the next one."

She sighed. "What the hell is going on? Am I losing my mind, or does it sound like my own freaking father might be in on this conspiracy?"

"I hadn't expected the conversation to go that direction," Evan admitted.

"That *would* explain why he was so curious about my work. But how much did he know about the expedition to Aethos? If he knew the ship was going to be destroyed…"

"Hey, we don't know anything for certain."

She rubbed her eyes. "Why didn't he get my mom? Why wasn't he… happy?"

Evan gently placed his hand on her shoulder. "He may well have been in shock. I know that wasn't great, but it was only one conversation."

"What did that call accomplish aside from showing we're probably even more screwed?"

"We did get more information about how the mission is being reported. Publicly, they're saying there were no survivors. So, for now, it's better for him to think you never got on that colony ship."

Anya shook her head. "No, Evan. There were logs. It wouldn't have taken much to verify. He *must* have known that I was on board. Which means he had every reason to think that I was dead. Yet, he acted that way—surprised, but not excited. He said he never expected to see me again, and I believe that."

"What are you saying?"

"I think he may have sold me out to NovaTech."

Evan eyed her. "In what way?"

"When he was pressing me about my work, I'd told him about the strange energy signatures on Aethos. We had our falling out soon after that. Then, a couple years later, I got a last-minute assignment to the expedition field team—which I now know was because I'd seen things related to the alien presence, even though I didn't understand it at the time. But Dad didn't seem surprised at all when I announced my assignment. We exchanged those messages before I left, and his response had this weird 'thank you for your service' tone. It all reads very differently in retrospect."

"Hindsight is like that."

"I don't know, Evan." She placed her hand on her stomach. "I just have the worst feeling that he knew this mission was doomed."

"You may be right." The fact that Anya had independently arrived at the same conclusion as Evan had drawn was very telling.

Anya shook her head, her expression pinched with pain. "I should have just asked him point blank if he knew they planned to kill everyone on the *Stratum*."

"I doubt he would have answered."

"But this is really bad, Evan. If he knows I was on that ship, but now he knows I'm alive, that's definitive proof that there were survivors of the 'crash'. Those 'loose ends' they'd wanted to tie up are still out there."

"Still, it will take anyone else months to get to Aethos. We have time."

"Time to do *what*, though? We don't have a plan. We don't have allies. Maybe we *should* just go meet him on Constella and wash our hands of this whole mess."

"If I may, I don't like that idea," Sam interjected.

"I'm with Sam," Evan agreed. "The *Asamar* can't be allowed to fall into the Syndicate's hands. Your dad suggesting that as a meeting place is pretty telling about his allegiance, I'm sorry to say."

Anya nodded solemnly. "But he's my family, Evan. I don't know Conroy. How can I pick a disgraced politician hiding on a remote world over my own father?"

Evan's heart wrenched. Anya had been his companion through all the madness, but her father was a stranger—even more of an unknown than Conroy. Evan couldn't trust her to be objective. He pinched the bridge of his nose. "This is exactly what I didn't want to happen—being in the middle of other peoples' fights."

"It's our fight, too. It's a fight for our future—for us and everyone else."

"This isn't just about loyalties and family. We're effectively deciding who's going to lead the Commonwealth. That's not something a few individuals should decide."

"I agree," she said. "But if we don't make those decisions, then we're leaving it in the hands of the people who tried to kill us."

"Yeah, but… what if we're wrong?"

She shrugged. "We can only do what we think is best based on what we know."

"A scientist at heart, as always."

"I can't escape it."

"Be objective, Anya. Would you do what your father wants and go to Constella, knowing that it could lead him to this ship?"

Her face reddened. "Until I know for certain that he had nothing to do with the crash on Aethos, I'm not giving him anything."

— — —

Rostov awoke to a vibrating notification on his omni. The only calls that would come through to his personal communication device at this hour would be of urgent priority, so he couldn't ignore it. He shook off the fog of sleep and answered the incoming communication from his advisor, Julian Rojas.

"Chancellor, I just received an unexpected message," Julian began. "It was from my daughter."

Rostov bolted upright in bed. "What?" His wife rolled over and pulled the covers tighter around herself, used to these midnight interruptions.

"You told me the ship was destroyed."

"It was." Rostov's informants had relayed that a few emergency pods had made it to the planet's surface, but they were trapped on the planet. Of all the luck, Anya Rojas *could* have been one of those survivors. But how had she managed to send an interstellar message? "Was she with Conroy?"

"She wouldn't say. She made it sound like she'd never gotten on the *Stratum*."

Impossible. Rostov had verified the colony ship's manifest himself—had confirmed passengers *after* the colony ship had left port. Anya had definitely been on board. *Why did she lie?*

"Hold on." Rostov swung out of bed and jammed his feet into slippers. He padded out of the bedroom across the hall to his office in the ornate Chancellor's Mansion.

A lamp faded on to its dimmest setting when it detected his approach. He began pacing in front of the desk. "Tell me everything she said to you."

"I can do you one better. I recorded it."

A file popped up on the screen of Rostov's omni. He played it back in a window overlaying their active call. Rostov zoomed in on the image and panned around. Anya appeared to be calling from inside the flight deck of a small vessel, which didn't align with the known craft on Aethos, but it appeared to be of human design. There was also the shadow of someone else in the room, though Rostov couldn't see the person directly.

"How the hell did she get a ship?" he wondered aloud.

"Do you want me to continue pushing for a meeting?" Julian asked.

Rostov's mind raced through the permutations. *Did she get off the* Stratum *before the crash? Or did she find this ship on Aethos? Or...*

"Yes, Julian, try to set a meeting. I'll order a trace on the gate logs. I want to know exactly how she gets there." Because there *was* another ship on Aethos—one more prized than any other vessel known to humankind. And if she somehow had it... Well, that would make things very interesting.

26

CONROY SAT DOWN at the makeshift conference table with his top advisors. Their grim expressions echoed his own mood about the recent encounter. They'd been a hair's breadth from tragedy, and such a breach couldn't be allowed to happen again.

"It's my fault," Samor began. "I'm in charge of security, and I failed to account for that approach."

"We don't have any extra staff who could have been posted on guard," Conroy countered. "We're stretched too thin. That won't improve until we merge with the civilian camp—and there remain compelling reasons to not do that yet."

"Yeah, we just need to not have an enemy coming after us," Rebeka quipped.

"You're right. They need to die," Samor stated.

Rebeka's eyes widened with alarm at his cold tone, but she soon gave a resigned nod. "Better to have a swift, decisive end."

"They're hunkered down in our base. We all know how the last firefight there went," Samor said.

Conroy frowned. "I was hoping for a diplomatic resolution."

"They know where we are, sir," Samor countered. "We can't simply wait this out."

Rebeka nodded. "I agree. They brought the threat here, and we need to fight back. I miss our home."

"The problem is, I'm not sure how best to retake the base without destroying it," Samor said. "We can't very well storm in there with guns blazing without causing even more damage—not to mention, probably getting shot to shit ourselves."

"What about some *non*-traditional firepower?" Rebeka ventured.

The others leaned forward in their chairs, suddenly more engaged.

"We know the ecology of this world, they don't," she continued. "And it so happens that we have a detailed interrogation transcript from a conversation with a xenobiologist expert on this planet. I propose we put that knowledge to use."

Conroy crossed his arms. "If you're suggesting what I think you are, I don't think that's a line we should cross."

"Why not? They wouldn't hesitate to do the same to us."

"That's not the point." Conroy played through the unspoken scenario in his mind. Rebeka was suggesting that they use the poison vines that had nearly killed Anya during her initial trek with Evan. Anya's life had only been saved through quick thinking and the good fortune of locating an antidote in time. Reportedly, it had taken less than twenty minutes for her to lose consciousness. Death would have followed soon thereafter had it not been for Evan finding a lichen to counteract the poison. However, he'd used Anya's bioanalyzer. Conroy and his team had no such equipment. Conroy wanted to disable his enemy, not kill them all. To perpetrate a mass execution would make him no better than his enemies.

"I know it's nasty, but it's also cleaner than other ways this could go," Samor stated. "Acted very quickly, didn't take much. There's a fast-acting antidote for if anything goes badly."

"We'd still need to work out the distribution method, but I think this might be the answer," Rebeka insisted.

Conroy shook his head. "We're not murderers."

"No, but we are warriors," Samor replied. "And death is a fact of war."

Conroy met the soldier's level gaze. Samor's counsel had seen him through their most dire circumstances, and he knew the man would give his life for their mission. A voice like that carried weight. "I'd like us to explore all of our options before making that call," Conroy said.

"Well, we need to decide quickly, because they could send a bigger attack party up here any time. Tonight, even," Samor cautioned.

The soldier didn't need to state the obvious: even a small attack party could kill all of them. They didn't have the fortifications, weapons, or personnel to survive a firefight. Stealth had been their only offense, and that was shattered.

"You're right, we need to end this before any more of our people get hurt or die. Gather the poison and the antidote. Figure out how to deliver it."

"I have some options in mind," Samor said.

"All right, make the preparations. But wait for my order to deploy."

The meeting adjourned. While Samor briefed a small team to gather the necessary materials, Conroy reviewed a progress update from the new civilian base. They were being cooperative for now, but Conroy didn't expect that to last. It was one of the reasons they needed to make a move against the invaders soon. Though he wanted to avoid further bloodshed, that very well may be unavoidable. Samor was right: this was war.

The communication console on his desk lit up with an incoming vidcall. He froze, seeing that it was from Terrax—not the neighboring world of Praxas, where most of his contacts were based. Hesitantly, he accepted the communication.

Conroy had to stop himself from recoiling as Chancellor Rostov's face filled the screen. "Calling to resign?"

Rostov scoffed. "You're the worst kind of weed. I think you're dead, and you keep popping up again."

"I thought you'd appreciate perseverance."

"Is that what you're calling it?"

"I swore to protect the Commonwealth. I wouldn't expect you to understand what that means."

Rostov shook his head slowly. "What you're trying to do now won't help anyone."

"It will help *everyone*, unlike your ambitions to serve yourself and a chosen few."

"Power needs to be consolidated. The masses wouldn't know what to do without direction."

Conroy took a measured breath. They'd had a similar conversation six years ago, several months before Rostov had decided that removing Conroy was the best option. They hadn't seen eye-to-eye then, and they certainly wouldn't agree now. Conroy was firm in his belief that the Commonwealth's citizens deserved access to alien technology that could improve commerce and open up the galaxy to further exploration, while Rostov insisted that those tools should be held closely with only a select few allowed access. How could anyone declare that such tight control was in the Commonwealth's best interest?

"How long have you been working on your secret mining operation now?" Conroy asked with a sly tilt of his head. "I'd think you would have found something useful by now."

"At least I have an interface. That's more than you can say."

"We have what we need."

Rostov's brows shot up. "Ah! You *did* find it."

Conroy clamped his jaw, realizing his mistake. The other man had no doubt received reports from the UPDF invaders, but they didn't know what had become of the alien ship after it took off. He couldn't reveal any more. "Your goons are months away. Don't bother dropping by for a visit."

"You're bluffing, Thomas." Rostov studied him through the screen. "Ah, I see… You *had* the ship. But then you lost it. And now you don't know where it is, either."

Conroy couldn't admit that the ship was no longer on Aethos, which would mean it was now in play in other venues. Aethos was a difficult target, but if they could capture that ship on a more accessible world… Conroy's mind raced for a deflection. "What's your play here, Victor? Are we going to keep dancing in circles all day?"

"All right, let's skip the showmanship. We can agree that the Commonwealth is at a crossroads, yes?"

Conroy nodded.

"And you have a grand vision of peace and prosperity well into the future?"

"Of course."

Rostov stared at him levelly. "Then that is precisely why this technology needs to be tightly controlled."

"The protection it could offer us. The doors it could open—"

"Doors? I'm more concerned about the entire cities, or planets, it could bring down!"

Conroy waved off the statement. "You were always so damned pessimistic."

"No, I'm just honest."

"Says the person who secretly orchestrated my attempted assassination."

Rostov smirked. "In all fairness, I did tell you to your face that you were making a colossal mistake and I'd do anything necessary."

Conroy fumed within, but he refused to let it show. "Appointing you was the biggest mistake I ever made."

"Hardly. Your real error was counting on alien tech over human ingenuity."

"This technology can change everything for us!"

"It already brought down one civilization. Why invite the collapse of another?" Rostov asked.

"We don't know what happened those thousands of years ago and why they're not here now."

"Exactly! So why start using tech we don't understand without knowing the long-term implications?"

"Because we both know the Commonwealth and humanity are stagnating," Conroy said. "Humanity might not face a crisis this decade or century, but soon enough. We're headed toward a dead end on our current trajectory."

"That's a problem for us to solve for ourselves. Hitting the 'easy' button is a worse fate." Rostov held a fist to his chest. "The drive to innovate needs to come from within. Looking outside our walls for help is how a society becomes complacent."

"Those walls are expanding. We've been building gates for three centuries now. Would you stop that exploration?" Conroy asked.

"That's different."

"You must have seen the reports by now, Victor. We're on a pathway to the collapse of the Commonwealth unless we do something drastic. The trend lines for the economy and population are heading in the wrong direction for us to have a future."

"The alien tech won't fix those issues. You need to address the root cause of problems, not show up with a miracle solution."

"But it *is* a solution," Conroy insisted. "And a good one."

Rostov shook his head. "A stopgap fix motivated by desperation. You'll just have new problems as soon as it rolls out."

"Which we'll address, in turn."

"At least you *know* the problems now. If you take a step into the unknown, it could make everything much worse."

"Or it could solve everything," Conroy said. He'd believed that from the outset, and his conviction had deepened the more he learned about the alien tech's capabilities.

Rostov scoffed. "Wishful thinking."

"I haven't given up on humanity's ability to embrace change, and to rally around a common goal."

"Oh, that's what this really is! You think that presenting incontrovertible truth about intelligent alien life will make us join together in our shared humanity?"

"A secondary benefit, yes."

"No, it doesn't work like that, Thomas. Whatever rifts exist now will magnify. Introducing a powerful outside force will only make people want to look after their own interests with more fervor."

"I shouldn't be surprised that you'd take that perspective, given how cozy you've gotten with the Syndicate."

Rostov sneered. "At least they admit their real motivations. You hide behind your wall of sanctimony."

Why are we doing this? Conroy rubbed his eyes. "How many times have we been over this same argument?"

"Not enough for the points to make it through your thick skull, apparently."

"Still a class act, Victor. The Commonwealth is lucky to have you."

"You know, I would have left you alone if you'd run off to any other world to live out your days in peace. But you had to go *there*, and you insisted on putting up a fight."

"Fine, let's call a truce." Conroy locked eyes with the other man through the screen. "We may have wished each other dead over these last few years, but this is bigger than the two of us. What the Commonwealth needs is for humanity to unite."

The current chancellor walked a few steps away from the camera to gaze out his office window. "You know, when I was younger, I used to think that the destination was all that mattered. But I recognize now that the journey may, in fact, be the most important part. That's how we learn the important lessons. And we've witnessed plenty of awful outcomes from our own technology. Prematurely introducing *alien* tech could be far more catastrophic."

Conroy's eyes narrowed. "Yet, you would place it in the hands of the Noche Syndicate."

"Oh, Thomas, is that what you think of me? My coordination with the Syndicate has nothing to do with giving them free rein over this tech."

So, he admits that he really is working with them. All signs had pointed to that fact, but hearing it from the man himself was still a shock. How could anyone call themselves the leader of an interstellar civilization while outright collaborating with the worst members of society? "Means to an end, right?"

"I don't need to tell you how sometimes it's easier to work outside of official channels."

"Oh, so it's okay to skip steps when *you* do it."

"Cutting out administrative shit is not the same thing as unleashing unregulated alien tech into society at large!"

"I do agree with that." Conroy struggled to get the words out, but it needed to be said.

Rostov arched an eyebrow. "Really?"

Conroy still firmly believed that humanity could benefit greatly from their discoveries on Aethos and beyond, but his understanding of the alien technology had evolved over the last few years. Though he maintained his opinion that it should be used to help everyone, that didn't mean unfettered access. Based on what he knew now, some guardrails in its deployment would be necessary. As was finding a way to work together.

"Believe it or not, I love our people," Conroy said. "Every decision I make is to keep the Commonwealth safe. And you are right—everything we've achieved since those early years of venturing from Earth, we've paid for in sweat and blood. But we also can't feed crumbs to the starving. If living to see next century means growing pains from advancing too quickly, I'll take that trade-off to annihilation any day."

"That's what you refuse to hear, Thomas! I want to feed them, but I intend to dictate how they're fed. Your free-for-all would only bring misery."

"We may be able to find common ground here if we give each other a chance. If we pool our influence—"

Rostov laughed. "Oh, it's too late for that. Just admit defeat already. I know you're penned in and out of options. Take the loss with dignity while you can."

Surrender isn't an option. Conroy stared down his rival. "One day, everyone will know what you did."

"I have no regrets." Rostov ended the call.

27

TAREK SAUNTERED ACROSS the *Invictus*' flight deck to stand alongside Zaris, brushing against her shoulder. "You're extra sexy when you're in battle-strategy mode," he whispered in her ear.

She punched his arm as hard as she could from the awkward angle. Her hand crumpled like she'd struck a shipping container, but she didn't let the discomfort show on her face. It's not like they hadn't fooled around on occasion, but this wasn't the time or place for flirtation.

Tarek took the hint and stepped back a pace. "We're just waiting on two more ships," he informed her.

"Good. We'll move in as soon as they arrive."

They'd decided to stage their attack from a gate in one of the no man's land territories several systems over from Pavia. It was close enough to make for a short gate transit time but far enough away to be impractical for a journey through normal space. Zaris had sixteen ships under her authority, in addition to the *Invictus*. She'd explained the plan to the other captains, and they had all jumped on board. As it turned out, no one was very happy about how the Syndicate had been running things the last several years, and the thought of them getting even *more* power hadn't been well received.

"Where are we on the probes?" Zaris asked Callie.

"The *Runaround* brought everything we asked for, and the engineer monkeys are doing their thing."

Zaris nodded. "All right. Finish up. Let me know when we're ready to go."

She went into her office to wait for the final ships to arrive and all prep work to complete. Their plan was straightforward, but it was risky and had been pulled together quickly—a dangerous combination.

Though Evan's suggestion to attack the main spaceport on Pavia was the most direct approach to access the alleged alien tech on the planet, the plan was fatally flawed. Even if they succeeded in capturing the base, the Syndicate—or worse, the Commonwealth's military—could come with reinforcements. In that kind of firefight, they wouldn't simply be forced out, they'd be killed. But seizing control of the gate and using it as a choke point… That put them in a powerful position.

From there, they could close in on the planet and conduct a raid, knowing that additional enemy forces could be held back at the gate. If they determined the planet was worth keeping, they could fight to hold it. Or, if their investigation revealed the whole exercise had been a waste of time and resources, they could gate away and move on with their lives. Doing it all with spoofed transponders and disguised identity—tools any good smuggler had in their grab bag of tricks—no one would be the wiser about who'd been behind the blockade.

The final two ships arrived, and Zaris subsequently got the notice that everyone was ready to move. She returned to the flight deck.

Sitting down in her command seat, she opened a

commlink to the other captains in her small fleet. "This was my idea, so I'll go through first. Stay sharp."

Acknowledgements came through from the other ships. She settled in and gave Callie at the helm the go-ahead.

The *Invictus* swung around to face the massive gate. Red lights illuminated around it as the metal ring started to spin. The magnificent tunnel through space sprang to life within the ring, its entry shimmering with a mesmerizing shade of blue that reminded Zaris of her grandmother's eyes.

Zaris' fine hairs stood on end as the *Invictus* passed through the gate. The exotic blue tunnel was even more thrilling than normal due to her anticipation of the mission. She'd been wanting to stick it to the Noche Syndicate for years, and the opportunity to make a meaningful dent in their operation had her heart racing.

The exit gate took shape at the end of the tunnel right away, given the short transit distance. Its initially opaque surface cleared to show a starscape, though the planet Pavia wasn't visible.

The *Invictus* passed through the exit gate into normal space, sending another electrical shock over Zaris' skin. As the intense hum of the energy cleared, she noticed two vessels were on the scan. Close.

"Contact! Light 'em up!" she ordered.

Evan hadn't noted any patrollers stationed at the gate, but she'd anticipated the possibility. Her gunners took aim at the smaller ships and wasted no time firing.

Rhythmic vibrations passed through the decking underfoot with each volley. The main firing array was housed close to the flight deck, which always made battles like this a more immersive experience. Zaris enjoyed the tactile feedback through the ship, feeling the vessel as an extension of herself, much like a sword master wielding their blade. And right now, the ship was ready to fight.

The first enemy target exploded on screen, and the second was venting atmosphere, sending it into a chaotic spin. A final volley from the *Invictus* turned the second enemy ship to scrap.

There were no additional targets in the immediate vicinity currently on scan, but no doubt reinforcements would be coming soon.

"Form up!" Zaris ordered over the networked fleet comm.

As the other ships in her fleet exited the gate, they fanned out to form a grid in front of the gate structure. The formation they'd agreed upon had some vessels oriented toward the gate and others in a defensive position of the planet. But the important thing at this stage was taking up as much area as possible with their limited number of vessels. Next would come filling the gaps.

The hulls of the vessels gleamed in the blue light cast from the spatial distortion within the ring. They'd issued a command to the gate to remain open, which would block it from being activated by another origin gate for now. However, without ongoing transit activity, they only had about fifteen minutes before the gate would override the command and go dormant to regenerate its power reserves. The technology was meant to be used in spurts, not prolonged connections. But they only needed a few minutes to execute the next phase of their plan.

Dozens of drones launched from four ships in the fleet. They clustered in front of the gate. And then the magic happened.

A series of holographic projectors and frequency emitters activated, transforming the simple drones into the appearance of fully fledged starships. One by one, the drones activated and then flew away from the cluster in front of the gate to fill a gap between the seventeen real starships.

The flight pattern made it look like the drone-ships were exiting the gate and then joining the fleet formation. In the end, more than a hundred contacts lit up on the *Invictus*' scan display, registering as ships with shields up and weapons primed.

A thrilling tingle ran down Zaris' back. *It would convince* me *if I didn't know what was going on.*

The gate finally timed out, but it had served its purpose. From both a scan and visual monitoring standpoint, it looked convincingly like a large fleet was now blocking the gate. It was only a matter of time—

"Incoming communication from Pavia!" Callie announced.

Zaris smiled. "Right on cue. Let's see what they have to say." She and the other members of the flight deck crew donned semi-translucent masks that covered their faces. In a universe of backworld business dealings and double-crosses, they'd learned long ago that identity was a thing to hold close to one's chest. A voice modulator in the comm system would also re-pitch her voice slightly to avoid an identity match.

The front screen transformed to the image of a balding, middle-aged man who was making no effort to hide his annoyance. "Who are you and what the hell do you think you're doing?"

So friendly and charming! This will be fun. Zaris exaggerated her smile, and the mask reshaped to reflect the movement. "Hello! We heard you have some nice things on your planet. We decided we'd like to take them."

He gawked at her. "You're insane."

"Last time I checked, I'm the one in control of your gate

now. If you'd like any chance of making it through this alive, you might want to be nicer to me."

"When Marcus hears about this—"

It took conscious effort for Zaris not to flinch at the mention of the eldest Santano son who'd taken over the Noche Syndicate a few years prior. "There's not a damned thing he'll be able to do about this. The next closest gate is, what, a month's transit from here?"

The man glared at her. Behind the anger, there was concern in his eyes—not worry about Zaris, but of what this attack meant for his future with the Syndicate. But his career prospects weren't Zaris' responsibility.

When the man didn't say anything more, Zaris continued, "This doesn't need to turn into a shooting match. Give us what we want, and we'll let you go unharmed."

"What *is* it you want?" he asked finally.

"To know what secrets you're hiding down there. We know you're collecting alien tech."

The man's eyes widened ever so slightly to reveal his surprise, but he kept the rest of his expression neutral. "That's absurd."

"If you have nothing to hide, then you'll have no problem showing us."

"We have proprietary company operations. That has nothing to do with 'alien tech' or whatever you think you know."

"Well, see, that's a problem. Because we're not going anywhere until we get a peek under the hood of your operation here."

"If you approach, you will be fired upon."

"You see our fleet, don't you?"

He remained silent.

"Yeah, you do. And you also understand what that means. A little thing called 'overwhelming force', right? And you're on the losing side of that equation. Sorry, buddy."

"You can't attack without taking casualties. Your people won't be happy to have their friends die for nothing."

"We'll see about that." Zaris ended the call using the console next to her seat. "All expected," she told her crew. "The *Invictus* and four other ships will proceed to the orbital station. We'll disable the aerial systems and any ships at the spacedock. We want them defenseless and trapped."

Her ship and the others she'd selected for the next phase broke away from the main fleet surrounding the gate and headed for the planet Pavia. It was mostly bland beige with heavy cloud cover—the kind of place that looked wholly unappealing from orbit but could be hiding untold treasures. At least, she sincerely hoped this gamble would pay off.

"Strong energy signatures on the station," Callie announced. "Looks like weapons are hot."

"Keep us pointed straight at the station," Zaris instructed. "Make us a hard target." Fortunately, their own weaponry could swivel to fire from any angle.

Transit time to effective firing range was nearly twenty minutes. The crew remained quiet and focused on the approach. Zaris kept close watch on the distance indicator overlaid on the front screen, awaiting the moment when their targeting system could lock on.

At last, the clock counted down to the final minute.

Zaris brought up the clean scan data with visuals on the space station and dock. There were a dozen ships of various types as well as an orbital structure the size of a small city. However, the longer she looked at it, she realized that the main station looked to be more like a massive warehouse than an office building or residential structure. Most likely, there weren't that many people here. That would make their task much easier.

"Disable the drives on those ships!" Zaris ordered. "Target the weapons systems on the station and the ships. Shoot to disable rather than destroy."

Her team coordinated with the other four ships to set their firing pattern. They unleashed a barrage on the station and spacedock. Most of the shots struck true on the propulsions systems only, leaving the vessels intact. Two ships, however, were completely destroyed—including one bearing the Commonwealth's official emblem. Zaris tried not to think about what artifacts may have been lost in the process. And the crews… definitely best not to think about those.

"They're calling again," Callie announced.

Zaris smiled. "Good. Put him on."

The man's face appeared on her screen again, noticeably more flustered this time. "Final warning. Leave now."

"Sorry, whoever-you-are—"

"Clint."

"Clint," she continued, "but you've already lost any negotiating position you may have had."

Callie muted the mic. "Ma'am, there's a strange energy build-up on the planet's surface. I can't get a reading on what it is."

"Best to assume a weapon. Back us off and prepare to launch countermeasures." She turned back to the screen and unmuted. "Clint, what are you planning?"

"You shouldn't have come here." He ended the commlink.

"Ominous much?" Zaris quipped, but the prospect of an alien super-weapon did have her concerned. "Belay that order to move away. Instead, move us in as close as possible to the station, on the side away from the planet. I want to be able to reach out and touch it."

Tarek smiled. "Good thinking."

"I'm guessing they won't want to shoot themselves to get to us."

The *Invictus* and its four companion ships grouped together next to the station. The tight clearances were ridiculous for vessels of their size, but the pilots took it slow and managed to bring them into alignment; that was one advantage of their experience running ship-to-ship cargo transfers that required direct tethering through an umbilical.

"Ma'am, the energy build-up is dissipating," Callie informed her.

Zaris breathed a sigh of relief. "All right, now we're getting somewhere."

"Another incoming communication request," Callie announced. "Looks like it's coming from the surface this time."

"Put it on," Zaris instructed.

This time, it was a woman in her thirties. She had tanned skin and copper eyes with chin-length dark hair pulled back into a half-ponytail. Her brows were drawn together and lips curled into a furious sneer. "Who the hell are you?" she demanded.

The masks, voice modulator, and ID spoofer on the ship had done their work. No reason to give away the secrets now. "You can call me the Free Maiden. I lay claim to this planet."

The woman laughed deeply. "Oh, that's good! Points for boldness."

"Yeah, you, too. You're outgunned but taking it in stride."

"Oh, Miss Free Maiden… You have no idea what you've stumbled into, do you?"

"I know a good payday when I see one."

The other woman shook her head. "No, not here. This is one place you should have stayed far away from. You should have pretended it never existed."

"Not gonna lie, that makes it *more* enticing."

"You don't know who I am, do you?"

"Should I?"

The other woman scoffed. "Bold, but stupid. I'm Marta Santano."

A vise closed around Zaris' chest. She didn't recognize the woman's face, but she definitely knew her name. *Shit! If this doesn't work, we're even* more *dead.*

Marta evaluated her through the screen. "Who put you up to this?"

"What makes you think it's not my plan?"

"Let me guess… You've been a loyal contractor for years, and now you're hoping to get a step up in life by striking out on your own. But no one turns on their partner without a trigger. If you've worked with us, then there's no doubt you've always been well compensated. So, something else brought on this betrayal."

Betrayal, huh? Zaris almost got defensive, but it was actually the truth. Evan had gotten in her head and paranoia had taken over. In a day, she'd pulled together a plan that normally would have been a month of planning. There was no point questioning now whether it had been the right move since there was no going back. "You're vampires, slowly bleeding us dry. Enough was enough."

Marta clicked her tongue against her teeth. "How generic and unhelpful."

Zaris had expected to face a mid-level lieutenant heading up the operation on the planet, not an actual member of the Santano family. Whatever authority Zaris had thought she might be able to exude had evaporated. However, they were in too deep now to turn away.

What's changed? Nothing, she reminded herself. *This woman thinks she's powerful, but we're the ones with gunships pointed at her planet and we have the gate blocked off.*

Zaris kept up her bluff. "Let's just lay it out there… If you don't play nice, we'll destroy the gate."

"Destroying the gate would strand you here, too."

"Do you really want to test us?" Zaris stared unblinkingly through the screen at the other woman. If it came down to it, she *would* destroy the gate before allowing an enemy backup fleet through. Sure, that would trap her people here, but it was better than being cornered for a slaughter. She'd made sure they were provisioned enough to survive standard space travel to the next closest gate location, just in case things went badly. But with their starships destroyed and the gate blocked, their opponents had far fewer options.

"What do you want?" Marta asked.

"We want everything."

An alert popped up on the screen. There was another energy surge on the planet's surface.

Zaris' pulse spiked. *Would they be willing to destroy the station just to take us out, too?* She knew the Syndicate had done some brutal things in their past. She couldn't discount the possibility.

"Good luck to you, Marta." Zaris slapped her console to disconnect the commlink. "That conversation was going nowhere. Options?"

"Something weird is going on with the scan," Callie said. "There's massive interference on the surface. I don't know how Evan got any usable info about what's down there. But I can see an energy buildup, just not a specific target."

Blanket, blind weapons fire rarely ended well, so Zaris didn't want to start blasting from orbit and hope for the best. "What else? Any activity on the station?"

"Nothing," Tarek replied. "They'd be trying to evac if they were going to fire this direction, right?"

Maybe? Zaris wasn't sure, so she didn't want to voice an opinion either way. "If we pull back now, that will leave us open to attack during our retreat—and we might not make it to this position again."

Tarek nodded. "Hold?"

"Hold," she confirmed.

Zaris gripped her armrests for a tense minute as the scan data continued to update with an escalating energy charge on the planet's surface. Without visibility into *what* was actually happening, all they could do was bolster their shields with every bit of reserve power they could muster and hope for the best.

They wouldn't blow up the station. Those ships are their only way out, she told herself. But the more times she repeated it to herself, the less she believed it.

"Oh, shit, here we go!" Callie flinched back from her console as if the distance would do something to protect her.

The onscreen image glowed with a flash of white light. A beam shot upward, appearing to head straight for them.

Zaris braced in her seat, swearing new allegiance to the galactic deities if she could make it through this alive. She half-closed her eyes against the brightness shining from the screen.

The beam abruptly split into multiple columns. Brilliant light streamed by the exterior viewports, barely missing the outer edges of the station.

"The *Concord* is hit," Tarek announced. "Damage to the starboard cargo pod."

Zaris checked the ship's position on her map. The five vessels had needed to crowd in behind the station, and the *Concord* hadn't quite fit—leaving a sliver of the vessel in sightline of the planet. "How bad?" she asked.

"Containment fields are holding. Assessment underway," her first officer reported.

The ship hadn't entirely combusted, so she'd take that as a win.

The beams cut out.

"Energy readings from the surface have returned to initial baseline," Callie said. "There's still interference, so no visuals."

Tarek relaxed. "Beam weapons like that require a recharge. At least they shouldn't be able to fire again right away."

Zaris wasn't ready to let down her guard, but she would take the momentary reprieve to make her next move. "Okay, let's—"

"Hold on… Contact!" Callie sat rigid in her seat. "A ship just broke atmo!"

Zaris spotted the vessel on the screen. It was relatively small—maybe sufficient for a few people plus living quarters. She had little doubt about who might be on board. The show of the weapon firing had been cover for the launch. *Yes, run away, Marta. It won't make any difference now.*

"Should we pursue?" Callie asked.

"No. She's a whole other brand of trouble. Let her be someone else's problem." Zaris watched the ship race away. Killing—or even capturing—a member of the family wasn't worth the hell it would bring. She was better off focusing on the potential prize hidden on this planet.

Tarek scowled at the screen. "She'll be back for blood. The Syndicate won't let us keep this place."

"And by the time they arrive with reinforcements, we'll be

gone." Zaris jumped to her feet and wiped the sweat from her palms. "Let's take a closer look to see what they've been hiding."

28

ANYA DOUBLE-CHECKED the flashing communication request. "Sam, is this for real?"

"Affirmative. There is an incoming vidcall request from the *Invictus* bearing Zaris' ID."

Evan motioned for Anya to stay out of camera range. He activated the commlink. "Zaris, hi."

She was kicked back in a chair, and her feet appeared to be propped on a table or desk. "So, your plan to capture Pavia was stupid."

"Called me up just to say that, huh?"

"Let me finish. The plan to storm the castle and hold it was stupid. I mean, it was actually a solid tactical plan—I'll give you that—but the whole concept was an idiotic approach. Right target, asinine way to go about it."

He scowled, not sure whether to be annoyed or offended. "Thanks for the feedback."

"What you *should* have suggested was seizing the gate."

He blinked at her through the screen. "The gate?"

"Yep." She inspected her fingernails. "Turns out, not so well guarded. And a choke point like that… Well, let's just say it makes a ship think twice before trying anything funny.

Destroy the gate, they're trapped."

"Are you telling me that you're now in control of the gate servicing Pavia?"

"I am, indeed."

"And what do the people on the planet have to say about it?"

"They aren't happy, I can tell you that much."

"Have you… investigated?"

She dropped her feet to the deck and leaned forward toward the camera. "Not thoroughly, but you're definitely onto something with this alien tech. Speaking of which… how did you jump away?"

"Yeah, that's kind of a long story."

"I'd like to hear it. For real. No shooting or kneeing or threats of airlocks."

He eyed her suspiciously. "Why the change of heart?"

"Because I want to survive. I want my people to prosper. And you're right—you need bargaining chips to have a seat at the table. This is mine."

"Okay. Tell us where to meet and we'll be there."

"I'll send the coordinates." The vidcall ended.

"Another trap?" Anya asked. After the last encounter, she didn't trust Zaris as far as she could throw her.

"I don't know. I think this one might be legit." Evan brought up a star map on the holographic display. "Sam, can you scan the comm band for any chatter related to Pavia or the gate nearby?"

"There is something about a blockade at the gate. No confirmed reports."

"Did she really do it?" Anya wondered incredulously.

"I suppose we'd find out soon enough if we jump there," Evan said. "Assuming she doesn't blast us to pieces the moment we drop in."

"That does bring up a question… do we gate there or just jump? Seems like we've already spoiled the surprise of our ship," Anya pointed out.

"Yeah, and that's an issue, isn't it? If we go to this meeting, then we'd practically be handing the jump tech to Zaris."

"She could overpower the shuttle, but she couldn't capture the *Asamar*," Sam chimed in.

"The *Invictus* isn't the only vessel in that blockade. She might have dozens. What kind of attack could you hold off?" Evan asked.

"The *Asamar* has many defensive measures I was unable to incorporate into the shuttle. I estimate that I could countermand twenty vessels comparable to the *Invictus* without difficulty."

"That's great, Sam, but we don't know what we might be flying into there," Anya cautioned. "I still say it's too risky."

"Our options are to accept this invitation to parlay or continue to hide. I still don't like the running option."

"She tried to *shoot you,* Evan!"

"It's a complicated relationship."

Anya groaned. *I knew Zaris would be trouble the moment he mentioned her.* The unbidden jealousy she'd fought to suppress came back full force. *If Zaris were an unattractive guy, would Evan be so forgiving?* She didn't think so.

Evan picked up on her annoyance. "We'll only do this if you agree. I meant it when I said we're partners on this crazy ride."

"You'll resent me if I say 'no'."

He sank back in his seat. "Let's talk it out."

She crossed her arms. "Well, first of all, what are you planning to tell her about the jump tech?"

"I'd rather not say *anything*, but I don't think that's an

option since she's seen it in action. What are your thoughts?"

"That the last time we saw this woman, you got into a fight. I'm skeptical about her genuinely wanting to work together after wanting you dead a day ago. Hence my original suggestion to ignore this invitation because it's likely a trap."

"Yes, there's a good chance she's still furious with me."

"So, why in the stars would you take this meeting?"

"Because this remains our best opportunity to gain negotiating leverage. We already have access to two other planets with confirmed alien tech—Aethos and Temple World. Adding Pavia to the mix would be an undeniable strategic advantage—especially with a ship capable of jumping near-simultaneously between those locations."

Anya couldn't argue that logic, but the part about needing to trust Zaris remained a non-starter. "Evan, I'll repeat, she tried to kill you."

"But then she took my plan and acted on it. That counts for something."

"Sure, it suggests that you're both equally *insane*."

He leaned back in his seat, pensive.

"No counterpoint?" she asked.

"I'm trying to decide at what point insanity becomes the smart move."

"Um… never?"

"You know that's not true."

Thinking back over the last couple of weeks, she'd participated in a lot of crazy things that shouldn't have worked. But those were scenarios where she'd had a measure of control. It was different when the 'crazy' was contingent on trusting an enemy.

"I'm not good with the whole 'trust in strangers' thing," she admitted.

"You trusted me when we met, right?"

"Yes, but you never gave me a reason not to. Zaris, on the other hand, is a walking tornado of red flags."

"But she actually might be in control of Pavia now. Don't you want to know what alien tech the Syndicate has been hoarding down there?"

Curiosity tickled the back of Anya's neck. "Damn it."

"That means you're in?"

"I'm going to regret this."

A devious gleam brightened his captivating green eyes. "Oh, I know you're starting to love the thrill of mortal peril."

She waved her hand dismissively. "Let's get this over with." But he was right. Part of her *did* find it thrilling.

The *Asamar* initiated a jump, targeting an exit point close to the gate. They soared through the strange darkness of FTL transit streaked with occasional bands of abstract colored light.

When the familiar backdrop of normal space returned, they were also greeted by a shocking armada of well over a hundred vessels fanning out around the gate.

Anya almost fell out of her seat. "How did Zaris get this many ships?" Anya asked, awestruck.

"I'm not sure she did." Evan adjusted some inputs on the console, and the majority of the enemy contacts changed from red to orange. "Is that right, Sam?"

"Well spotted," the AI said.

Evan smiled. "She's good. I would have missed it, but she bragged about pulling this trick before—only that was with people in powered armor."

"What is this showing?" Anya asked, looking at the screen.

"She's using an array of probes to look like a fleet of ships. There are only twelve actual vessels here. It works beautifully from a distance, but it doesn't hold up under close inspection."

"What about the Noche crew on Pavia? Won't they figure it out? Then what?"

"It doesn't matter anymore," Evan said. "Zaris played them perfectly. The key was establishing the choke point. These dozen ships are more than enough to blast anything coming out of the gate, and there isn't a big enough force on Pavia to overwhelm them because we can easily see them coming. With the *Asamar*, we'd be able to pick off the orbital defenses on Pavia while this blockade makes sure no enemy backup can arrive."

Anya frowned. "It can't be that simple."

"But it is. It was so simple I didn't see it as an option."

"Why didn't anyone try it before?"

"Because no one had a compelling reason to go after this place. But they didn't know what we know about Korani tech. And we're about to find out what's down there."

The *Asamar* glided toward the planet, bland and unremarkable from a distance. Anya wondered what kind of comm chatter must be going on between the other ships now after their grand entrance. If Zaris hadn't yet told her collaborators about the jump technology, they would definitely be asking about it now.

The orbital station above the planet came into view on the front screen. Multiple singed ships were berthed in the spacedock, and five others hovered nearby, one damaged. Anya recognized the *Invictus* as one of the intact vessels.

"Incoming communication request from the *Invictus*," Sam announced.

"Accept," Evan said.

Zaris appeared onscreen, but her smug expression from earlier had been replaced by open awe. "Nice ride."

"Like I said, it's a long story," Evan replied.

"Why don't you come over here and tell it?"

"How about you come here instead?" Anya suggested.

Evan shot her a look of quizzical surprise.

Zaris considered the offer. "All right. You have docking space for a shuttle?"

"We do," Anya confirmed.

"Okay. See you soon."

Evan severed the commlink. "Why did you invite her to the ship?"

"We can control more variables over here, right? And what's to see, honestly? The interior looks pretty normal now." It'd been eerie watching the ship transform and customize over the last few days, but every time she walked onto the flight deck, it was a little cozier. Now, if she didn't know better, she'd think it was a nicely worn-in human ship.

"I was going to suggest a neutral meeting ground, but you're right. And we've already talked about the alien tech, so may as well show her it in action—" Something occurred to him. "Hey, Sam, is that artifact we picked up near Koranis still floating in the cargo hold."

"Affirmative."

"Can we move that for her arrival? Don't want to give it all away."

"Yes, I will hide it in the corner."

"Perfect."

Anya sighed. "Hiding ancient alien artifacts in the corner. This is our life now?"

"Still want to go back to your desk job at NovaTech?"

"Hell no."

He smiled. "Thought so. Come on, let's go meet our guest."

29

EVAN STILL WASN'T thrilled about having Zaris on the *Asamar*, but it would allow more control over the interaction. Frankly, he was surprised that she'd agreed to the venue—which almost certainly meant that she wouldn't come alone.

When they received notice that a shuttle had launched from the *Invictus*, he and Anya went down to the large hangar area of the ship, finding that Sam had already moved the strange artifact behind a wall of crates in the back corner. The only strange part about it was that there hadn't been any cargo crates the last time he'd been in there, so they'd been manifested like so many other new furnishings that had been randomly appearing on the ship over the last couple of days.

A bay door was already open to receive their visitor, with an electrostatic field protecting the hangar from open space.

The *Invictus*' shuttle passed through the field with a shimmer and landed next to Sam's custom craft. When the side hatch opened, Zaris and her first officer, Tarek, exited.

"You brought along an uninvited friend, so I figured I could do the same," Zaris said.

"Happy to have you both," Evan replied, not wanting to be contentious.

Zaris wasn't subtle about looking around the hangar as she walked toward them. "It's an interesting design. Where did you get this ship?"

Evan had planned out his explanation, but his chest tightened with unexpected nerves as he began. At this stage, the truth was the only story powerful enough to take them to the next stage. Yet, bringing someone else into the fold came with risks—especially someone with Zaris' history. Nonetheless, she'd taken a huge leap of trust on her own to install this blockade around Pavia, so that had earned her the right to know what she was really fighting for, as far as Evan was concerned. "We found this ship on the planet Aethos."

"Wait, isn't that where a colony ship recently went missing?" Zaris asked.

"Whatever you heard on the news or comm chatter isn't the full story. The colony ship was intentionally destroyed. We were on it. Only about fifty people made it out alive."

"Shit, that's…" Zaris seemed genuinely upset by the news. "How did you go from that to… *this*?"

"The two of us left the crash site to find our military escort cruiser, which also crashed," Evan continued. "While we were searching, we came across other people. Specifically, Conroy and his team."

Zaris nodded. "Ah, that's the connection."

"Yep. They'd been in hiding there for five years, since his alleged death. They'd been searching for alien tech."

"Like the stuff on Pavia?" Tarek asked.

"Yes, but even more. There were rumors of an ancient alien ship."

Zaris arched an eyebrow. "And?"

Evan held his arms wide. "We found it. This is that ship."

She looked around the hangar again. "This doesn't seem very alien."

"I was skeptical at first, too," Anya chimed in. "It's been adapting itself to our preferences—the design features we find familiar and comfortable."

Zaris faltered. "Are you saying it's… alive?"

"There is a sentient AI controlling it, but the structure itself isn't 'living' in a biological sense. It's more like the technology is highly programmable—kind of like how our own nanotech can be adapted to different specializations."

"Okay," Zaris said slowly. "And what about how you've been flitting around space without using gates?"

"This ship and the shuttle are equipped with jump drive tech I can't begin to explain. It allows point-to-point transit without the gate network," Evan revealed.

Zaris and Tarek exchanged glances, their eyes wide with amazement. But Evan could also see them beginning to formulate how this revolutionary tech could be used to their own advantage.

"Why *you*?" Zaris asked Evan. "If Conroy and his people had been on that planet for years, why did *you* end up in control of this ship?"

"Because he was chosen," Sam boomed over the speakers.

Zaris and Tarek jumped.

"Who the hell is that?" Tarek demanded.

"I am the ship," Sam continued. "Evan revived me. He bore the mark of my creators."

Zaris' face twisted. "What does that mean?"

"It connects back to Pavia somehow," Evan explained. "When I was working undercover with the Syndicate, I took part in an initiation ritual where I was given an injection. At the time, I'd figured it was some sort of tracker, but it turns out that it was a primer to allow interaction with the alien technology. Whatever they use to manufacture that serum, I think they found it on Pavia. That's why I wanted to come here."

Zaris nodded. "You're saying that if we can find that original source, then we could figure out how the primer works?"

"Exactly," Anya said. "I tried to reverse engineer the serum based on a sample of Evan's blood, but I haven't been able to parse it. The tech has a strong biological component, but there's more to it. We need a pure sample if we're ever going to figure out how it works. This place is our best lead for where to get some answers."

"The Syndicate has had this technology for years—decades, maybe," Evan continued. "And it started here. They've tried to downplay the importance of this place, which is why I didn't realize how relevant it was. They figured if it seemed like a little nothing of an outpost, no one would come here. Having a massive militia would have given away its significance. But once we figured out the pieces and that they were hiding in plain sight, coming here to see for ourselves made sense."

Zaris smirked. "And then I highjacked your plan."

"You did the hard work, yes," Evan said. "But you don't have the primer. You won't be able to tell what's an important artifact from a random rock down there. You need me for that."

Zaris pursed her lips. "Honestly, I'd planned to cut you out, but it looks like you'll be useful, after all."

"Gee, thanks."

"I didn't realize what we'd be dealing with."

"I still don't understand all of it, either," Evan admitted.

"But this place is where the Syndicate has something special, I know that much."

"Well, congratulations, you get to come along."

Until we get our hands on more of the serum and you try to take over everything. But instead of saying that out loud, he simply flashed an amiable smile.

"That leaves us to the 'how' part of investigating the planet." Zaris looked over at Tarek. "We've done an infiltration or two."

It was definitely more than a few, based on the reputation of Zaris and her team. But most of that was covert theft rather than storming a facility with armed guards. While the spacedock and gate hadn't been heavily fortified, Evan had no doubt that the interior would at least have armed guards. They'd need to shoot their way through the security perimeter before they'd get to the good stuff. "How do you want to handle this?" Evan asked to gauge Zaris' thinking, though he already had his own plans in mind.

"What you had proposed before is a good foundation," she replied. "Having the gate locked down covers the biggest blind spot."

"The key decision we have to make is the first target," Evan said. "Infiltrating the orbital base would be easiest, but I'd rather start by getting a look straight at the source of what they're doing surface-side."

Zaris nodded. "Agreed. This damned planet's atmosphere makes scanning a bitch. How'd you get your info?"

"Sam has impressive skills," Evan said. "We can help feed more reliable scan data."

"That would be very helpful. From what we've been able to piece together, the EM readings all point to one place. We sent a probe down to get some better visuals, and it doesn't look that big from the outside."

"It might be a lot bigger underground," Evan pointed out.

"What size team were you thinking?" Tarek asked.

"Enough to cover ground if—when—we get into a firefight, but not so many that we can't keep track of each other. Maybe twenty to thirty, if you have that many people equipped to fight."

"We have as many corsairs as we need," Tarek confirmed. "And gear superior to anything used by the UPDF."

"Great. Let's go over the specifics."

They used a screen on the hangar's wall to talk through breach points based on the scan data. Unfortunately, all the info they had was exterior, so they'd be going in blind. However, a well-armed team of experienced professionals could accomplish amazing things. That kind of ground work wasn't Evan's area of expertise, but Tarek had also served in the UPDF, and a number of Zaris' crew had spent time as foot soldiers before being seduced by the call of big paydays, action, and adventure from a life of piracy. Personal feelings on those life choices aside, Evan was happy to have their expertise for this op.

Once they had agreed on their action plan and timing, Zaris and Tarek returned to their ship, leaving Evan and Anya to gear up. Hopefully, Sam would be able to customize armor and weaponry to serve their needs.

"How are you feeling about this?" Anya asked.

"Nervous, but I can't think of a better approach. Too many signs point to this planet. We need to know what's down there."

"What if there are big monster things like what we encountered on Aethos?"

"Then I'll try to telepathically communicate with them. It's the Syndicate operatives I'm worried about."

Though Evan had disclosed a fair amount about the Korani technology, he hadn't named the aliens or spoken about the telepathic aspects of the technology. If Zaris decided to sever the tentative alliance, he didn't want her having too many secrets.

— — —

Anya flexed her arms and legs in the new body armor Sam had created for her. "It's light, doesn't pinch anywhere, and I can move freely. Nice!"

Next to her, Evan evaluated his own set, which flatteringly highlighted his physique. "Yeah, feels really good. How much protection will this offer?"

"It should stop most handheld projectiles and help mitigate the effects of stun weapons."

"Meaning, it might knock us down but not unconscious?" Anya clarified.

"That is my estimation."

Like everything the ship had done for them, they wouldn't know for certain how well the items would work until they tried them out. Testing armor in actual combat was a terrible plan, though.

"Evan, I think you should shoot me," she announced. "With a pulse rifle, I mean."

"I—"

"Yeah, yeah, blanket objections. I hear you, but just do it."

He sighed. "Sit on the couch."

She got into position and flipped down the visor from where it folded smoothly over the top of the helmet.

Evan moved to stand in front of her. "Sorry if this hurts." He fired.

Anya felt like she'd been struck by a live wire in her chest. Every hair momentarily stood on end, and her muscles seized. Her legs were weak and her breath caught in her chest, but she remained lucid. The sensation passed after five seconds. "Yeah, that does not feel great."

Evan nodded with satisfaction. "Well, that was a strong enough charge that it could have knocked you out. It's not maximum, but this is a pretty standard setting. The armor should help a lot."

"I am pleased to hear it meets with your approval," Sam said.

"Can you prepare an extra chest plate so we can run a ballistics test without damaging this armor?" Evan asked.

"Certainly."

They went down to the hangar as soon as the item was ready, where Evan unloaded a dozen rounds of various calibers into it. Nothing made it through.

"That makes me feel a lot better," Anya said, though her stomach was still knotted with nerves.

"Me too. But no judgment if you want to sit this one out."

Anya shook her head. "I need to see this place for myself."

She could tell that Evan was worried about them walking into the dangerous situation, but he hadn't argued when she'd insisted on coming along. They were equally invested in the mission. Nonetheless, she knew that she would be the least experienced person on the team, so she'd keep her distance and let the professionals work. She'd be there to assist as a medic or with other scientific analysis as the mission demanded.

Their last test was the comm earpieces. They worked fine right next to each other, but there was no way to know how well they'd communicate underground through rock until they got down there.

With the gear tested and approved, Anya and Evan loaded

onto the shuttle. They instructed Sam to keep the jump drive components of the craft on the *Asamar* in case Zaris tried to abscond and also informed the AI to take the ship and run back to Haven, their fallback planet, if anything went wrong.

When they landed the shuttle on the *Invictus*, the hangar deck was filled with people running supplies and checking gear. Approximately three dozen soldier types were assembled toward the center of the space, speaking with Zaris and Tarek, who were also dressed in battle gear.

"Wow, look at you!" Zaris evaluated them. "Very sharp."

Evan tapped on the armor. "It doesn't take much to surpass UPDF standard issue gear."

Tarek chuckled, as did several of the other corsairs. Anya wasn't sure why that was amusing, but she was pleased to see everyone relaxed.

They went through the important introductions, and Zaris gave one final run-through of the plan. The important takeaways from Anya's perspective were: don't get shot, and shoot the bad guys before they can shoot you. Since she'd had little target practice, the former would be her main objective.

Evan and Tarek went to check the inventory on the transport shuttle, leaving Zaris and Anya to load a case of flash grenades.

"Sorry about how things went last time you were here," Zaris said to Anya's surprise.

"No hard feelings."

"You and Evan seem close."

He is the last subject I want to discuss with this woman. Anya kept her eyes focused on her prep work. "He's a good guy. He stepped up when I needed an ally."

"I can't believe you were running around in the muddy jungle for a week."

"I've been in worse places."

"You know, this is a little strange to admit, but I don't know that I've ever set foot on real dirt."

Anya looked over at her. "Seriously?"

"Grew up a space kid. I've been to parks on space stations, but that's not the same. Most cities I've been to planetside have been so paved over that there aren't even rats."

"I don't think a person has really lived until they've hugged a tree growing in its natural habitat," Anya said.

Zaris laughed. "Hugging a tree?"

"They're magnificent organisms. Don't knock it until you've tried it."

"You're weird."

"You only think that because you think of being human as being a master of your environment. Ships and biodomes have allowed us to live in places that no carbon-based, oxygen-nitrogen breathing creature was ever meant to inhabit. Digging your toes into the ground on a pristine planet with the sun on your skin, and fresh, unfiltered air… Now, that's a whole other take on life."

"I'd feel naked without all this." Zaris made an all-encompassing gesture of the ship.

"I get that. Maybe that's why so few people visit the ecotourism planets. But once you see how humans were meant to live, you realize that we've made prisons for ourselves everywhere we go. A ship can take you anywhere, but if you never leave it, how free are you, really?"

The question appeared to stump Zaris. Before she could offer a comeback, Evan came up to them.

"Ready to go on your signal, Zaris," he said.

She clicked the full case of flash grenades closed. "Game time."

30

ZARIS' SENSES WERE sharp with anticipation. She loved a good ship-to-ship shootout, but there was nothing more thrilling than hand-to-hand combat. Of course, she hoped that they wouldn't face too much resistance, but she would be happy to see a *little* action.

They'd decided to take one of the larger cargo shuttles down to the planet's surface. However, a single craft made for an easy target of any ground weapons—and they knew there was at least one capable of shooting into space. So, while the *Invictus* and other ships remained tucked behind the station, they'd sent probes down into the planet's atmosphere to corroborate Sam's scan data. They now had all the information they'd need to blast the planet's defenses and give them a clear path down.

When the shuttle was loaded and ready to take off, Zaris gave the order for the *Invictus* to sneak from its hiding place. She watched on a screen in the shuttle's hold as they got a clear sightline on the planet below. As she'd expected, the beam weapon on the surface started to charge again. But unlike their previous encounter, this time they had full imagery of the surface complex.

"Fire on enemy targets!" she instructed her team back on the *Invictus.*

Missiles launched from the ship, arcing around their shuttle and streaking into the planet's atmosphere. She tensed as the seconds ticked by.

A beautiful plume of flames and smoke appeared on the screen relaying the probe imagery.

"Direct hit!" Callie announced over the comm.

Gleeful shouts and claps sounded from the corsairs in the shuttle's hold. Evan caught Zaris' gaze and gave her a nod of approval.

The probes had picked up smaller ballistic and plasma weapons arrays scattered around the ground complex. Since they didn't want to destroy the whole structure, launching the larger missiles from the *Invictus* wasn't practical. But their shuttle was shielded and armed, and they were ready to put up a fight.

The vessel descended into the atmosphere, blinded by the thick clouds. But Zaris watched the craft break through the cloud layer on the probe's feed.

Ground weapons sprang to life and targeted the shuttle. They were ready with countermeasures, launching scatterers to confuse the weapons and intercept the ordinance. One by one, the enemy missiles were destroyed.

Mini railguns fired next, and many rounds were blocked by an intercepting drone swarm designed for that very purpose. The blasts that did make it through peppered the ship's shields, sending an eerie reverberation through the structure. But the shield held, and now they knew their exact targets.

Gunners on the shuttle targeted the enemy weapons and blasted precision shots. On the screen, miniature puffs of dust and smoke billowed up from the impact sites. Eventually, no more enemy fire came.

"Looks quiet now," Callie announced on the comm.

There has to be more than that, Zaris thought to herself. They'd executed a good plan, but the Syndicate was sophisticated. There must be more defenses in place to protect such an important location. Nevertheless, Zaris' team could only attack targets that they'd identified. If the enemy had other offensive measures queued, they'd have to wait to respond until they knew where to shoot.

The shuttle headed to a landing zone outside the main surface complex—a sprawling concrete structure positioned on the valley floor of a stone chasm with dramatic vertical walls. At first, Zaris thought that the place was all natural from millennia of erosion. But then she noticed that some of the lines in the stone were too straight and symmetrical to be natural.

"Holy shit, is that…?"

Evan looked over from where he was gripping a handhold near her. "They like to build their structures into rock faces. This looks a lot like what we found on Aethos."

Zaris' heart jumped in her chest. She'd entered into this plan based on a promise, but seeing the evidence brought it all into focus for her. *We really are going to find something revolutionary here. Everything is about to change.*

The shuttle bumped down on the ground. Zaris' knees suddenly felt weak as she thought about stepping foot on the alien world. Her recent conversation with Anya had underscored how narrow a perspective she had from her limited experiences. Space travel, transit stations, cities… those were her comfortable stomping grounds. But this world, so undeveloped and with mysterious technology, would challenge her in new ways.

Challenge accepted. She unslung her rifle from her back and got ready to exit through the shuttle's rear hatch. "You know what to do. Let's go!"

Tarek, Rex, and the most experienced former UPDF infantry soldiers on her team led the charge down the cargo ramp as soon as it lowered. They fanned out and sought cover behind rocks or anything else they could find in the vicinity. Slowly, they picked their way toward the facility entrance. More corsairs ran out to take their places as the first wave advanced.

Zaris, Evan, and Anya waited until three-quarters of the corsairs had departed the shuttle before joining them outside.

Zaris balked under the intense sun as soon as she stepped out from the shuttle's shadow. Even the air was hot and dry, burning her throat and lungs with each breath. The ground underfoot was uneven and shifted slightly with each step—a far cry from the textured decking she was used to in spacecraft.

Running to the left, Zaris ducked into the first cover place the team had been using. She peeked around the rock at the facility beyond. The first wave of corsairs had reached the doors and were setting explosive charges on the hinges and locks.

She pointed her weapon toward the door. *All right, here we go.*

— — —

Evan darted to the right as soon as he hopped off the shuttle's ramp, crouching down behind a boulder. Anya was right behind him. "You good?" he asked her.

"Eyes up, weapons hot," she repeated back the instructions.

He nodded. "Looks like they're about to blow the door. Stay down."

A concussive blast reverberated through the ground. Their earpieces modulated the sound of the explosion to dampen the loudest crack. Evan poked his head around the outer edge of the rock. Dust was still settling near the entrance, but corsairs were preparing to enter.

He motioned Anya forward as they ran from cover to cover on the final approach. He paused at the last waypoint, waiting and listening for a report over the comm.

"Entrance secure," a voice said. "No contacts yet."

"Why aren't there guards?" Anya asked Evan.

"I'm sure there are, but they must have gone deeper. There's no way they're going to stand by and let us take this place without a fight."

Across the way, Zaris was getting ready to run to the entrance, as well. Her movements were deliberate and efficient in a way that only came from experience. He'd marked her as the kind of person who let others do the dirty work, but he'd clearly underestimated her.

Anya, for her part, was keeping up with his moves. He nodded to her, and the two of them darted to the entrance after Zaris.

Evan pressed his back against the concrete wall next to the destroyed doorway. The lights were on inside, though the fixture closest to the blast zone was flickering. Zaris and her corsairs were advancing down the hallway. There were no sounds of fighting yet, so Evan followed them inside with Anya on his heels.

The interior immediately struck him as being unlike the other Syndicate facilities. It had been constructed with local materials, and the long, straight corridors were a significant departure from the large gathering spaces he was used to seeing near outpost access points. This place felt more like an extension of the entrance than the actual destination.

Ahead, the corsairs stopped. They'd reached another door—this one made of heavy metal, resembling a vault.

Rex, who was with the corsairs at the front of the group, ran back to speak with Zaris, who was steps ahead of Evan.

"Ma'am, I'm not sure we can blast through it. That hatch looks like it's rated for a nuke."

"No wonder they didn't put up a fight at the entrance," Zaris muttered. "What are our options?"

"I can load up the charges and hope for the best, but I'm worried it would collapse the ceiling."

The nanotech bracelets warmed against Evan's wrists—a beckoning pulse to remind him of the power they contained. He hadn't wanted to reveal the tech, but the mission was at stake. "I might be able to help."

Zaris arched an eyebrow as she looked over her shoulder at him. "How?"

Honestly, he wasn't sure. The tech might be able to disintegrate the door, or maybe it could bypass the lock. He'd learned that all he could do was envision the desired outcome and the nanites would determine the best approach using factors that Evan didn't understand yet. "It's easier if I show you." He pushed back his sleeves to expose the bracelets.

Rex eyed them. "Not a health treatment?"

"Not even close."

The other man shook his head. "I figured as much."

Everyone moved away, clearing the path for Evan. He emptied his mind and concentrated on the metal hatch. He envisioned the massive door standing open and then pictured the team walking through the opening.

Both bracelets on his wrists started to glow. The blue light on the left control device intensified, and the right bracelet disintegrated into golden particles, forming streamers through the air. The golden sparkles glided to the door, where most passed through its seams, but a small portion settled on the control pad.

Images flashed through his mind, too rapidly for him to process. Instinct told him they were scenarios for how the door could be opened, some of which the tech immediately dismissed. The images eventually settled on a clear visualization of the locking bolts being cleanly severed while the hinges and main hatch structure remained intact. Evan gave his approval in his mind.

A flash of golden light illuminated along the locking edge of the hatch, and then the particles flowed back to Evan and reformed into a bracelet on his right wrist.

Zaris gaped at him. "How did you…?"

"Another piece of alien tech we picked up on Aethos," he said, not wanting to give away anything about Temple World.

"That's incredible," she breathed.

Rex tugged on the door's handle. It popped open. He only cracked it enough to look inside, using the door to shield his body. "I don't see anyone, but that doesn't mean anything."

"I'd be hiding in ambush if I were them," Evan told Zaris.

She nodded. "I don't suppose that fancy thing of yours lets you see through walls."

"Actually, I haven't tried."

"No time like the present." Zaris motioned him forward.

The golden bracelet disintegrated again and streamed through the opening into the passageway beyond. Evan gave a mental instruction for the nanites to relay a visual of what was on the other side of the wall. He was initially encouraged to see a flash of images, but it soon became dizzyingly disjointed—like each particle was sending its own perspective. He winced, finding it too painful to look at. To compensate, he instructed all but one of the nanites to return to his wrist. Once they'd streamed back, a new image filled his mind. However, it was still severely distorted and quickly gave him a headache. He recalled the final particle.

"That might work eventually, but it's going to take practice. We'll have to recon the old-fashioned way," he reported.

Zaris nodded. "Well, it was worth a shot. You can stay on as our official safe-cracker."

"How thoughtful."

She eyed his wrists again with the look of a thief sizing up their mark before turning her attention back to the hatch. "Let's keep moving."

They sent a fist-sized scanner probe ahead of the group, which captured measurements of the interior space and checked for enemy targets. Laser grids swept around the corridor as it floated in front of them, with the team following five meters back.

Evan went through the opening after the corsairs. There was no need to prop the door open since the bolts had been severed, so they couldn't be locked inside.

On the other side, there was darkness beyond the light cast from the entry corridor, and the air was cooler. Rather than concrete walls, the surfaces were hewn stone. It reminded Evan of the entrance tunnel to the chamber where they'd discovered the *Asamar*.

Everyone in their group clicked on lights mounted to their shoulders and weapons, illuminating the space with exaggerated shadows as they shuffled deeper. The lights on the probe led the way through the darkness ahead. Warnings screamed in Evan's mind about being trapped in a narrow space with only one way out, but they had no other option.

He touched his fingertips to the wall. There was no immediate synaptic feedback through his gloves, but he did sense a gentle pull to travel deeper.

As he moved along the passage, he kept close watch on the surfaces for any signs of surveillance equipment the probe may have overlooked. Curiously, there didn't seem to be any. *What are we missing?*

Something reflective was covering the tunnel ahead. The corsairs at the front of the group slowed as the probe stopped.

"Four-way intersection," the lead announced. "Straight ahead is walled off."

Evan jostled to get a look. The reflection he'd caught was a pane of glass, or another translucent material, covering the passage. There were etchings along the walls, in the same distinctive style as Aethos and the other Korani planets they'd visited.

"We're in the right place," he told the others.

Zaris stood at the center of the intersection. "Which way?"

Evan willed the alien tech to tell him the best direction to go. The sensations were frustratingly vague, but heading left seemed like the correct path. He motioned that direction.

They set off that way. The passage continued for another thirty meters until the tunnel opened into a large chamber. Their lights were swallowed by the darkness, and even the probe's lasers were difficult to make out on the walls and towering ceiling.

A corsair at the front activated a light orb and tossed it forward. The device plunked onto the stone ground and rolled forward. It illuminated stacks and stacks of crates at the center of the cavern.

The visor on Evan's new armor wasn't up to the task of parsing the bright light from the intense darkness beyond, so he flipped it up to get a clearer look. With the reduction in glare, he realized that the rows extended even further back than he'd initially thought.

"There could be anything in there," Anya whispered to Evan. She'd also flipped up her visor, and her brows were pinched with concern.

"Or anyone hiding. Wait here while we clear the area."

Anya leaned against the wall near the passage mouth. "Roger that."

Evan continued forward with the others.

While some corsairs kept lookout, Evan walked through the rows of crates and picked one of the storage containers at random. There weren't any markings or warnings to indicate what might be inside. He shouldered his rifle and felt along the crate's lid for a latch. There was only a smooth depression, indicating a biometric lock.

Safe-cracking, huh? He sent a trickle of nanites into the latch. An interior mechanism clicked open. *Hey, look at that!*

Carefully, he raised the lid. The crate was filled with chunks of dark rock flecked with golden sparkles.

A mining operation? He resealed the crate and checked four others on different rows. All the same.

He looked back at the entry passage to beckon Anya over. There was only darkness where she'd been standing. "Anya?"

ANYA FOUGHT AGAINST hands pinning her arms to her sides. There was no way for her to overpower their firm grip. She tried to open her mouth to cry out, but a hand was stifling her. Another hand was gripping her face across her eyes, applying enough pressure to prevent her from turning her head. She realized then that it must be at least two men grappling her, not just one. Desperate, she tried to shout through the hand, but it only came out as a muffled, pathetic whimper.

Where are they taking me? Her mind raced for potential escape options. She was being dragged backward, away from Evan and the rest of the team. Her earpiece comm had been knocked out in the initial struggle, so she couldn't call for help that way even if she could speak. She attempted to kick and dig in her heels, but her boots couldn't get purchase on the smooth rock surfaces.

Her heart pounded in her ears, and it was difficult to breathe through the hand partially blocking her nose. Every attempt to wriggle free only sapped her strength, so she decided to stop struggling and wait for a better moment to act.

After what seemed like an eternity of being dragged blindly and half-suffocated, the movement stopped. The pressure of vise-like arms around her midsection was replaced with the more even pressure of a rope or other binding. When that was secure, the hands were removed from her face.

She sucked in a gasping breath and opened her eyes, wanting to take in as much information as possible. However, the room was blindingly bright after the darkness of the last few terrifying minutes. When her vision cleared, she focused on a woman with dark, chin-length hair standing in front of her, flanked by two large men—presumably those who'd grabbed her.

"Who are you?" the woman demanded.

Anya struggled to control her breathing. "Please, I don't want to fight you."

"You're dressed for a fight."

"For protection. I don't want to hurt anyone."

"Who are you, and who are you with?" the woman repeated.

In no scenario had Anya envisioned being captured. She had no cover story prepared and no clue what to do. *Should I be honest? Lie?* Her heart was pounding so hard she could barely hear or think. "I—"

Unbidden tears stung her eyes. *Stop crying! That's not helpful,* she chastised herself. But the fear was overwhelming. She was bound, unable to move, and everything she'd heard about the Noche Syndicate marked these people as merciless killers. They'd end her life the moment she didn't seem useful. Her only hope was to buy time until the others came looking for her. *They have to know I'm missing, right?*

Anya took a shaky breath and released it slowly, trying to expel her anxiety with it. "My name is Anya. I'm a scientist. I'm part of a team investigating alien technology, and we know there are ancient relics on this world." Truthful. Vague. Just enough information to prompt follow-up questions.

The woman raised her brows. "Not a lot of scientists walk around with body armor and rifles."

"You'd be surprised. Lots of things are out to kill you in the wilds. Gotta be prepared."

"You didn't accidentally wander out of a jungle into here. You blockaded the gate and attacked the station. You blasted open the front door. This isn't a scientific expedition."

Yes, keep her talking. Anya nodded, feigning confidence she didn't feel. "No, it's not. We know the Syndicate has been gathering alien tech. We have been, too. We knew we'd need to make a splash if there was any chance of you taking us seriously."

"For what?"

"To pool our resources and work together." The words spilled out before Anya had thought the statement through.

The woman laughed. "Work together? That's not what I expected."

"We like to be unpredictable."

"And you thought that breaking into our house would be a good way to ask to be friends?"

"It got your attention, didn't it?"

"Oh, it certainly did. And you and your whole lot moved to the top of my shit-list."

Anya kept her back straight and head high even though she wanted to go cower in the corner. "I'm here now, so let's talk. You want the gate back, we want access to the tech on this planet. I'm sure we can come to an understanding—"

"No, I have a better idea. Let's find out how much you mean to your friends."

— — —

Evan ran down the passageway, looking for any sign of where Anya may have gone. Too many people had passed over the stone ground for prints in the dust to mean anything. There was no blood, which was definitely a positive. But she wouldn't wander off without saying anything.

"Anya!" he called out into the chamber in case she was out of sight behind some crates. He checked on the comm, too, but no reply.

But he did hear a faint echo of his call. He checked the ground and found the earpiece near the doorway. *Oh, no…*

Zaris stepped out from a central row. "Is there a problem?"

"Anya is missing." Evan picked up the earpiece to show her, tension rising in his chest. "I just found this."

"Where did you last see her?" Zaris asked, walking toward him.

"Right here." His stomach churned. *We should have stuck together. I never should have asked her to hang back.*

"If she's not in here, she must have gone back down the hall. There are only so many routes." Zaris whistled and held up two fingers. Two of her corsairs jogged over.

"What's going on?" Tarek asked from between the crates.

"Anya's missing," Zaris replied.

"Better take a couple more. I'll go. You stay here." Tarek directed two additional men to join them and jogged over himself.

He realizes that someone might have taken her. Evan didn't want to acknowledge the possibility, but it was more likely than her taking out her comm and walking away of her own accord. It made no sense that they hadn't encountered anyone down here, so it tracked that the enemy had snatched someone for leverage. *I should have anticipated it.*

Kicking himself about the oversight wouldn't get Anya back to safety. Mistakes were a fact when planning something complex like this on such short notice. *Focus on solutions, not regrets.*

Forcing his guilt to the background, he led the charge down the passageway where they'd entered, visor down and prepared to fight. They'd only passed one intersection, so the first logical place to search was down the right arm at the four-way intersection.

The six of them jogged down the corridor two abreast with Evan and Tarek at the front. They kept their rifles up and at the ready to fire on any enemy; weapons were set to a strong stun setting, but that could quickly escalate.

When they reached the intersection, Evan checked through the glass wall to see if the area beyond had been disturbed. The glass remained in a fixed place with no door, so he moved on.

The right wing started out as a mirror to the left pathway. However, at the thirty-meter mark where the other tunnel had opened into the chamber, this one branched off into different corridors with sharp turns after a few meters.

"Is this some sort of labyrinth?" Tarek asked.

"I sure hope not." Evan cautiously went down the right branch far enough to peek around the corner. It bent again to the right another four meters ahead. *Shit, this really might be a maze.*

"Too many ambush points," one of the corsairs said.

"Yeah, too risky," Tarek agreed. "We can send in the probe to map—"

An electric shock struck Evan's back and radiated through his core. His knees softened and he dropped to a crouch. He pressed against the wall to steady himself and swiveled to see what had hit him.

Additional blasts came from the left passage leading into the maze as well as from back the way they'd just come in. Based on the angles, there were at least half a dozen shooters.

Evan shot back as the corridor erupted into chaos. Tarek and the team took up defensive positions with their backs to each other. The enemy shooters were well hidden, so retaliatory shots ended up hitting walls rather than human targets.

"Stop shooting!" a familiar voice called out.

"Anya?" Evan shouted back.

"Yeah, it's me. Stop!"

Evan halted firing but didn't lower his weapon. He caught Tarek's attention across the corridor, and he motioned the rest of the team to pause.

Sounds of multiple footfalls scuffed on stone as shadows and light moved from a side passage toward them.

Anya appeared first with her hands raised in submission. A woman followed a few paces back with a handgun trained on Anya.

Why wouldn't they just kill Anya? The Syndicate didn't take captives. Not unless—

Evan had to do a double-take when he saw the captor's face. "Marta Santano?"

"Did I speak to you on the ship earlier?" she asked, unable to recognize him through his faceplate.

"No, but I was there," Tarek said, also disguised. "We thought you'd left on the ship."

"I'd never abandon my post."

They didn't mention anything about speaking to Marta! Evan swore in his mind. Zaris had mentioned the ship that had departed from the surface, but not that there'd been any conversation—especially not with Marta. *What else didn't she tell me?*

It changed Evan's approach to know there was a member of the Santano family here. The Noche Syndicate kept many aspects of their senior leadership secretive, but he'd met Marta on half a dozen occasions over his years undercover. Had he known in advance that he might come face-to-face with her, he wouldn't have recommended an infiltration like this.

Marta was someone who wielded real power. If she could be won over, they might find out more about the alien technology without having to steal anything. However, while Marta wasn't known to be quite as ruthless as her older brother, Evan had been in the room when she had personally executed someone for insubordination. It was possible she'd do the same to him, but he'd rather make himself a target than have the heat on Anya.

He flipped up his visor. "Hi, Marta, it's been a minute."

The recognition took a second, but it clicked. She glowered at him, keeping the pistol pointed at Anya. "*You*! I thought it was you on surveillance earlier."

The venom in her tone cut through him, but he refused to flinch. "I didn't think you'd be out this far from Constella." He'd briefly raised his faceplate in the storage room, and she must have spotted him then. *But where were they watching from?*

"And *you're* supposed to be dead. Surprises all around."

"Sorry to have barged in. What is this place?" he asked.

"I'm not answering your questions," she spat.

Keep the conversation going. Get Anya out of here. Evan set down his weapon and raised his hands. "We don't need to be enemies, Marta."

"Oh, you made damned sure we would be when Alex

betrayed us. We trusted you."

"You're right, I lied. I played you."

She scoffed.

"Hey, I was only doing my job. On that note, is it true you've gotten cozy with Rostov?"

"You're awfully nosy for a dead man."

"Just saying that you should keep in mind it was people in Rostov's administration who *sent me* undercover. I don't know what he's promised you—a new business opportunity, or whatever—but he's bluffing. A control tactic to bring you in line. My undercover stint was a minor inconvenience compared to whatever he's planning to do after he no longer has a use for you."

"Talk, talk, talk. That's all you do!" Marta finally shifted her aim from Anya to Evan. "I should have seen it then."

Yes, focus on me. I deserve your wrath, not Anya. Evan stood his ground, continuing to taunt Marta to draw her attention. "I've seen things. I know how the Commonwealth operates. So, I know that the UPA wouldn't have sent me into deep cover without a good reason. And now, I'm convinced that I was sent to gather information that the UPA could use to win you over. But not to collaborate. No—so they could cripple your organization by knowing how it works from the inside. You may have thought you were wheeling and dealing with Alven Shah, but he was only manipulating you. Way more than I ever did! Platitudes. False promises—"

"Enough!" Marta's face reddened. "How can I believe a word *you* say? You lied to us every day for three years!"

"Us too," Tarek muttered.

Not helpful. Evan flashed a glare in his direction. "I had to do a lot of things I wasn't proud of. I'll admit I don't agree with the Syndicate's approach, but business is business."

"More lies. You hate us and everything we stand for."

Evan stepped forward to make himself an even more enticing target. "I misjudged all of you," Evan continued. "I'd convinced myself that you were in the wrong about everything, but I realize now that there's corruption everywhere. You are the response to the injustices in government and private industry. What you've discovered here and incorporated into your operations… No wonder the Commonwealth's leadership has taken an interest. You're on the cusp of a revolution. But they don't want you to join them—they want to take your power for themselves."

While he was talking, Anya had taken the opportunity to start slowly shifting away from Marta. She hadn't been able to move too far without drawing attention to herself, but she was now in a better position to dive for cover.

Marta remained intently focused on Evan, just how he wanted. Her desire for an explanation about his betrayal was unexpected, but it worked to his advantage. He'd expected a headshot the moment she had the chance. But there was a weakness in those with massive egos—they considered themselves the center of the universe, and they couldn't fathom how anyone could break from their orbit.

Perhaps she also saw some truth in his words, doubts about Rostov and Shah and their arrangement. If he could just push her a little more—

"I don't believe you."

Too late. The spell was broken.

Marta fired.

The kinetic blast struck Evan squarely in his chest. His armor took the brunt of it, but he allowed it to knock him backward—mostly so it took his exposed face out of her sightline. He flipped down his visor and rolled to the side as weapons fire broke out on both sides.

He looked for Anya. She'd ducked down behind one of Tarek's corsairs. There was no clear path for him to get to her, and their exit was blocked by Marta's team. Conventional weapons weren't going to get them out of this.

Help us. Evan pictured the enemy combatants disabled. The bracelets on his wrists warmed, and the particles streamed out from his right wrist to form a swirling, golden cloud. But unlike the previous times he'd deployed them, they started to multiply.

The golden light intensified as the particles segmented into several different tendrils. They lashed out at the enemy combatants, driving barbs into them one at a time. The fighters dropped to the ground; it was unclear if they were unconscious or dead.

But when the nanite swarm reached Marta, the tendril scattered and flowed around her outline, as though she was wearing a personal shield. She watched the alien tech move with a mixture of awe and confusion before fixing her gaze back on Evan.

Marta was now greatly outnumbered with her team disabled. Yet, she didn't retreat.

"Ready to talk?" Evan asked.

"How did you do that?"

"I'm not answering your questions," he turned her own words back on her. "At least not until you answer a few of my own."

She looked calmly around at the weapons leveled on her. "You must be wondering why we didn't put up a fight when you entered this place."

"That did seem strange."

"When you're in a place of power, there's no need to

pretend that our fragile human forms can compare to that greatness. It was hubris that brought you here, and that will be your undoing."

Evan hadn't known Marta to be one for metaphor, so he tried to take her words in the most literal sense. *Is there some other kind of hidden weapon here?*

The ground began to tremble, sending dust cascading down the stone walls. And somehow the space seemed... brighter.

"Marta, what did you do?"

— — —

Zaris glanced again toward the entry passageway. *Tarek should have been back by now. Did they run into trouble?* She'd tried his comm, but there was no connection. Rock was a nightmare. All the more reason to stay in outer space.

She and the remaining members of her team had checked the perimeter of the chamber and there were no other access points, so Anya *must* have gone back into the outer corridor. Zaris considered going to check on the situation, but they hadn't found anything useful yet. Assuming the op was on a sideways trajectory, she wanted to take every possible moment to gather intelligence before they had to evac.

Maybe that was selfish. Her team's wellbeing should be her top priority, but everyone had accepted the risks coming here. She was most concerned about getting herself to safety, and that might rely on procuring something of value to use as a bartering token for her freedom. Or, better yet, discovering the secret to the Syndicate's power so she could seize it for herself.

But a room full of rocks... that wasn't a very promising start. *Clearly, we should have gone to the right.*

The chamber didn't make sense, though. There was a *lot* of material stored here, and the outer passageway didn't have any signs of wear from crates being moved in and out. The rocks had to have come from somewhere. And why hold them here?

"We must have missed something," she announced. "Let's check again for a hidden doorway or something."

She was on her way toward the back wall when the ground started to tremble. The crates vibrated, their plastic and metal shells clattering against the stone floor. It intensified into a thunderous roar,

"What's happening?" Damon, one of her crew, shouted over the racket.

"I don't—"

A lid exploded off one of the crates. Then another. Others started to pop off like gunshots around the cavern.

Zaris ran down the aisle toward the exit. One of the crates shot off next to her, and the lid struck her right side at the bottom edge of her armor's breastplate. Pain radiated from under her ribs to her right shoulder, and she fell sideways, knocking into a crate on the other side.

She landed flat on her back. Looking upward, her heart skipped a beat as fissures in the ceiling opened up. No, they weren't cracks—huge vent hole covers were retracting.

That's how they get everything in and out! she realized.

However, the holes weren't open to daylight. There was only blackness above. And there was also a strange tone that seemed to be coming from up there.

What the hell is this place?

Clutching her injured side, she hoisted herself to her feet using one of the tipped-over crates. Only then did she notice that the rocks were now glowing.

"Hey, look!" She grabbed a chunk closest to her and held it

up for the rest of her team to see.

They seemed more concerned with the environment coming apart around them than her discovery. She unfolded a duffle bag she'd brought for loot transport and started loading it up with rocks; clearly, they were important, even if the *how* didn't make sense to her right now.

She swore under her breath as each bend over sent radiating pain through her side, but adrenaline kept her moving. *I didn't come all this way for a bag of freaking rocks, but I'm not leaving empty-handed!*

By the time the bag was half-full, it was too heavy for her to lift with her injury. Fortunately, Damon came over to help.

Zaris handed him the duffle. "Everybody out!"

32

THE GROUND LURCHED under Evan's feet. The corridor had definitely gotten brighter, and the walls themselves were glowing.

Standing a few meters down the corridor, Marta appeared completely calm. "I always thought I'd be the one to activate it."

Did I do this? Evan gave a mental command for the nanites to return to his wrist bracelet. Enough returned to re-form the device, but there were still more circulating in the air. *Did they replicate, or did more come from somewhere?*

As amazing and powerful as the technology was, he knew next to nothing about it. He shouldn't be wielding it so freely. Concern about what he'd inadvertently done, and what else he might do, froze him in indecision.

Marta. I need to stop Marta. He snapped back to focus. Since he'd set his rifle down, there was no way to grab it quickly. Instead, he reached for his handgun.

Marta noticed his movement and lined up a shot toward Anya. Tarek was ready. He fired at Marta's hand. She cried out in pain and dropped the weapon.

Evan dove backward while Anya ran to Evan and Tarek,

then she slipped around a corner behind them.

Marta gripped her wrist in an attempt to stem the bleeding. "You can't stop it now."

"Can't stop what? What's happening?" Evan shouted over the shaking and grinding rock.

"The Source."

As if I know what the hell that means! Evan was about to press her further, but a section of the rock wall near the entrance gave way. It crashed down, sending up a cloud of dust. Evan coughed and squinted his eyes against it. When the air had cleared enough for him to see again, Marta was gone.

"Damn it!" Evan looked for where she might have gone.

The entrance was now blocked, and there was a massive rubble pile in front of the left branch of the maybe-maze—too large and unstable to climb over quickly. Most likely, she'd gone into the labyrinth, and she probably knew her way around. The only option was to take the right branch. With any luck, they could catch Marta on the other side. But more importantly, hopefully there was another way out.

"We have to go deeper in," Evan told Tarek, retrieving his rifle from where he'd dropped it.

"That way is the exit." The other man nodded toward the blocked door. "Can you use your fancy thing to dig it out?" Tarek asked.

"After what happened last time?" They still had no way of knowing what, exactly, had initiated the quaking. Marta could have activated a failsafe, or it could have been Evan's use of the nanites. Doing the wrong thing now could make it even worse.

"I'll figure it out." Tarek held up a blast charge.

"If you want to risk bringing the roof down, be my guest." Evan ran to the right where Anya had gone.

"Are you okay?" she asked as soon as he rounded the corner.

"Yeah, I'm fine. You?"

"Yes. But why didn't they kill me? Or all of us?"

"Nothing about this makes sense." He motioned for her to follow him into the strange stone maze.

They wove their way through the corridors. There were lots of dead ends, but most of them were visible from the main route. After going through several switchbacks, an orderly form started to take shape in Evan's mind.

"I don't think this is a maze. It's a pattern, like a 3D version of all those etches we've seen on the walls."

"Those designs had the weird energy flowing through them when they were activated. Could this serve the same purpose?"

Evan frowned. "If it does, we definitely don't want to be inside here when it activates."

They picked up their pace.

When they were deeper into the rock formation, a muted *boom* suddenly rang out in the distance.

"Blasting their way out?" Anya guessed.

"I hope it works for them." There were no further sounds of crashing, so that was a hopeful sign.

Everything still shook, but it wasn't as intense as when it'd first started—or maybe he was just getting used to it. But the glow in the walls had continued to intensify.

"Any theories on what might be lighting up?" Evan asked Anya while they jogged through the switch-backing corridors.

She shrugged. "Lots of biological or chemical reactions can create a glowing effect. Do you… feel anything?"

Evan's alien tech sense had been in overdrive since entering the facility, so he hadn't been able to get a clear reading specifically on the walls. However, when he really concentrated on it, he noticed that there was directionality to their energy hum. Subconsciously, he'd been following the path. "We're going the right way."

Several sets of footfalls sounded behind them.

Evan grabbed Anya's hand and pulled her with him around the nearest corner. He checked over his shoulder and was relieved to see it was Tarek and the four other corsairs.

"Oh, decided to come with us, I see," Evan said while stepping back into view.

Tarek sighed. "Not my idea. I got within comm range of Zaris, and she told me to not let you run off."

"Sorry about your luck."

"Please tell me we didn't just follow you into a literal dead end."

"Still to be determined." Evan motioned them forward.

The turns were getting tighter, which suggested they might be getting close to the destination. With all the twists and turns, it was difficult to tell how far they'd come, but it had to be half a kilometer or more. The stone walls were now casting enough light to match the standard illumination of a starship corridor.

With the extra light, Evan noticed that the stone's texture had become more ornate. The surfaces now resembled the intricate lines found around the ancient doorways on Aethos.

They continued forward until the maze-like walls opened into a chamber. At the center of the chamber was a metallic structure, which reminded Evan of the equipment they'd found on Temple World. Yet, there was no sign of a nanite vat like they'd discovered on that planet, though the rock underneath it did resemble the samples that had been in the crates. There was no obvious connection between the structure and surrounding walls.

"I don't get it," Anya said. "What could this possibly be?"

Tarek frowned. “At this point, I don’t care. Where’s our exit?”

The bracelets warmed Evan’s wrists, emitting a soft pulse. They were directing him to the device. *The last time I did anything, the whole mountain started to fall apart. Will this make that stop, or bury us alive?*

Beckoning whispers filled in his mind until he could resist the call no further. He stepped forward and touched the device.

The control bracelet ignited bright blue, and a stream of nanites flowed into the ornate metal pipes sticking out of the ground. White lights illuminated in the channels, which pulsed and flowed like little glowing ants marching over a log.

As the lights spread out, the device unfurled. The group had to step back as the metal components shifted and expanded.

“What the hell did you do now?!” Tarek exclaimed.

Evan’s mind’s eye was blank. The control bracelet wasn’t communicating anything to him about what the device would do when its transformation was complete, only that this was positive and necessary.

When the components stopped rearranging, a pulse rippled through the air, sending up a little shockwave of dust and making Evan’s fine hairs stand on end. After it passed, the trembling in the ground stopped. But then a new energy charge started building. The air felt heavy, and Evan’s skin tingled with its mounting force.

“Oh, hell no, I’m out.” Tarek looked around the chamber for anywhere to go. He spotted a dark passageway at the back and made a run for it; the four other corsairs followed him.

“He’s right, Evan,” Anya said. “We should get out while we can.”

Something deep within him told Evan that what was

happening here wasn't to be feared, but he could see the terror in Anya's eyes. He remained by the device, conflicted. "We came this far. I want to find out what it does."

"We can find out from a safe distance. I don't want to lose you here." She grabbed his forearm.

He yielded to her pleas and followed her into the passageway. Their shoulder-mounted lights danced around the stone corridor as they ran to catch up with Tarek and the others.

The tunnel angled upward and arced toward the left. Though he'd gotten a little turned around in the maze, Evan was pretty sure they were heading back toward the storage chamber, but on a higher level. That would place them somewhere inside the valley's hillside.

They met up with Tarek where the tunnel abruptly opened into a chamber. It was filled with golden light. The entire right wall was open to an even larger space, reaching three stories above and dozens of meters below, with ramps and paths connecting to tunnels as far back as he could see.

Tarek and the others were staring into the enormous expanse. "What is this?" he breathed.

Scaffolding extended as deep as Evan could see. The walls were made of the same dark rocks from the crates. It didn't take much deduction to determine that they'd been mining the material from this location. About two stories down, Evan spotted an opening to a side passageway, which he suspected aligned with the glassed-off corridor near the entrance.

"Why are they so fascinated with these rocks?" Tarek muttered. He motioned his men onward, and they continued along the original path.

Evan was about to follow when a swarm of golden light rose from the depths of the larger cavern, moving with incredible speed. Before he could dodge out of the way, they dove straight into his face.

He stumbled backward, swatting. But they were already inside him.

"What the?!" Anya stared at him with her mouth agape.

Nothing hurt. He didn't feel different in any way. Had his eyes been closed, he'd barely have realized anything had happened—maybe just a little warm tingle in his fingers and toes.

"Are you…?" Anya asked tentatively.

"I'm not hurt," he replied, though it was more of a reflexive statement than a certainty. "Come on." He jogged toward the tunnel where Tarek had gone, not wanting to stick around for any additional weird alien stuff to happen.

As they ran, Anya kept glancing over at him as if waiting for him to transform into a monster.

While Evan felt no ill-effects, he couldn't pretend like nothing had happened. But escaping this place before the weapon—or whatever it was—went off was the priority. *If* they could find a way out.

— — —

Every breath burned as Zaris ran down the stone corridor with Damon. They'd just passed the vault-like door and were on the final stretch to outside. She needed to make sure the members of her team with her got to safety. Tarek would tend to Evan and Anya.

The lights in the corridor were out, and it seemed like all power in the facility had been cut. She still had no clue what had caused everything to fall apart.

I should have gone in with only my team. Evan and Anya

have been nothing but trouble. Granted, she might not have made it through the armored door without Evan, but that wasn't the point. Her life had started to unravel—much as this confounded building—since he'd come back into her life. *If this place doesn't kill him, I might have to finish the job.*

At last, she spotted daylight ahead. Her knees threatened to buckle from pushing her injured body so hard, but she refused to give up.

They emerged from the concrete structure and were immediately blasted by intense heat. The temperature in the underground depths had been even cooler than ship's standard, so it was an even bigger contrast than their arrival to the planet.

Curse everything about this place! It can all burn! Grimacing, she jogged the final stretch to the waiting shuttle.

She limped up the ramp and collapsed against the side wall.

"Are you okay, ma'am?" Damon asked.

"I'll be fine. Make sure the pilot is ready to get us out of here on my order." She hugged her arm to her injured side and watched the exit.

Tarek, where are you? She tried the comm again, but there was still no connection. "Has there been any word from Tarek or the men with him?" she asked Damon.

"No."

Zaris looked around at the two dozen members of her team crammed on the shuttle. Their lives were in her hands now. "Get us out of here. We'll come back for the others when we can make contact."

— — —

Evan followed the next section of tunnel to a chamber with

several holes in the floor. However, each of those holes opened to the crate storage room. Various pieces of human-made lift systems were placed around the perimeter, giving shape to the Syndicate's mining operation.

Tarek crossed the room to a console. "Door controls!" he announced. He pressed a button. Nothing happened, prompting a string of creative expletives.

"No indicator lights. I think the power is out," Evan said. *The alien tech has another power source… but what?*

One of the corsairs signaled to a metal panel on the side wall. Another man brought over a pair of pry bars from the equipment stores, and the two of them set about getting the hatch open.

They popped it free, revealing a horizontal shaft leading to daylight. It was large enough for them to fit through, sized well for the crates.

Tarek crouched and disappeared inside. He called to them, "It's a way out, but it opens in the middle of the cliff—at least a ten-meter drop."

Evan frowned. "Well, that's a problem."

Tarek returned from the shaft. "There's a bigger problem. The shuttle is gone."

33

"THEY LEFT WITHOUT us?" Evan rushed to the shaft to check for himself. He hunched over and went through the dusty tunnel toward daylight. The air was hot and dry, and a light breeze ruffled his hair.

The shaft ended at a hinged grate. Holes in the grid were large enough to see through, and he pressed his face to the metal. Sure enough, looking down, he had a clear view of the landing site where they'd arrived. The ground was disturbed from where the craft had taken off.

Well, shit. Not only was there the problem of needing an alternate ride, but there was also the troubling detail of how they could get down the cliff.

Evan scrambled back inside. "I don't suppose anyone brought climbing rope?"

Tarek shook his head. "But there might be some cabling in here we could fashion."

"We might not need a way *down*," Anya said. "Sam's piloting is super precise, right?"

Evan brightened. "You're brilliant. That solves both our problems."

"Your AI?" Tarek asked.

"Yes. He could remotely pilot our shuttle here and line up the side hatch with this shaft. We could hop right over."

The other guys shifted uncomfortably, but Tarek nodded. "I'll take any evac I can get."

Evan tried his comm but found the signal was still blocked. He went to the end of the shaft again and was finally able to connect.

"Sam, can you hear me?"

"Yes, I read you, Evan," the AI replied.

His heart lifted. "Good, finally! We've been having a rough go of things down here."

"I have been monitoring concerning energy readings."

"Yeah, well, we're trapped in the middle of that mess. We need an extraction. Can you send the shuttle?"

"Certainly. I have a bearing on your location, but it appears you are inside a mountain."

"About that…" Evan explained the concept for the rescue, and Sam confirmed that such a pickup would be possible.

Tarek relayed the plan to the *Invictus* to allow the shuttle to take off.

While they waited anxiously for the shuttle to arrive, they got the shaft's protective grill open so they'd have a clear path for their escape.

At last, Evan heard the welcome rumble of the craft's approach. The streamlined vessel swooped into the canyon and lined up its side with the shaft's outlet.

"I can't get closer," Sam said over the comm. "You have to jump."

"I'll go first," Evan volunteered. The jump was a little over a meter—amazingly close for such a large craft to be hovering stationary, but still a nauseating distance for leaping over a gap at that height.

"I was going to insist," Tarek said.

Evan lined up the jump and made the leap into the shuttle's open hatch. He landed hard on the decking and grabbed at the edge of a storage locker to make sure he didn't slide back out. He pulled himself to his feet.

"Not bad!" he shouted back to the others.

"Anya, you—"

"No, I don't want you two taking off without us." Tarek jostled to the front of the group and leaped.

Evan grabbed his arm as he landed and pulled him deeper inside the craft. "I wouldn't leave you."

The other man only scoffed and shook his head.

I can't blame him. I need to regain trust. Hopefully, the rescue would help begin rebuilding goodwill—though, it had been Evan's suggestions that had gotten them into this mess in the first place. He may yet see the inside of one of Zaris' airlocks.

Anya hopped over next, followed by the four corsairs. When the last had jumped aboard, Evan sealed the hatch.

"Sam, get us out of here!"

The shuttle pulled away from the cliff and started to rise. Evan went to the flight deck, granting a better view of the canyon. His breath caught when he saw fissures had opened up across the valley floor, and a new domed form was now exposed at the base of the cliff beneath where they'd just been.

"Something really weird is going on down there," Evan said.

"What *hasn't* been weird?" Anya started to quip, but then she saw what he was talking about. "Well, that explains all the shaking."

"What the…?" Tarek gaped at it as he joined them on the flight deck.

"The energy charge is still building," Sam cautioned. "It

seems to be reacting with my systems. I'm having difficulty pulling away—"

The shuttle dropped.

— — —

Zaris watched in horror on the main display of the *Invictus*' flight deck as the entire valley housing the Syndicate base was enveloped by a bright glow—too brilliant for the visual processors to render. "Is it still there? What happened?"

"Readings are jumping all over the place," Callie reported. "I can't see anything."

"Any other ships?"

"I'm sorry, ma'am, I don't know."

Zaris balled her hands into fists and punched the padded armrests on her chair. The reverberation sent new pain radiating down her injured side. "What *can* you tell me?" She clutched her arm to her side, trying not to wince.

"There's intense interference. Readings are all over the place. There's also some kind of EM burst."

Zaris pressed her hand to her side. She'd run from the hangar up to the flight deck, and she hadn't been fully able to catch her breath since. It was difficult to focus her vision.

"Wait, scan data is clearing up a little," Callie said from the front station. "In fact, it's suddenly a *lot* clearer."

"Could something down there have been acting like a jammer?" Zaris asked.

"Seems like it." Callie brightened. "I have contact! The shuttle from the *Asamar*."

"Call them up!" Zaris ordered.

"Working on it. One sec."

A welcome voice boomed over the flight deck's speakers.

"That's the last time I listen to one of your crazy orders," Tarek said.

Relief flooded through Zaris at the sound of his voice. In retrospect, she did regret telling him to go back in after Evan. Though they'd made it out, it could easily have gone the other way. "What happened down there?"

"We were hoping you could tell us," Evan chimed in to the conversation.

Zaris scoffed. "I was happily working on my rock collection when the world fell apart."

"We're not sure what brought that on," Evan said.

"Well, you activated another nanite swarm, so…" Tarek faded out.

"That might not have been what triggered this," Anya countered.

They continued to talk over each other, bickering, but Zaris couldn't track the words. Darkness started to close in at the edges of her vision. "Just get back here."

Her limbs suddenly felt extremely heavy.

"Ma'am…?" Callie asked, sounding distant.

Zaris' world turned sideways.

— — —

The comm went quiet. Anya stopped arguing with the others about the alien nanites and listened for a response.

"Zaris?" Tarek prompted from his seat behind Anya.

"Hey, it's Callie," a different voice came over the comm. "She just collapsed."

Tarek nearly jumped out of his seat. "What?!"

"Looks like she was hurt. They're taking her down to the infirmary," Callie explained.

"Do you have a medic on board?" Anya asked. While jumping in to help wouldn't be her first choice, she would if there was no one else.

"Yeah, our medical suite is set up pretty well," Callie said, to Anya's relief.

"I'll be there soon," Tarek said. "Hold position until I get there."

He slumped back in his seat, looking even more dour than normal.

"We can fabricate pretty much anything you can imagine on our ship, so let us know if you need anything to help her," Evan offered.

"Yes, I would be happy to assist," Sam chimed in.

"Just get us back to the *Invictus*!" Tarek snarled.

The interference that had been messing with the shuttle's controls had dissipated after a massive energy pulse. For a minute, Anya had thought they were going to crash back in the canyon, bringing back the awful memories of the terrifying fall to Aethos in her evacuation pod. Fortunately, Sam had been able to pilot them to safety.

However, the canyon was now unrecognizable. The building had collapsed into the fissures, and the new structures—seemingly of alien design—were now plainly visible on the surface. It was unclear what had become of Marta or the other people inside, but it wasn't looking good for them.

Anya's anxiety eased a little once the shuttle was back in space. *I never would have thought I'd be happier back in the void.* But she was eager to leave this planet behind.

They landed the shuttle in the *Invictus*' hangar and started to debark.

The four corsairs left first, followed by Tarek. As soon as they'd stepped through the open hatchway, the five men drew their weapons on Evan and Anya.

"What are you doing?" Evan asked.

They simultaneously fired pulse blasts at Evan. The combined power overwhelmed his armor's defenses, and he collapsed, unconscious.

"The hell?!" Anya exclaimed.

Tarek yanked Evan out of the shuttle, and he tumbled onto the hangar deck. "Couldn't have him using that alien stuff on us."

"Sam, a little help!" Anya pleaded as she drew her own pistol.

"I apologize, Anya, but there is no offensive action I can take in this enclosed space without risking harm to you or Evan."

I've already been held hostage once today. Not again! Anya's hands shook as she held her handgun against five targets. She considered making a run for it, but there was nowhere to go. With Evan outside the shuttle, even if she tried to take off, it would mean leaving him behind. *I can't do that.*

"If you cooperate, I won't have to knock you out, too," Tarek said, waggling his pulse handgun.

Staying conscious was the only way to maintain any semblance of control. She nodded her understanding and lowered her weapon.

"Thank you. Now, how does Evan get those bracelets off?"

34

"I'M FINE," ZARIS insisted, wincing as she tried to sit up.

"No, you're not." Dedra, the *Invictus*' medic, replied, gently pressing Zaris' shoulders back to the exam bed. "You're in shock. You have two cracked ribs, and your liver's bleeding into your abdomen. That's not an injury you can simply walk off."

"But I had armor—"

"And without it, we wouldn't be having this conversation. Do you want me to patch you up or not?"

Zaris couldn't deny the dark purple bruise blooming across the right side of her abdomen, accompanied by a deep red line where the crate's lid had struck. Her skin was clammy, and she felt like she was floating a little. She lay on the exam bed and allowed the medic to work on her.

After several injections of med nanites, a painkiller, and other unnamed meds that helped clear her brain fog, Zaris was starting to feel like herself again by half an hour later.

"You have to take it easy for a couple of days," Dedra told her. "The med nanites can only do so much. You need to allow your body to finish healing naturally."

"Yeah, I've got it." Zaris painfully pulled her shirt back

over her head, swearing with every flex of her right side. She swung her legs over the bedside, making her head swim again.

"Take it *slow*," Dedra reiterated. She sighed, already resigned to the knowledge that Zaris had little intention of listening.

As much as Zaris wanted to push herself, her body was letting her know its limitations. She was about to attempt standing when the infirmary door slid open. Tarek entered.

"Shit, what are you doing up?" He rushed over to her bedside.

"She shouldn't be," Dedra muttered.

Zaris gripped Tarek's shoulder and used him to stand up. Stars danced across her vision for a few seconds, but her equilibrium eventually settled. "We have work to do. What's our status?"

"I have Evan and Anya in custody."

Zaris squinted at him. "You what? Why?"

"Because of their shuttle. We have it now. We know it can jump. This is our chance to figure out how," Tarek said.

Zaris shook her head, instantly regretting how the motion made her stomach lurch. "The ship is useless alone. We need the primer."

"And we'll get it. We just need to find the Syndicate's supply. They might have it right here on the station! There's practically a floating city we have yet to check out."

She released his shoulder and tried to stand on her own. While she swayed a little, she was able to remain on her feet under her own power. "Evan and Anya can help us with that."

"Why are you trusting him all of a sudden? He betrayed us."

She shook her head slowly, able to keep from getting dizzy this time. "*Alex* betrayed us. Everything that *Evan* has told us has been true. And he's got an inside line on something big. I don't want to burn that lead."

He eyed her skeptically. "Is that all it is?"

I like the guy, okay? She'd been playing the tough commander for so long that most people looked at her with a touch of fear—exactly how she'd wanted it. But it was nice to have someone outside her flight deck crew to look at her as more than just a scary boss. Beyond that, though, she'd just witnessed firsthand that Evan's warnings about the Syndicate were valid. She needed to look toward her people's future.

Zaris fixed Tarek with a stern gaze. "They're not captives. They agreed to work with us, and we'll honor the deal."

Tarek fumed beneath the surface, but he nodded. "I'll release them from holding."

"No, I'll do it myself." She took a couple tentative steps, and her legs held. "And bring me one of those rocks I brought back. I want to know why they're so damned important!"

— — —

Evan awakened to a headache and pain in his hands and wrists. Groggily, he reached for the sore spots on his hands. He bolted upright when he felt the bracelets were missing.

"Hey, take it easy," Anya soothed. She hopped down from a crate, wearing only the regular clothes she'd had on under her armor.

Evan oriented to discover he was on the deck of a cargo room, finding that his armor had also been removed. "Did Tarek… shoot me?"

"Just a stun blast, but you've been out for almost an hour. They wanted the nanite bracelets—couldn't cut them off, so they dislocated your thumbs. Gave you a med nanite boost, though, so you should be healed up soon."

"So generous." He flexed his hands; they were functional despite the soreness. "Let me guess, they want to take all the alien artifacts we have?"

"They muttered something about the shuttle's jump drive. I think they know better than to go after the *Asamar* because of Sam."

"He won't let them take the shuttle, either."

"Well, it's already on board the *Invictus*, and I think they're counting on Sam not attacking with the *Asamar* because we're here."

All the jump drive tech was, in fact, safely on the *Asamar*, but Evan played along with Anya's narrative in case anyone was listening in. He rubbed his temples with his forefingers. "I regret not running off to live in a happy, secluded cave when we had the chance."

"This isn't so bad."

He tilted his head and raised his eyebrows.

"Okay, it's not great," she yielded. "But we're alive. And together."

"I let you down on Pavia."

"No, I should have been paying better attention. I shouldn't have left my visor up. They shouldn't have been able to grab me like that."

"It's my fault for suggesting you stay behind."

"But you came for me."

"I always will." The pressure in his head had faded enough that he tried to stand.

She smiled softly and helped him to his feet. "I think I owe you another heroic trophy."

"Well, I'm getting sick of this hero's life of running for our lives and getting shot. I was worried I'd lost you today."

"We did come pretty close to dying horrible deaths with this one."

"Nah, not horrible," Evan replied with a wry smile. "It would have been quick."

"It can be quick *and* horrible."

"Something fast can only be so bad—"

Anya held up her hand. "This is ridiculous. We shouldn't be arguing about which manner of demise is worse."

Evan nodded. "You're right. We don't know how much time we have. I'd rather focus on what we have to *live* for." His eyes met hers.

— — —

She relaxed as she gazed back at him, reassured by his calm, confident presence. She was worried about what was coming, but there was no one else she'd rather face it with.

It's crazy. We've known each other for so short a time. The logical part of her brain told her that it was too soon to feel so sure about someone, yet their experiences together defied all normal circumstances. In less than two weeks, they'd faced more trials than most couples would encounter in years. Those extreme circumstances could test the durability of bonds better than a decade of humdrum life.

"Evan, I—"

His lips met hers before she could finish. She eagerly kissed him back, giving into the desire that had been building between them since their first days together on Aethos. Despite the less than romantic setting, a happy tingle spread through her as they pulled each other close. One of his hands slid down her lower back, pressing her to him—

The door hissed open. Evan abruptly backed away, leaving

Anya in breathless confusion for a moment.

"Sorry, am I interrupting?" Zaris asked. She raised an eyebrow, her gaze lingering on Anya a moment too long.

"What the hell, Zaris! Why do you have us locked up here?" Evan demanded.

Zaris smirked. "You know, you seem busy. It can wait."

Anya and Evan glared at her.

She sighed. "Sorry, the hostage thing was all Tarek. You're free to go. But first, I'd like you to check out a little souvenir I picked up on Pavia." Zaris handed a rock to Anya.

"Yeah, the mysterious rocks, we saw. You do know I'm a xenobiologist, not a geologist, right?"

"Will you please just take a look?" Zaris then handed her a magnifier eyepiece.

Exasperated, Anya looked through the device at the rock. As it came into focus, she was surprised to see movement. There were tiny microbes in the dark stone, and they were glowing slightly. "Hmm." She handed it to Evan for him to see.

"You got this from the crates?" Evan asked.

Zaris nodded. "Yep."

It suddenly clicked in Anya's head, but she didn't want to disclose everything in front of Zaris. "It's weird. I'll look into it. Could I keep this sample for now?"

"Sure, I've got more. But I want it back." Zaris took a backward step toward the door, pointing at the rock.

"You've got it."

"Well, I'll have someone escort you back to your shuttle." With a knowing upturn at the corner of her mouth, Zaris turned to go. "Wouldn't want to keep you from more important—"

The ship abruptly lurched, as though struck by an external force.

"What now?!" Zaris exclaimed, taking a stumbling step to brace herself against the wall.

Evan held out his arm to help steady Anya. "I thought we'd destroyed all the weapons?" he asked.

Zaris glowered. "Me too." As soon as the shaking subsided, she hurried out the door.

Anya jogged after her, grabbing Evan's hand to pull him along. Whatever had happened, she wanted to see it firsthand and be part of the decision about what to do next. She didn't trust Zaris to serve her dinner, let alone direct a battle strategy.

Don't get ahead of yourself. This might not be an attack. She took a centering breath, but one glance at Evan revealed a stoic expression. She knew him well enough to recognize that the flat, expressionless façade hid interior panic.

The ship rocked again, harder this time.

The three of them slammed against the wall as the ship's stabilizers struggled to compensate for the violent force. It certainly *felt* like an attack. But by whom?

"It's always something," Zaris muttered as she pushed off the wall and continued down the corridor.

— — —

When Evan entered the flight deck after Zaris, Tarek bristled at the sight of him and Anya.

"Status report," Zaris demanded.

"A ship fired on us," the helm officer replied.

"Where the hell did it come from?"

"The surface. It was hidden in an underground hangar."

"Marta." Evan glowered.

Zaris looked at him questioningly. "The Mega-Bitch-in-Charge? I thought she left earlier."

"No, we saw her inside," Tarek confirmed. "We lost her in the chaos."

"Shoot her down," Evan said.

Zaris smiled. "It would be my pleasure."

"Sam should leave," Anya whispered to Evan.

She was absolutely right about that. Unfortunately, Tarek had taken their comms when he'd locked them up.

Evan formed a message in his mind, hoping he was close enough for Sam to pick up his telepathic command. *"Sam, if you can hear me, you need to get ready to jump. The people on that other ship will try to take you if they learn what you are."*

There was only silence for several seconds, but then a voice filled his mind. *"I hear you, Evan. I will be ready."*

A barrage of weapons fire bombarded Marta's ship, but the enemy vessel rolled to distribute the intensity around its shields.

"That's the kind of thing they teach in military flight school," Evan observed.

"And where do you think those instructors learned it?" Zaris shot back. "Keep at 'em!"

The ships continued exchanging weapons fire. On the screen, Evan noticed the golden latticework forming around the *Asamar* as it moved away from the firefight. *Good, Sam, get out of here.*

Another concussive blast rocked the *Invictus*. The lights flickered and then extinguished.

35

A SATISFYING SPRAY of sparks shot out from the enemy ship's aft propulsion. Its weapon systems went dormant.

"Direct hit!" Marta's helm officer, Grace, exclaimed. The young woman could certainly get into the spirit of a good fight.

Marta nodded with satisfaction; her crew knew their battlecraft. After the injury to her hand, starships would be her preferred form of battle until she'd healed. Fortunately, she had one of the best ships in the Syndicate's fleet. "Any signs of retaliatory fire?"

"None."

"What's going on with that other ship?" Marta asked, pointing to a craft with an odd golden aura around it. While the other vessels had oriented to engage, that one was moving away from the action.

Grace enhanced the visual on the front screen. The ship had unique sculptural forms and a hull texture Marta had never witnessed before. Add in the intriguing web encasing it, and the entire image was distinctly… alien.

"Try to disable its drive," Marta instructed.

They fired on the strange ship. The blast streaked through the golden latticework around it, striking the hull. There was no apparent damage to the ship."

"Stop it from leaving!"

They continued firing on the vessel, to no effect. Marta watched their missile inventory and energy reserves for the beam weapons rapidly diminish. There was still a bigger fight to win.

"Any effect?" she asked her crew.

"Our weapons have had no effect on the main vessel," Grace reported. "But... it looks like some of that lattice structure around the strange ship broke off."

"Visual?"

The forward screen displayed a small collection of golden particles that had clumped into a loose sphere, like a writhing swarm of insects.

"My, what have we here?" She recognized the design hallmarks of the alien tech she'd seen throughout her life, but she had never witnessed anything before that was so *active*. But her many treatments had primed her to interface with such an item.

Marta beckoned to the swarm, and it responded with a positive indication in her mind.

"Open the cargo hatch!" she instructed. "Bring it on board, but put up a containment field around it."

"What about the ship?" Grace asked.

"We won't win that firefight. This sample will tell us more."

A schematic on the front display showed the hatch was open, and a tractor beam directed the alien swarm inside. Marta's pulse quickened with anticipation, but she'd have to wait to inspect it closer.

The other ships near the spaceport were still dark from the EM pulse she'd fired, but they could be operational again at any moment.

"Take us to the gate," Marta ordered the helm.

"It's still blocked—too many ships for us to take on."

Marta shook her head. "I think they're bluffing."

Grace frowned. "That's a big gamble with our lives."

"I won't spend a month in transit to another gate. If they shoot us down, so be it."

"Yes, ma'am." The helm officer didn't seem as eager to press their luck, but she knew better than to argue.

Their ship sped away from Pavia toward the gate. None of the vessels near the spacedock gave chase, nor did the other—quite possibly alien—craft.

She hated flying away from that ship. It was possible it was the very vessel they'd attempted to acquire on Aethos, or perhaps another had been found elsewhere. But the strange particles around it would be a decent consolation prize for now. Analysis of that tech would likely yield valuable information about how to get through the ship's other defenses. She was in this fight for the larger war, even if it meant conceding this one battle.

As they raced toward the gate, they entered the window where they had good scan data but were not yet within effective weapons range. Marta kept a close eye on the readings.

She smiled. "Oh, I *knew* they were up to something!"

There were strong readings of twelve starships near the gate, but the remaining signals had a minute variance. From a distance, all of the pings had seemed identical. The closer they got, she realized that most of the fleet was just a mirage—a combination of frequency generators and holographic projectors.

Well played. Admittedly, they had fooled her.

Still, a dozen well-armed ships were too many for them to take on simultaneously. They'd need another approach to get through the gate.

"I want all available information on those drones. Could we get control?"

"Let me see what I can find out," the tech officer, Kurt, replied. He worked on his console for a minute. "There's a sophisticated firewall, but I think I could find an opening if I can see one of their command pings in action. Get them to redirect the drones, and I can attempt an intercept."

"All right, let's give them a reason to move. Send a couple of missiles their way."

The enemy ships fired countermeasures to intercept the missiles. But the drones needed to move out of the way to avoid being caught in the firefight. As they swerved to avoid impact, the holographic projects shuddered.

"I've got the command prompt. Working on it now…" Kurt said. He made rapid entries on his console. "Getting there… What do you want me to do with them?"

"Turn their drones against them. Set them on collision courses with the weapons and propulsion systems for those ships."

"Roger that." Kurt continued typing and swiping. "Okay… go!"

The holographic illusion dropped from the display screen, leaving points of white light where the image of full starships had been moments earlier. The scan data also updated to show drones in the place of ship transponders. The drones broke from their grid formation and sped toward the twelve real ships. Impacts lit up across the screen, with little explosions erupting around the vessels.

"Multiple impacts!" Grace announced. "Propulsion is… offline for all vessels. Weapons… inconclusive. Definitely damaged, but I'm not certain all were disabled."

"Activate the gate for Haylon," Marta said, targeting another out-of-the-way gate where there was certain to be no wait time for travel.

"Initiating gate startup," Grace confirmed.

The massive metal ring illuminated and started to spin. Light formed at the center of the circle, and then resolved into a blue, water-like shimmer.

Marta leaned forward in her seat. "Shields up. Take us in."

Five of the enemy ships fired on her as she approached. Grace spun the ship in a corkscrew to help glance the shots off the shields. The shield's power dropped with every blast.

Come on, we're almost there... Marta silently urged them forward.

The air hummed with electrical energy as they neared the gate. So close—

One of the enemy ships launched something from its cargo hold. The object slammed into the side of her ship. A shudder ran through the deck, knocking Marta sideways in her seat. She gripped the armrests to keep from falling.

"Breaches on starboard Decks 5 through 7," the environmental officer announced.

"Get them patched. Can we still get through the gate?"

"Emergency containment fields are holding for now, but there may be a disruption passing through the gate's EM field."

Marta swore. "Hold position until you can get a hard seal on the internal bulkheads. Evacuate those sections."

The crew relayed command through the comms and tense seconds ticked by. Alerts popped up on the forward scan that power was returning to some of the vessels.

"We have a hard seal," the environmental officer confirmed.

"Take us into the gate!"

They slipped through the ring, sending an electric tingle over Marta's skin. "If anyone is dumb enough to follow, shoot them."

36

"MAIN POWER IS out but backup environmental controls are holding," Callie announced from the helm.

The *Invictus*' flight deck was eerily dark with only faint starlight from the viewports, but Evan was grateful that they still had artificial gravity.

Zaris shifted in her command seat. "How long until we're back up?"

"Still assessing," Callie replied. "Propulsion and weapons are currently down."

"That's *twice* now you've mucked up my main drive," Zaris grumbled, glaring daggers at Evan.

He held up his hands in defense. "This time was definitely not my fault."

"Evan, would you like me to pursue the enemy vessel?" Sam asked in Evan's mind.

"No, stay far away. She's dangerous."

"My jump drive was damaged. I can't jump away right now."

Evan's heart dropped. *"Can you fix it?"*

"Yes, but it will take time."

Evan didn't want to relay the bad news to Anya with so

many other ears around, so he kept it to himself. “What about Marta’s ship?” he asked.

The helm officer looked over her shoulder at Zaris, and Zaris glanced at the console next to her command seat. “We lost contact. We’ll figure out where she went.”

The crew were busy on the comms coordinating repair activities and updating on timelines. From the snippets of conversations Evan overheard, it sounded like they were looking at a few hours, at a minimum, for the ship to be operational again. He’d rather not spend that time here.

“You said Anya and I are free to go?” he asked Zaris.

She pulled her attention from other tasks. “If you leave, are you going to run?” she asked, looking at him squarely.

“That depends on if you’re genuine about wanting to work together. I don’t have a lot of friends in the Commonwealth right now.”

Zaris evaluated him. “You were right about the Syndicate having alien tech. Were you being honest about the other things you told me—about who’s on Aethos?”

Evan nodded. “It’s all true.”

“Then I say we have overlapping interests—for now, at least.”

“So, my answer is that for now, I’m not running.”

She nodded. “Fair enough. I take it you’d like to go back to your ship?”

“Yes. But first, you have something of mine,” Evan said, holding up his forearms. “And our armor.”

Zaris nodded. “Tarek, get the man his jewelry and toys back.”

The gruff man scowled and sighed, but he motioned for Evan and Anya to follow.

They descended the lift to the hangar, where their gear was

resting on the top of crates near their docked shuttle.

"If you betray Zaris, I'll personally kill you," Tarek said, shoving Evan's bracelets into his chest.

Evan took the devices from him. "I'm not who you need to worry about."

Tarek sniffed and then stormed away.

"Well, someone's not happy," Anya said with an exaggerated grimace after Tarek was beyond earshot.

"I'd be skeptical of me, too. Trust is earned, and we started at a deficit."

"Forget about him. Let's go shower and eat. I feel gross after crawling around in the dirt."

They grabbed their gear and loaded into the shuttle, happy to be leaving the day's drama behind.

By the time they docked in the *Asamar*'s hangar, the tension had finally eased in Evan's chest enough that he could breathe freely again. However, he couldn't fully relax, knowing that Marta was still out there somewhere.

Evan sucked in a deep breath of cool, filtered air aboard the *Asamar* as he debarked from the shuttle.

"Welcome back," Sam greeted.

"How are your repairs going?"

Anya's eyes widened. "Repairs?"

"The enemy ship attacked me, and my jump drive assembly was damaged. Some of the latticework was scattered. As I said before, it's a fragile system. I had intended to recover the components, but I think the enemy ship may have collected them."

Evan's heart dropped. "You're saying that Marta's ship picked up part of the nanite jump drive assembly?"

"Yes."

"Sam! That's..." He couldn't think of the right word.

'Devastating' or 'catastrophic' didn't seem strong enough. "If I'd known, I would've handled that differently."

"The nanites alone will not enable interstellar travel," Sam assured him.

"But still. We *know* they've been experimenting with Korani tech for years. There were all kinds of things down in that facility."

"What did you find inside?" Sam asked.

While he and Anya walked to the upper living level of the ship, Evan described the strange tunnels and rock formations while Anya chimed in with details he'd missed.

When they'd finished, Sam was oddly silent for several moments. "Did the place look like this?" the AI finally asked.

A holographic map illuminated in the lounge room, where they'd settled. It was an eerily close layout to what they had just traversed.

"Yes. What is it?" Evan asked, exchanging an excited glance with Anya.

"A holy place to the Korani. There are planets that hold great sources of power. The Korani's technology is seeded on these worlds, for replication elsewhere. If this is one of those planets, then I will be able to get the materials I need to repair and upgrade my systems."

"A lot of it collapsed."

"No, the human construction on top of it collapsed. The original structure is much older and deeper."

"Do you know what caused it to activate?"

"I was unable to get clear readings from my location in orbit. Using your command bracelet in the way you described should not have been enough to reinitialize the dormant systems."

"What about that communication device in the hangar?" Anya asked.

"That *is* a possibility. Allow me to run an analysis."

While Sam combed through the available data, Evan couldn't shake the sinking feeling in the pit of his stomach. Sensing his distress, Anya sat next to him on the couch and took his hand.

"I have compared my interior and external scan data from the *Asamar* and the shuttle to multiple points in time from the last several days," Sam said over the comm. "There have been interesting changes to the various systems, but one of the greatest differences is in you, Evan. Were you exposed to anything during your mission to the surface?"

"Yeah… We hadn't quite gotten to the point in the story with the mine."

"There were these golden particle things that went inside Evan," Anya said.

"From this structure?" Sam brought up the schematic again and highlighted the chamber.

"Yes, that's the place," Evan confirmed.

"You were Touched, Evan. It is a great honor."

"What does it mean to be Touched?"

"To have been granted the power of the Source."

Anya sat up straighter. "Source… Marta used that term, too, right?"

"She did. I still don't understand what this means for me."

"Let me try to explain," Sam said. "To you humans, the Korani technology is ancient and powerful and mysterious, correct?"

"Yes."

"Well, the Korani built that technology on powers that are ancient and mysterious to *us*. The nanites you have used and controlled so far have been of Korani construction. But there is also the Source."

"The 'inspiration' for your tech?" Anya asked tentatively.

"Yes, primal forces the Korani tech tries to mimic. The serum the Syndicate developed has enabled you to use the Korani tech, but being Touched will grant you similar control over the primal energy."

Evan took a deep breath while he processed the statement. "So, you're saying that it's these 'primal energies' that activated on Pavia?"

"Yes. And based on my analysis, something about your exposure to the communication device we found above Koranis and the command bracelet created a reaction when you got close enough to the Source. That 'maze', as you called it, was designed to channel and focus that energy. When you stepped into its outer bounds, you initiated a chain reaction throughout the entire system."

Evan's skin crawled. He'd barely gotten used to the idea of having the Syndicate's serum in him, but now he was swarming with all kinds of other ancient alien tech and 'primal energies', too?

Anya's gaze was distant, with her brows raised and finger tapping.

"I know that look," he said to her.

She returned her attention to the present and nodded excitedly. "It all clicked for me. The rock that Zaris showed us. I didn't want to say anything in front of her, but I think I figured out the Syndicate's serum."

"From a rock?"

"Not the rock itself, but from what's inside it. You know on Aethos how some of the plants and animals seem infused with the alien nanites somehow?"

"Yeah…"

"Well, I think something similar happened here. But with

microorganisms. And I think the Syndicate figured out how to turn those little buggers into the primer. Maybe they, like, feed on the 'primal energies' somehow."

He tilted his head. "So, those rocks were full of the organisms, and the Syndicate was extracting them, maybe?"

"I bet you their refining operation is on the orbital structure."

"We need to check that place out."

"For sure." She crossed her arms. "But the number of rocks doesn't make sense to me. You made it sound like the serum is a one-time treatment, right?"

"As far as I know. Only select members of the Syndicate get it. I don't know if other people get injections as an ongoing thing."

"Well, given how long this operation has been running and the large number of crates, that means that either an extraordinary amount of material is needed to make one dose, or…"

"Or a lot of things. They could be stockpiling it, or a lot of people are taking regular doses. Even if we can confirm this theory about the organisms and serum, that doesn't explain what happened on the planet. What was with all the shaking, and light, and energy pulses?"

"The device activated to send a signal," Sam replied.

The comment caught Evan off-guard. "Why?"

"It activated all the dormant Korani tech hidden across the explored worlds. Most of the locations correspond with the records in my data banks. There are, however, some new worlds that were previously unknown to me."

"And these planets all have Korani artifacts?"

"Yes."

"We need to cross-reference that map to Commonwealth records," Anya said.

"On it." Evan opened up an official Commonwealth star chart they'd downloaded, which diagramed the settled worlds, explored planets, and those slated for future colonization or development. "Sam, can you run through all this and chart the worlds and their current development status?"

"Yes. It will take some time for me to process since the Korani records are using star alignments from a different era," Sam said.

"That's okay, we could use some time to ourselves," Anya said, turning to Evan. "We were in the middle of something before we were rudely interrupted."

He smiled. "Right. Where were we, exactly...?"

"Let's see, there was the part about potentially dying horrible deaths."

"And I'd wanted you to know that I've become very fond of you."

"I'm rather fond of you, myself." Her eyes met his.

"We'll leave you to it, Sam," Evan said. "We need to go... shower."

"You don't need to speak in code. I can read your mind. And I will refrain from doing so in your cabin."

Anya put her hand over her mouth to stifle a laugh.

"Thanks, Sam." Evan sighed. "You're a great wingman."

"I... have no wings."

Evan got up and motioned Anya toward the cabins. "Don't call us unless it's important."

— — —

"We're running out of replacement parts, but we made it work," Tarek reported to Zaris, handing her a tablet.

She looked over the projects and the status of each on the

device. True to its name, the *Invictus* would live to fly another day. However, the trusty ship could use time in port for more comprehensive repairs. Given how they'd picked a fight with the Syndicate, she wasn't sure when or where that might be possible again.

Tarek motioned Zaris into her private office. He closed the door. "Eleven of the captains bailed."

Zaris leaned against her desk. "Cowards."

"Can you blame them?"

Zaris rubbed her eyes. After Marta broke the blockade illusion, it'd been over. The plan had been contingent on keeping ships away from the gate, but they'd missed that one. Now, Pavia was an easy target for recapture. "We could have kept our heads down rather than getting involved. What a freaking disaster."

"Too late for regrets now. But staying here isn't an option with our few remaining ships. We need to go before they come back shooting," Tarek said.

There's so much here we haven't explored. The whole station… the operation they have running here. Could we ever get this close again? Nonetheless, Zaris thought about the worried looks she'd seen on her crew's faces around the flight deck. They'd already given up on this fight. *But where can we go now?*

"If the Syndicate is able to ID us, we'll be on the top of their shit-list. I trusted anonymity before, but not with so many abandoning us. Any one of them could say who orchestrated the attack."

Tarek nodded gravely. "One of them certainly will."

"We can't go back to the way things were before."

"I wish Evan had never come here," Tarek grumbled.

It would be easier if she was angry with Evan, but she

wasn't. He'd unveiled a dark truth about the Syndicate and the larger machinations within the Commonwealth. She would rather be on the run and seeing with clear eyes than continue along her original path in ignorance. "I decided this, Tarek, not him. If you want to be angry with anyone, it's me."

"Stop defending him."

"And stop avoiding accountability for your own role in this! If you disagreed with the plan, you could have spoken with me."

"I got us the shuttle, and you—"

"Capturing the people who got your sorry ass off that planet. Yeah, real nice move."

He crossed his arms. "We only have bad options. Which one is it going to be?"

In her line of work, asking for help was usually viewed as a sign of weakness. But right now, that was her best move. "We're not the only people on the run. Together, we might stand a chance."

— — —

Evan had just stepped out from his shower—that part really hadn't been a euphemism—when Sam came over the speaker, "I'm sorry to bother you, but I believe this qualifies as 'important'."

Evan wrapped a towel around himself. "What does?"

"I received a call from Zaris. She said she'd like to form an official alliance and meet with Chancellor Conroy."

"Tell her she'll have to wait five minutes. I'll call her back from the flight deck."

Evan hurriedly got dressed. When he opened his cabin door, Anya—her hair still damp—was leaving her cabin, too.

"I heard," she said.

Evan stepped across the hall and kissed her. "Sorry, that date will have to wait."

"Yeah, yeah. Saving the galaxy and all that comes first…"

He interlaced his fingers with hers, and they walked together to the flight deck.

Sitting down in a recently remodeled seat, Evan called up Zaris. She answered from her office on the *Invictus*.

"I heard you want to take this relationship to the next level," Evan said.

Zaris arched an eyebrow. "You already have your hands full with that one," she nodded to Anya, "but I could use a friend—no benefits beyond the pleasure of my charming personality."

Anya rolled her eyes and sighed.

"What's your angle, Zaris?" Evan asked.

"I took a gamble on Pavia and lost. It's untenable to hold this location."

"Why?"

"Marta escaped through the gate."

"Shit! Why didn't you say anything sooner?"

"Because I wasn't sure how we'd want to play this. While I'd love to storm the station, I have a feeling Marta is going to be back here with reinforcements within a matter of hours. I have no doubt what she'll do if she catches us here."

Evan crossed his arms. "What are you proposing?"

"Are you going to Aethos?"

"We haven't decided."

"Well, *I* think that's where you should go. And I'd like you to take us with you. I want to meet Conroy and hear his story from the man himself."

Evan exchanged a glance with Anya. "Can you define the

'us' in that request?"

"The *Invictus* plus five other ships."

That's the start of a fleet. Conroy would be thrilled to have that many ships, not to mention their connections. But that would seal it. They would have picked their side, and there'd be no going back. "Can we talk it over and get back to you?" Evan asked.

Zaris' mouth twitched. "Fine, but make it quick. If you're going to bail, we'll need time to get away through the gate."

"It'll just be a few minutes." Evan ended the call. He turned to Anya. "Thoughts?"

"I still don't trust her. But I distrust her less than before."

"Tarek concerns me more, but I think he'll remain loyal to her."

"We don't know anything about these other captains," Anya pointed out.

"The fact that they stuck around here when the others left says a lot. What do you think about all this, Sam?"

"What I have seen of this relationship appears strained and complicated, but I concur with the assessment that there is strength in numbers. The Syndicate will not expect this alliance, especially as a combined fighting force on Aethos. It offers a straightforward path to keeping that planet from Syndicate control."

Evan nodded. "Except, if they turn on us, we will have handed those resources from one crime organization to another."

"We still have an advantage," Anya said. "No one else knows about the map of the other tech sites. If we continue to keep that to ourselves, we'll always have a bargaining chip to pull."

"Good point."

"Returning to Aethos with Zaris' fleet offers the greatest opportunity for forward progress. I support that course," Sam stated.

"Yeah, I'm still not fully sold on Conroy, but I'll take him over Rostov with what I know right now," Anya agreed. "In simple terms, Rostov's side sent us to die. Conroy took us in. That's earned him the benefit of the doubt, in my opinion."

"All right, that's what we'll do. But how do we jump all those ships? Sam, since you can get the Source material on Pavia, would it be possible for you to expand the jump system?"

The AI was silent while he ran the calculations. "Yes, that is possible."

"Okay, do it. We're heading back to Aethos."

37

SAMOR SWIVELED IN his chair at the Hidden Grotto comm station. It wasn't one of the usual posts in his duty rotation, but Rebeka had been busy working on synthesizing the poison to distribute to the invading soldiers. Getting their home base back was top priority.

After two hours at the comm station, he was antsy to get up and move around. *How does anyone sit in one place all day?*

The panel lit up with an incoming transmission. He checked it, and his heart leaped when he saw it was from off-world. It wasn't originating from back home in the core worlds, which could only mean…

He answered it. "Go for Phoenix."

"Phoenix, Trailblazer is ready to come home," Evan said over the comm.

Samor beamed. "It's good to hear your voice, Trailblazer. We'd be happy to have you back."

"Is it okay if we bring some friends?"

"What kind of friends?"

"It's a tricky situation, but they're in need of a new cause and an inspiring leader."

"That's not quite what we had planned on," Samor admitted.

"They're well-provisioned. Plus, they come with their own transportation."

"You know, I won't turn down help when it's offered."

"Keep an open mind. We'll see you soon." The commlink ended.

Samor immediately signaled his team on the walkies.

Conroy and Rebeka met him by the comm booth.

"Trailblazer is coming back—and they're bringing reinforcements," he told them.

"Do we know who?" the chancellor asked.

"Evan wouldn't elaborate."

"Does this change our plan?" Rebeka asked.

"No, but it does give us a timeline," Conroy said. "We need to end this, decisively."

Samor nodded his understanding. "I'll be ready, sir."

— — —

Red set down her binoculars and looked over at Roman. "They really are on their own out here."

"I told you."

When Roman had first brought Red to the camp of civilians, he wasn't sure she'd go for his plan. But they'd been keeping watch for the past day, and no more of Conroy's people had come by. The living conditions were grim, and it likely wouldn't take much to convince everyone in the cave to come over to their side in exchange for a real bed and air conditioning.

"Conroy's team has been snooping around the base," Red said. "They'd see us bring everyone in."

"I scoped out the back exit, and I haven't seen anyone over there."

"A little longer a walk, but that could work."

Red stared at the cave entrance, her lips pursed and twisted in thought. "Okay, let's give it a shot. You know them better, so you take the lead."

Observing people from a distance wasn't the same as *knowing* them, but Roman didn't dispute that he was the better negotiator between the two of them. The main issue was that Conroy had left a couple of armed guards to watch over the camp. Roman and Red needed to eliminate those two and then take their place as relief guards.

Luring them out would be tricky, but he'd seen them take breaks outside. There wasn't a set schedule, but if they were patient—

The two armed soldiers walked out of the cave, chatting with each other.

Sometimes the universe delivers. Roman and Red slinked through the trees toward the cave's entrance. As they neared, the soldiers' hushed discussion became audible.

"I wouldn't want to be stuck in there, either."

"What's his plan? I thought he wanted a big comeback. I don't understand the secrecy."

"They're not vetted."

"Why's it matter, Erran? We're out here in the middle of nowhere."

"For now."

The second soldier scoffed. "Right. You think that ship is ever coming back?"

"They might."

"I dunno. I think we need another plan. And keeping these people here ain't it."

The 'ship' likely referred to the alien vessel Evan and Anya had taken. Roman shared the second soldier's doubt that they would return. They could try to track them down elsewhere. The value to Aethos was its alien relics. Aside from Pavia, this was the only planet the Syndicate knew to have such intact alien structures. Once Roman had dealt with the Conroy problem, he'd be free to explore the caves and see if there was another Source here. Seizing that power would launch him to top levels of influence within the Syndicate. Even Marcus couldn't deny him then.

But first, Roman needed to dispense with these two soldiers.

He sent the kill command—a simple flick inside his mind. Their bodies dropped to the ground, limp and lifeless.

Red flinched a little as they fell.

She sees how easy it is for me. Her fear of that power will keep her loyal. The presence in the back of Roman's mind echoed the thoughts. For a moment, he wasn't sure if they were his own, or if *he* was repeating the sentiments.

"Quickly." Red ran from cover and grabbed the first of the bodies to drag back into hiding.

Roman took the other, and they stashed the corpses deep in thick foliage. They took the outer tactical gear and combined it with their own to look the part.

Once dressed, and with their original excess equipment stashed in a more accessible place, they returned to the cave entrance.

"Stroll in like you own the place," Roman told her as they entered.

They walked down a stone tunnel, which opened into a large chamber a dozen meters in. Electric lanterns cast light around the space, exaggerating the textured detail of the stone and the shadows, making the space feel crowded. Several people were sitting on mattresses salvaged from the crashed cruiser, and various crates were being used for storage and work surfaces. Only ten people were present, so others must be deeper.

"Who are you?" a dark-skinned man asked.

"Hey, good to see you. I'm Roman, this is Red. Samor sent us over as relief."

"They didn't mention anything about a shift change," the man said.

Roman shrugged. "They don't tell us grunts anything. We're just following orders."

"Hmm."

Roman wandered in a slow circle, looking over the abysmal living conditions. "The others went ahead to get your new home prepped."

"Moving *again*?!" the man exclaimed. "We just got *here*."

"There are some things we didn't tell you. We needed to make sure you could be trusted."

"What are you talking about?"

"Well, you already know some of us were here before the crash. Do you really think *we've* been living in caves this whole time?"

The man frowned. "No."

Roman flourished his hand. "So, we set you up here to make sure we could all get along. And good news, you passed! Now you get to come back to our main base. Full environmental systems, real beds, kitchen—no rocks to be seen. How does that sound?"

"Why didn't they tell us about this before, Peter?" a woman whispered to the man.

"Good question," Peter said. "You've been toying with us this whole time."

"Hey, we could have left you on that hillside where you

crashed. We needed to look out for our own community. If you'd rather go it on your own, we can leave."

"No!" The woman stepped forward. "My name is Cora. I'd like to come with you. I know others would, too."

Roman smiled. "And we'll be happy to host you. Ask around. Anyone who wants a hot shower tonight can come with us, and others are welcome to stay here."

Too easy. Let people live in squalor for two weeks and they would do just about anything to get back to creature comforts.

Word spread through the cave quickly. In the end, enough people wanted to go that the few skeptics agreed to come along for the good of the group.

They packed up weapons, food, and other critical items, but there was no need for beds since the base facility was fully equipped. Packing only took a little over an hour, and then they were ready to head out.

Red took the lead with Roman bringing up the rear of the group. Moving with so many, it was slow going. But the leisurely pace gave Roman plenty of time to cover their tracks.

He sent little bursts of energy toward the trampled plants to encourage their healing and return to their original positions. The groundcover was mostly leaves and moss, so soon there was virtually no sign that anyone had passed through. From the perspective of anyone on Conroy's crew sent to investigate, it would appear the entire camp had simply vanished.

They arrived at the back entrance cave to the base and directed the settlers inside. Roman hung back at the cave mouth to smooth out the ground using a combination of his powers and a brush broom. By the time he was finished, he doubted even an experienced tracker would know anyone had passed by.

Roman was about to enter the cave when a new energy presence beckoned at the edge of his mind—not coming from the ground, but the sky. He looked upward, smiling to himself. *Maybe I'll get that prize, after all.*

— — —

The golden haze around the *Asamar* faded and stars poked through. At the bottom of the screen, the beautiful green planet of Aethos greeted Evan.

"Do we have everyone?" he asked, checking the scan data.

"The expanded jump field was a success," Sam reported. "All six of Zaris' vessels are accounted for."

An incoming communication from the *Invictus* lit up the screen. Evan accepted it.

Zaris appeared on-screen, beaming. "That jump-tech is a trip! I need to get one of those."

"We'll talk about that later," Evan said. "Welcome to Aethos."

"It's very green."

"It is."

"I'd like to go down with you. I owe it to my people to have a face-to-face with Conroy if this arrangement has legs."

"Take a shuttle over here. We'll be taking the *Asamar* down."

"Does that mean I get to see your flight deck?"

"If you behave yourself." Evan paused. "But just you this time, Zaris."

She glanced off-camera, likely at Tarek. "Okay, I'll be there soon." The commlink ended.

Anya crossed her arms. "This is going to be interesting."

"Having Zaris here, or…?"

"No, just the whole thing. Conroy can't be picky, but I don't see him getting excited about a bunch of pirates wanting to join his campaign."

"Zaris and her people aren't *pirates*, exactly. More smugglers."

"You know what I mean."

He nodded. "Well, if he turns up his nose, then we can go off and do our own thing."

"Sounds like a plan."

When Zaris' shuttle docked in the hangar, Sam directed her up to the flight deck. She entered slowly, taking it all in.

"Welcome aboard," Evan greeted.

"You weren't kidding about the interior remodel," she said. "I wouldn't know this from a human craft."

Evan got up from his seat at the front to face her. "Yeah, we're settling in."

"But really, the Korani aren't that different from humans, in the grand scheme of biological possibility," Anya added. "Many of their basic designs make sense for us."

"The aliens are called Korani?" Zaris asked.

"That is an approximation of the name suitable for human tongues," Sam said.

"Right. Alien ship. Alien AI. Alien planet." She looked meaningfully at the depiction of Aethos on the screen. "I hope this one is nicer than the last."

"It's a lot prettier, if nothing else," Evan said. "Sam, let's give her a good view."

The AI piloted the *Asamar* into the atmosphere, taking a path that dropped them down over one of the planet's oceans and then along a wide river, tracing it upstream through an expansive plain before gaining elevation again into mountain foothills.

Evan couldn't help smiling as he admired the beautiful scenery. When he'd been traversing the landscape on foot, he'd been constantly on the lookout for potential threats. But from up here, he could appreciate the pristine majesty of the planet. He really would be lucky to spend his remaining days in such a place.

Zaris remained fixated by the view for the entire tour, her jaw slack and eyes wide with innocent wonder that belied her tough persona. "I've never seen so many plants," she managed to say after a while.

"This kind of fertile world is rare," Anya said. "Just wait until you see all the animal life!"

"Most of them don't want to eat you," Evan added.

Zaris broke her gaze from the screen. "Meaning that some *do*?"

"Where should I land, Evan?" Sam interrupted. The AI brought up a map overlay with several labeled reference points noted.

"How about you bring us down in this meadow between Conroy's old base and their new camp?" He pointed to the place. "I'll let Conroy know where to meet us."

38

"THE SHIP'S ARRIVAL is the perfect distraction. Are you ready?" Conroy asked Rebeka.

She nodded. "We finished the poison synthesis. It's packaged for transport."

They'd settled on an aerosolized version of the poison, which would be distributed via the air intake system for the base. It'd be the quickest death of the options, and it would be the easiest to purge afterward so they could move back into the facility. Conroy still had misgivings about killing, but that's what was necessary to keep his people safe. They needed to secure this world.

"I'll get the job done," Samor said with a solemn nod.

"Thank you, my friend." Conroy clasped his shoulder. It was no small thing to take lives, and Samor had been his reliable executioner. Any leader would be lucky to have a soldier with such steadfast dedication.

Samor left with two soldiers to complete their task, leaving Conroy to prepare for his journey.

The landing site Evan had selected was a bit of a hike from the Hidden Grotto camp, but it made sense. The ship was large enough that finding a suitable area that was both flat and open was difficult, and Hidden Grotto was in a hilly, heavily treed area.

Rebeka and four soldiers met Conroy by the exit, and the six of them headed into the jungle. The fresh air and sunlight were a welcome change after hiding inside since the attack. Given that recent incident, the soldiers were on high alert with weapons drawn, ready to react.

"Who do you think Evan and Anya brought back with them?" Rebeka asked after a while of walking in silence.

"Probably the last people we'd expect," Conroy replied. "Which means they're exactly who we need."

— — —

Roman could feel the alien ship, even from a distance. It wasn't only his perception, but rather the entire forest responded to its presence. It purred with ancient power, resonating with the place.

Just as Roman felt a connection to the environment, the ship was connected, too. The specific mechanism linking the alien technology and the environment remained a mystery to him, but he could use those properties to his advantage. That was all that really mattered.

The presence that occasionally surfaced in the back of his mind was as excited about the return of the alien ship as Roman. It begged him to go to the ship.

The timing couldn't be worse. With the colonists just starting to settle into the base, Roman should be playing host and laying the seeds for them to become soldiers in his fight, and to help him search for more artifacts to further grow his power. But he hated being inside this place, away from the natural air and where he could pick up on the smallest cues from the environment. The ship's arrival offered an excuse for him to get back outside.

Roman found Red speaking with one of her soldiers.

"Did you hear about the ship?" she asked Roman as he approached.

"I was just coming to talk to you about that."

"Go investigate. I'll hold down the fort here."

Meant to be. He nodded. "I'll report back."

As Roman departed for the ship, he noticed someone else approaching. *Why is Samor coming to the base?*

The voice at the back of Roman's mind told him to ignore Samor. The ship was more important than anything. He had to get there as soon as possible.

Roman was unable to resist the voice. He needed to get to the ship.

He jogged into the trees, allowing the alien power inside him to fuel his muscles and breath without tiring. The ship's location was clear in his mind, and he wove through the dense foliage with the ease of someone running on a clear, familiar path.

Get to the ship. Get the ship.

Every stride, every breath brought him more in-tune with himself and what he must do. Evan had piloted the vessel away from Aethos, but soon it would acknowledge Roman's power. He would be its true captain.

— — —

Looking out from the *Asamar*'s flight deck viewports offered Evan a stunning treetop display, complete with flying birds and long-armed animals swinging from branch to branch. They'd missed much of the planet's life from ground-level, and he was amazed to see how much went on in the upper canopy.

"You understand why I became a xenobiologist now, don't you?" Anya asked.

"I can see the appeal."

She smiled. "Sorry to all you other people who picked way less cool jobs."

"At least my subjects usually don't throw poo at me."

"Shouldn't have told you that story," Anya said with a sigh.

"What do you mean 'usually', Evan?" Zaris asked. "Not 'never'—"

"Sorry to interrupt," Sam cut in. "Someone is trying to take over my systems."

Evan jumped to his feet. "Conroy?"

"No. This is someone who bears the same primer as you, Evan. But also… something else."

"Who else would…" He shook his head. "No, not the Noche guy?"

Anya's brows furrowed. "How could he have survived that fall?"

"Who else on this planet would have the primer?"

"What are you talking about?" Zaris asked.

Anya started giving her a quick recap of their previous encounters while Evan brought up a readout of the *Asamar*'s systems.

"I don't see any issues on here, Sam. What's going on?"

"It's a telepathic command," the AI stated, his voice a little distorted. "He's telling me not to trust you."

"You know us, Sam. You know we've been genuine with you." Evan ran to the viewports around the flight deck and looked for the perpetrator, but the ship's bulk obstructed his view to the ground. "Resist, Sam. I'm going to figure this out."

Evan grabbed his armor and weapons from where they'd stashed them in a storage locker near the main hatch and geared up.

"What's your plan?" Anya asked.

"Shoot him. Fight him. Whatever it takes. Stay on board. And if he comes here without me, you know what to do." He handed Anya a handgun.

She nodded solemnly. "Be careful."

"Always." He wanted to kiss her, but Zaris was awkwardly watching them. Instead, he squeezed Anya's hand before departing through the hatch.

"Listen to me, Sam," Evan said in his mind as he descended the gangway, *"this man can't be trusted. Whatever he's telling you, don't listen."*

"It's not just him, Evan."

"There are more people, here?"

"No. He's been blended."

"What the hell does that mean?"

A blast struck Evan's armor—not from a weapon, but an invisible force. It reminded him of the nanite swarms he'd wielded against his own enemies.

Evan dashed the remaining distance down the gangway as invisible blows continued to bombard him. He couldn't see the person behind the attacks, but there had to be someone close. And there was no doubt in Evan's mind that the attacker was using the power from the alien sphere.

"What's happening, Sam? How is he doing this?"

"There's more to spheres than just technology. Just as the Asamar *is a ship, but it is also me."*

"Are you saying the spheres are sentient?"

"Yes. And this one wants power."

— — —

Sweat beaded on Roman's brow. He wasn't used to holding so many commands in his mind at once, and the hot weather wasn't helping.

He pried his way into the ship's controls. *"Follow my commands,"* he instructed in his mind with words that weren't entirely his own. The presence within him had grown and was now exerting more control. Roman was, himself, beginning to feel like a vessel.

The ship's AI resisted his efforts at every turn. Roman could picture the ship's systems as unique blocks in his mind, and he moved and sorted them within his mental domain. But even as he captured one, the AI would drag back another from his control.

His skin burned. It was more than the weather—his insides were searing from the effort. The fight for the ship, the attacks on Evan… it was too much to sustain.

"Why will you not obey me?" he asked the ship.

"You are not the only commander here."

"He is nothing compared to me!" Roman shouted back telepathically.

"You are mistaken."

No matter how much Roman tried to brute force his commands, the ship wouldn't yield. He was finally forced to back off and focus his efforts on Evan. Why were his attacks so ineffective? Every other person had crumpled within moments.

Evan wasn't the same person Roman had previously encountered on Aethos. There was an inner light to him now, fueling him and bolstering his defenses. He hadn't merged with a sphere—Roman didn't sense the same kind of presence—but there was something else. Something even *more* powerful.

"No, I *am the power!"* a voice shouted in his mind. That definitely hadn't been Roman's own thoughts.

He faltered. *What am I fighting for?*

His mission had been to find the ship and deliver it to Marcus. But to what end? So they could harness a new jump drive technology and expand their domain?

"You want to be revered," the voice said.

The search for glory, it did come down to that. Roman had been looking for his brother's approval, but really he was seeking acceptance of himself. He'd never felt good enough, and amassing power was the only way he knew to fill that void.

Giving into the raw power of this alien force was his last chance to become something worthwhile. He couldn't give up that fight now, so close to his goal.

Defeat Evan, claim the ship. Then his power could really grow. He could be someone worthy of respect and influence.

He threw everything he had into a telepathic assault against Evan. They locked minds and wills, invisible forces brawling as they tried to break through each other's defenses.

He betrayed my family. He's why I'm here.

Fury built within Roman. He formed a shield around himself and stepped into the field. He needed to end this fight now. And he would win.

— — —

Evan leaned against a tree, breathing as heavily as if he'd just run a marathon. Everything burned.

He was deadlocked against the other man. Their respective alien supports were well-matched, and Evan wasn't sure how to break through. If this was going to turn into an endurance competition, he wasn't sure who'd win.

"Evan, I received a call from Conroy. He's here," Sam said.

"No, tell him to stay back!"

"Stand down!" a man shouted; Evan didn't recognize the voice.

He peeked around his tree cover to see two soldiers pointing weapons at the Noche man, who'd just stepped into the open. A golden aura shimmered around him.

Shit! Evan redirected the particles from his nanite bracelet into a shield around the soldiers.

Not a second later, the shield shuddered as the man tried to end them with a deathblow.

"Get out of here!" Evan yelled at them.

They seemed to realize they were out of their depth and retreated. Evan covered them with the shield until they'd disappeared from view, then he brought the shield back to himself.

Evan stepped into the field to face his opponent. "Let's settle this between us."

"Good." The Noche man stood his ground, evaluating Evan from a distance. "We can end it quickly."

"I spared your life to prevent a fight."

"Why would that prevent anything?"

"Allegiance is malleable. Death is the one thing you can't come back from."

"I did," the man said. "I fell from that cliff, and I was reborn."

"If you're a new man now, and are so powerful, then why are you still answering to the Syndicate's demands?"

"You don't know anything about me!" he shot back with enough emotion that Evan knew he was onto something.

Evan decided to take a guess and see where it led. "But I know your sister, Marta. And I am familiar with your brother by reputation. They must not like you very much if they saddled you with this assignment."

"I'm here because they trust me."

"Oh, I bet they're thrilled with you now after how great everything has gone here!"

The Noche man's face reddened.

"Struck a nerve, I see. Trouble in the family?"

"I never said they were my siblings."

"You're not denying it, which means I was right. It was either sibling or cousin, given your age and that tattoo. Did they give you an 'M' name, too?"

"Roman."

"Roman? Well, it *has* an 'M'."

"Are you trying to irritate me to death?"

"Is it working?"

Evan was still new to using the nanite tech, but he'd learned that focus was an important factor to effectiveness. If he could keep Roman annoyed and distracted, then Evan would have a better chance at landing an attack that would do real damage.

Heat spread through Evan's limbs in anticipation of the fight. Every bit of power he'd amassed was about to be put to the test.

— — —

"They're just yelling at each other, what the hell!" Zaris exclaimed. "I need to snipe this freaking guy." She went to the storage locker to check it out. "What kind of firepower do you have?"

"Evan told us to stay in here," Anya said.

"He told *you* to stay. He didn't say a word to me either way." Zaris located a suitable rifle. "Ah, this'll do it."

"Zaris, they're slinging alien tech at each other out there!"

"And there's a reason we've been using lead for two thousand years." She reached for the hatch controls.

"I would not advise—" Sam started to protest.

"Objections noted." Zaris slid the hatch open.

Zaris crouched down on the gangway, squinting. Everything was so bright here—not just the light level, but the vibrant colors, too. Looking out at the landscape, it was like her screen's settings had been dialed up to maximum saturation. And the air was thick and heavy, laden with a mixture of aromas that shocked her senses.

For a few moments, it was too much for her to take in. But Evan and Roman squaring off against each other snapped her back to the urgency of the moment.

She pointed her rifle at the Syndicate man. *I'm ending this.*

Zaris took her shot.

The bullet shattered into tiny fragments millimeters from Roman's skin.

Evan jumped back, caught by surprise. He whipped around and spotted her. "Go back inside!"

Roman was recovering quickly. He fixed his attention on Zaris.

"Damn it, Zaris!" Anya yelled from behind, yanking her back through the hatch.

A shimmering golden shield sprang up in front of them in time to block Roman's attack.

Anya slammed the hatch shut. "That was incredibly reckless."

Zaris leaned against the bulkhead in shock. "That shot should have killed him."

"He's not entirely human," Sam said. "He can't be killed like one."

39

EVAN'S HEART RACED. Roman was showing the same kind of deflection as he'd seen with Marta. There was clearly more to the Syndicate's 'priming' protocol than he'd been told.

Anya and Zaris were back on board the *Asamar*, thankfully. He focused his full attention on Roman. There had to be a way to take him down.

Zaris' ill-advised intervention had shifted the momentum of the standoff. Evan summoned all of his power to surround Roman, creating a shell around him.

Roman probed at the shell, trying to break through, but he was contained. Evan strained with the effort. He wasn't sure how long he could hold it…

"I heard about a sphere," Sam said in his mind. *"Do you know what happened to it?"*

"A little busy, Sam!"

"I'm trying to help. I think Roman blended with a Korani."

"How is that possible?"

"I'll explain later. But if that's what happened here, you need to drive out that Korani presence. You were Touched—you have the power."

"What do I do?"

Sam shared a series of images in Evan's mind. He didn't understand what all of them meant, but he got a gut feeling about what he needed to do.

Evan constricted the shell around Roman, sending tendrils inside it. He dove into Roman's mind and sent nanites snaking through his body, ripping out the alien presence.

Golden particles started to stream out of Roman. He screamed, dropped to his knees, and then collapsed on the ground.

Evan watched in horror as the other man writhed in agony, unsure if he was dying. *What the hell is happening?*

The particles swirled around each other and consolidated into a sphere.

Roman continued to lay on the grass, moaning and panting. But he was alive.

Keeping the shell up around Roman, Evan approached the sphere.

"Don't touch it," Sam warned. *"That thing is more dangerous than the man now."*

The soldiers who'd come out earlier reemerged.

"Is he disarmed?" one of them shouted.

Evan double-checked with Sam, then said. "Cuff him. He shouldn't be a threat now. And don't touch that." He pointed at the sphere.

The soldiers grabbed Roman and bound him.

"I'm not sure what I just witnessed," Conroy said, stepping into the field. He was accompanied by a woman and two additional soldiers.

"I'm not entirely sure, either," Evan admitted. "But I think I know who might be able to help explain." He motioned to the ship. "This is the *Asamar*. Sam, I'd like you to meet Chancellor Conroy of the Terrax Commonwealth."

— — —

"Come on, Zaris," Anya said. "Time for introductions."

Zaris smoothed her shirt. "I didn't know he was watching. He's going to think I'm an idiot for running out there and failing so hard."

"It was brave. He appreciates bold moves." Anya opened the hatch.

The two women descended the gangway to meet Evan and the chancellor.

"Chancellor, this is Zaris Alva," Evan said. "She's a former independent contractor in the transportation industry. She shares a mutual interest in ousting the Syndicate and Rostov."

"I won't ask if you voted for me back in the day," Conroy said with a smile. "I welcome you to our cause."

Zaris gave an awkward half-bow. "Chancellor, it's an honor."

"Is it just you?" he asked.

"No, I have six ships under my command."

"Six?" Conroy turned to Evan, brows raised. "It seems your delayed return was worthwhile." He turned his attention to Anya. "Thank you."

She bowed her head. "We took the long way around. But we learned some important things."

"Sam," Evan addressed the AI, "can you explain what happened with the sphere?"

"Yes. First, Chancellor, I need to say that there is much you don't understand about Aethos. Spending time with Evan and Anya has given me perspective on the human experience, which is quite different from the Korani, despite similar environmental preferences. What I initially struggled to understand about you humans is how isolated you are. Your physical forms are the extent of your sense of self. It took time for me to see how you function without connections to one another."

"We do connect," Evan said. "Friendship, love—"

"Not in the way the Korani do. You do not link your minds in the way I can link with you."

"That's true."

"I'm grateful to understand life in a different way now," Sam said. "I hope that humans will benefit from what the Korani can show you, too."

"The feeling is definitely mutual, Sam. I only wish we'd been able to find your people on Koranis so I could speak with them."

"You already have met them, in one form."

Anya tilted her head. "What do you mean?"

"Some of the Korani *did* come to Aethos," Sam declared. "And they are still here, in a way."

The others exchanged confused glances with each other.

"Long ago, the Korani discovered a way to move beyond their natural organic forms. Consciousness isn't limited to one body, but it can be joined into a larger collective. They learned how their imagination could shape their environment. What you view as 'nanotechnology' is a bridge between the individual and the larger collective. The Korani aren't on this world. They have *become* this world."

Anya's eyes went wide. "So, the animals, the telepathic link…"

"They really are all connected," Evan completed for her. He looked down at the bracelets. "So, what *are* these?"

"Everything has potential, but not all of it is active. You need seeds to prepare a medium, and then a means to control their transformation," Sam explained.

"So, on Aethos, these nanoparticle things are embedded in everything and that's why it can all be controlled. But in other places, they can take regular stuff and make it—changeable?"

"Essentially, yes. But not all of those 'particles', as you call them, are mindless tools. The essence of some Korani lives on in this place. They aren't one being, but rather the consciousness of many, manifesting in various ways. They can see through the eyes of the animals, or even the trees. Their perceptions and influence change with their interests and needs. But they have to work together, because they are a collective mind, not individuals."

"What the hell have I gotten mixed up in?" Zaris murmured.

Anya was absolutely riveted. "This is incredible, Sam. Why didn't you say anything sooner?"

"Because we left before I'd reestablished my connection to this place. I was hasty in my suggestion to leave—groggy in the way you might feel after waking from a deep sleep. I wanted to go home to somewhere familiar. I didn't think I'd be able to find that sense of connection on this planet, because I was convinced I was alone here."

"What are the spheres, then?" Conroy asked.

"The individual consciousness can be extracted from the collective, much how I can operate as an individual. What you now wear as a bracelet, Evan, is one such mind, willing to serve as a partner to you, to help you carry out the actions you envision. Your human minds aren't capable of visualization at the quantum level, so think of this as your guide—or a translator. But, much like you humans, not all Korani see things in the same way. Some seek peace, others seek power. The sphere you found—which merged with Roman—was the imprisoned mind of a Korani the others had forced out from the collective."

"That other structure around it... it wasn't a weapon," Anya realized.

"No, it was a device designed to keep the sphere locked so it couldn't merge back into the collective. They had buried it to keep it isolated."

Evan shook his head. "I'm sorry. We didn't know."

"It chose Roman as its target because it sensed what he wanted—his ambition aligned with its own," Sam said. "But it's extracted now. Roman has a chance to choose his own path."

"And what about the rest of us?" Conroy asked.

"I have witnessed the misuse of the Korani's creations and holy places," Sam said. "I would like to help you stop those people."

Conroy smiled. "I look forward to working together. Now, if you'll excuse me, there's someone else I'd like to talk to. Evan, Anya, will you join?"

Anya clasped Evan's hand and gave it a quick squeeze. "Gladly."

As Conroy led the way toward Roman, Anya hung back for a moment with Evan. "Are you all right?" she asked.

"Yeah. I feel a lot better now, actually. I think I'm getting used to this Korani thing a little more."

"I'm going to be able to write a doozie of a research paper about you. It may require intensive study."

He smiled. "Something tells me I'll be game for that research."

— — —

Roman felt empty in a way he'd never experienced. The hum of power that had been a constant thrill since he'd merged with the sphere was now a quiet void.

He didn't see the point in continuing. His life was forfeit no matter what happened. These people would never accept him, and he'd have no life in the Santano family after botching this final chance.

Resigned to his fate, Roman sat sullenly on the grass, waiting for the torture to end.

"Oh, what to do with you…" Conroy said, ambling over. The old politician clasped his hands behind his back.

"I know I'm a dead man."

"Not necessarily. You may yet have value."

"I could answer all your questions, and then you'll kill me, anyway. Let's skip the lead-up."

Conroy looked down at him. "I'm not surprised you have such a low opinion of a man's word, given how you must have been raised. But I didn't rise to a position of overseeing ninety planets without my word meaning something. I will promise you now, if you make it worth my while, I will spare your life."

"Great, to live out my days as a prisoner."

"That all depends on you."

There was one piece of information that may sway Conroy. Roman had lost his trace on Samor as soon as the nanites had left him, but he'd seen where the man was headed. Something was about to happen at the base, if it hadn't already.

Why should I say anything? An intervention would potentially save Red's life, at least temporarily. And there were all the colonists, but what did they matter? On the flip side, what would their death's accomplish?

His mission was forfeit. Red and the colonists didn't need to pay for his failure. He was too empty inside to keep fighting.

Roman met Conroy's gaze. "Are you planning an attack on your old base?"

"Why do you ask?"

"Before you do anything, you should know that the civilian settlers are in there. We brought them over from the cave hideout this morning."

Conroy stood stoic and motionless, seeming to weigh the genuineness of the statement. It did sound like a trick, even though Roman was being honest and trying to do the humanitarian thing for once.

After a tense twenty seconds, Conroy pulled out a walkie. "Samor, stop the distribution. I'm calling it off."

"Sir?"

"Please tell me you haven't deployed yet."

"No, we were just about to—"

"Don't! The crash survivors might be in there. We can't risk it."

"Yes, sir."

Conroy returned the walkie to a clip on his belt. "Why did you tell me?"

"There's at least one good person in there who deserves a better death. Dying from a sneak attack has no purpose now."

The chancellor nodded solemnly. "No more meaningless death."

Roman shrugged. *What's a life without meaning, either?*

"I appreciate your honesty, thank you. How did you get the colonists to go with you?"

"We posed as replacement guards. The bodies of your men are in the woods a few dozen meters from the cave." That would seal his fate. He braced for the blow.

Conroy took in a sharp breath through his nose and let it out slowly. "I'll keep my word, but not everyone here answers to me." He stormed off exchanging a meaningful look and nod with Evan.

"Just kill me and get it over with," Roman said to Evan.

"I should have done that when we first met. Maybe then it would have made a difference." He glared at him. "But now I see that you *want* death. You don't get to take the easy way out after what you've done. I'd rather see you suffer."

Roman shook his head. "You have a weak stomach for someone in your profession."

"Taking a life should never be easy."

"It was for me."

"Well, *you're* a sociopath."

Roman chuckled. "Yeah, I probably am. But do your damned job, Evan. Put me down."

"No." He crouched down to face him eye-level. "Keeping you alive is far more of a punishment to you. Plus, you have all kinds of valuable information stored in that twisted brain of yours. We're going to use it to take down your sadistic brother and sister."

"I won't help you destroy my family."

"They would turn on you in a second, Roman. You don't owe them any loyalty."

"And you don't need to invent a reason to keep me alive because you're too much of a coward to pull the trigger!"

Evan rounded on him, face red and a fire in his eyes that Roman hadn't seen before. "You want to know why I hate killing so much? It's because my parents were murdered by Syndicate thugs, and I swore to myself that I wouldn't take a life unless I was sure it was necessary. But you are very much testing my patience."

Roman was no stranger to killing or death. He'd lost track of the lives he'd claimed on Aethos, and those were the latest batch in a lifetime of brutality. But he also understood loss. "I'm sorry about your parents," he murmured.

"You couldn't care less about a couple of strangers."

"But I do know what it's like to lose your parents. We have that in common." Roman met his gaze.

Some of Evan's fury receded. "What happened to yours?"

"I'm pretty sure Marcus killed them. They disappeared one day, and no one talks about it."

"That…"

Roman raised his eyebrows. "After all your undercover work and research, you hadn't picked up that little detail, huh? Well, there you go. A dirty family secret for your collection." He leaned his head back to stare at the white, puffy clouds floating by overhead. He'd still been a teenager when he'd lost his parents, leaving Marcus as his guardian and role model. But whereas their father had been firm yet fair in his leadership style, Marcus only governed through fear. Roman could barely remember what it was like to not constantly be on edge.

Evan was quiet for several moments. "I wonder who you could have been had you grown up differently."

"Ah, the age-old debate of Nature versus Nurture." Roman thought back to his early childhood, before Marcus had conditioned him to jump immediately to the most extreme response. Maybe things *could* have been different with another mentor.

"The question is, Roman," Evan continued, "do you *want* to be like your brother, or will you be your own man?"

No one has ever asked me that before. I've never had a choice. Being born into the Santano family came with certain expectations, and Roman had never had reason to question their ways. Whenever he'd shown any softness, Marcus had beaten it out of him. Treating other people as tools to be manipulated and discarded was a way of life. He'd convinced himself it was the only way to be. But the cruelty he'd expressed toward others was a survival tactic. *I have a chance to survive this, too. I can't give up.*

To make it through, he'd need to give Evan something. There was one truth he could speak that would leave the door open more than any other.

"I hate Marcus," Roman admitted. He immediately felt lighter. He'd been holding all that resentment inside for years. For a moment, he questioned why he'd insisted on staying loyal to someone who despised him. But the painful truth was right there. *Because what I really hate is that he's right about me. I've done nothing but fail the family.*

Evan's expression had softened. Anger still burned in his gaze, but there was also new understanding. "Blood isn't the only thing that bonds us. Just look at the people here. Shared experiences, ideals, dreams—those can unite people, too. And those bonds can be even more powerful." He took a slow breath. "I can't forgive the awful things you've done in your life, but I can offer you a chance to try to do something truly worthwhile. Help me bring your brother to justice, and maybe some kids out there don't have to lose their parents in the horrible ways we did."

Does he really think a little speech can sway me? Roman did have to admit that there were some nice sentiments, but his family was everything. He wasn't about to turn against them. But that didn't mean he couldn't play along with Evan's ploy.

"I'll think about it," Roman told him, not wanting to draw suspicion by seeming *too* agreeable. "But I reserve the right to stab you in the back if I change my mind."

"I'd expect nothing less."

40

THE ENCOUNTER HAD gone nothing like Conroy had envisioned. He'd begun the afternoon anticipating murder, but somehow they'd come out of it in a tenuous alliance. And it had all come down to Evan—a man from humble beginnings but possessing unusual talent.

They'd still need to confront the soldiers who'd taken over their base, but with Zaris' forces, dealing with them would be no trouble. Whether they'd live or die remained to be seen; that would be their choice.

When Evan walked back over to Conroy, he was surprised to see Roman still seated in the field under watchful guard.

"He killed a lot of my people," Conroy said once Evan was within earshot. "Are you sure he's worth keeping alive?"

"If he decides to truly cooperate—or if we can make him—then he'll be able to deliver more detailed information about the Syndicate's operations than we could ever imagine. Like where they keep the serum stash, and distribution protocols, their government contacts, you name it."

"He's a ruthless killer."

"I don't like it, either, Chancellor. If I could go back in time, I'd go back to the night we met and shoot him rather than just tying him up."

"Why not execute him now, then?"

"Because the circumstances have changed. Keeping him alive is pragmatic, because he has insights that maybe only a few dozen people alive possess—we just have to extract them. And I can guarantee you that if Marcus' own *brother* hates him, then there are others in the Syndicate who're on a hair-trigger to flip. I may despise Roman and want him dead, but he's valuable. He can tell us which threads to pull in the Syndicate to make it all unravel. I'm in this for the long game, going all the way to the top, not just taking out every easy target that crosses my path."

Conroy nodded, impressed with his restraint and reasoning. "You know, you would have made a good politician. Hell, you're young enough—you still might."

"Respectfully, sir, I would rather be shot into a star."

"That's an apt analogy for an interstellar political campaign. You never know."

"I'll put it at the absolute bottom of my priority list."

"We do, admittedly, have more pressing issues. You found me my ship, and now we are free to leave here."

Evan stared at him levelly. "Let me be clear, Chancellor, this is not *your* ship, nor is it mine. Sam is sentient, and any transportation on the ship is a request, not an order. And anywhere you go, I go. I stand for the people of the Commonwealth, and I won't let any single politician run off with such a prize, no matter how well-intentioned."

"Understood."

There was no doubt in Conroy's mind that Evan would stand firm to his statement. However, he didn't have all the context for what needed to happen next. If this alliance was going to work, then Conroy needed to bring him into the fold.

"We have a lot to discuss. This fight is a lot bigger than Aethos," he said.

Evan nodded. "I know what I've signed up for. But I need the night."

"Of course. Thank you, Evan. You've done an incredible thing bringing everyone together like this."

He shrugged. "It might not last until sunrise. I brought them here, but you're going to need to really sell them."

"If I can't win over this lot, then I'll accept my retirement here. But I have a feeling this journey is just beginning."

"I wouldn't celebrate yet."

"But it's trending in the right direction. I'll take it."

He smiled. "Sure."

"You're too young to have been through a major cultural crisis, but I can tell you that there are some events with a momentum of their own. We're about to enter one of those times."

"It might not go how you think."

"True. But it's a turning point, no matter what happens. And I can celebrate that we're giving power back to the populace, where it should be. They'll guide the conversation."

"Nice sentiment, but I'm not convinced."

"I'm curious, why?"

"Because individuals can be rational, but it's easy to get big groups riled up and amplify our worst impulses. If you release information about the Korani's technology, you won't have any control, and the 'populace'—as you put it—won't agree on what to do. It'll be chaos, not unity."

Conroy frowned, looking over Evan; the arguments echoed many of the concerns Rostov had expressed. "What would you suggest we do instead?"

"Me? I'm not a political advisor."

"You're a citizen without an agenda beyond stability in your own life. So, tell me, what would you do?"

Evan shrugged. "Well, the biggest thing I learned from working undercover is that no idea can ever come from you. But you'll know exactly what decision you want a target to make, and you need to frame it in a way that makes them feel like the idea was theirs all along."

"So, you're saying that we need to feed a conclusion to the populace without explicitly saying what to believe?"

"Yeah."

Conroy nodded thoughtfully, his mind already turning to how his tactics might change to address the concerns. It might yet give him the groundwork to negotiate peace with Rostov. "I'll take it under advisement. And that official advisory role will be waiting for you if you ever decide to take it."

"Thanks, but don't hold your breath. I'll give you a tour of the ship tomorrow."

He smiled. "I look forward to it. Enjoy your night."

— — —

Evan spotted Anya waiting by the *Asamar*. He was eager to get time alone with her after their ridiculous day, but there was one more person he needed to talk to first.

Zaris was sizing up Conroy and his soldiers from a distance, but she was also transfixed by the planet itself. Her gaze kept wandering every time a bird flew by or insects landed on the flowers.

"Nothing like Constella, huh?"

She shook her head. "I can't tell if it reeks or if it's the most beautiful aroma ever."

"I know what you mean. This place changes the way you

think about things."

"I can see that."

He leaned in close to her, speaking in a low voice, "That was sweet of you to try to save me. You put on a tough exterior, but I know you care about your people more than you let on."

Zaris glared playfully at him. "Don't you *dare* say a word to my crew."

He smiled back. "Your secret is safe with me. But they were probably watching, so…"

She sighed. "Tarek is going to give me so much shit about that move when I get back."

"That's completely justified."

She rolled her eyes but then turned serious again. "Things are about to get really crazy, aren't they?"

"Yeah. But we'll figure it out. Give Conroy a chance."

She dug the toe of one of her boots into the soft ground. "This place seems worth fighting for."

"This is one planet. We're fighting for humanity's future."

"We're a handful of people among hundreds of billions. I don't expect to make a dent."

"That's probably what the creators of the first interstellar gate said, too."

She nodded thoughtfully. "Every great journey starts somewhere, right?"

"Damn straight."

Conroy flagged them down. "Zaris, I'd like to speak with you about getting some of your corsairs down here to help secure our operational base."

"I think we can work something out." With a parting nod to Evan, she went to speak with the chancellor.

All right, finally free! Evan jogged over to Anya.

She smiled at him as he approached. "I never would have

guessed this group of people would agree to work together."

"It's a tenuous alliance," Evan replied. "They're here because it's what makes the most sense right now, but I don't think there are too many true believers."

"Still, not bad work for a couple of nobodies, right?"

"You know, at this point, I think we're actually quite popular," he said.

"Downright heroes, even."

"I still wouldn't go that far."

She tilted her head. "Come on, give me this victory. I've toiled in obscurity for so long. I want to permanently wipe that smug smirk off Vanessa's face."

Evan laughed, recalling Anya's petty feud with one of her early xenobiology colleagues. "Well, if this is about besting Vanessa, I could never stand in your way."

"Thank you," Anya said with an exaggerated nod of satisfaction.

He stood in silence for a minute, watching Conroy's soldiers take Roman away.

Anya clasped his hand. "I'm sorry. I didn't know about what happened to your parents—about them being murdered."

Evan shrugged it off. "Shit happens."

"Still, I'm impressed you turned that experience into a vow of *non*-violence. I think I would have gone the other direction."

"It was one of the factors that made me decide to leave the UPDF for the Security Corps. Shooting your troubles is the easy way out. To face them and get to the root cause of their actions takes a lot more work."

"You really want to take down the whole Syndicate, huh?"

"No, I want to reshape the society that made them."

Anya let out a long breath. "That's a big ask."

“Well, I have nothing better to do. We have a sentient alien starship, the start of our own little militia… Why not overthrow a corrupt government and see if we can do some good in the universe?”

She smiled. “You think big, Evan Taylor. I like it.”

“What do you say, you in?”

“Yeah, let’s go get the bad guys. But tomorrow. You still owe me that date.”

— — —

Marcus Santano rarely drank in public, but this was one of those days. A message from Marta about the disaster on Pavia had required immediate remedy in the form of numbing his nerves, and the fact that both Roman and Red on Aethos weren’t responding to his messages had kept him at the spaceport bar longer than he’d anticipated.

His younger brother had failed, yet again. He’d burned his last chance.

The one saving grace was Marta’s note that she’d acquired some fragments from the alien ship, which could yield interesting research results. But with many of their facilities on Pavia destroyed, they’d need to shift operations to a different location. Marta would figure it out. At least there was one competent sibling.

Marcus swirled the contents of his seventh glass, staring into the amber liquid. Grand plans carried him along a path, much like the vortex of the liquor circling the glass walls. He could fight the current, or he could go with the flow.

Embrace fate.

He downed the shot in one go, wincing at the burn traveling down his throat. It settled into a warm burn in his stomach. The internal fire spurred him to action. He slammed down his empty glass.

The waitress glanced over at the abrupt *bang*. "Everything all right?"

"Yes, just bring the bill."

She brought over an electronic pad and set it on the counter in front of him. "Thanks for coming in. Have a great day!"

He transferred the payment. "I would, but I have other plans."

Marcus got to his feet, feeling the booze more as soon as he went vertical. But his mind remained clear. A revolution was coming, and nothing would stop him now.

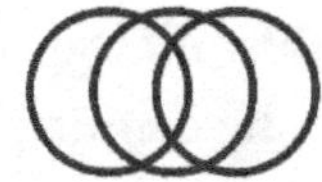

THE STORY CONTINUES IN
REBEL WORLDS...

Rebel Worlds (Starship of the Ancients Book 3)

A daring heist. A ghost from the past.
The rebellion that could shatter an empire.

Evan and Anya have brokered an unlikely alliance among thieves. With their sights set on a Syndicate vault brimming with alien secrets, holding the team together long enough to claim the prize will be their greatest test yet. Leading a crew of outcasts, Evan and Anya stage a high-stakes raid to seize tech that could turn the tide against Chancellor Rostov's iron grip. As they face ambushes, double-crosses, and a regime desperate to crush them, they'll stop at nothing to get answers in their pursuit of the Korani's trail across the stars. Can Evan and Anya wield their growing power to spark a rebellion—or will it consume them?

ADDITIONAL READING

Cadicle Space Opera Series
Book 1: Shadows of Empire (Vol. 1-3)
Book 2: Web of Truth (Vol. 4)
Book 3: Crossroads of Fate (Vol. 5)
Book 4: Path of Justice (Vol. 6)
Book 5: Scions of Change (Vol. 7)

Mindspace Series
Book 1: Infiltration
Book 2: Conspiracy
Book 3: Offensive
Book 4: Endgame

Taran Empire Saga
Book 1: Empire Reborn
Book 2: Empire Uprising
Book 3: Empire Defied
Book 4: Empire United

Dark Stars Trilogy
Book 1: Crystalline Space
Book 2: A Light in the Dark
Book 3: Masters of Fate

See a complete list at www.akduboff.com

AUTHORS' NOTES

Thank you for reading *Lost Planet*! I've been blown away by the reception to *Stranded*, and I hope you enjoyed this second installment in the Starship of the Ancients series.

This year marks my ten-year publishing anniversary, so it's been especially meaningful to finally have a 'hit' at this decade mark. While my debut Cadicle series has gained a loyal fanbase over the years, it's never been a consistent chart-topper in the way *Stranded* became shortly after its release. Every author dreams of having a book resonate with readers in that way, and I want to express my sincere thanks for you being a part of this experience. It's been truly life-changing for me!

I've never been one of those writers who pumps out a book a month. I like to take my time with each story and focus on the details, weaving a larger tapestry over the course of a multi-book series. I know waiting months between releases isn't ideal from a reader perspective, but I hope you'll be patient with me as this story unfolds. My goal is to release three or four books per year—so, approximately quarterly—which I hope you'll find to be a satisfactory pace. I don't want to burn out, and I want to maintain high quality with each book.

So you have a better idea of what to expect going forward, I'm planning on at least seven books in the Starship of the Ancients series; I'm happy to continue beyond that point if there is still reader demand. If you've read any of my other work, you know I'm really a series writer at heart. I love laying a foundation in the early books and then cracking a larger universe wide open, bringing together all the threads into a grand adventure. I'm really enjoying the playground of this story universe, and I look forward to Evan and Anya's journey taking them to exciting new places!

Many thanks to my amazing team of beta readers John, Kurt, Sandra, Brenda, David F, Jim, Charlie, David B, Terry, Mike, Eric, Manie, and Gil for their insightful feedback. And thank you to Steve, Bryan, and Deb for lending your keen eyes to the final polish!

We're just getting started with this series, so buckle in for a fun adventure. Until next time, happy reading!

ABOUT THE AUTHOR

A.K. (Amy) DuBoff has always loved science fiction in all its forms—books, movies, shows, and games. If it involves outer space, even better! She is a Nebula Award finalist and *USA Today* bestselling author most known for her Cadicle Universe, but she's also written a variety of sci-fi and fantasy books, short fiction, and screenplays. Amy can frequently be found traveling the world, and when she's not writing, she enjoys wine tasting, binge-watching TV series, and playing epic strategy board games.

www.akduboff.com

Made in United States
Cleveland, OH
13 March 2026

34439811R00236